THE PROPHECY OF THE SEVEN

THE STARSEA CYCLE BOOK FIVE

KYLE WEST

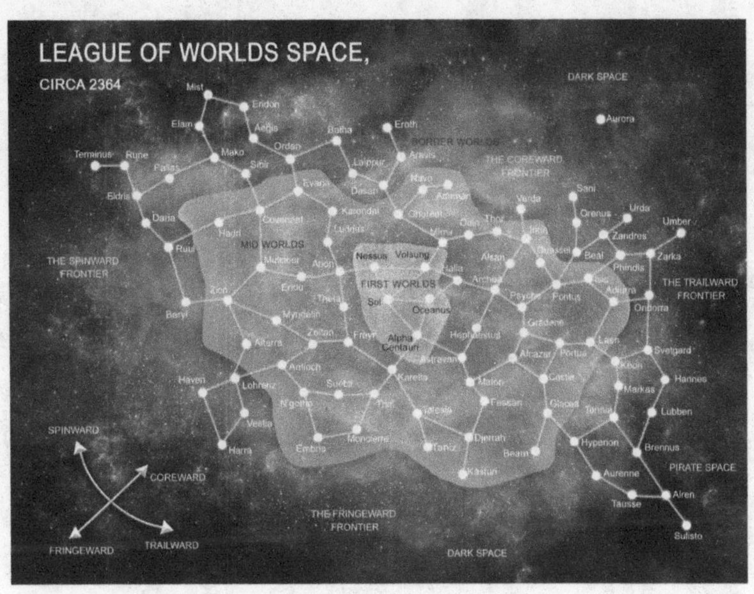

LEAGUE OF WORLDS SPACE,
CIRCA 2364
DARK SPACE
Aurora
Mist
Eridon
Elam
Aegis
Batha
Eroth
Ordan
BORDER WORLDS
Anvis
THE COREWARD
FRONTIER
Terminus
Rune
Mako
Laippur
Sibir
Pallas
Navo
Sani
Evaxa
Dasan
Ammon
Varda
Orenus
Urda
Eldris
Coruscat
Kasondai
Ghylad
Odin
Thor
Iris
Zandres
Umber
Daria
Hadri
Ludius
Mirru
Alsan
Brassel
Beal
Zarka
MID WORLDS
Ruu
Muldoor
Abon
Nessus
Volsung
Halia
Archea
Isis
Phindis
Adiarra
THE SPINWARD
FRONTIER
Zion
Eridu
FIRST WORLDS
Psyche
Fontus
THE TRAILWARD
FRONTIER
Theta
Sol
Onborra
Beryl
Myndelin
Frayr
Oceanus
Gradene
Lash
Zeitan
Alpha
Centaun
Astravan
Hephaestus
Alrazar
Portus
Svetgard
Altarra
Antioch
Karetta
Costa
Kron
Hannes
Haven
Lohrenz
Sueta
Malon
Markas
N'gorna
Thif
Vatesta
Fessan
Glacas
Tennil
Lubben
Veeta
Djerrah
Hyperion
Brennus
Harna
Embris
Mondrene
Taniz
Beam
PIRATE SPACE
SPINWARD
Kasturi
Aurenne
Alren
THE FRINGEWARD
FRONTIER
Tausse
COREWARD
DARK SPACE
Sulisto
FRINGEWARD
TRAILWARD

THE SHABBY TRANSPORT SHIP, with the trapezoidal insignia of Caralis Intergalactic on its hull, idled under Halia's eternal night sky. Lucian, Fergus, and Serah waited just below the top of the shaft that led to the temple beneath the ice. Lucian kept watch with his head above ground, since he was the only one with cold weather gear, while Fergus and Serah waited on the ladder below.

The frigid temperature was far worse than anything he'd experienced on Volsung, including the north side of the Isle of Madness. The ship *should* have picked up their thermal signatures by now, so why in the Worlds was it just *sitting* there?

In the sub-zero temperatures of Halia's dark side, waiting was anything but easy. Even with a Thermal ward, it was rotting cold. But as soon as they were on the surface, they'd have to cut the stream. A Thermal ward strong enough to keep them warm would emit red light, a dead giveaway of what they were. Any display of magical abilities might get them reported to the League Health Authority. And the LHA would do everything in its power to ship them back to Psyche, and that was the last thing Lucian wanted.

But for now, while the shaft hid them, it was possible to keep somewhat warm.

Lucian ran over the story they'd concocted, a story he hoped adequately explained how they came to be out here. They were part of an archeology expedition, but their dropship had taken off when the pilot had betrayed them to Carthago, a corporate rival of Caralis. It wasn't the *best* story, but hopefully it was enough to get out of this alive. And that was all they needed.

Lucian was still trying to smooth things out by the time the transport's blast door opened, revealing a single figure wearing a white thermal suit, including a respirator mask. Lucian knew it was a man, judging from the broad set of shoulders and unusual height, probably just short of two meters. The man descended the ramp and approached the shaft where Lucian, Fergus, and Serah were sheltering.

Confident that the man had seen him, Lucian lowered his head into the windless shelter of the shaft.

"Taking his rotting time, isn't he?" Serah said.

"The sooner we're on board, the better. Let's go."

Lucian couldn't imagine their discomfort as Serah allowed the Thermal ward to dissolve. Both began shivering almost immediately. Even in his thermal suit, the cold biting wind was almost painful. Serah and Fergus shuddered, still wearing the space jumpsuits they'd picked up aboard *Wayfinder*.

The white-suited man came to a stop, regarding them for a moment behind his cold weather mask.

"You just going to let us freeze?" Serah asked.

The man shifted his feet awkwardly. "Ugh, no. This leads down to the ruins, right?"

This guy wasn't inspiring much confidence.

"Get us on the ship, first," Lucian said. "We lost most of our cold weather gear when the ship took off."

The man watched him for a moment, as if to ask how they got in this predicament, but the dangerous look on Lucian's face must have stopped him.

"Right. Well, let's go back then. You have some explaining to do."

The man walked back to the ship, much too slowly. It was torturous. It would only take fifteen minutes or even less for Serah and Fergus to get frostbite on their exposed skin. Lucian felt guilty for wearing his suit, but it didn't have auto-tailoring, meaning he couldn't let Serah have it. It felt wrong to use it while the others had nothing.

The man cleared his throat. "The archeology teams are usually a bit more . . . prepared." The man picked up his pace only marginally. By now, they had reached the boarding ramp. He stood before the door, puzzled. "Shit. What was the code again?"

"Are you serious?" Serah asked. "I'm going to blast that thing open if you don't figure it out in five seconds!"

Thankfully, the man didn't seem to question *how* she would blast it open. The man knocked on the door, and it slid open automatically. Someone from the inside must have opened it.

They hurried inside, the warm air tingling the skin on Lucian's face. When the door slid shut, the three of them stood huddled, jumping up and down to generate warmth.

The man took off his mask, revealing a long, solemn face, droopy eyes underlined with dark circles, and a mouth that seemed to hang eternally agape. Something about this man seemed familiar to Lucian, though he didn't know why.

"I'm Adam," he said, putting out a hand. "Adam Abrantes. My father sent me here to investigate your claim."

At that name, Lucian realized why this man looked familiar. Adam was his *cousin*. For now, it didn't seem as if Adam recognized him. Lucian had only been eight or nine when they'd last seen each other. He'd expected his Uncle Ravis to send someone under his employ, but not his firstborn.

He tried to hide his surprise, though it wasn't easy. For now, it might be best not to say anything. It could complicate things. "Well, the ruins are right below our feet. We want to talk to Ravis personally. I know he'll want to hear from us."

Adam's slightly droopy eyes narrowed. "That's *Mr.* Abrantes to you. He's a very busy man. Besides, I'm *more* than capable of handling any information you have." From Adam's tone, it seemed he was trying to convince himself of that as much as them. "Anyway, you're with the archeology department? No one told us you guys were out here."

"Secret mission," Lucian said. "We had a bit of a cave-in down there, so we lost a lot of our equipment, including our direct line. There are too many spies in the department, and Ravis . . . I mean, *Mr. Abrantes* . . . wanted this under wraps."

"I . . . see. Yeah, we've had our suspicions about Carthago." He looked at him suspiciously. "I'm sorry for saying, but none of this makes sense."

"Is it just you here?" Lucian asked, ignoring his point.

"Me, plus the pilot. We were the closest ship on call, but trust me, more will be arriving. Mercs, too. We've got to set up a perimeter, anti-space batteries. The usual to keep prying eyes away. So, was it a good haul?"

"A great haul," Serah said. "The best haul anyone could ask for."

Lucian resisted the urge to shoot her a look.

"A perimeter, then?" Fergus asked, focusing on Adam.

"You guys claimed this area, but until we have boots on the ground, Carthago might contest it. And we're far enough away from League authorities for blood to be spilled. Of course, Portnov will be here soon, and you can talk to him when you do."

"Of course," Lucian said, easily, not having the first clue who Portnov was. After dealing with everything he had gone through, he found it easy to lie through his teeth. The thought was a little scary, but he would do whatever he could to get out of this situation. "However, we report directly to Mr. Abrantes. Trust me, we have things he wants to hear. Things that will change the balance with Carthago Corp entirely."

Adam's sad eyes widened ever-so-slightly. "You think Portnov might be in on it, too?"

Lucian wasn't sure what this Portnov guy might be "in" on, so he also didn't want to throw him to the wolves for no reason. "No reason to think that. The only person I really trust is Mr. Abrantes."

"I see," Adam said, seeming to consider. "Well, I can put in a request, I guess. I doubt it'll lead anywhere."

Lucian thought it might be easier to tell him the full truth, or at least the relevant parts. All this lying could backfire at some point. Then again, saying that the three of them were mages was the worst thing possible. But if admitting as much could get him to Ravis, maybe telling the truth was safer.

Then again, all of this was speculation. During Lucian's debriefing after his metaphysical, his mother had mentioned possibly sending him to Halia to be closer to his uncle. The government here didn't ban mages outright, the last Lucian checked. It was possible she had mentioned him to Ravis already.

"Wait a minute," Adam said. "I know you, don't I?" The realization seemed to hit him all at once. His mouth hung even more agape.

"You know me? I don't believe we've ever met."

"Lucian? How in the Worlds...? What are *you* doing here?"

The jig was up. It was time for Plan B. "It's ... a long story."

"I thought you'd gone to Volsung for training. We thought .. ." He trailed off. Making a snap decision, he raised his slate to his ear. "Yeah, we have an issue. I'm going to have to bring the archeology team directly to you."

"Issue?" Serah asked. "*What* issue?"

Lucian heard what sounded like his uncle shouting at his son on the other end of the line.

"Let me talk to him," Lucian said.

Adam shook his head. "Change of plans. As soon as more of our ships touch down, we're heading back to the estate."

"The estate?" Serah asked.

Adam ignored her. "Here. Take some seats. Won't be long before we arrive."

———

THE SHIP ROSE PONDEROUSLY from the thick ice sheet, burning through the atmosphere east. Adam sat with them, surrounded by a couple dozen unoccupied seats. It seemed this was a private company transport, and a dated one at that, judging from the rough interior, peeling paint, and rattling chassis. There was not even the benefit of a viewport. The hull clattered fiercely until they were out of the atmosphere. Lucian floated against his restraints. No AG field turned on, meaning they had to stay seated. He wouldn't have been surprised if this vessel predated the Mage War.

Lucian slept, such was his exhaustion, but not for long. It couldn't have been twenty minutes before they were burning through the atmosphere again. Lucian ground his teeth. The inertial dampening system was out-of-date as well, unable to take much of the edge off. This hunk of junk needed *thousands* of creds in repairs to be truly serviceable. He had to wonder why Ravis would give his son such a crappy ship.

Another few minutes saw them touching down on an unknown part of the planet.

Outside the transport's blast door, Lucian was greeted by a

strange sight. A flat expanse of land covered with tall, black grass stretched before him. It extended at a slight downslope until it reached the edge of a cliff a few hundred meters away. Beyond the cliff lay a violet-tinged sea, its water dark, choppy, and violent under a perpetual evening sky. The sun shone like dull copper, about halfway up in the sky, where it had *always* shone on this world with only the slightest of deviations too small to bother with. On a tidally locked world like Halia, the sun always stayed in the same position, which was usually the case with red dwarf star systems.

On that grassy field, hundreds of strange, shelled creatures reminiscent of snails grazed—if a snail could be as large as a horse. A rainbow of colors painted those shells, and even in the dim twilight, they seemed to glow from the reddish sunlight.

The wind from the north blew cold. Judging by the position of the sun, the dark side of the planet was only a few thousand kilometers away.

As he, Serah, and Fergus took in the sight, Adam ignored it, walking under the ship toward a large mansion rising above the black-grassed plain. Gloomy clouds loomed over the western horizon, thick and turbulent, while yet more of the shelled creatures scuffed about in the dark grass.

"This is the Abrantes Estate," Adam explained. "Only a short flight from Halisport, and not too far from our holdings in the Western Rift."

"There are rifts here, too?" Serah asked.

Fergus shot her a look of warning to not mention where she was from. But Adam seemed blind to the blunder. "Halia is rife with rifts, most naturally made. It's from these that the Corporation extracts the planet's mineral wealth."

Whatever that wealth was, it was most definitely not available to Lucian's part of the family. He knew his Uncle Ravis was well off, but judging by the size of the estate ahead of them, he was far richer than even Lucian had imagined. That mansion was almost large enough to be a small palace, and had to have more space than Ravis and his family ever needed. It was the type of mansion that was common in the South Florida Shoals that required armies of servants just to keep livable. But unlike that environment, this mansion and its attendant support buildings were the only sign of civilization.

They entered through the large double doors, to be greeted by a grand foyer with double staircases leading to a second-floor mezzanine. The surfaces were of pink marble, richly carpeted in red, the walls decked with artwork of various modes and styles. Standing before the righthand staircase, browsing his slate, stood a dignified man with snow-white hair and a trim beard, wearing an expensive designer suit with a white flower pinned to his pocket. When he looked up, his eyes seemed to find Lucian's first. His gaze was shrewd and inscrutable.

"My dear nephew," he said, breaking into a practiced smile. "Having you here is . . . quite the surprise."

From his tone, it was hard to tell whether that surprise was good. "Trust me, I'm just as surprised as you are."

Ravis's white eyebrows arched at that. "Come. Let's go to my study. You're in awful shape, but we'll fix that up soon enough." He looked at his son. "Have the kitchen prepare something warm and substantial. Nothing too fancy. Good, hearty food that warms the bones. Maybe some Ajiaco Cubano." Ravis winked. "That should remind you of home, eh? Not like your abuela, but close enough."

It was something his mother used to make, his grandmother's recipe. It stood to reason Ravis would know it, too. Lucian tried not to look too excited about the prospect of food, even if he was ravenous. There was a reason his mother didn't like her brother, and he would not let his guard down. "That'll do just fine."

"I'm on it," Adam said. He stood for a moment, as if waiting for something more from his father, but already Ravis was leading them up the stairs and had forgotten his son.

Ravis didn't say a word, not until he'd led them down the mezzanine and through a richly decorated door. The air inside was deliciously warm, allowing Lucian to thaw for the first time in days. They entered a sumptuously appointed office, the walls of which were lined with hundreds of books. A massive desk set before wide bay windows overlooked the dark plain below, with the shadowy sea in the distance. A light sleet fell. Lucian had rarely seen a gloomier scene. He could see why this world had been sparsely settled, despite its nearness to Earth and the First Worlds.

"Pull up some chairs," Ravis said, sitting behind his desk. "We've got a lot to go over."

They found some chairs on the room's periphery and pulled them forward. If Ravis seemed uneasy about their general appearance, he didn't give any sign of it. As for their shockspears, they were well-hidden beneath their jumpsuits. Lucian had peeled off his cold weather gear by now, having left it on the ship.

"Thanks for taking us in," Lucian said.

"Of course, of course," Ravis said. "I would be remiss. Your mother and I had our disagreements, it's true, but I was sorrowful to hear of her passing." He sighed. "That's over a year ago, now."

"We don't have to talk about that."

"If you wish. So, business. I must ask the obvious question first. My son told me a wild tale of how you were a part of my archeology division, and that I'd cleared an exploration mission? Why the lie? And how did you find the Builder ruin in the most forsaken part of our planet, in a place no one would dream of looking?"

"That's a long story."

Ravis shrugged. "We have time. I've cleared my schedule for

the next two hours."

Lucian felt wary. His mother hadn't told him much about his uncle, but when she talked about him, it was never nice. He trusted his mother's judgment and wanted to respect her memory.

"You don't have a ship," Ravis began, "so the only other option is someone dropped you off there. Scanning my company's traffic logs, we noted a vessel touching down a few days ago on the dark side, only to depart a short time later. The transponder code was not in any of our registers, and we've catalogued millions. Went by the name of *Wayfinder*."

Lucian decided that concocting a web of lies would just be a waste of time, and pointless in the end. His uncle already knew he was a mage, and likely his friends, too.

"I'll just tell you the truth, since any other story would sound more ridiculous. I want to know something about you, first."

"I'll bite. What?"

"My mom always told me you guys had a falling out, but she never said why. Could you explain the reason?"

Ravis's face became stony. "She was a good person, despite our differences. But the nature of our disagreement was legal, and unfortunately, the law was on my side."

His manner seemed detached, as if he were not as regretful as he made himself to be. "Legal, how?"

"It's not your concern," he said, voice stern. "Now, you must tell me what you were doing on the dark side, and how you found that ruin. My archeology team is already telling me the excavation must have taken years, and it's a find that will change our understanding of the Builders forever."

"I can't tell you that until you come clean."

Ravis's eyes narrowed. "What do you mean? You claimed the site in my company's name, and you don't want to reveal how you found it in the first place?"

"It's complicated."

"I tire of this, Lucian. Just tell me what happened, and I'll tell you about your mom and me."

From his uncle's no-nonsense expression, Lucian saw that there was going to be no way out of this. All he could do was jump off the deep-end and hope for the best.

"So, I guess my mom told you about what happened to me?"

"Of course she did. Some of it, anyway. She reached out to me for the first time in years, so I knew something was wrong. She said you'd tested positive for metaphysical emergence. But then I never heard from her again. So, I knew you were one of them. Figured she probably wanted me to sync some creds to her, but it was nothing like that. She wanted me for a backup plan, in case the academy thing fell through. So when Adam told me who you were, I connected the dots. I figured you were in those ruins on some sort of Academy business and things went south. Hence, why you're here. The only thing I *don't* understand was why you would turn over the discovery of that site to me instead of your masters on Volsung. Don't tell me you've gone rogue, because I'm not sticking my neck out on the Warden chopping block. Not even for family."

It seemed there was no choice but to tell the truth. That was, if he wanted his uncle's help.

"We called you because we need your help. Because you're the only one who *can* help."

Ravis leaned back in his chair, his face one of mild surprise. "Is that so? You know, telling me that doesn't help your position much. I don't help family members for nothing. So, you must convince me. You're doing a piss-poor job of it so far."

Lucian sighed. "*Fine.* I'll tell you what happened, but you won't believe me."

"Try me."

2

WHILE EATING dinner in Ravis's office, Lucian told him everything. From his concerned expression, it seemed Ravis wished he hadn't heard a word. He didn't interrupt, much to Lucian's surprise, except to call his secretary and cancel the rest of his appointments.

At last, the old man leaned back in his chair and sighed.

"See?" Lucian said. "I knew you wouldn't believe me."

"I never said that." His eyes went to Serah. "You're from Psyche, then?"

At her nod, Ravis swiveled his chair and looked over the black, grassy fields. It felt late in the day, but the twilight was the same as it had ever been while the sleet was still falling. It was hard to tell what Ravis was thinking.

Still facing the window, he broke the silence.

"You know, it's my duty to turn you over to the League."

The sting of betrayal was intense. "What do you mean, *turn us over*? Did you not hear *anything* I said?"

"I said it's my duty. Didn't say I'd do it." He swiveled back around. "Family comes before government. I don't care about the League. Greedy bastards, trying to steal every sub-cred I earn. I'm under investigation, you know." He gave a sardonic smile. "We'll figure something out."

Lucian didn't like the sound of that. "We need to go after Vera. And for that, we need a ship. If we can't chase her, they'll find the Prophecy of the Seven. If they find that, then we've got much bigger problems."

"I need to digest all this. You expect me to agree with you right off the bat? How do I know Vera and Xara don't have the right of it?"

Did Lucian *really* have to explain that? "Because they're power-mad."

"And you're not, Lucian?" There was a good-natured twinkle in his eye. "Don't lie to me and say that kind of power wouldn't feel good."

"I don't want power. If I had my way, things would just go back to normal, but obviously we're past that point. Now I just want to keep *them* from getting the prophecy."

This point didn't seem to matter to Ravis. "If Xara is *really* alive and powerful enough to save us from the Swarmers, well, that's good for business. I can't make money if the Swarmers destroy us. Already, the markets have plummeted." He gave a good-natured smile. "You should've taken their money, nephew. With that fifty thousand, just think of what you could've done."

"I don't care about money. What does money matter if we're all dead in the end?"

"Well, you need money now. Fifty thousand could've gotten you off this world and more besides. Could've even *bought* you a ship, even if it was a clunker. Point being, Xara's feeling more like this Chosen One than you. She has two of these Orbs, and from what you've said, she knows how to use them better than you. And if she actually gets all the Orbs, and the fraying ends for good, *that* will be the best thing that could happen. And she's got a head start on you, too."

"What's your point?"

"In business, it's best to back the winning horse."

"And none of that about the Immortal fusing with her mind, ruling over humanity, concerns you in the least?"

"I don't buy all that. Sounds far-fetched."

"How are you determining what's far-fetched and what isn't? Supporting your family is a bridge too far?"

Before Ravis could respond, Serah huffed. "You only care about money."

Ravis smiled, as if conceding that point. "Money is my legacy and power. It's what makes me strong, and my family strong. It has me in reach of taking control of Caralis for good and securing my legacy forever." His smile wavered as his expression darkened. "Unfortunately, my sons are no good and my daughters are more interested in pissing away my wealth rather than building it."

"What do you mean?" Fergus asked. "Adam seems a dutiful son."

Ravis waved his hand, almost disgustedly. "He's my best choice, but that's not saying much. Drug problems. His wife divorced him. I wouldn't care about all that, but he just doesn't have the heart of a cold-blooded killer. You need that to run a company, especially one as big as Caralis Intergalactic, to survive the jackals on the board. Here on Halia, I basically run Caralis however I see fit." He gave a sharp smile. "You need to be a cold-blooded killer if you're going to sit behind this desk, with the fate of tens of thousands in your hands, all of them trying to stab you in the back. Adam wouldn't last two months as the patriarch of my estate."

"That's harsh to say of your own son," Serah said. "You should be ashamed."

It shocked Lucian that he was even saying this much to them, but it seemed the man had much pent up inside of him.

It was obvious why his mother disliked him. He was reprehensible and probably sociopathic.

"So, how *did* you screw my side of the family?" Lucian asked. "Because I'm assuming you did."

Ravis gave a slimy smile. "Well, Dad willed the estate to me. It shocked both your mother and me when we found out how much he'd squirreled away. I needed that money to build this franchise out here. It's what Dad would have wanted. Mira didn't see it that way, though. She wanted her money up front, but the trust said the money couldn't be dispensed in that manner. She refused to play ball, so I had to take it. I invited her out to Halia for a job, but she stayed home. Out of spite, I guess. Wouldn't accept any of my help, either. Not even when it might've helped you."

"That's an awful thing you did," Serah said. "If not for you, she'd still be alive today."

Lucian knew all that was true, and it filled him with a fury such as he'd never known. And the way his uncle looked at him, his brown eyes mocking, just made him want to teach him a lesson. With magic, if it came to that. But he willed himself to calm down. Nothing good would come from losing his temper, and as much as he hated to admit it, he needed his uncle's help.

"No one regrets her death more than I do," Ravis said, though from his tone, it didn't seem that was the case. "But let's be realistic. People make their own choices, and she made hers. It might've been different had she not been so stubborn. I loved her, but don't say she wasn't stubborn."

"You shouldn't speak ill of the dead," Fergus said.

Lucian knew the warning wouldn't matter. He instantly saw that Ravis cared about no one but himself, and he only cared about his family as much as they reflected his legacy.

"You're obviously interested in the Builder ruins on the dark side of this world," Lucian said. "Maybe we can start there."

"And you said the inner sanctum only opens upon the

alignment of all the planets beyond Halia's orbit? I don't have seventy years to wait."

"There's nothing inside. Xara took the Orb of Gravitonics, but your company can still make a mint from monetizing the site."

"And I suppose you want my thanks for that? I already saved your life. What more could you want?"

"I already told you. A ship. If you really are on Xara's side, as you seem to be, you'd want me to find her, right? We'll fight, and one of us will take the Orbs from the other, speeding up the end of the Starsea Cycle before the Swarmers kill us all. You don't have any other idea for how to use me, so use me that way."

Uncle Ravis watched him in silence. He still wasn't convinced.

"You're harboring a rogue mage," Lucian went on. "Even if you kicked me out of here, you know things now that could get you killed."

"Is that a threat?"

"It is for the rest of your life, Ravis. It's in your best interest to help me, and I know you have the resources for it." Lucian smiled. "Consider it . . . an investment. Even if you believe Xara will ultimately triumph as the Chosen of the Manifold, don't you want to place a hedge on me? Give me a ship, and a fast one." Lucian thought for a moment. "And one thousand credits that I'm free to use however I want."

Ravis laughed derisively. "One thousand credits? You don't know the first thing you're asking, kid."

But something in Ravis's composure told him that wasn't true. His uncle was negotiating.

"Just the ship, then. And five hundred creds."

"Get out of here. You mentioned what the League would do to me if they found you here. Just think of what they would do if they found out I gave you money."

"This would hardly be the most illegal thing you've done, right? Make it untraceable. That's not too hard."

Ravis cracked a smile, but he gave no answer. "Let's not talk business tonight. It's getting late."

Ravis was about to get up when Lucian extended both of his hands. He reached for his Focus, willing both the Orb of Psionics and the Orb of Binding to materialize in his hands. Their twin lights shone brilliantly as they obeyed Lucian, doing exactly as he specified. Ravis's face went ashen as he shielded his eyes against their resplendent auras.

When the lights faded, coalescing into the two Orbs, Ravis uncovered his eyes and watched. Even Fergus and Serah stared wide-eyed, never having seen the two Orbs in person. Ravis stared in shock.

"They're mine to command," Lucian said. "I intend to keep it that way."

"What is this, some display of power? If you think that'll change my mind . . ."

"I'm just trying to show you how serious I am. These are the Orbs of Binding and Psionics. I've gone through terrible things to get both. And I won't let anyone stop me from getting the rest. You least of all."

Lucian absorbed the Orbs again, each streaming down his arms and toward his heart.

"You want a ship? I'll get you a ship." Ravis smiled wickedly. "My ship will take you directly to Halisport and drop you off on the edge of town. That's the best you'll get from me."

"Seriously?"

"You should be grateful," Ravis said. "No roads out here, and a skycar taxi this far out would probably cost you ten full creds."

"You're throwing us to the wolves, Ravis."

"I already helped you by saving your miserable mage lives," Ravis said. "And to borrow a term you used several times with me in your long story, you should be rotting thankful."

Lucian saw he was going to get nowhere with him.

"I wish I could help, Lucian. I really do. But if I give you a ship or any money, the League will be onto me. I already told you I'm under investigation. Every transaction is being monitored. You know they don't let mages outside the communes here. If anyone finds you, they'll send you right back to Psyche. In fact, if I turned you in, it would do a lot to get the League off my back."

"You wouldn't dare," Serah said.

"No," Ravis said. "I wouldn't." He watched all three of them candidly. "There is one thing I can do, though." He opened a drawer in his desk and retrieved what looked like a credit stick.

"What's this?"

Ravis looked at him matter-of-factly. "It's yours. The League gave it to you . . . for your mother's funeral. They sent it to me after a time, I guess because you were in the Academy." He shrugged. "The amount is so inconsequential to me, I haven't added it to my account. Don't know why I've been keeping it like this."

"How much is on it?" Lucian asked.

But even he remembered the number and knew the answer before Ravis gave it to him.

"2.5 creds," he said. "Not much. It can't get you off world. But maybe it's enough to send an encrypted light-message back to Volsung."

Lucian *could* do that, if only he knew how to reach the Volsung Academy. They had already destroyed and discarded the old slates Vera had given them. They were a liability, as Vera probably had a way of tracking them.

"I don't have the Academy's contact info," Lucian said. "What am I supposed to do with 2.5 credits?"

"It's all I can give you," Ravis said.

"You're serious?"

Ravis nodded. "I'm sorry, Lucian. You've been dealt a rotten hand." His shoulders relaxed a bit. "For the record, I hope you emerge as this . . . Chosen. I don't think it likely, but it's something I would like to see."

"I don't care what you want. So, are we responsible for finding our own way to Halisport?"

"I can have someone drop you off on the edge of town discreetly. Thankfully, the city isn't watched too closely. At least, not all of its quarters. I can do that much. As far as what you do after . . . well, that's up to you. You'll have 2.5 credits to work with. I've had far less in my pocket before."

2.5 credits was actually a healthy sum of money. It might afford one-month's rent in a crappy apartment in Miami's crime-ridden west side, or an incredibly posh meal at a high-end restaurant. What it couldn't buy, though, were three tickets anywhere in the Worlds, and probably not even as far as Halia Station in orbit.

If Ravis wouldn't give them anything more, they'd have to earn it.

"It's late," Ravis said. "It won't harm either of us if you stayed a night. You're safe enough here. For one night, at least."

All Lucian could manage was a nod. It was hard not to feel defeated. He didn't want to accept that hospitality, if it even *counted* as hospitality, but they had been without adequate sleep and warm conditions for several days now. It was better than being dumped on the outskirts of Halisport, the only city of any note on the surface.

Lucian didn't bother masking the sarcasm in his voice. "Thanks for your generosity."

Ravis pretended not to notice and stood. "It's late, and I expect you are ready to retire. I certainly am."

Ravis had one of the house servants lead them to their rooms.

3

LUCIAN'S ROOM was as pointlessly large and opulent as he had expected. It overlooked the black, rolling hills extending toward the west. The sleet pelted the wide bay windows. It was the perfect complement to his mood.

Such was his exhaustion that he couldn't stay awake for long. He slept for a good while in the soft, lavish sheets, feeling as if he was melting into them. After a few hours, there was a light knock at the door. Serah stepped inside and closed the door behind her. There was no bashfulness or asking permission before she slipped under the covers. After months of fighting their way across entire worlds, they were well beyond that point by now.

"I think I'd go *crazy* if I had to live here," she said.

Looking out the window, Lucian felt much the same.

"How are you holding up?" she asked.

Lucian propped his back against the pillows. Serah rested a hand on his chest as she laid her head on his shoulder.

"Well, my mom was right. That's all I can say."

"Yeah. He's an asshole, but we knew that going in, right? At least we don't have to walk to Halisport."

He held her close. "I miss this. Just the two of us."

"Well, I've *always* been here."

Lucian felt a stab of guilt. During the voyage to Halia, he'd prioritized learning magic with Vera over spending time with Serah. He'd learned a lot, but there was some distance to mend.

She had a right to be a lot madder at him than she actually was. And the worst part was, he wasn't sure if the lessons had been worth it.

"Sorry for that."

She remained quiet. His eyes went to the mottled skin on her arm. Thankfully, it hadn't grown since Psyche. They'd been using far less magic, nothing beyond what naturally accrued.

"I can't believe she's alive," he said. "That she has two Orbs."

"I know. It's crazy. Are you doubting yourself or something?"

The question didn't sit right with him. "How could I not? Maybe Ravis *is* right. If there is a Chosen of the Manifold, what if it's her? What if Vera's right, and my job is to hand over what I already have? How could I be so arrogant as to think *I* have the right of it?"

Serah just watched him, not seeming to have an answer. Not that Lucian expected one.

"For your faults, you're a good man," she said. "I don't know much about Xara. All I know is she doesn't seem like you. Whatever she wants deep down, it's not what's best for everyone. I don't know what gave it away. Probably her entire scheme to fuse with an ancient, evil alien."

Lucian cracked a smile. "Oh, is *that* what gave it away?"

"Well, it should go without saying. But maybe it's not for the morally deficient. Take your uncle, for example. He seemed quite comfortable with that concept."

"Well, it's common sense. Anytime an evil alien overlord

takes over the mind of the most terrifying mage in history, it's great for the economy."

She snickered. "Stop." She looked up at him. "My point being, you *can't* give up, Lucian. You've come too far, and the fact you're even *entertaining* the idea that you made a mistake . . ."

"I'm *not* giving up. I never said that."

"You need to believe you're right."

He had to push down his irritation, but he couldn't help but feel like he was being lectured. "Am I not allowed a bit of self-doubt now and then?"

"I understand. It must have blindsided you, being betrayed like that." She paused for a moment thoughtfully. "Even if the rest of us saw it coming from a thousand light-years away."

That wasn't completely true. He'd never trusted Vera. Not really. But the betrayal still stung because it came at such an unexpected time. It was worse because Vera probably didn't even see it as a betrayal. To her mind, he had a different role to play than he'd first imagined. Why else would she have bothered with training him if she didn't think he had *some* role to play? Even *he* doubted he was the Chosen of the Manifold, and it had taken a long time for him to embrace it.

And now that he *had* embraced it, the Chosen was supposed to be someone else all along? He didn't know *what* to think anymore.

"None of this will sort itself out soon," Lucian said. "I'm . . . glad you're here, Serah. Makes it easier to bear."

She watched him sadly. "I can't imagine what's going on in your head right now."

Lucian couldn't, either. "Maybe I just need time." He laughed bitterly. "Don't know what the hell we'll do when we're dumped on the side of town like trash being taken out."

"We'll figure it out. There's still the Prophecy of the Seven to find. Somewhere."

Lucian didn't respond. All of it seemed so insurmountable, and he was still so tired. Too tired to be thinking of solutions to the coming galactic apocalypse, anyway.

All he could do was hold her. Like that, they fell asleep.

————

He was back in the temple under the ice. His heart pounded as Vera and Xara waited in the wings, their hands glowing with potential, unreleased magic, cruel smiles stretched on shadowed faces.

He reached for the Orb of Psionics. Magic overflowed his Focus, but he was still too weak to counter both of them. His Focus collapsed, his defenses shattered under their dual assault. Their gleeful smiles widened, victory assured.

Lucian?

A familiar voice entered his mind from some faraway time. And at its sound, Vera and Xara shrunk into the background. A new setting replaced the ice temple.

Lucian stood on a cliff high above a tumultuous gray ocean, beneath the boughs of a flame tree laden with snow and ice. Transcend Mount on Volsung.

He turned to see Emma, her face narrow and somber. She wore the gray robes of a Talent and the green sash of a Radiant. Instantly, he knew this was no mere dream, and he was only here with her because he was streaming from the Orb of Psionics. But he had not sought her out. Somehow, she had found *him*.

Despite himself, his heart ached at seeing her. In a dream, it was difficult to push feelings away.

She kept a distance from him. It wasn't like his former dream of her, under the tree in her old village on Aurora. There was no preamble as she spoke.

"You need to come to Volsung, Lucian."

Was she serious? "Volsung? Why?"

"Transcend White needs to speak to you. It's . . . important."

What did she tell her? Terrible memories returned, and he could still see the Transcends leering down at him from their high seats.

"Emma . . . what have you done?"

"I had a dream of you, Lucian. I saw you with who I thought was Transcend White in this temple under layers of ice. It . . . felt important."

Lucian felt his eyes widen in shock. "You *saw* that?"

Emma nodded. "I had to tell her. How could I not, after what you told me on Psyche? It was only after that I realized that it probably wasn't Transcend White at all. It never occurred to me it might be Vera . . ."

"It was Vera. Listen, a lot has happened. Too much to say in a dream." Lucian already felt the connection weakening. "I can't come back to Volsung. Do you know what Transcend White *did* to me? I can never forgive her. If she wants to speak to me, why can't she just . . ."

No, she couldn't reach him here telepathically. He and Transcend White had never formed a link, and they didn't have a strong connection like he and Emma.

"A lot has changed here, too," Emma said, keeping her face neutral. "If you come back, it would not be to send you to Psyche again. That much I can promise."

Trading one conniving twin for another was the last thing Lucian wanted. "So, she wants to use me for something. I won't allow that, Emma. I'm *done* being used."

Emma went on as if he'd said nothing. "Don't be stubborn. Just this once. As soon as I told her about that dream, she told me to tell you to come back. I've been trying to reach you almost every night since, but this is the first time I'm able to speak to you. I don't know why it's worked this time."

"It's because I'm holding the Orb of Psionics," Lucian said.

"What's the Orb of Psionics?"

"Remember that story Transcend Blue told us about the Aspects of Magic during lessons?" At her nod, he continued. "They're real, Emma. I've found two of them."

"Seriously?" she asked, skeptically.

Lucian felt the dream fading—talking across such an extreme distance was taxing, even with the Orb of Psionics. "I don't know how much longer I can hold the connection."

"If you want to explain, return to Volsung. Find a way if there isn't one. I'm sure you know how dire things are at the moment, not just for the mages, but the Worlds. Somehow, you're a part of all this."

"I . . . don't want to face her again."

"You must. For what it's worth, I don't believe she wishes you harm. And . . . it would be good to see you again. Alive and well. From here, it looks like you've been through things."

He couldn't help but laugh. "Things" was an understatement. "That obvious, huh?"

Lucian had to admit, seeing her again would be good. But his old feelings, mixed with his feelings for Serah, were a complication he didn't want to deal with. Emma had likely moved on, and he had, too. At least, that was what he thought. He couldn't think straight, especially looking her in the eyes right now.

He cleared his throat. "I . . . should go. I'll think about it. It depends on a lot of things, most outside my control."

"Find a way. We need you. I don't know how or why, but we do. The mages are preparing to enter the war. The only reason we haven't yet is because Transcend White is balking."

"Why?"

"My guess is because of you."

"Because of *me*?"

"Transcend White wants to speak to you before she loses

the chance forever. That's what I think. If the mages travel fringeward toward Kasturi, we would be worlds away ..."

"I can't trust her, Emma."

"I know you can't. I'm still angry at them, too. But I haven't forgotten you. I . . . still think of you, sometimes." Her cheeks colored. "I'm sorry. I won't tell anything you've said to me to Transcend White. I'll leave it for you to decide. Just come back."

Lucian watched her for a long while. Long ago, she'd asked if he might help her if she ever asked. He couldn't betray that, as foolish as it sounded.

"I'll be there. As soon as I can."

Before she could respond, the dream slipped away, and he awoke in his suite on Ravis's estate.

4

THE NEXT MORNING, if the eternal twilight outside could even be *called* morning, Ravis led them from his estate toward the spaceship launchpad. Though the sleet had stopped, it was still gray and dismal. On the launchpad rested the very ship that had taken them here. The clunky transport looked as if it might disintegrate at the slightest breeze.

"Are you *sure* this hunk of junk can get us to Halisport?" Fergus asked.

Ravis seemed irritated by the question. "If my technicians say she'll fly, she'll fly." Ravis reached into his jacket pocket, producing three slates and handing them off. "These are yours."

"You can't access the GalNet without an identity," Lucian said. "As soon as I log in, they'll realize I'm off Psyche. Fergus, too. And as far as Serah, she doesn't *exist* as far as the League's concerned."

"I've already thought of that," Ravis said. "As my parting gift to you, these slates have identities preloaded. Identities you

27

must use from now on. You can use these IDs to access the GalNet and hold currency accounts."

"How did you get those?" Lucian asked. "A verified identity is far more expensive than the credits I asked for."

"Unlike credits," Ravis said, "no one can tie these IDs to me. Consider it a proof that I'm doing all I can for you, even if it doesn't look like it. Obviously, anytime you're dealing with someone, you need to go by your aliases. You'll find the details on your slate."

The slates Vera had given them worked similarly, although out in the Mid-Worlds and beyond, the system security networks didn't care as much about identity. But if they were going back to the First Worlds, where League presence was thicker, it paid to be careful.

Serah swiped her slate open. "Esmerelda Hodgman? Do I *look* like an Esmerelda to you?"

"We randomly generated the names," Ravis said.

"It's a beautiful name, Esmerelda," Lucian said with a smirk.

She stuck out her tongue.

"Looks like I'm Roger Varner," Fergus said. From his tone, he also seemed disappointed.

Lucian opened his own slate. "Marvin Hudson. That's an old man's name."

"Can we choose different names?" Serah asked.

"I'm afraid not," Ravis said. "You should be thankful. Fully verified identities aren't cheap."

Lucian didn't want to know how Ravis arranged it. The details were probably sordid. "Won't they conflict with facial recognition technology?"

Ravis shook his head. "Well, they don't even have information for Serah. You'll notice on your passports that all of you are from low development worlds, so no one will think your lack of biometric IDs strange. Keep a low profile and you'll be fine." He gave them a somewhat sarcastic salute. "Best of luck to you."

He was already turning around without sentimentality. If he cared so little for them, he probably wouldn't have bothered with the slates and new IDs. Lucian got the feeling they were an inconvenience Ravis was more than happy to get rid of. Which, he supposed, was understandable.

And truth be told, he was ready to get out of here, too, even if they only had 2.5 credits to share between them. It was enough to survive in a hotel for a few nights and get some takeout.

Clearly, they needed to get more money if they planned on getting off-world. Lucian didn't know how, but somehow, they had to make it happen.

The three of them boarded the transport and took up the middle row of seats. As soon as they'd strapped themselves in, the pilot announced departure. They lifted off from the cold tarmac.

"Only one question," Fergus said. "How do we get off-world? And *where* are we going?"

Lucian didn't have the faintest idea about the first question. On the second, though, he had some thoughts. "I had this dream last night. It was my friend from the Volsung Academy. Emma."

Both of them looked at him with interest, but it was Fergus who spoke. "What did she say?"

"Transcend White wants to talk to me. That . . . it was important."

"Seriously?" Fergus asked. "Then we must go at once."

Serah just watched him with suspicion. "How do you know it's not a trap?"

Lucian told them the details of the dream over the next couple of minutes. Once done, Serah frowned.

"She must be a good friend then."

Lucian tried to ignore the slight edge in her voice. "Either way, we have nothing else to go on. She said Transcend White was holding up the mages joining the war because she wanted to speak to me first. If that's true, then I want to hear what she has to say."

"Well," Serah said, "I'm for it, since we've got nothing else."

"What about the Orb of Thermalism and Hephaestus?" Fergus asked. "Might it be better to go straight there?"

"A ticket to Volsung is cheaper, since it's closer. And maybe Transcend White can help us, as much as I hate to admit that."

Fergus leaned back in his chair. "If you think we can learn more by going to the Volsung Academy, I say we go."

Lucian stared at the bulwark ahead, trying not to think about what had happened a year and a half ago, when the Transcends had sentenced him to Psyche. "I won't ever forgive Transcend White for what she did. But if she hadn't done it, I wouldn't have met either of you or found the Orb of Psionics."

"That's . . . accurate enough," Fergus said. "You're set on Volsung, then?"

Lucian nodded. "Yeah. It's all we have to go on."

Serah remained silent, keeping her arms crossed.

"Volsung it is," Fergus said. "Let's try to survive Halisport first."

———

The trip to Halia's capital city took less than an hour, and it took less than a minute for them to gather what few things they had, step off the ship, and watch the transport blast off into the low, gray clouds. The air was humid and warm here, telling Lucian Halisport was located more sunward than Ravis's estate, backed up by the additional brightness of the sky. The outskirts of the city were perhaps half a kilometer off, its outer ring of buildings forming a sort of wall. Farms of wheat and pastures of those strange, shelled creatures populated the land in between, and where there weren't farms, the tall black grass rose to their knees.

"On our own again," Serah said, staring across a field. "I'm hungry again."

"Doesn't look like there's much out here," Fergus said.

Lucian spied what appeared to be an auto-taxi rental place, standing alone on the side of a highway.

"We don't have much money," Lucian said. "Not that I condone stealing, but we've got to do what we've got to do."

"Stealing?" Serah said, clutching some imaginary pearls. "How *dare* you entertain the notion, Lucian Abrantes?"

Lucian smirked. "I might be honorable, but Marvin is a right bastard." He nodded toward the building with the taxis. "Maybe we should see how much one of these costs. We need to get to the spaceport, eventually."

They made their way through the dark grass. The stuff was rubbery and had the consistency of fake indoor plants. It was very much alive, though, oscillating in the breeze. He hoped there wasn't the equivalent of an alien lion out here stalking them.

It felt good to reach the road, and they walked up to the line of ground cars outside the small kiosk, approaching the first one in the queue. A touchscreen displayed a map of the surrounding area. Lucian zoomed it out, until he could see the full city to the south, along with its spaceport, which was centrally located by what appeared to be a large lake or sea.

"600 sub-creds to get to the spaceport," Lucian said. "That's a quarter of our stash. Maybe we should just walk."

"Twenty kilometers," Fergus said. "We've certainly walked farther on Psyche."

"Not in *this* gravity," Serah said. "But I understand. I hate this money system you guys have. Makes no rotting sense. Why can't everybody just take what they want?"

"It's how the galaxy works," Lucian said. "Unfortunately."

Complaining wouldn't get them anywhere, so they set off walking.

After a few minutes, Serah's face seemed to brighten. "Hey, I've got an idea that'll *really* speed things up."

"*No magic*," Fergus said.

"What? Why? No one's out here."

"Because," Fergus said, with forced patience. "mages are banned in this area. If anyone catches us, off to Psyche we go. It's not worth the risk."

"I guess," she said glumly. "Maybe just a *tiny* bit of magic?"

They fell into silence as they walked up the road. Within twenty minutes, they were between the first of Halisport's buildings. The city had a sterile look, with little paint or ornamentation. Dull metal surfaces surrounded them, the expansive, box-like buildings having the feel of a temporary colony rather than a permanent settlement. A lot of Border Worlds were like that, to Lucian's knowledge, but Halia was almost close enough to Earth to be a First World. Weeds grew between cracks in the pavement, and only a few ground cars zipped around the narrow streets, which went every which way with little planning. There were few pedestrians, the road network seeming very car-centric. They had to walk in a line along the sidewalk or else be in danger of being run over. They had to consult their slates constantly to make sure they were on the right track.

"Remember your names," Lucian said. "Everything has to match up with our IDs."

"I've been reading up on myself," Serah said. "Esmerelda is from Pallas." She looked at Fergus. "Do you know what a Pallan accent sounds like, Roger?"

"No clue," Fergus said, his mouth twisting a bit. He must have really not liked his name. "I doubt anyone will care to ask."

They entered a pedestrian mall with a large fountain in the middle. It was nice to have a break from all the cars speeding by.

"Hey," Serah said, stopping in front of a large, shabby building with plenty of people filtering in and out. The sign, lit with bright neon light, proclaimed the place to be "The Den of Iniquity."

"Oh, that sounds fun!" Serah said.

From the place's dingy appearance and gaudy lights, including a treasure chest filled with chips, Lucian could easily guess the building's purpose.

"A casino."

"Oh! Can we go in? Maybe we can win enough to get off this hunk of rock!"

Lucian saw that there were multiple such casinos on this strip. The Pirate's Treasure, The Golden Goose, The Tree of Money, the Reel Steal, Sapphire Star, among others. It was like a mini Vegas, though decidedly less glamourous.

Lucian looked up at the Den of Iniquity doubtfully. "This place looks a little sketchy." He looked down the street, at the Sapphire Star, which was larger, brighter, and had a cleaner appearance. "Sapphire Star seems classier."

"Only the best for Marvin," Serah said.

"We're not going into a *casino*," Fergus said. "They're designed to make you lose."

"Unless you have a proverbial ace up your sleeve," Lucian said quietly.

Vera had taught him a few things about psychic streams on board *Wayfinder*. You couldn't read thoughts with purely a Psionic stream. It required a Binding *and* Psionic dualstream.

And thankfully, he had access to both Aspects through his Orbs. He could read minds with impunity, as long as he streamed in amounts small enough to obscure the manifestation of magic.

"Vera taught me about psychic streams," he said. "I'm good enough to read thoughts. When I set my mind to it."

"Okay," Fergus said. "If you think you can get away with it without being caught . . ."

"What number am I thinking about right now?" Serah asked.

Lucian focused on her eyes and reached for both of his Orbs. He didn't open himself to them fully. He allowed a trickle of ether to combine into a dualstream and connected his Focus to her mind.

"Two and four?"

Her eyes widened. "Rotting hell! We're going to be so rich!"

"Try me," Fergus said.

Lucian obliged. "Seventy six point forty-two."

"Damn," Fergus said. "Well, color me convinced." He looked at the marquee for The Den of Iniquity. "We've been hanging outside too much. It'll look suspicious."

"Sapphire Star, then?" Lucian asked.

Serah rolled her eyes. "Okay, fine. *If* they let you in."

She walked on ahead before Lucian could respond.

"I don't know how you keep up with her," Fergus said.

Lucian sighed. "I don't."

5

THE SAPPHIRE STAR CASINO was far less posh than its name suggested. It was clearly the busiest though, which Lucian took for a good sign.

That was probably why they had a fifty sub-credit cover per person, which quickly knocked their stash down to 2.35 credits. They went toward the bar first to get the lay of the place, walking between glitzy slot machines, roulette, holo-kazan boards, Pai Gow tables, along with various other games of chance. Young female servers in tight-fitting dresses balanced trays of twenty or more drinks, expertly weaving through the crowd, while dressed-up crowds laughed raucously from the bar area and tables.

The bar was in the middle, on a platform that floated on a sort of indoor lake. They crossed a short bridge to get there, realizing they'd only seen a small part of the casino. There was a whole other side, with more slots and tables.

"What are you thinking?" Fergus asked Lucian. "Cards is probably your best bet."

Lucian nodded. "Makes sense. I can't read the mind of a machine."

"What about *that* one?" Serah said, pointing. "The one with the ball and wheel. How does that work?"

"That's roulette," Fergus said. "And it's the fastest way to lose your money."

"You seem to know your way around games of chance," Lucian said.

Fergus shrugged. "I've dabbled."

"Blackjack might be easiest," Lucian said. "I'm only playing against the dealer, not others."

"While that's true, the dealer has no agency in Blackjack. They follow rules, and will only look at their hands if a 10 or ace is showing. You need a game where you have an advantage for having information you're not supposed to have access to."

"What game would that be?" Lucian asked.

"Ideally, a game with hidden cards where you play against *other* players. A good one might be poker, particularly Pontic poker. You'll find it in most casinos in the Mid-Worlds."

"Okay. I can play poker, but how do you play that?"

"Well, Pontic begins with each player having one card showing, and one in the pocket."

"What's that mean?" Serah asked.

"Face down, so no one can see it. Each player bets, and with each round of betting, the dealer gives each player another card face-down, but also a face-up community card. And it goes like that for one more round, until each player has four cards, one face up and three face-down, and two community cards. If players are still in after that, one last card is drawn that all players can use. So, the end is that each player has four cards, and they can use the three in the middle to complete their hands."

"I see," Lucian said. "Sounds like a kind I played back on Earth. So I play other players, not the dealer, right?"

Fergus nodded. "That's right. The casino makes its money by taking a five percent rake off each pot."

From Fergus's description, it seemed a simple game, one where reading minds would come in handy, though it still wouldn't be a sure thing. A lot of it depended on how the community cards upset the balance.

They went through the rules several times until Lucian was sure he had it.

"All right," Lucian said. "Let's look for a table."

They scoped out the tables, walking through clouds of smoke and raucous, drunk patrons. A group of rowdy men were playing craps at a table they passed, shouting victoriously as the dice came up at seven. Serah watched with wide eyes, seeming to want to partake.

"That looks like a good one, too," she said.

"Too random," Fergus said. "We want something that's as close to a sure thing as possible."

When they found a poker table, a nervous weight formed in Lucian's stomach. They had so little money as it was, and even with a perfect, undetectable psychic stream, it was still possible to lose if he was unlucky. A sign on the table declared the blinds to be 250 sub-creds, about ten percent of his stash, so it would only take ten unplayable hands to lose it all.

He didn't want to think of that possibility.

Lucian took up a chair and inserted his credit stick in the table's slot, keeping his eyes forward and holding his Focus to calm his nerves.

"Welcome, sir," the droid dealer said, passing him the proper amount of chips. It was a piddling stack compared to the two others sitting at the table. The left was a gruff-looking man with a gray beard, protruding gut, and a pipe in his mouth. His dark eyes were half-hooded, as if almost asleep. The woman on his right was a late thirty-something in a red cocktail dress, smoking behind a heavily painted face.

"Good luck, Marvin," Serah said, kissing his cheek.

Lucian nodded and paid up his blind. Ten percent of his stash staked already. The droid dealt his cards. Lucian took a peek. Queen of hearts in the pocket, with a ten of clubs showing. Not terrible, but not great.

He was wondering how he should play this. With two players at the table, it might be difficult to maintain two separate streams. It would be better to wait and see if one of them folded early before opening a stream. There was less chance of his magic being detected if he was only reading one mind.

When the players had paid up and no one raised, the droid dealt Lucian his next facedown card, the jack of diamonds, while the community card came up as the four of clubs. Still nothing in his hand, with only a marginal chance for a straight.

The old man placed a sizeable bet based on his showing ace of diamonds. The bet was big enough for Lucian to have to call half his stack if he wanted to stay in. The middle-aged woman's mouth twisted, and she folded. The man watched Lucian intently.

Why would the man bet so much on such a small pot? If he really had something good, wouldn't he *not* want to scare Lucian off? Or was he counting on Lucian thinking that?

Well, he could have the answer to his question with a psychic stream. He had to do it now, otherwise he would be too nervous.

He opened his Focus to both Orbs, reaching for the man's mind.

The old man had a two of clubs and a four of hearts in the pocket. With an ace high, he was beating Lucian handily. But Lucian still had two more cards he could be dealt, and two more community cards to consider.

But it was too great a risk. He folded, and the man raked in the tiny pot with a self-satisfied smirk.

The old man bled him out like this two more times until

Lucian only had seventy percent of what he started with. The old man also took a sizeable chunk of chips off the middle-aged woman, winning with two-pair, while she had pocket aces. Lucky bastard. She got up in a huff and cashed out.

When the droid took her chips, Lucian and the old man were the only ones left. On the next round, Lucian had an ace of hearts face-up and a king of diamonds in the pocket. After calling the blind, the droid dealt his next card. *Another* king.

Reading the psychic stream, Lucian knew the man had a pair of eights hiding under his hand, with a queen showing. The man bet heavily, the entirety of Lucian's chip count.

Here, his psychic stream meant nothing. He had to call it.

"All-in," he said, pushing his chips forward.

They flipped their cards, and the man frowned at seeing Lucian's two kings against his two eights. Insult was added to injury as the dealer dealt Lucian *another* king, while the old man got nothing. Once the droid dealt the rest of the cards, the old man only had two pair.

Lucian's pot doubled as he raked his winnings in.

"Lucky bastard," the old man said.

Lucian just shrugged.

"What's your name, son?"

"Marvin."

"Marvin." He gave a slight chuckle. "I'm Owen. Owen Bradford. That was a ballsy play. But it'll get you wrecked soon enough."

"We'll see."

Serah leaned down and whispered to him. "So, Roger and I just looked it up. Getting three tickets to Volsung will be about fifty credits."

Lucian tried not to make his eyes pop. He'd have to *double* his stack four or five times to afford that. Eyeing the man's chips, he *could* win that much off him. It felt bad to cheat, but it was the only way he could see them earning enough money to get off this world.

They traded back and forth a few times, the man betting more carefully now. Over ten hands, Lucian was three credits richer and Owen three credits poorer. Lucian's stack was 6.5 credits now.

"Quite the shark," Owen said. "Where the hell did you come from?"

"Just looking for a way off this world."

The droid dealt another hand. Lucian tried not to betray his surprise when he had *another* ace showing and one in the pocket.

"What the hell you got over there, son?" the gambler drawled.

"Two aces."

The man guffawed. "Even *you* aren't that lucky. I'd have to shoot you dead."

Lucian kept his face expressionless. One benefit of holding his Focus was that he could be as emotionless as the droid dealing to him.

From his psychic stream, Lucian knew Owen was just trying to get into his head. The old gambler was nervous. He still had upwards of fifty credits in chips, and he was sweating after losing a few here and there. He didn't lose often. Owen was a rancher. A very rich one. This was just play money for him, a way to blow off steam, get off the ranch and gamble, drink, and whore his way across Halisport while his wife was off-world. He had two kids who'd left home young, and his major regret was not spending more time with them. He came to town because the ranch was cold and lonely, and he just wanted to feel the thrum of human life around him sometimes. He'd married three times, and things were not going well with the current one. He . . .

Lucian shut off the stream of thoughts. He was digging too deep. He just needed to know the man's cards, not his life story.

For now, Owen had a pair of kings he felt strongly about, but little did he know, Lucian actually *did* have pocket aces.

Before the droid dealt the last card, the man called the size of Lucian's pot. After all but the last community card had been dealt, it was still kings against aces.

Lucian called, knowing that whatever that last card was, it could end him.

The droid flipped the card. Jack of clubs, which didn't help either of their hands.

Lucian revealed his two aces and took the pot.

"Son of a whore," the old man breathed.

Lucian was nearly up to thirteen full credits. It would've been higher if not for the casino's rake. It was more money than he'd ever earned in a single night. "Had enough?"

Lucian wasn't trying to drive the man away, but taunt him. From his stream, he knew the old man wouldn't back away from a direct challenge.

Owen's expression reddened. "I'll clean you out before the night's through. You'll see, gosh darn it."

They'd gathered something of a crowd by now. Apparently, Owen was a regular, had even won several tournaments at various casinos in Halisport. The man's pride was shaken that this young upstart was reading his every move.

Lucian lost a few hands because of bad luck, but thankfully he could limit his losses. Whenever Lucian bet too big, it spooked the old man into folding too soon. He lost some potential that way. He also bluffed twice, knowing Owen would fold.

Then Lucian had a string of bad hands. The old man raked in the small pots, only marginally adding to his stash. Lucian knew exactly when to duck out.

"Think I'm about done here," he said. "Maybe got one more in me."

The droid dealt, and Lucian had a seven and nine of clubs. By the time each of them had four cards and two in the middle showing, Lucian had a flush. Owen had nothing but two-pair, twos and jacks.

Owen watched his cards for a moment, seeming to think. His bushy eyebrows drew down, and he let out a sigh.

He bet everything he had to clean Lucian out.

Lucian called. The only way he could lose was if a jack or two showed up that would give Owen a full house.

The dealer flipped the last card…

Ace of diamonds.

The old man cursed. Lucian took the pot, with nearly twenty credits in chips on the table.

"I've had enough of you," the old man said, his face fuming. "You're cheating. I don't know how, but I ain't ever seen someone play like you."

The droid turned to the old man. "Accusations of cheating are prohibited at the Sapphire Star Hotel and Casino. The casino scans every patron for illegal cybernetics upon entry. This is your first and only warning, and any further breaking of rules will see you removed."

"Pshaw," the old man said. "You're one lucky son-of-a-bitch is all I've got to say."

The old man walked off in a huff, puffing his pipe madly.

In a daze at having so much money, Lucian pushed them toward the droid. "Can you load these?"

"Certainly, sir," the droid said, taking the chips. "Congratulations on your winnings."

A little ding sounded, and a light above Lucian's credit stick blinked. Lucian withdrew the stick, and upon his hand touching it, the small screen illuminated, revealing the sum of 18.93 credits.

Someone touched him on his arm. Lucian turned to see a

young woman with perfect features that could have only come from very expensive surgery.

"Congratulations, sweetie. Want to go celebrate?"

"Get lost, you rotting hussy," Serah said, drawing him to her arm.

The woman just smirked and walked away to find a new mark.

"You must be careful, Marvin," Fergus said. "You attracted quite the crowd over here. In a place like this, that can be a bad thing."

A server walked up to him, flashing a radiant smile. "Congratulations, sir. Have a drink, on the house."

"No, thanks."

He led the others a fair distance away until the crowd stopped trying to talk to him.

"So, we need a little over ten credits more," Lucian said. "I doubt anyone wants to play poker with me now."

"Probably not," Fergus admitted. "At least, not here."

"What do we do, then?" Serah asked. She lowered her voice. "Wait. You think you can control one of those roulette balls?"

Lucian shook his head. "That would take too much precision."

A suited pit manager walked by, flashing Lucian a shark's smile that didn't reach his eyes. The smile was clear. He had his eye on him.

"Maybe we should go," Lucian said, once he'd passed. "New place."

"That's a good idea," Fergus said.

They left the Sapphire Star and walked several doors down to Fortune's Favorite. After several hours more at the medium stakes Pontic poker table, Lucian more than doubled his stack to forty credits.

One player, named Isaiah, was easy to take advantage of. He

talked a big game, but he bluffed almost every hand, his face going red with rage every time Lucian called.

"You'll regret this," he said, getting up and ripping out his credit stick. Before the droid could reprimand him for the threat, he was stalking out of the casino.

"This doesn't bode well," Fergus said.

"We're rich!" Serah said. "Fer . . . err, Roger, do you have your wallet open?"

"I do," he said. "Marvin, can you sync the creds to me?"

Lucian did so. Despite everything they'd been through, it still felt strange indeed to sync that amount of money to someone. Within moments, the digital wallet on Fergus's slate received the money.

"Good. Found a ship that leaves Halisport in three hours, and a liner from Halia Station that leaves in five."

"The sooner we're off this rock, the better," Lucian said. "As long as you think we can make it in time."

"I can book the trip and we'll still have eight credits leftover. More than enough to travel in comfort."

"Let's go," Serah said. "I'm *so* ready to get out of here!"

6

WHEN THEY LEFT THE CASINO, an auto-taxi Fergus had hailed was waiting for them.

But so was a mob of four men, led by Isaiah, all bearing shocksticks.

"Give me that credit stick," Isaiah said. "Or else!"

"Already spent," Lucian said. "Get lost."

From Isaiah's expression, it didn't seem he would do that. Isaiah raised his shockstick, and the others followed suit.

"Here we go again," Serah said.

The crowd cleared as Lucian withdrew his shockspear, extending it with a flash. He blocked Isaiah's shockstick with ease. Two men fell on Fergus, while one attacked Serah. Serah didn't even take out her spear, instead wrapping her hands with silvery Gravitonic Magic. When Serah's fists landed, Lucian heard ribs crack. Though Serah's fists weighed nothing to her, they punched with the weight of ten gravities.

Fergus easily dealt with his two, opting not to kill, but to land hard blows with the butt of his spear, knocking both out.

Lucian dealt with Isaiah simply by tethering his feet together, causing him to go down.

"What the . . .?"

"Stay down if you know what's good for you," Lucian said.

From the crowd's reaction, it seemed none of them detected the use of magic. Or at least, they were too shocked to respond to it.

Either way, the taxi was waiting.

The three of them piled in and fled the scene, Lucian letting go of his Binding stream. Isaiah bounded up and watched them leave, though his three cronies remained grounded.

"That was almost too easy," Serah said.

"We're not to the spaceport yet," Fergus said. "Still about half an hour."

The self-driving car took them on a highway that rose above the buildings below. In the distance, Lucian could see the sea tinged the color of wine in the distance, and a vast spread of buildings before him. Halisport didn't have many tall structures, opting instead to spread out. It was an ugly city built in a hurry and without planning, and the gloomy weather certainly didn't help the aesthetic.

But this city wouldn't be his problem for much longer. The taxi dropped them off at the front entrance of the spaceport.

"Will they let us take these on board?" Serah asked, pointing to her retracted shockspear.

"You'll have to check it in," Fergus said. "It'll fly in storage."

"Won't they know we're mages by carrying these?" Lucian asked.

Fergus shrugged. "Mages are hardly the only people who use shockspears. Soldiers sometimes have them, though the electric outflows come from a battery."

That ended the debate right there. They had nothing else to check in besides those spears. The baggage attendant handled them with a professional mask and asked no questions while placing them in a magnetically sealed crate.

A few hours later saw them in orbit and docking with Halia Station, and another hour saw them on board the *Great Venture*, a Pan-Galactic vessel that was smaller than the one Lucian had taken almost two years ago.

In twenty days, they'd be docking with Volsung-O and on their way to the Academy.

7

THE PASSAGE to the Volsung Gate only took three days, such was the small size of the Trappist System, but from there, it was a long slog to Volsung. Its orbital path placed it on the opposite side of its parent star, adding seventeen days to their journey.

From the beginning, Lucian could tell this passage was going to be far different from his first. Most of the people were traveling alone and stuck to themselves. There were no rowdy fleet recruits, or people who looked like they were going to cause trouble. Not that such a thing would concern him anymore, but the passage would be a rare opportunity to rest after what they'd been through.

Lucian, Serah, and Fergus alternated their between training in their private cabin and staying occupied with the on-board entertainment. Lucian loved seeing Serah react to a lot of his favorite holos, and she never seemed to get sick of them. She absorbed everything. Her father had taught her to read on Psyche, but they had little besides some old tomes Elder Erymmo kept in his hut.

"All this stuff I'm learning, you learned it in school?" she asked.

"Some of it," Lucian said.

"The Climate Wars, the Solar Expansion, the Stars Diasporas . . . how do you keep it all straight? Not to mention all the stuff that happened *before* space travel."

"To be honest, I don't. Most people don't, actually."

"It's all so fascinating," she said, holding up her slate. "With this, I can learn what people were thinking back then. Can even hear them talking about it! Have you looked up your ancestors?"

Lucian smiled. "Yeah, but it's been a while."

She waved a finger at him chidingly. "You don't appreciate what you have. I don't know who my ancestors are, or I'd look them up."

"You could probably learn, if we submitted your DNA for testing."

"Can we do that?"

"Maybe," he said. "If we ever get some downtime."

She sighed. "I'd like to do something other than fighting. Just . . . live a normal life."

"That's impossible for us. Even without all this Orb business."

"You're depressing me." Her expression suddenly darkened. "So. Who's this friend of yours on Volsung? Emma, was it?"

Lucian repressed the urge to swallow the nervous lump in his throat. "Yeah. We trained together for a while. Met on the way from the Solar System."

"I see. Anything still there?"

"What do you mean?"

"Don't play dumb."

"You cut right to the chase, don't you?"

"It's what I'm known for."

Honesty would probably be the best policy. "Well, I had a

thing for her in the past before I left for Psyche. I think she did for me, too. Nothing happened, though. It would've been impossible, anyway."

He remembered the kiss they shared on the way to the Academy while crossing the ocean, what seemed so long ago. That kiss hadn't turned into anything as much as Lucian had wanted it to. Things had changed. Maybe some feelings still lingered. He didn't know what would happen when he saw Emma face to face again. Hopefully nothing. He was happy with Serah, and he didn't want weird feelings gumming up the works.

She watched him closely, not seeming to miss a single detail. "Impossible, why?"

"They forbid romance at the Volsung Academy. Among many other things. They claim it impedes the training."

"Do you still have feelings for her?"

Lucian resisted the urge to squirm. "It's been a really long time."

"Huh." From her glowering expression, Lucian got the impression that he'd answered wrongly. "Which of us is prettier, then?"

"Are you serious?"

"Come on. Hit me with the truth. I can take it."

Lucian wished he could just walk away from this most uncomfortable situation. "You, of course."

Her eyes narrowed a bit. "You *sure* about that?"

"Yes," he said. "You're not just prettier." He pulled her closer, and her blue eyes suddenly widened. "You're far more irrepressible."

"Is that what you like?"

"Maybe," he said.

He kissed her, and she seemed to soften somewhat, much to Lucian's relief.

He pulled back. "I don't want you to worry. I'm with you. We've been through a lot. More than Emma and I ever have."

She looked into his eyes. "Which of us do you *like* more, though?"

"Why are you so insecure suddenly?"

"I don't know. I just . . . see your face when her name is mentioned. It makes me think you're lying."

"I'm not."

"See? Your voice is tense. You have feelings for her still. Just admit it."

"What do you expect me to say? I was honest about that. It's complicated, but you're my girl."

From her smile, it seemed she liked the sound of that. "I'm supposed to be mad at you."

"Mad, why? I'm doing my best, here."

She sighed. "I know. I'm not being fair. Just . . . rotting feelings. I hate them sometimes." Her blue eyes glimmered. "I can be a wee bit crazy."

"Maybe just a little."

She let him hold her, for which Lucian was grateful. Serah had given up everything to come with him, which only made him feel guiltier. The answer should have been simple, but it wasn't.

"Well, I'll tell you one thing," Serah said. "If you fancy having two girlfriends, I'm just going to let you know I don't share. The last time a woman tried to steal my man, I punched that bitch." Her eyes glinted dangerously. "My fists and Gravitonic Magic make a *very* dangerous combination."

Just the idea of Serah giving Emma a beat-down almost made Lucian choke. "Err . . . that won't be necessary."

"I won't bother you anymore. I've said my piece. It's . . . okay if you're confused, I guess. Just . . . don't string me along. If you want her more, just cut me loose. It'll hurt a lot less."

Lucian said nothing. What *could* he say to that? They went

back to watching holos, though the mood wasn't the same. A relationship between him and Emma was impossible, anyway. He might not be a mage of the Volsung Academy, but Emma was. She wouldn't jeopardize her station for anything.

But there was always a sliver of doubt. In the end, he was there to see Transcend White, not Emma.

At least, that was what he told himself.

———

A FEW DAYS left until Volsung, the three of them were in the mess hall eating breakfast when a newscast began playing on the television.

The sleek-suited anchor delivered the news. "Chaos in the Djerrah System as the Swarmer Fleet blasts through the Kasturi Gate, inciting fear and panic on the distant desert planet. Evacuations are underway as a flood of refugees pours toward the inner worlds. The League Fleet, currently based at Alpha Centauri, is expected to deploy to Astravan to block incursions to the First Worlds."

"Jesus," Lucian said. "Look at the size of it."

The screen displayed a truly massive fleet, filled with dozens of supercarriers and thousands of tiny, angular strike craft.

"It's beginning," Serah said, faintly.

"Kasturi is far, and so is Djerrah," Fergus said. "It'll take several months before they reach Astravan, even assuming they don't stop to pillage the worlds on the way."

"And how many worlds on the way?" Serah asked.

"There are two worlds between Djerrah and Astravan. It's likely they want to get to Alpha Centauri, because that will lead them directly to Earth. The question is, will they try to get to A.C. through Astravan, or through Karelia?"

"Is there a difference?" Serah asked.

"Both would take the same amount of time. At least three months if they're going top speed and meet no resistance, but likelier it'll be closer to half a year."

Three months was about how long it took the smaller Swarmer fleet that had killed Lucian's mother to reach Alpha Centauri. But that fleet had stopped for nothing.

"There's not much time," Lucian said. "Three Orbs left to find, plus the two Xara has. I can't do that in six months, much less three."

Everyone went quiet at that. Probably because they knew Lucian was right.

Earth would fall before he could gather them all. And if Earth fell, what was the point?

"We can only hope the League is powerful enough to stop their advance," Fergus said, though his tone said he doubted that.

And it was easy to see why. During the First and Second Swarmer Wars, the Swarmers had never had over ten carriers in *any* fleet. This one held at least a hundred. True, the League fleet was stronger than it had ever been. But there was no way it was strong enough to challenge *this*.

"Hephaestus borders Astravan, doesn't it?" Lucian asked.

Fergus nodded. "If the Swarmers are going for Alpha Centauri, like they think, then the bulk of the fleet won't head for Hephaestus. It's possible they'll pass it over entirely."

"It's an important source of metals for the League," Lucian said. "If I'm remembering right."

"You are," Fergus said. "Losing the Elevator would be an immense blow to the League's industrial base."

"Hephaestus is where the Orb of Thermalism is, right?" Serah asked.

"If Vera is right," Lucian said. "If the Swarmers get there first, then I'll have no hope of getting it."

"Should we try to get on a ship once we reach Volsung-O?"

Lucian shook his head. "Maybe after we speak to Transcend White."

"We need to be careful when dealing with her," Fergus said. "Remember Vera?"

"I'll never make the mistake of trusting anyone outside this table again," Lucian said. "It's the three of us against the galaxy. Transcend White will have information. Information that might change the equation."

"You mean *Vivienne*," Serah said.

Yes, there was that. Lucian wondered how she would react if he called her by her proper name. It seemed like something Vera would do. For that reason alone, he decided not to do it. No need to disrespect Transcend White unnecessarily.

"Three days until we're there," he said. "I'll be close enough to Emma to let her know we're close. I can wait until we're in orbit, at least. That way the connection has no chance of failing."

Either way, it was just a matter of time. Lucian willed down the nervousness bubbling up in his stomach. He wondered how Vera and Xara were reacting to the news of the Swarmers. They probably already had a plan in place. Hell, they were probably well on their way to finding another Orb by now.

Lucian wasn't giving up, though. This was far from over.

8

ANOTHER THREE DAYS and they had docked at the dilapidated Volsung-O, which orbited a planet whose upper hemisphere was half-encased in ice. It must have been winter down there.

He'd established a link with Emma thirty minutes before without issue. A few minutes later, Emma assured him they didn't need to go to Karendas, but an Academy mage would be on the station waiting to take them by shuttle directly to Transcend Mount. Lucian wondered why he and Emma hadn't gotten that treatment on their first trip, but perhaps it was a matter of priority.

As soon as they stepped off board, a gray-robed Talent with the gray sash of a Gravitist was waiting a few meters from the boarding tunnel. The exiting passengers gave him a wide berth, watching him fearfully.

Lucian approached, and the man lowered his hood, revealing a mage he'd never met before with brown skin and a trim goatee.

"I'm Talent Yorus," he said. "I'm to lead you to the shuttle."

"Lucian," he said, giving his real name. "These are my friends, Serah and Fergus."

"Yes, the Spectrum has apprised me of their arrival. You must come with me."

Without waiting, Talent Yorus turned and stole into the crowd. With a shrug, Lucian followed.

As they walked, a bubble surrounded the gray mage, as if at any point he might lash out and attack. The teeming crowds swarmed around him like a school of fish would a shark. Talent Yorus paid no mind, picking his way through the dark corridors to the underside of the orbital.

After a few minutes, he passed through a coded sliding door, which took them into a private and empty waiting room. On the other end of a single airlock was a waiting shuttle, large enough for perhaps ten people. The door slid open.

"Please, it's time to board," Talent Yorus said formally.

"We're going straight to the Academy?"

Talent Yorus nodded. "Yes."

"You're piloting?"

Yorus nodded, but offered nothing more.

"I thought the Volsung Mages didn't use advanced technology."

"Some do."

Yorus offered nothing more, so Lucian ducked inside the vessel, followed by Serah and Fergus.

There were two rows of seats in the tiny craft. Lucian and Serah took the front row while Fergus plopped down in the back. As soon as they'd strapped in, Yorus breezed by, entered the cockpit, closing the door behind him. A minute later, the engine powered on and the ship detached from the spinning orbital. Lucian felt himself lifted against his restraints as he looked through the left-hand viewport.

Within moments, they were angling down into the pristinely blue atmosphere toward the vast ocean below.

"A water world," Serah said. "I never dreamed of such a place before this."

"More like an *ice* world," Fergus said. "Must be winter."

"I've had my share of ice," Serah said.

Lucian remained silent. Being so close now, he was feeling nervous.

The sky below was clear, revealing a seemingly endless sheet of ice stretching in all directions. This far north during the Volsung winter, the sea was a frozen waste, almost as frigid as Halia's dark side. At first, there was no evidence of the island. But eventually, it revealed itself, a lone bastion rising above the whitish-blue ice sheet.

Within minutes, the Volsung Academy materialized from the snowy surface of the island's flat top, seeming to claw at them with its lofty dilapidated towers and battlements.

Lucian held his Focus, hoping it would steady his nerves. It was . . . *strange*, to be back here again. He would have never dreamed it to be a possibility. Old fears pulsed within, even if he had grown enough to face them.

The snow-filled training yard was empty as the shuttle landed and powered down. Lucian looked out the porthole at the massive edifice. Ice encased its sides, hanging from its battlements and arcades.

"This place looks rotting creepy," Serah said. "You sure it's not haunted?"

"Worse for the wear, isn't it?" Fergus asked. "The Mages' Tower on Irion is far more modern."

"The design is a conscious choice, trust me," Lucian said.

Yorus seemed to want to stay in the cockpit, so Lucian waited.

At last, a lone figure materialized from the Academy's yawning mouth. At first, the completely white robes made Lucian think it was Transcend White herself. But the person's broad shoulders dashed that notion. It could only be Psion Gaius.

A surge of anger burned through Lucian. Just remembering how the Psion had tormented him during his passage to the Isle of Madness was enough to boil his blood.

"We don't like him, I take it?" Serah asked.

Lucian didn't answer as more Psions emerged from the cavernous entrance. Violet, Green, Gray, Blue, Red, and Orange all filed out onto the snowy grounds. Almost all were faces he recognized. They had escorted him to the Isle of Madness, after all. They stood silent as statues, seeming to judge from a distance, their gazes unrelenting.

Last of all came Psion Yellow, and to his surprise, it was Khairu. She wore the yellow robes of a Psion's station. She had fully ascended, then. Lucian wondered what had created the vacancy: the death or exile of Transcend Yellow, or the death or exile of the former Psion. Changes happened here, Lucian realized, albeit slowly.

The eight Psions of the Volsung Academy wore somber expressions as they approached in a perfectly straight line, each of their hands hidden within the billowing sleeves of their robes. That was where they no doubt kept their shockspears.

"Quite the welcoming crew," Fergus said.

Lucian waited, but no one else came out of the entrance. He wondered why Transcend White wasn't here to greet him herself. Was she afraid to face him? Or was she trying to play her power games?

"Let's go," Lucian said.

The three of them headed for the blast door. Still holding his Focus, Lucian forced calm throughout his entire being. The Orbs of Binding and Psionics were ready and willing to be used, if it came to that. They almost *ached* to be used. He hadn't streamed beyond what was necessary during the long voyage, and only in their shared cabin. He had to admit, it would be nice to push the Psions around and teach them a lesson.

But the last thing Lucian needed was a confrontation. That would get him nowhere.

He needed Focus. He needed calm.

Obediently, his emotions subsided. *He* was in control. That he had become a powerful mage without their help would be the greatest revenge.

When he pressed the button to open the blast door, Fergus and Serah fell in behind. It felt good to have them at his back rather than having to face this place alone. He'd come far in the past two years, but he'd only come so far because of his friends.

When the breeze swept across into the ship, it was bitingly cold, stinging Lucian's face and nostrils. The yellow sun radiated little warmth. It was deep winter now, and the island was a world of gray and white. Even so, the fresh air was welcome after several weeks on board a spaceship.

When the Psions didn't make a move, Lucian approached them until he stood about ten meters away. Lucian kept his gaze level with Psion Gaius the entire time. The White Psion looked much the same as before—solid face, bushy eyebrows, humorless brown eyes. His expression was inscrutable.

Though Lucian didn't want to talk to him, there was no other way forward. "Where's Transcend White?"

Gaius responded as if it pained him to do so. "Her High Eminence awaits you in her tower."

"Not the Spectrum Chamber?"

"She would have words with you privately first. It would seem the two of you have much to discuss."

Lucian wondered just how much Gaius knew. Lucian rankled at the fact that Transcend White might have told him some of it already. It was impossible for Transcend White to know more than what he'd told Emma, so at least there was that.

"Lead on, then."

Gaius's eyes went to Serah and Fergus. "Your . . . *companions* . . . must remain on the transport."

There was no way Lucian would allow that. "Gaius, I didn't travel all this way to turn around. Transcend White wanted to see me, and there's no rotting way I'm going in there alone."

Gaius's eyebrows arched in surprise. "Only ascended mages have the privilege of stepping within our hallowed halls."

Lucian couldn't help but smirk a bit at that. This place was a lot of things, but it certainly wasn't hallowed.

"Is there something amusing, Exile?" Gaius asked.

"Quit pretending you're my better. I've been through a lot of shit, and I'm not here to play stupid power games with you. Take us to Transcend White. Now."

Fergus stepped forward, his expression somewhat placating. "Fergus Madigan. Radiant Mage of the Irion Academy." Some of the Psions' feet shifted at that. Clearly, they had not expected this. "By your own words, I have every right to step into the Academy. You said *ascended mage*, and I am one. Just from another academy."

"And I'm Serah Ocano," Serah said. "The best Gravitist in all the Worlds." Psion Gray, an overweight man in his fifties, narrowed his eyes at that. "I'm also an ascended mage of . . . the Riftlands Academy."

Psion Gaius arched an eyebrow. "There *is* no Riftlands Academy, and if there were, it would be a rogue academy."

"She's coming," Lucian said. "That's final. Either that, or her High Eminence can come out here in the cold to talk to us."

Psion Gaius let out a labored sigh. "*Fine*. We will escort you there now."

Gaius glared a moment longer. Maybe he thought it would save his pride, but to Lucian's mind, it didn't in the least.

The White Psion turned around, leading Lucian, Fergus, and Serah toward the front entrance. The other Psions fell in around them, forming a protective barrier. As if *that* could stop him if he wanted to break out. Lucian almost felt bad for them. He held two Orbs of Starsea, and he had been through things they would never believe. In just a year and a half, life had tested him far more than they ever would be.

If it came to a fight, they wouldn't stand a chance. Not even if they worked together.

His nerves vanished once he passed the dark threshold, entering the familiar anteroom filled with its massive black granite columns and wide central brazier. Memories of his Novice days returned to him. Sweeping the floor. Dueling Khairu before the fire. Warming himself by that same fire with Emma. It was like remembering another life.

"Where is everyone?" he asked.

"Quiet hours."

Lucian had almost forgotten about that. "Well, don't worry about us. I'm not here to hurt anyone."

"That's the least of my worries, Nov . . . I mean, Exile."

For the first time, Lucian's eyes met Khairu's, who was walking beside him. As usual, she seemed angry for anger's sake. She kept her gaze steady.

"Good to see you, Psion Khairu. Congrats on your promotion."

Her cheeks reddened, though her expression didn't change.

"Be silent," Psion Gaius said. "Insolence will get you nowhere."

"I'm not a Novice anymore," Lucian said. "You can't tell me what to do."

"You impudent scamp," Psion Gray rumbled. "What could her High Eminence *possibly* want with such an upstart?"

"That is not your concern," Psion Gaius said coldly.

Psion Gray's jaw hardened, but he did not offer a counter-argument.

Within a few minutes, they were standing before Transcend

White's oaken door on the Academy's third level. Soon, he would be face to face with her. His nerves returned, but his feelings were nothing he couldn't control. His Focus steadied his resolve.

"Enter," came a reedy voice from within. A voice that was nearly identical to Vera's.

"Sounds just like her, rotting hell," Serah whispered.

"Let me do the talking," Lucian said.

Serah stuck out her tongue at him, and with that, the three of them entered Transcend White's study, leaving the Psions behind.

———

THE ROOM WAS JUST as Lucian remembered it. Cold, bare, with little in the way of ornamentation. Transcend White sat behind her large desk, hands folded neatly on its pristine surface. Her gaze was dark, her expression inscrutable, almost completely hidden by dancing of shadows cast by the low fire on the hearth. The air was warm, heady with the fragrance of incense.

Lucian stood before her, and all his former resolutions to remain calm faded into the distance. She studied him for a long moment, seeming to see to the marrow of his bones. Lucian tried to return the favor, though he suspected it was with less effect. He had formed a Psionic ward before meeting Talent Yorus, but being face to face with Transcend White made him wish he'd refreshed it.

A mere glance at her tired expression revealed many less-than-peaceful nights. Questions ruminated over for months. Perhaps even years. The weight on her shoulders, it seemed, was greater than the weight on his.

That humbled him, if only a little.

At last, she shifted in her seat, and her voice came out cool and collected. "I would speak to you alone, Lucian."

Lucian. Not *Novice* Lucian. It was hard not to reel at that.

"I would rather not be alone, Transcend White." He nodded toward his friends. "This is Fergus Madigan and Serah Ocano. I met them on Psyche. They know everything I know. Whatever you tell me here, I'll just tell them."

Transend White's practiced gaze went to Serah's left forearm, which was not completely covered by her jumpsuit. She was a bit too late in hiding it.

The Transcend, however, made no comment about the fraying wound. "As you wish." Her jaw tensed. "Perhaps . . . it would be better to clear the air first. Such as we can."

"If you're wanting forgiveness, I have none to give. You Transcends are nothing but a bunch of backstabbers."

Transcend White nodded, as if expecting that answer. "The choice wasn't easy, Lucian. We did the best we could with the information we had. I don't expect you to understand, but that's what it came down to."

"Your Psion said the same thing on the way to the Isle of Madness. He seemed happier about it than you, though."

"Not even the wise can see how things will turn out. And sometimes, we Transcends can be greater fools than anyone. And when we are fools, millions die." Her deadened gaze almost gave Lucian a chill. "We err on the side of conservatism, because rocking the boat, or allowing someone to exist who *can* rock the boat, has proven disastrous in the past. But for all our conservatism, inexplicable paths manifest in the most unlikely of moments. That is something you should understand very well. For without our intervention, you would have never unearthed two of the lost Aspects of Magic."

So Emma *had* told her that much.

"From your indignation, it would seem you think your friend betrayed you. She said not a word."

"Then how do you know?"

Transcend White gave a small, cunning smile. "Her mind is

no match for my will. Everything you've told her since you've left Volsung, I'm now privy to."

"You had no right to read her mind."

"The fate of the Worlds is greater than any one individual's rights."

"Your sister said a similar thing. More than once. Along with the likes of Ansaldra."

If that name surprised Transcend White, she gave no sign. "The fate of the Worlds is in the balance, Lucian. Don't you see that?" She watched him critically for a moment. "Of course, I know you mixed yourself up with Vera. I assume she somehow extracted you from the Mad Moon, something I didn't think possible. And you've found two of Arian's fabled Orbs." She paused again, as if to let him digest the weight of that. "Well, perhaps those Orbs are *not* so fabled now. Your role is far greater than I could have imagined, and the mystery that brought you here in the first place is being answered. Worse, you might be our only hope against the coming darkness."

"What do you want from me? Why did you want me to come back?"

"Because I need to know your story."

"No. If you want to help me, that's one thing, but—"

Her face tightened in severity. "For the stars' sake, don't be a fool, Lucian. For once in your life." She sounded very much like her twin. "Telling me your story—*all* of it—is how I help you."

"Or maybe it will give you an opportunity to betray me again."

"Things have changed, Lucian. Even you should be able to see that. As great as your dislike for me is, as understandable, you must set it aside. Otherwise, you can get right back on that transport and seek Arian's prophecy on your own."

He couldn't help but widen his eyes. "What do you know about that?"

"More than you think. Obviously, you've gathered two of the

Orbs, and that you've come here tells me you have no clue what you're doing, otherwise you would have ignored me. You need The Prophecy of the Seven to find the rest of the Orbs. Until Emma came to me, I was doubtful of their existence. But now, nothing else makes sense. The Orbs are real, and *you* must gather them. And I imagine Vera means to use you to find the Orbs for her own ends, which would be an unmitigated disaster."

She knew more than Lucian would have guessed. "Where is the prophecy, then?"

"I'll tell you what I know. But only when you tell me everything that's happened to you. There are missing pieces, tremendous gaps in my knowledge. I need to know everything Vera is up to."

It was going to be like that, then. And it wasn't like he could lie. She would detect that immediately, unless he drew from the Orb of Psionics and shielded his mind entirely.

"You've got a lot of gall," he finally said.

"I'm Transcend White," she said. "I'm *nothing* but gall."

"Then this had better be worth it."

They talked late into the night. He left no detail out. She even learned about Linus and Plato, somehow clawing that information out of him. If she seemed surprised they had survived the Isle of Madness all these years, eluding capture, she gave no sign. The one thing that surprised her was that the Orb of Binding's location had been on Volsung itself.

When he talked about Queen Ansaldra, she asked sharp questions until she knew as much as him, and perhaps even more. A few more clarifying queries, and some honeyed tea to soothe his sore throat, and he finished the full telling.

Transcend White was no longer sitting at her desk, but had dragged her chair before the fire as Volsung's nighttime cold seeped into the tower. The wind howled outside the thick walls, and darkness had long fallen. She just stared into those flames intensely for what felt like hours, though it couldn't have been over fifteen minutes. The silence seemed to stretch forever.

When Lucian thought about interrupting, she stirred like a statue coming to life.

"It's much worse than I thought. They have the likely location of one Orb, that of Thermalism, if her suspicions about your vision are true. But even if they know its exact location, I don't believe they are going there first."

"Where are they going, then?" Serah asked.

Transcend White watched her intently. "They want the same thing you do: The Prophecy of the Seven. The authentic version, written by the hand of Arian himself. The Chosen of the Manifold is the subject of that prophecy, along with his or her path to find the Orbs."

His or her. Was she tacitly admitting Xara might be the Chosen? Lucian ignored that point.

"Where is it, then?" Lucian asked, his voice somewhat raspy. "I left nothing out, so now you've got to keep your promise. If you don't tell me where it is, we're done here."

"I don't know where it is."

Instead of feeling a surge of anger, Lucian only felt disappointment. Disappointed that he had believed she would actually tell him. It seemed to be his fate. Falling for people's tricks over and over.

"However," she said, "that doesn't mean I don't have a lead."

"Well, don't leave us in suspense," Serah said.

Fergus held up a hand to defray Serah from antagonizing Transcend White. But proper decorum seemed to be far from the Transcend's mind.

"We have three secondary copies of the prophecy here in our library, protected and safe on the third level."

Lucian knew the Academy's most valuable texts were there, including the writings of the Old Masters, the original Eight

Transcends who founded the Academy during the dawn of magic.

"Vera referenced those," Lucian said. "She told me bored Novices and Talents translated them and they didn't do a good job of it."

"I'm afraid that's accurate," Transcend White said. "But it's from these copies that Vera herself composed two master copies, which she took with her. To this day, only one copy of that remains with us, less pure than the one she took."

"So this translation might point me to the real prophecy?" Lucian asked.

"Perhaps," Transcend White said. "If you read it in a state of Psionic hypnosis. It would require great power. More than even I could marshal."

"The Orb of Psionics could point the way!" Serah said.

"That's what I'm hoping," Transcend White said. "And if not, there is one lead you can follow, anyway."

"What's that?" Lucian asked.

"Something led Vera and Xara to Isis long ago before the Mage War. Above even the Orbs, they were looking for a clue that might lead them to The Prophecy of the Seven. For the prophecy is the key to finding the rest of the Orbs. It stands to reason there might be some clue on Isis, some bit of research conducted during the days of the Mage War. If so, it would be at the Starsea Sanctum."

"The Starsea Sanctum?" Fergus asked.

"It was the name of their old academy. It lasted just over a decade. Isis, of course, remains a depopulated wasteland, off-limits to the public and guarded by the League Wardens, though not to the extent Psyche is. After listening to your story, I've surmised that Isis is likely where Xara found the Orb of Atomicism. Sometimes, I wondered how she might have been powerful enough to lay waste to that entire world. But now it all makes sense. Now that I know what the Orbs are capable of, it is paramount we keep them out of her hands."

"Is Atomicism Xara's primary?" Fergus asked.

Transcend White nodded. "You might say that, but she is proficient in every Aspect. But especially so in Atomicism, Dynamism, and Thermalism. And she is more powerful in her weaknesses than many are in their strengths. She stands above even Vera, and her strength is the chief reason Vera believes her to be the Chosen." She smiled bitterly. "The only thing Vera respects is strength, whatever form it takes."

"So even without Orbs, she's a tough fight," Serah said.

"Indeed," Transcend White said. "My heart quails knowing she's been walking these Worlds the past fifty years, unseen, unknown."

"And there's someone else who's found an Orb, too," Lucian said. "Someone we don't know about." He watched Transcend White. "Before coming here, I thought it might be you. Or maybe one of the other Transcends."

"Me?" She chuckled darkly. "I'm an old woman playing guessing games. But Vera and Xara are, too. At least, we hope that's the case. We have little else."

"They might be heading for Isis, too, if what you're saying is true," Serah said.

"Yes," Transcend White said. "During the Siege of Isis, it's inconceivable that they could have rescued all of their knowledge. But assuming not, it's clear as day what a fool I was."

"What do you mean?" Lucian asked.

Transcend White smiled bitterly. "Why, it's because of *me* that they escaped Isis at all."

9

LUCIAN BROKE THE FOLLOWING SILENCE. "What do you mean, it's because of you?"

"Do you have siblings, Lucian?"

He shook his head. "No. I'm an only child."

"Spilling the blood of one's own family isn't a simple thing, and few outside the psychopathic can do so. Add to that, I was the only one who knew she was on that ship trying to run the League blockade. Indeed, the only one who *detected* her. Ultimately, I was the only one who could have given the order."

"You let them escape?" Fergus asked.

Transcend White nodded. "She was using Radiance and Psionics to shield her vessel from detection. Despite her skill, I still recognized her emanations within the Ethereal Background. The Ether was tumultuous then with so many mages streaming, so not even I was sure it was her at first."

"The Ether?" Serah asked.

"An archaic term for the Ethereal Background. Sometimes, us old ones still use it." She paused before going on. "I could have destroyed her utterly. It . . . was my great test. My great test, and I let her go. In hopes, perhaps, that we might reconcile in some far future day." She went silent, her expression darkening. It gave Lucian a chill, watching the firelight dancing in her eyes. "But as we all know, that was not to be. Whether it was by my mercy, or the Manifold itself, my hand was stayed. Vera lived, and for decades thereafter, she worked unseen and unknown. Without even a rumor of her over the long years, I feared she might truly be dead." Transcend White's eyes went to Lucian. "Until *you* showed up."

"Because of your choice, we're in this mess now," Lucian said.

He immediately regretted saying that. Transcend White gave a ghostly smile. "Are we? Perhaps I spared her so she might set you on your proper path. It's impossible to say. One thing we can be sure of is the Manifold guides all things. After so many years, I see the truth."

"What is that?" Fergus asked.

"Why I made that decision. She has some part to play still, as we have seen with Lucian. Even if I had ordered the lances to fire, some miracle would have saved her. Her purpose was not complete."

"*Fate* saved her?" Lucian asked in disbelief.

"Is it really so unbelievable, after everything that's happened? Do you not sense something larger at work in the galaxy?"

Lucian knew what she was getting at, but he didn't want to admit it. That the Manifold lurked in the background, inexplicably guiding all events in subtle ways, was not something he wanted to entertain. The Shadow Realm would always remain that: a shadow cast by the Manifold, the ultimate truth.

"If all this is fate, then what's the point of action? Why not let Xara gather all the Orbs?"

"Perhaps *you* are fated to do so," Transcend White answered. "Fate does not mean inaction. It does not guarantee success or failure. It means something is guiding at least some of our actions. The important ones."

"What is important is making sure she never finds another Orb," Fergus said.

"On that, we agree," Transcend White said.

"What about the *Alkasen*?" Lucian asked. "How are we supposed to stop them?"

"It's a race against time. At the rate they're going, they won't reach Earth for another six months, if not longer. We are only now seeing them fall upon the Djerrah System. From there, the speed at which they get to Earth depends on whether they go through Fessan or Talesia. If they spend as long in each system as they have in Kasturi, it would be two years before they reach Earth, assuming we don't turn them back first."

Lucian had the feeling it wouldn't take that long. Why give the League a chance to defend itself? Unless the Swarmers were so many that it simply didn't matter.

"Getting to Isis, like you're suggesting, will take at least five months," Lucian said. "The benchmark is about a month between gates, right? Isis is five Gates from here, unless I'm misremembering."

"Five *months*?" Serah asked. "And I thought it took forever to get here. I'd die if it was any longer than that."

"Space is vast," Transcend White said. "But I'm afraid we have little choice."

Fergus cleared his throat. "Assuming no slowdowns between gate passages, it might be less than five months. Most of space travel is getting up to speed or slowing down. Usually, there's enough time to maneuver between gates for no slowdowns at all. That alone can save us weeks on a long journey, if not months, depending on Gate positions and such. Of course, it will be impossible to know until the navigation computer plots the course."

"Fergus is right," Transcend White said. "Assuming a fortuitous alignment of the Gates, you shall reach Isis in about three months. Five months if you are unlucky. Of course, the three of you will not be going alone. Three is not enough to accomplish a task of this size." She considered for a moment. "I've been considering whether my Psion, Gaius, should go with you."

"No," Lucian said. "Anyone but him."

Transcend White's eyes seemed slightly amused. "However, I thought it might be best for you to be accompanied by someone you are already familiar with. Psion Khairu will make the perfect companion. Highly capable, and as a Dynamist, her magical abilities will complement you and your companions perfectly."

Lucian was at a loss for what to say. *Khairu*? They'd murder each other before they even reached the Halia Gate. "Are . . . you sure we can't take someone else? Khairu and I don't really see eye-to-eye on a lot of things."

"Then learn to work with her." Transcend White gave a small shrug. "Of course, her apprentice will join her, since it seems she's mixed up in this, too."

Her apprentice?

"Normally, I would not let someone so young join you on such a dangerous mission, but I fear *all* Talents, whatever their age, will be in great danger soon. Emma Almaty has already asked about helping you, such as she can. And her progress has been enough that I wouldn't lose too much sleep over it. Of course, it's contingent upon her agreement."

Lucian nodded, hardly believing what he was hearing. If he could get Emma, then maybe he could tolerate Khairu. He knew that was selfish. To accept Emma meant putting her in danger, but as Transcend White said, she would be in danger, anyway. And besides, this was Emma's call, not his.

He would see her again after nearly two years. He was all too conscious of Serah watching from beside him. He held his

Focus more deeply and cleared his throat. "I would welcome both of their help."

"Make no mistake," Transcend White continued, "their loyalty is to the Volsung Academy, not you. While you would be in charge of the overall mission, they will report directly to me. If you expect Emma to choose her friendship with you over her loyalty to the Academy, you will be in for a rude surprise."

What was *that* supposed to mean? A sliver of doubt entered Lucian's mind. Had he misjudged Emma's intentions?

"Well, it seems our interests are aligned. For now."

"So it would seem. Now, do you have questions?"

Lucian wasn't even sure where to begin. "There's something I've been wondering for a while. How did Vera find me in the Golden Palace on Psyche? She *knew* I was there, but how did she pinpoint my location exactly?"

Transcend White gave a knowing smile that gave Lucian the creeps. "You haven't guessed?"

Why was she toying with him like this? "If you know something, just tell me."

"During your first voyage to Volsung, Vera almost certainly placed a brand on you. And a powerful one at that, to have lasted this long."

"A brand? What kind of brand?"

"A Psionic brand of her own devising, sealed with at least five of the Seven Aspects, if not more, to ensure longevity. You wouldn't have felt a thing, as limited as your powers were. It's likely she did so upon your first meeting."

It was hard to remember back that far, but Lucian had almost felt a certain . . . *pull* . . . emanating from Vera from the moment they'd met. She had drawn him toward her, trapping him like a fly in a spider's web. *That* had been magic? He felt faint at the idea. She knew where he was, even now? Could she hear him speak? Read his mind? The very notion made him want to heave.

Transcend White seemed to guess his thoughts. "It works better with proximity, but yes. My sister knows the general direction in which to find you, and the closer she is, the more powerful she can feel her brand. It also gives her the power to affect your dreams, perhaps even to speak to you directly, though such a thing cannot be easy at great distance."

As soon as Transcend White said those words, Lucian remembered how Vera had spoken to him under the Sea of Storms, during the Gravitonics Trial. That hadn't been a hallucination at all. She *had* been keeping tabs on him.

"I feel sick," Lucian said.

"Fear not. She can't know your exact location. Not unless she's within several kilometers, at least. But she knows in what direction to find you, and by that alone, she might deduce your location. She likely knows you're here, for example."

"They might set up a trap if we come after them!" Serah said.

"They might," Transcend White said. "It's a possibility you must be ready for. If she knows you're here, it might please her you're far from Isis, assuming that's where they're going. She knows that I'm likely to be working with you. That is something she assuredly *doesn't* want. Time is on her side, unfortunately."

"What do you suggest?" Fergus asked.

"What I said before. Psion Khairu and Talent Emma will be at your disposal, along with purest translation of the prophecy we possess. It might be of some help to you, though I wouldn't hold my breath."

"I read part of it once," Lucian said. "While I was a Novice."

Transcend White watched him with interest. "Did you, now?"

"I checked it out by mistake. I was looking for a copy of Manifoldic Theory, also by Arian. Anyway, I remember going into some sort of trance. I thought it was gibberish, and I'd almost forgotten about it."

"A trance?" Transcend White asked.

Lucian nodded. "It was during the Trials, so I tried to put it out of my mind. I heard a voice in my head, talking about Starsea and the Orbs. I . . . think it might have been Arian himself."

It sounded completely crazy to say aloud, but Lucian had gone through far crazier in the last two years. The others watched him with interest.

"You never mentioned that before," Serah said.

"Like I said, I forgot. At least until Transcend White mentioned it again."

Transcend White ruminated for a moment. "Perhaps that translation isn't as useless as I thought. If there was time, I'd want you to stay here and ponder it for weeks for even the faintest clue of unraveling its meaning. However, time is not a luxury we have. Whatever studies you want to make of it, it will have to be in transit."

"We're leaving soon, then?" Fergus said.

"Within hours, if possible. Even a few minutes might be the difference. Before you go, there is one last matter to take care of."

"What's that?"

"The three of you are rogue mages, legally speaking. The Spectrum must convene to see that doesn't remain the case."

"So, you're letting me back into the Academy?" Lucian asked incredulously.

"It's legally necessary. The situation is . . . unorthodox. I don't want you to be hindered for any reason during your travels. To get here, you had to assume fake identities. But doing that long-term is extremely risky, and no longer necessary. Because of the war, Academy Mages now have carte blanche to travel wherever they will in the Worlds, with the notable exceptions of Psyche and Isis. But that only works if you *are* an

Academy Mage. We can write off your imprisonment on Psyche as a clerical error."

"No one's going to believe that."

"Why not? The only people who saw you go were here and on board the *Worthless*. And our committing you to Psyche is easily explained by an absentminded Talent making a recording error." She smiled. "We need not specify who."

"If . . . you say so."

Transcend White's eyes took in Fergus and Serah. "Though I haven't looked up your details, Fergus Madigan, I sense you are speaking the truth about your origins. And we can easily enter Serah Ocano into our rolls as a Novice, recently promoted to Gray Talent." She looked at Serah's arm. Though her fraying wound wasn't showing, it might as well have been from the way Transcend White was watching it. "I'd keep that well-hidden, were I you. Others . . . might not understand."

Serah's face paled, and she said nothing.

"What if the other Transcends don't want to reinstate me?" Lucian asked.

"It's not a question of want, but need. I will meet with them after this, and tell them most of what you've told me. Ultimately, they will vote the way I tell them to."

One other thing was bothering Lucian. "You knew they were lying about me during my sentencing. And you said nothing in my defense."

"Of course I knew. We Transcends are not paragons of virtue. We never have been. We do what suits our purposes, and sentencing you to Psyche did. Much went into that decision, and your performance at the Trials was probably only a quarter of it."

"Then why should I trust you now? Your own sister betrayed me, and now, I'm supposed to believe *you* won't?"

"I suppose you must make your own decision."

"Even that's asking a bit much."

"Do you have a choice?"

Lucian realized he didn't. The feeling was terrible. "Can you remove this brand Vera placed on me, at least?"

"That remains to be seen." She rose from her desk. "I have much to do. If you wish for a warm meal, our larders are open, but you wouldn't offend anyone if you remained on the ship, if that would be more comfortable. We can bring food to you there."

"We'll go back, then."

"When the Spectrum is ready, we will summon you."

10

A FEW MINUTES after they had returned to the transport, a pair of Novices delivered a pot of stew, which the three of them shared on the deck of the main cabin. Though Lucian remembered the Academy's meals as being mostly tasteless, it was far better than the slop Pan-Galactic doled out.

A couple of hours later, Psion Gaius himself entered the transport, snow having collected on his shoulders from a light flurry outside.

"The Spectrum has summoned you," he intoned somewhat ceremoniously.

Everything seemed to be an act for him. Still, Lucian made no comment, standing to follow the Psion out into the cold.

This time, they didn't see fit to guard him. They followed Gaius across the dark, snowy grounds leading into the Academy. The only light came from the sphere Gaius had streamed.

"Colder than the Upper Reaches," Serah said.

The inner antechamber was warmer, the fires helping to push back the chill. Psion Gaius led them through dark corridors, weaving his way to the deepest parts of the Academy.

Within minutes, they were standing before the entrance to the Spectrum Chamber. It took Lucian back to that horrible night, where Psion Gaius had awoken him from his sleep. Within moments, he would be face to face with the same people who had consigned him to a fate worse than death.

Against all odds, he was here. They would soon learn that their sentence had only strengthened him. Now the tables had turned. *They* needed *him*. It was hard not to feel good about that, even if he didn't expect them to grovel.

There was little time to ruminate. Psion Gaius gestured toward the archway, and Lucian walked through, followed by Serah and Fergus.

When he reached the dais before the Eight High Seats, he didn't bother to bow. That wasn't his place anymore, and he wasn't their subject. He would refuse even when they raised him to the mantle of Talent. There was no way he would bow after the hell they'd put him through.

Instead of lowering his face, he raised it toward the eight resplendent figures sitting before him, each of their robes shining like the surface of a star. But beyond that blinding light did not sit gods, but humans. And humans were fallible, prone to mistakes. Lucian understood that well, and it gave him confidence. If Transcend White was an old woman stumbling in the dark, how much more so were her underlings?

"Let's just get this over with," he said.

Their silence seemed to stretch for an eternity. Even Fergus looked at Lucian, as if shocked at his defiance. It shouldn't have come as a surprise, given Lucian's history with these frauds.

Transcend White was the first to move, her robes shining like a nova bursting into life. The light on her robes dimmed, and the rest of the Transcends followed suit. Now able to see their features, he took them in one by one. Transcend Red's beautiful, sharp features were appraising. The portly Transcend Orange looked ready to scold him. Transcend Yellow had not been replaced, and she now looked at him as if he were a viper about to bite, though Lucian knew full well she was the true viper. Transcend Green looked somber, while Transcend Blue contemplative. When Lucian's eyes went to Transcend Gray, he already looked half-dead, his figure emaciated and slumped. How had he not been ousted by now? The man clearly had the fraying. Not that Lucian believed *any* mage deserved the cruelty of Psyche, but it was strange how the Transcends' justice fell more swiftly on Novices and Talents than their very own.

Last of all, Lucian watched Transcend Violet, whose dreamy expression seemed far away from this place.

"It's time," Transcend White said.

At that moment, each of the Transcends stood in eerie unison.

"What are you doing?" Lucian asked.

"What we must. Kneel."

"No. I refuse."

"Imbecile," Transcend Red said, her blue eyes furious. "This is more than you deserve!"

"Watch your rotting mouth," Serah said, her hand going to the shockspear hidden beneath her robes.

Transcend Red's eyes widened slightly before she broke into a small smile. It was nice to know Transcend Red was as psychotic as ever.

"Stay your hand, Serah Ocano," Transcend White said. "We are going to remove the brand my sister placed on Lucian."

"You could've just said that to begin with," Lucian said.

As far as Lucian knew, until today, none of the other Transcends knew of Vera's existence. That news couldn't have been easy for them to take in. He wondered just how much Transcend White had elected to tell them.

It took a moment for him to sink to his knees. He didn't

trust them to so much as fetch him a glass of water. But he had no choice. He wanted that brand gone. This was the only way.

"This may be . . . uncomfortable," Transcend White said. "There is no guarantee of success, even with our combined powers."

"Do what you must. Just don't kill me."

"We aim not to."

Before Lucian could question further, each of the Transcend's hands rose, palms outward, becoming alight with the colors of their respective Aspects. A terrible coldness overwhelmed him, as if they'd poured water beyond freezing over his body, penetrating him to the very marrow of his bones. He stiffened, his breath leaving him in a sharp gasp, his vision darkening, his body wrenching but somehow remaining rooted in place.

How long that lasted, Lucian couldn't say. He was blind to everything and everyone. Blind to everything but the pain. It couldn't have been more than thirty seconds, but it felt like an eternity.

Then, the cold pressure released. The Transcends sat back in their seats as Lucian tried to catch his breath. They, too, seemed to be strained, as if they had just run a lap around the Academy.

It was a moment before Transcend White spoke again. "We tried. Any longer, and you would have been in danger of dying."

"The brand's still there?" Serah asked.

"Yes," Transcend White said. "It's beyond our power to heal. And if we can't heal it, you may be sure there are probably none in the Worlds who can."

"There's seven of you, though," Serah said. "Only one of her!"

Her shoulders slumped, as if she were suddenly very weary.

"It's not as simple as that. Perhaps the Masters of Irion or Mako could do better. I don't know."

"I don't have time to go to either planet," Lucian said. "Is there really no hope?"

"Only her death, or yours, can undo that brand. Or if she were to do it of her own will. Her Focus is the key. As much as we might try, we cannot replicate something so unique. Great care and power went into the making of that brand. She meant it to last a lifetime."

That was it, then. No matter where he went, Vera would have a rough approximation of how to find him. And when he pursued her, she would know weeks or even months ahead of time that he was coming.

It felt pointless to go on when the odds were so stacked against him. And yet, he didn't have a choice. Not if he wanted to stop Vera and Xara from gathering the Orbs and unleashing their madness on the Worlds.

"The next item of business," Transcend White said. "Your reinstatement to this Academy as a fully-fledged Talent, and the induction of two new mages into this Academy, each to be raised to the mantle of Talent, with all the rights and privileges afforded thereto."

She watched him, as if it was his turn to speak. Lucian didn't know what she expected him to say.

"I don't care about becoming a Talent," he said. "All I care about is stopping Vera and Xara. If that sounds good to you, then let's finish this."

They watched him gravely. It was Transcend Blue who broke the silence.

"Yours was a . . . special case. That the Manifold would see fit to return you here, after so many trials, is a testament that it means greater things for you. Mind that you lay down your pride. In fact, I would see these Orbs. Not that I doubt Transcend White's words, but—"

"He has them," Transcend White said. "They are his to command. I would not risk them being displayed in their raw power."

"If he could have a teacher—"

"No," Transcend White said.

That told Lucian all he needed to know. Even Transcend White didn't trust her colleagues to restrain themselves at the promise of holding an Orb. That he held the Orbs of Binding and Psionics might make him the object of envy of Transcends Blue and Violet in particular.

"Then what do you propose, your High Eminence?" Transcend Blue asked. "Surely we cannot send these three, along with Psion Khairu and Talent Emma, on such a dangerous journey across the Worlds with no preparation."

Several heads nodded, including Transcends Red and Yellow.

Transcend White's face held barely restrained, cold fury. "Did you not listen to a word I said, Transcend Blue? There isn't time for training. I suspect Lucian's trials in the last two years have been far greater than anything we could offer. Psion Khairu has received instruction at the feet of the Transcends. She will share that knowledge as she sees fit."

At this, the Transcends had no response. Lucian got the feeling that Transcend Blue, along with the others, wanted him to stick around for more nefarious reasons. The longer he stayed, the more time Transcend Blue had to figure out how to get a hand on Lucian's Orb.

But none seemed to want to challenge Transcend White, at least here in the open.

"We must raise all three to the mantle of Talent immediately. Do any oppose?"

No one voiced protest. None looked happy about it, but they were following Transcend White's lead. For now.

"If there is no dissent," Transcend White said, "each of you must choose your favored Aspect."

Lucian's jaw tightened. "If you think that means we're going to follow what you say—"

"Do it," Transcend White said. "I have no more patience for this. We must register you with the League, and we can only do that if you choose an Aspect."

"Well, I'm a Gravitist," Serah said. "I suppose that would make me a Gray Talent."

Transcend White nodded. "Very well. Do you accept her, Transcend Gray?"

Silence stretched for a long moment, to where Lucian didn't think Transcend Gray even heard her. Perhaps he had even died on the spot. He remembered Linus's story about competing with Transcend Gray to become Psion decades ago. He wasn't sure why that memory returned to him at that moment.

"I accept," he rasped.

"And you, Fergus Madigan? Toward which Aspect shall you dedicate yourself?"

"I choose the Radiants."

"We are called the Green Mages here," Transcend Green said.

"The Green Mages, then."

"And you, Lucian?"

He didn't want to choose *any* of them. But there was only one choice that made sense. The one that wasn't frothing at the mouth to get a hand on his Orb.

"I'll go with Transcend Violet, I guess."

Transcend Violet smiled. "You *guess*?"

"This is only a formality in my book," Lucian said. "You threw me to the wolves as much as everyone else."

Transcend White's gaze was icy. Lucian expected her to scold him, but she didn't. Instead, she stood, removing from her robe something previously hidden. It was some sort of book, and from its tattered edges, Lucian knew what it had to be.

"The Academy's most pure translation of Arian's *Prophecy of the Seven*." She stood before him, handing it to him reverently. Standing just a couple of steps away, Lucian could see just how frail she was with age. But her eyes were hard. Harder, perhaps, than even her twin's. "It's yours. I hope it may be of some use to you, but don't lose hope if it's not. More mages than you know have wasted decades trying to glean some kernel of truth from his madness."

It didn't feel appropriate to thank her, so Lucian merely took the delicate book.

At some unseen signal, Psion Gaius entered the Spectrum Chamber.

"Take them to the *Ethereal*," Transcend White said.

"At once, Transcend White."

"The *Ethereal*?" Lucian asked. "What's that?"

Transcend White watched him for a moment. "How did you expect to get to Isis, Talent Lucian? Even if there *were* a passenger ship that went that way, none would stop there. You must take one of the Academy's vessels, and *Ethereal* is among our fastest."

"Wait . . . you have *ships*?"

"Yes," she answered, as if that were a foregone conclusion. "And more than that, you'll need a pilot. Another reason for Talent Khairu to join you."

"She's a *pilot*?"

Transcend White ignored his question. "There are five of you now, and despite your talents and abilities, the galaxy is a dangerous place. Have a care, Talent Lucian. Though it is too soon to say, my hunch is that the fates of billions rest on your shoulders." She looked at her Psion. "Take them, Psion Gaius. There's no time to lose."

"Follow me, Talents," he said.

Lucian watched Transcend White a moment longer, hardly able to believe this was over. But once he saw she was completely serious, he couldn't get out of there fast enough. He left the silent Transcends behind and followed Psion Gaius through the cold, dark halls of the Volsung Academy.

11

PSION GAIUS LED them to the third level of the Academy in complete silence. Once they were walking down a long, cold hallway, Lucian was feeling suspicious.

"I know there's no ship up here, Gaius."

"It's *Psion* Gaius, now," he said, smugly. "And you are a Talent of the Academy. You had better conduct yourself as one."

"Rot that," Serah said. "No one tells *me* what to do."

"She's right," Fergus said.

"Where's the ship, then?" Lucian asked.

"You'll soon learn that," he said coldly.

From his tone, Psion Gaius clearly realized he held no cards. He couldn't punish them, he couldn't lord his power over them, and he couldn't do anything against Transcend White's wishes. She had relegated him to an errand boy. Lucian had to admit that it was nice to have the tables turned.

"Lead the way, Psion," Lucian said.

Lucian thought he might have heard a growl, but he wasn't entirely sure.

They passed empty halls and offices, most dark, cold, and

disused. It recalled long, bygone days where the mages were more plentiful, in those decades before the Mage War where magic had seemed the solution to all of humanity's problems, rather than the source of them. Lucian tried not to think of those lives and stories, many likely cut short because of the war. Save for the Transcends themselves, no one occupied this floor any longer, but clearly, it was not always so. It seemed a terrible waste.

"The Transcends sure are living high and mighty," Serah said. "All of Kiro Village could fit here."

Gaius regarded the dark, passing rooms. "It was not always so, but that is before my time. None but Transcend White remember those days."

He said nothing more, turning down a central corridor which ended in a stone staircase spiraling into darkness. They were probably somewhere in the middle of the Academy, but this was not a staircase Lucian recognized. It may have led to the Talents' level one floor below, but it almost certainly did not lead to the main floor.

"This is the central tower, isn't it?"

"Yes," Psion Gaius said. "It is only accessible from here."

To Lucian's surprise, Gaius took them down the staircase rather than up. The stairs went around and around until they had to be far underground. It reminded him of his descent into the Mountains of Madness on Psyche.

After fifteen minutes, the stairs came to a sudden end, revealing a short corridor. A pair of thick metal doors stood at the end of the passage, looking extremely out of place among the heavy stonework. It was too high tech for the Volsung Academy.

"I'm guessing not all electronics are prohibited on the grounds," Lucian said.

Gaius input a code on the nearby reader. "You should have guessed that when you saw Talent Yorus piloting a shuttle."

Serah glanced at Lucian and rolled her eyes.

The hangar doors slid open, revealing a vast hangar bay sprawling before him, large enough to hold multiple vessels. Not just surface-to-space transports, but fully outfitted spaceships fit for Gate travel that could crew ten or more.

However, only one ship occupied the cavernous space right in the center. *Ethereal* had a sleek, aerodynamic shape typical of ships designed not only for space travel, but for atmospheric operations. Its hull was glossy and black, larger even than Vera's *Wayfinder*. Lucian knew little about personal spaceships, but from a glance, it looked as if it could compete with Vera's vessel. At least, he hoped it could.

"Has this been here the whole time?"

"*Ethereal* has not stirred since the close of the Second Swarmer War," Psion Gaius said simply. "Transcend White must truly believe in your mission to give you access to her personal vessel. She could have given you a much slower one."

"The Academy has other ships?"

"Yes. They are docked on Volsung-O."

Lucian knew Psion Gaius was hinting he should feel grateful, but it was hard to forgive Transcend White for what she did, even if she was giving him access to *Ethereal*.

Standing before the extended boarding ramp leading into the ship were two familiar faces. The first was Psion Khairu, who watched him with brown eyes set in a heart-shaped face. Instead of her customary yellow Psion robes, she wore the gray robes of a Talent, electing not to wear their yellow sash. And beside her stood Emma, tall and willowy in comparison, wearing similar garb. She was as beautiful as he remembered, and perhaps even more so since the last time he saw her, which wouldn't help matters with Serah.

Both Emma and Khairu took in Serah, Fergus, and Psion Gaius as they approached.

"Who would have ever thought this was down here?" Emma asked, trying to break the ice.

"We should get moving," Khairu said, all business. "We'll have months to get acquainted, and Vera and the Dark Psion have a head start on us."

"The Dark Psion?" Lucian asked. "You mean Xara?"

She nodded. Apparently, that was a name for her that Lucian knew nothing about.

"I guess Transcend White updated the two of you on everything?"

"She gave us the gist of it," Emma said.

Without waiting for anyone to follow, Khairu went up the boarding ramp and scanned the door open with her slate.

"I'm Emma," Emma said, giving a graceful half-bow to both Fergus and Serah. "I didn't know Lucian had returned with anyone. What are your names?"

"Talent Emma," Khairu said, with a slight edge. "We must prepare the ship." She entered the open hatchway.

Emma's cheeks colored. "Right. Looks like we're about to take off."

"She always talk to you like that?" Serah asked. "I'd slap her silly."

Emma's eyes widened, as if such a thing were unimaginable. "She outranks me."

"Still . . ."

Serah looked as if she was about to say more, but Lucian broke in. "Introductions can wait."

Just as he said that, *Ethereal's* fusion drive warmed up with a hum that resonated within his very bones.

"See you all on board," Emma said, smiling at Lucian before ascending the ramp.

Once she had disappeared inside, Serah crossed her arms. "*She* looked awfully cheery."

"Try to do a better job of hiding your jealousy," Fergus said.

"I'm not jealous!"

Fergus smirked. "*Sure* you're not."

Fergus was the next to go on board.

"It won't be like this the whole time, will it?" Lucian asked.

"Like what?" She was silent for a moment. At Lucian's stare, she sighed. "Okay, I saw she was looking at you. Like a rift adder in the wet season!"

"Whatever that means . . ."

"We have a saying on Psyche. Eyes can't see themselves."

Lucian was still trying to make sense of that one as she walked up the boarding ramp. Adding Khairu's usual cheery disposition to the drama might make three months feel more like three years.

———

WHEN LUCIAN BOARDED *ETHEREAL*, he entered a small airlock chamber, beyond which lay an open wardroom, not unlike *Wayfinder*, but more spacious. He heard voices emanating from the direction of the bridge, so he walked down a short corridor, joining the others there. All the surfaces shone brightly, obviously state-of-the-art. Even the spaceship *smelled* new, of metal and clean, sterile air pouring through the lower vents. It was a far cry from the smelly liner the three of them had taken from Halia.

"It's all ours," Fergus said with a smile.

"Hardly," Khairu said. Their eyes met for a moment. Fergus smiled at her intense glare, which caused Khairu to just shake her head and look away.

"Have you plotted a course yet?" Lucian asked.

"Navi-computer is still trying to find the best solution to the Isis System," Khairu said.

"Can we make it all the way on a single tank of He-3?" Lucian asked.

"We can, but that could be risky." She went back to her work at the computer terminal behind the pilot's seat, not explaining exactly *why* that could be risky. "Should be a few more minutes."

They waited in silence. Emma sat in the co-pilot's seat, her eyes on her own terminal, while Serah stood nearly in the doorway, as far from her as possible. From her intense glare, it seemed she was making no attempt at being subtle. Thankfully, Emma didn't seem to notice, or was pretending not to.

At last, the terminal projected a holo showing all of League space, zooming in on the route between Volsung and Isis, along with the four systems in between: Halia, Archea, Psyche, and Pontus.

"Ninety-nine days," Khairu said. "Could be far worse."

"Rotting hell," Serah said.

Emma looked at her. "What was that?"

Serah gave her a fake smile. "I said *rotting* hell. It's a Psyche thing."

"I see. What Academy are you from?"

"The . . . Riftlands Academy."

"I'm not familiar with that one."

Lucian wondered if he should intervene, but he also valued his life. He resisted the urge to squirm.

"You probably wouldn't have. It's on Psyche."

Emma's face blanched at that. "I take it that's where you and Lucian met?"

"Met," Serah said. "And . . . other things."

As Emma's expression reddened, Lucian cleared his throat. "Khairu? Can we move?"

"Strap in," Khairu said. "We're about to take off."

"Wait," Lucian said. "There's somewhere I want you to go first."

She glared at him. "Even a day's delay could add a week to our journey, if not more."

"This shouldn't take more than a few hours." He looked at the others. "I met two other mages on the Isle of Madness. Both are completely healthy and not frayed. I couldn't live with myself if I didn't get them out of there."

"Linus and Plato, right?" Fergus asked. "I remember you talking about them."

"Absolutely not," Khairu said.

Lucian firmed his expression. "I'm in charge of this mission, per Transcend White. I'm ordering you to do it."

"You don't have the authority to do that. If you want to override the flight plan, then contact Transcend White."

She gave a smug smile. She knew Lucian wouldn't do that.

"I'm dead serious. Do it, or I'll make you."

"How?"

"You don't want to find out."

Emma looked from Khairu to Lucian uncomfortably. "There's no need to fight. We should stick to the mission. The League doesn't allow the mages to avert their prescribed courses."

"The League doesn't *know* about this mission," Lucian said. "And even if they did, Transcend White told me herself we have carte blanche to go wherever we want."

Ethereal edged out of the hangar, where at the other end, a large pair of doors was sliding open, perfectly blended into the gray rock. The ship ascended toward the starry sky.

"Change course for the Isle of Madness," Lucian said. "Do it now."

Khairu's jaw tensed, but it was clear she had no intention of following that order.

Lucian had no choice but to make good on his threat. If he didn't, Khairu would never take him seriously again, much less anyone else on this ship.

If he was in charge, he had to act like it.

Lucian reached for the Orb of Binding, streaming its power

in full. He tethered the nose of *Ethereal* itself to the face of a rock jutting out from the island below. At once, the ship slowed, as if a leash were pulling it.

"What are you doing, you fool!" Khairu almost screeched. "We're going to crash!"

He felt her reaching for his Focus to block him. But with the Orb of Psionics already shielding, she had no chance at all.

"Change course, Psion Khairu."

Her expression went pale. "Impossible."

"Just do it," Fergus said.

The ship was still slowing, its thrusters fighting Lucian's magic. More and more magic went into the tether, ripping from his Focus. He didn't know how long he could hold *Ethereal* back. His vision was blackening, reality being replaced with a matrix of blue lines, all converging on his Focus before diffusing into his tether. The ship's fusion engine whirred as its engines worked twice as hard to move.

"Fine," she hissed. "Have it your way."

Lucian cut off his stream as soon as Khairu canceled the course. She manually took control, steering east across the ocean.

"That wasn't too hard, was it?" Lucian asked.

Khairu remained silent. If she didn't hate him before, she certainly did now.

Emma's eyes were wide, and she was probably just as much in shock as Khairu. Fergus and Serah seemed to take it in stride. To them, it was just another day with Lucian Abrantes.

"I didn't want it to come to that," he said. "But when I give an order, I mean it. Transcend White put me in charge. I know that must hurt, but the chain of command must be adhered to."

He watched for a reaction, but Khairu said nothing.

"If I give an order that doesn't explicitly go against something Transcend White told you, you must follow it. End of discussion."

"You must really want to save them," Serah said.

"There's no way I'm leaving them behind. They saved my life. Shouldn't take more than a few hours to pick them up and drop them off wherever they want to go."

"They are exiled mages," Khairu said. "There's no place in all the Worlds they can go! Don't you see that? We only have supplies for five people. That's more fuel and more food, and they can never leave this ship. At least, not in a public place that requires GalNet ID verification."

"They can be added to the Academy's rolls, just like we were," he said.

"You know nothing," Khairu said. "Transcend White will not stand for this, and you can be sure I'll be telling her in my first report!"

"Is that supposed to scare me or something? I'm only a Talent because of formalities. You're here to help us, not the other way around."

Serah nodded approvingly.

"If you think I, a Psion, will follow you, a mere Talent raised on this very day . . ." Khairu said coldly.

"Titles aren't worth rot out there in the stars," Serah said. "If you'd been out there, you'd know that. The Swarmers are back. Do you think *they* care who's in charge? All they care about is killing."

"Looks like *she* might kill *you*," Fergus said to Serah.

"I'm not leaving my friends to die on the Isle of Madness," Lucian said.

"They could be frayed by now," Emma said.

"They won't be," Lucian said. "They've figured out a way to block their own magic."

"How?"

"They can explain when we get there."

"Madness," Khairu said.

What had taken days by boat only took an hour by air.

Reluctantly, Khairu angled the ship toward the island's relatively flat southern shore.

"Head for the island's western part," Lucian said. "That's where they'll be."

She ground her teeth, but didn't offer a counterargument. They flew low over the gray tundra, Lucian keeping his eyes peeled for the steaming hot springs. That would be easy to spot.

Within minutes, they'd found them. "Head west of those springs until you reach the cliff before the ocean."

"This better not be a waste of time. Or worse, a waste of life."

"It won't be. Bring her down. Shouldn't take more than an hour."

12

WHEN LUCIAN STEPPED off the ship, a strange sense of familiarity struck him. The cold, bare land stretched before him. The rainbow auroras he still saw in his dreams danced above his head. Serah looked up in awe as a light snow fell from a cloudless sky. Fergus was stoic, staring across the landscape toward the western cliffs. Khairu and Emma came from behind, both keeping themselves separate for now.

Lucian felt guilty about using his magic to make a point, but it was important for Khairu to understand that the Transcends weren't in control anymore. They could give their advice, even lend their ship, but that didn't mean Lucian had to follow every order.

Just by being here, Khairu and Emma had thrown their lot in with them. Transcend White had to have known that, though she had never explicitly said it.

"This way," Lucian said.

He still knew the way as clearly as if it were yesterday. He found one of the main trails. Just half a kilometer more and they'd be at the seaside cave.

97

"They might expect us to be wardens, so don't be surprised if they're a little shy."

"Are you *sure* they won't attack us?" Fergus asked.

"Not when they see it's me."

"If you say so," Emma said doubtfully.

"I think it's good, what you're doing," Serah said. It was as if she wanted to take the opinion opposite of Emma's.

Khairu was only silent.

When they reached the cliff, Lucian came to a stop. "Probably best if I go on alone."

"I won't allow that," Khairu said.

"I'll be fine."

"Not happening."

He saw he would not change their minds. "All right, then. Just hang back so they see me first."

Lucian went down the trail. Everything was exactly as he remembered. The ocean's frozen surface looked cold and forlorn under the starlight. They rounded the last bend, finding themselves before the massive cave entrance.

"Looks like a pair of wyverns might come out any moment," Serah said.

"No wyverns here," Lucian said.

The cave was dark, which somewhat worried him. There was *always* a fire roaring in the winter months. He realized they could've put it out as soon as they landed. That would have been the smart thing to do.

Within moments, he was entering the cave's dark mouth. The smell of smoke tinged the air.

"Hello?" Lucian called. "Linus, Plato? It's Lucian."

There was no response. Lucian immediately got a bad feeling. Had the same prison ship found them, too? Had they been on Psyche the whole time, dead in some forgotten rift?

Then, there was a sudden shifting of rock that made the hairs on his arms stand on end. He streamed a powerful light sphere, brightening it until the entire cavern stood revealed. The remains of the fire stood just a few meters away, while old pots and pans were strewn about, along with discarded shells of crustaceans, baskets of mushrooms, and frost fruit gathered from Plato's gardens.

Lucian smiled. "If you two want to be rescued, you'd better show yourselves now."

That was when two old men stepped into the light, blinking drearily. Linus, dressed in nothing more than leathers, fell on his bony knees and placed himself prostrate before Lucian.

"We surrender, almighty one! We will do whatever you ask, only spare our miserable lives!"

Plato stepped forward, too, his gut even *more* prodigious than the last time they met. It was clear they didn't know who Lucian was, or perhaps didn't hear him call out earlier. Either his appearance had changed, or the sphere's light was too much.

Lucian allowed the sphere's intensity to ebb. When he spoke, he couldn't help but do so with a thick voice. "It's me, guys. I'm back."

Linus looked up, unsure. "Lucian? Are you a phantasm come back to haunt us? Please have mercy! We thought you were right behind us, we swear!"

"I know. I went to Psyche. But now I'm back, and I have a ship."

"Is it truly you, Lucian?" Plato rumbled, stepping forward. "This isn't some Sea Drink hallucination?"

"It's him," Serah said, somehow stepping up beside him.

"Ye gods, a woman!" Linus said, as if she were a ghost.

"Yes?" Serah said, raising a quizzical eyebrow. "Have you old ones never seen a woman before?"

Plato sank to his knees next to Linus and closed his eyes tightly. "This . . . can't be happening. It's impossible! The fraying has reached my brain! My brain is all I have!"

"It's real," Lucian said. "I have a ship up there, if you guys want to leave."

"A ship!" Linus nearly screeched.

The others were eyeing the two exiles doubtfully. But Linus's face underwent a transformation, from being completely overwhelmed to suddenly beaming a wide and manic smile. "Be welcome, friends! Welcome to the Isle of Madness! I'm Linus. Linus Wander. Isle of Madness mayor of these environs for over four decades. We have food and drink in plenty, for it would appear we have much to speak of."

"Whatever speaking we have to do, let's do it on the ship," Khairu said. "We have a narrow window to make our passage."

Linus gave a somewhat crazed laugh. "*Leave*? Now? Nonsense! My poor mind couldn't take it." His wide blue eyes went from one person to another, running them over with no sense of proper etiquette.

Plato stepped forward. "Lucian, my boy, it's so good to see you. It's been rough ever since you left. The guilt has been eating away at me for so long . . ." He looked at the others, clearing his throat. "Err . . . I'm Plato. Plato Albach, if last names matter."

"It's my fault," Lucian said. "I got caught on purpose. For reasons I'll explain soon."

"So what is on Psyche, then?" Plato asked. "Did you truly go there? How did you ever escape?"

"I'll tell you everything," Lucian said. "But you need to come with me. Introductions and stories can wait."

The two of them just stared at him as if he had spoken a foreign language. After so long on the Isle of Madness, the possibility of escape was beyond their comprehension.

Plato seemed to accept reality first, but Linus still had not.

"Leave," Linus said. "Leave?"

Plato put a beefy hand on his shoulder. "Now's our chance, friend. The time has come."

He looked around at the cave, as if seeing it for the first time. "Forty years . . ."

"It's time to start the rest of our lives," Plato said. "What's left of them, anyway."

"We should get moving," Khairu reminded them.

To Lucian's surprise, Linus nodded. Perhaps all he needed was that little push.

"Where are we going, then?"

"That's the thing," Lucian said. "We probably don't have time to drop you guys off anywhere before we reach our destination. So you'll have to be okay with us going to Isis."

Plato looked at him somberly. "Isis? Are you mad?"

"I'm sorry you have to decide this quickly, but—"

"Let's away," Linus said, puffing out his chest. "I'd say *yes* even if we were going to Terminus or outside of the League forevermore." He gave a somewhat crazed laugh. "Not like we have anywhere to be, or anyone who's waiting for us."

"It's settled," Lucian said. "Let's get back on board. We'll have plenty time to get everyone up to speed."

Within minutes, they had left the caves behind, taking with them some food the men had gathered that would stretch their reserves. It would be nice to have proper food.

The others led the way, but Lucian hung back with the two of them.

"You saved my life, once," Lucian said. "Now, it's my turn to return the favor."

———

UPON SEEING THE SHIP, Linus and Plato's eyes seemed to pop out of their sockets.

"Glorious," Linus breathed.

"We need to get into orbit," Khairu said.

Linus and Plato watched as she stalked for the bridge.

"She's the pilot?" Plato said.

Though Lucian hadn't questioned it before, he wondered how Khairu had gotten training in something as complicated as piloting an interstellar spaceship. Perhaps that was a question for Emma, who was watching Linus and Plato almost with pity.

"I'm sure we have something warmer you can wear on board," she said to them both.

Before either of them could respond, *Ethereal's* fusion engine revved up as it prepared for liftoff.

"She's waiting for no one," Fergus said.

Lucian resisted the urge to shake his head. It seemed Khairu was trying to buck whatever authority he had. She was right, in a way. They had a narrow window to make all the Gate passages. Being delayed by as much as a day could be disastrous.

"Let's strap in," he said.

Lucian remained behind with Linus and Plato in the jumpseats in the wardroom, while the others went on ahead.

"Seems you have a fair amount of story to tell, boy," Linus said, once they were all secured.

"You don't even know the half."

"Or a quarter, I'd imagine," Plato said.

Their conversation cut off as the ship veered upward, though the inertial dampening field easily redirected the G-forces, so Lucian barely felt the ship's movement. If this ship was better and faster than *Wayfinder*, which he hoped, maybe they could make up some ground.

Within minutes, Lucian was floating against his restraints. When gravity returned, he sunk into his chair at a third of a G, the standard for most spacecraft.

"Space," Linus said. "It seems like a dream."

Plato smiled wistfully. "Last I was in space, I was Lucian's age, escaping war and hoping for a better life." He went silent for a moment. "It took a long time, but perhaps today is the start of that better life. I'd like to hope so."

Lucian hoped so, too. "Let's go up front."

"Wait a minute," Linus said. "Isis, you said? What in the Worlds are we going there for?"

"I'll tell you in a minute. Shouldn't be long for Khairu to set the course."

By the time they joined the others on the bridge, the terminal was displaying the ship's trajectory through all the Gates that would lead them to the Isis System. It was still only ninety-nine days, despite the detour they'd taken.

"We're lucky," Khairu said. "We're about ready to get going."

The ship changed directions for a few seconds more, the stars spinning above them. The spinning slowed until it was pointing directly at the Halia Gate, the first of four they would have to pass to reach Isis, the former capital of the short-lived Starsea Empire controlled by Xara Mallis.

"Ready?" Khairu asked. "Course plotted. Ninety-nine days, four Gates, average speed of 4.5 percent light, with a time-debt of two hours and fourteen minutes."

"Time-debt?" Serah asked.

Fergus cleared his throat. "Basically, we're going so fast that we'll be on the ship two hours longer compared to someone outside of it."

"That makes no sense."

"You should look up time dilation on your slate," Fergus said. "Should make for some light reading."

"Gate fees will be sixty-two credits," she said. "Half of that being the Isis Gate. Guess they're trying to keep people from going there."

"We don't have that much," Serah said.

"Well, the Academy has seen fit to provide me with a sizeable stipend," Khairu said.

Lucian watched her warily. Was *that* how she was going to hold the strings?

"How much, if you don't mind me asking?" Fergus asked.

"Five thousand credits."

Linus nearly choked. "That's nearly enough to buy an entire ship!"

"A clunker, maybe," Plato said.

"Still . . ."

"They don't want this mission to fail," Khairu said, turning to Lucian. "Now that everything's settled, Transcend White said you'd fill us in on everything."

Lucian nodded. "Well, it's going to take a while. Might want to grab some food or a hot beverage."

"Hot . . . beverage?" Linus asked. "There's coffee?"

"Should be," Khairu said.

"Ye gods," he said.

Within minutes, all had gathered in the conference room with coffee. The hum of the air recyclers and fusion drive emanated throughout the vessel. Linus sipped from his mug deeply, closing his eyes in sheer joy.

All waited for Lucian to begin. He couldn't count how many times he'd had to tell his story, and each time he did so, the telling seemed to take hours longer.

He started at the very beginning, with the discovery that he was a mage, along with the strange visions he'd received from the mysterious voice. That voice, at least, now had a name. Vera had called him the Ancient One, but he was also the Immortal Emperor of Starsea. The Starsea that had existed over a million years ago. He recalled his meeting with Emma and Vera on board the passenger liner to Volsung, and his choice to train at the Volsung Academy rather than accepting Vera's offer of training. He only got in because of Transcend White's curiosity about her sister, who she'd believed dead for decades.

Next, he recounted his time at the Academy. Things had

come slowly to him at first, but over the months, he had become more proficient. So much so that he did well on most of the Trials, to the point where all of the Transcends were vying for him. However, Lucian couldn't bring himself to choose one, and for that, they decided *none* could have him. From their perspective, without a Transcend to oversee his training, he was simply too dangerous to keep around, especially considering Vera's interest in him. They remembered well what had happened with Xara Mallis, how the Transcends' decision to train her had led to the Mage War. Even if there was a minor possibility Lucian was the next Xara Mallis, that was enough grounds to exile him.

Khairu's and Emma's face had paled somewhat. By this point, they had probably only relied on rumors.

Emma shifted in her seat. "I knew you had done nothing wrong. Everyone was saying it was because you overdrew on all your Trials."

"That's what I believed," Khairu said. "Though you admitted to overdrawing on two of them. That alone should have been grounds to expel you."

"Believe what you want," Lucian said. "Just telling you how it happened."

Khairu didn't have a response to that. "Continue."

He went on, describing the Isle of Madness, his meeting with Linus and Plato, and finally, his first revelation from the first Oracle of Starsea, Rhana, and gaining the Orb of Binding.

This was where Khairu stopped him.

"Wait. This can't be real. I thought we were being sent to hunt down Vera and Xara, and stop them from reforming the Starsea Mages."

"That's only part of it," Lucian said. "Our mission is much bigger than that. But yes, we have to stop them. But stopping them is only the first step."

Doubt entered her features. It was clear she was reeling

from the fact that stopping the two most dangerous mages in the Worlds was merely the first step. She motioned for Lucian to continue.

He told them then about Psyche, meeting Serah, Fergus, and Cleon and his quest to find the Orb of Psionics, and his conflict with the Sorceress-Queen of Psyche, Ansaldra, and Cleon's sacrifice. Emma watched in wide-eyed amazement along with Linus and Plato. Khairu's face was skeptical, but that was no surprise. After he had secured the Orb of Psionics, he turned to Emma.

"This was when I had my first vision of you," he said. "With the Orb, I could talk to you. At least, I could at that moment."

"So, that's when that happened," she said.

Lucian explained how he had used the Orb to reach Vera, the only way he knew to get off Psyche. He then described how he, Serah, Fergus, and Selene had flown across the desert using the ruins of the Queen's airship, their meeting with Jagar, and eventually facing the Sorceress-Queen again to secure her translation of The Prophecy of the Seven, and meeting Vera herself in the Golden Palace. Lucian told them of his vision during the prophecy's destruction, and how that vision revealed the location of each of the Orbs—though they were nothing more than images. More important were Arian's words, telling him to find the Dark Gate, whatever that was, and that the Chosen would know the way.

He concluded with their stop on Kandi, the kerfuffle on Archea Station with Zheng Yang's agent, and finally, the revelation that shook him in the temple under ice of Halia's dark side. That Xara Mallis was still alive, and that Vera was still working with her. She believed *herself* to be the Chosen of the Manifold, and she took the Orb of Gravitonics from under Lucian's nose.

Once he'd finished, he couldn't believe just how much they had gone through. It felt like many details were missing, but thankfully, the others asked the right questions.

Khairu was the first to speak. "Can I see them?"

Lucian didn't have to ask what she meant. He knew he should say "no," but a large part of him wanted to prove he wasn't lying.

He reached for his Focus, outstretching both hands. Almost immediately, the room brightened as two lights, one blue and the other violet, manifested from within his chest. The lines flowed outward, down each of his arms, until the light pooled into two spheres, one for each hand. A sudden flash of brilliance, and then the light faded, revealing the two resplendent Orbs of Starsea.

Everyone stared open-mouthed at the display, even Serah and Fergus, who had seen them before. Even Lucian looked at them, as if in disbelief they were actually there.

"I went through hell to get these," Lucian said. "I never wanted to do it, but it seems I'm the only one who can. For now. Unless we want Xara getting them."

Emma shook her head somberly. "This . . . was the last thing I expected when Transcend White asked us to help you."

"Honestly, the whole thing feels like a joke. I'm not even sure I'm the Chosen of the Manifold. I spent all my time on Psyche trying to convince myself of it. When I succeeded, the rug got pulled."

"You want my opinion, boy?" Linus asked. All eyes went to him. "You're worrying too damn much."

Was he being serious? This was his *life*. How could he *not* worry about it?

"Prophecy, schmophecy. Maybe you're the Chosen, maybe you're not. Are we really set on doing this mad quest, returning these Orbs to this Heart of Creation place?"

"I've got nothing else to go on," Lucian said. "Unless you have a better idea . . ."

"Well, I'm not trying to denigrate the idea. I know you're trying to do the honorable thing. Honor is overrated. I just have a few questions about it, is all. We know this First Gate is *deep in dark space*, according to this Oracle lady on Volsung. We don't know where that is, and right now, we're hoping Arian's prophecy will tell us where. Too many ifs, maybes, and buts for my liking."

"We've got nothing else," Serah said. "Lucian has found two Orbs so far. If he's the Chosen, he's destined to find more."

Linus's expression told Lucian he very much doubted that. Lucian found he agreed.

"Perhaps it would be helpful if we were all on the same page about what *needs* to happen," Plato said. "Those Orbs need to be found. It's the only way to stop the fraying that we know about."

Heads nodded all around.

"The key question," Plato said, "is what to do with them. There are two options. Lucian keeps them, but that would make his mind fuse with this Ancient fellow. The Ancient One told Lucian that on Psyche, and Xara herself confirmed it would happen. So we can only assume it's true."

"He's not doing that," Serah said.

"I agree," Emma said, quietly. "There has to be a better way."

"Well, there is only one other way," Plato said. "One other way that we know of. We have to take the Orbs to this Heart of Creation place. But we don't have enough information. As impossible as both tasks are, it's easy to see why Xara chose the first one. It's easier."

"It also gives her the power she wants," Serah said.

Plato shrugged. "Well, that goes without saying."

"That doesn't solve the problem of the Swarmers," Lucian said. "They are the response to the return of magic. The *Alkasen* are the emissaries of the Light Realm, sent here to get the Orbs back. In that strange way, they want the same thing we do."

"What are you saying?" Khairu said. "That the Swarmers

are our *allies*?" She shook her head. "I don't buy that. They've killed tens of millions by now, if not more."

Lucian had to agree that it didn't seem likely. "Well, it's impossible to communicate with them, so it's pointless. All we have to go on is what I learned from Xara. I don't believe she was lying about that."

"There are other things to consider," Emma said. "The option of returning the Orbs, if carried out, would destroy the Gates, or at least cause them to cease functioning. The Oracle of Binding said returning the Orbs would end magic. That alone could kill billions of people. Why would we ever do that? Are we *sure* we're on the right side here?"

That was something Lucian had considered as well, that he could be wrong and Xara could be right. "Are you saying I should've given the Orbs to Xara?"

"No. But maybe you need to keep them for yourself. And fight this Ancient One when he tries to fuse with your mind."

It was an idea, Lucian supposed. Xara welcomed that fusion with open arms. But what if he were to gather the Orbs and resist that takeover, if such a thing were possible?

The Ancient One seemed to suggest that resistance was futile, but isn't that what he would *want* Lucian to believe?

"We don't know nearly enough," Lucian said. "That's the real problem. We have to get to Isis first. Maybe there'll be answers there."

"What if we find nothing?" Khairu asked. "Transcend White gave us the coordinates to this place, but it's been over five decades. What if the League destroyed it during the bombardment?"

"You're asking me like *I* know."

"So, you have no plan other than hopefully finding this prophecy that's been lost for almost a century. After that, you hope to find all these Orbs that have been lost for over a million years?"

"That … about sums it up."

At that moment, Khairu looked as if she wanted to turn the ship around. Lucian didn't blame her.

"I need to get some air," she said, stepping out of the wardroom.

Once she had left, Linus looked around at the others. "Should you tell her, or should I?"

"What?" Plato asked.

"There's no air out there."

13

THOUGH LUCIAN DIDN'T WANT to, he followed Khairu out of the conference room to the cabin she had claimed sternward. When he knocked on the door, there was no answer. She had probably locked it, since she had full control of the vessel. He didn't bother trying to convince her to open it.

"She just needs to blow off some steam."

He turned to see Emma behind him. "Yeah. Probably."

"Can we talk?"

"Sure."

Instead of talking to him there in the corridor, she led him sternward, toward the engine room. They walked down a set of metal steps and past a thick metal door that contained the engine room. On the other side was the spherical fusion reactor, powering the ship on its burn toward the Halia Gate. A viewscreen stretched across the surface of the rear wall, revealing a vista of stars, at the center of which shone the faded blue dot of Volsung, quickly receding into the black of space. Transcend White had not been bandying words when she said *Ethereal* was a speedy ship.

They stood facing each other awkwardly for a moment, neither meeting the other's eyes. Two years, and they were almost strangers again, though not a day had gone by where he hadn't thought of her. In his times of darkness on the Isle of Madness, and in his cell on the way to the prison moon of Psyche, thinking of her had been the only thing that kept him sane, even if he had known deep down he'd never see her again. It was hard to look her in the eyes, to know that he might communicate all that with a single glance.

He was with Serah now. He had to keep a proper distance, but undoing everything that had happened with Emma, both in real life and in his head, wouldn't be easy.

All he could hope was that she had kept herself busy enough to forget him.

"I've missed you," she said. "Good friends are hard to find."

He nodded. "Same. I . . . guess you're a Talent now? How did you pull that off?"

"It wasn't easy. I was so sure I failed my Trials. I was surprised when I passed."

"I wouldn't have been surprised. You're still too humble."

She gave a small laugh. "All right, I guess I'm pretty amazing at what I do."

"So, what did you want to talk about?"

"I . . . guess I should get right to it. I guess you and Serah are together?"

"Yeah," he said. "We have been since Psyche."

"She's pretty. And . . . spirited."

"Yeah. That's one way of putting it. I'm sorry if she's coming across too harsh. Things are just done differently on Psyche."

"I understand. I'm sure you talked about me to her, if only in passing. Since this is out in the open, I'll just be blunt. She has nothing to fear from me."

"I understand," Lucian said, cutting her short. "We . . . really don't have to get into it."

Emma nodded. "Good. As long as we understand each other. I'm a Talent of the Volsung Academy. I have new priorities. I was already heading that way, even before you left. Which we've talked about before."

"Of course."

There was an awkward silence. He hated that awkwardness, but if they were going to be on the same ship, everyone had to be on the same page. They didn't have to all be friends, they at least had to work together.

"Glad that's out of the way," she said. "It's good to be here. It's a little surreal being outside the Academy for once."

"What've you been up to?"

"Well, I've been busy, as you can imagine. I trained hard after you left. I knew an injustice had been done, but somehow, I put it out of my mind and focused on my training." Her eyes became distant for a moment, and she seemed somewhat embarrassed. "It was far easier to believe you had brought it upon yourself. It was . . . the only way I could go forward. I apologize for that."

He nodded. "It's all right. You had no way of knowing what really happened."

"Well, I always knew. I told you they'd fight over you, but I never imagined that outcome."

"So, you're saying I should've listened."

"I have a knack for being right." She paused for a moment, signaling a change in subject. "There's something strange I noticed about Linus and Plato."

"What's that?"

"It's their auras. They're like nothing I've ever seen."

Lucian remembered Emma's strange ability. At a glance, she could tell if someone was a mage or not without streaming magic itself.

"Their auras are . . . suppressed, for lack of a better word. Linus seems to be a Gravitist, but hardly any light escapes his Focus. And Plato is much the same, except he's a Thermalist."

"It must be because they've blocked themselves. They figured out a way to stop streaming, which is how they've lasted this long without fraying."

"Before you told me about that, I wouldn't have believed it possible."

"It's incredibly dangerous, but both of them managed it. I did it myself, though by the time I got to Psyche, I had to unravel the block to survive."

"I remember your story. Well, Serah is a strong Gravitist, that much I can see, and Fergus is as strong in Radiance. It's . . . strange."

"What is?"

"This. On this ship, everyone is uncommonly powerful in their own way."

"We've all been through a lot."

"Maybe," Emma said, doubtfully. Once again, her brown eyes became distant. "You, though. When I look at you, it's almost blinding. It's hard to ignore."

"Blinding?"

"Your aura. I can see it floating in your mind, two stars, blue and violet. I noticed when I first saw you, which is why I acted so surprised."

"I thought it was because you were surprised to see me."

"Well, that too. But the aura overshadowed everything."

"Hopefully it's not too distracting."

"Just thought I should mention it. Psion Khairu and I are here to help you. To be upfront, we will report to the Academy regularly. Khairu will be the one doing that, but I just thought you should know."

"Don't leave a detail out. Just don't tell her my bathroom schedule."

Emma didn't smile. "Just be careful, Lucian. I know you

have those two Orbs, and I know that amount of magic can be addicting. It probably makes you feel invincible. Though Transcend White is my leader, I'm your friend. I don't want us to be at cross-purposes. For me to be forced to . . . choose."

Lucian nodded. He didn't want that to become a possibility, either. "I understand. There won't be much to report over the next few days. Few months, even."

"Well, once we're beyond Archea, things will get rougher. And with the Swarmers fringeward in Kasturi, it might cause things to fall into disarray sooner rather than later."

"In disarray, how?"

"Piracy has always been a problem in the Border Worlds. Even in the Mid-Worlds, depending on where you are. And of course, you guys had a run-in with one of Zheng Yang's agents."

"You think she can catch us in this ship?"

"They don't need to catch us," Emma said. "If they can get close enough, a pirate vessel just has to threaten us with torpedoes, which are faster than *any* ship. They may not want to mess with a bunch of mages, though. Our transponder reveals what we are, though I guess if they don't like mages, that can be a liability, too."

"I didn't come this far to get blasted by pirates," Lucian said. "We'll make it to Isis. You'll see."

"Well, I'm heading to the galley for some food. It was good catching up with you."

She left him there in the engine room, where he gazed out the back viewscreen, where Volsung was already hard to pick out among the background of stars.

AFTER HALF AN HOUR, Lucian went to get a meal and coffee in the galley. The shipboard clock said it was 1830, so most had probably eaten by now.

He had just warmed up an instameal, something that approximated lasagna, when Linus entered the galley, too. He sat on the counter across from Lucian, looking rather sheepish.

"Could you, ah . . . help me with making food?"

After forty years on the island, it seemed Linus had forgotten how technology worked. "Yeah, sure."

Lucian went to the standing freezer built into the wall and opened it up.

"Pick your poison. We've got spaghetti, curry, chicken teriyaki . . ."

"Ooh, that last one. Haven't had chicken in . . . well, not since I was a kid."

"Chicken it is. Just don't expect it to taste like the real thing."

Lucian showed him how to warm it up and poured him a coffee, too.

"That's the stuff," Linus said, after taking a long, luxurious sip. He closed his eyes in satisfaction. Lucian reminded himself to get a proper cup of joe, something that wasn't instant, once they'd gotten some place safe.

Linus tucked into his meal like a starving man. Though the food he'd eaten on the island was undoubtedly fresher and more nutritious, it seemed novelty won out over everything.

"Maybe I should try that one," Lucian said.

Linus smacked his lips. "How're you holding up, boy?"

"Fine, I guess."

"You've grown. That much I see. Sporting a fresh scar, that's for sure. Me, though? Time stands still on the Isle of Madness. We gained one and lost one, since you left. All the others stayed in the village and went on to Psyche. You were the worst to lose. One of the good ones."

Somehow, Lucian doubted that. "How are you holding up?"

Linus gave a somewhat crazed laugh. "I should be as happy as a shellock in a thermal vent. I long ago gave up the idea that I might leave the island, except maybe on a prison barge. So this seems unreal. I'm sure I'll wake up any second."

"I have the same feeling, sometimes. How's Plato?"

"Ah, I don't care. Probably hogging all the hot water or something." His bushy gray eyebrows, now flecked with white, scrunched up. "Say. What made you come back for us? What good could two old magicless geezers be?"

Lucian took another sip of his coffee. "I couldn't just leave you there. Not when I had the chance to get you out."

"I appreciate the thought, but now you've roped me into saving the universe or something."

"You want to go back?"

Linus gave a humorless smile that was missing several teeth. "Well, not so much. What I mean to say is, I don't intend to stream again, my boy. If you're all right with that, then maybe I can make myself useful being ship janitor or something. Even a ship needs a janitor, wouldn't you say?"

"You could cook some of that food you brought aboard," Lucian said. "Though most of our meals are instant since it saves on space."

"I hear you. Well, I'm not sure how my skills will translate to a modern kitchen, but I'll do what I can."

Despite Linus's words, Lucian could tell the man was shell-shocked. He wasn't making much eye contact and kept looking at the sleek technology of the surrounding ship instead of focusing on the conversation.

"Maybe we can worry about all this later," Lucian said. "I'm glad you're here. You and Plato both. You saved my life, so I just wanted to return the favor."

"All right. Well, I'm going to rest up. I think I found an extra pod in Fergus's cabin. If he'll have me." He leaned forward. "Between you and me, it'll be nice to get some space from Plato's snoring for once."

"I'm sure," Lucian said.

"Tootles."

Linus left, and Lucian headed up the central corridor toward the bridge to check on the ship's progress. He passed Fergus on the way, who stopped him with a hand on the shoulder.

"Lucian, we have an issue."

"What's that?"

"Food," he said. "At the Academy, they gave us enough for five people for six months. However, we have two more mouths to feed, and the food Linus brought aboard will only last us about a week."

"I see. When do we run out?"

"Well, after Isis, admittedly. But we won't have much of a chance to resupply in the Border Worlds. If we resupply at Archea Station, it'll slow us down, but will ensure we have enough food to remain self-sufficient."

Lucian scrunched his brow. "How much will it slow us down?"

"About eleven days, by Khairu's calculations."

"Eleven days? How does that work out?"

"Well, it takes time to slow down. If you overburden the dampeners, we'll be in for a bad time. Of course, loading new food and topping our fuel tank will take about a day, and of course, it'll take time to get back up to speed."

"Why not Halia Station? It's one Gate closer."

"The Halia Gate shifts more than any of the others, since it orbits close to its parent star. Stopping there would throw off the schedule too much. The later we stop, the less hang-ups down the line, if that makes any sense. The Psyche System has no options, and the Pontus System has rampant piracy. Archea Station is far bigger and is a central hub. It'll have more options."

"I see. What about the little kerfuffle that happened last time?"

"Well, it's your call. Given the options, I still say Archea is best. It's not likely anyone will recognize *Ethereal*. Khairu said that from the ship's logs, it's been six years since the ship was last used."

"Six years? That's a long time."

"Transcend White said it herself. The mages only have free rein to travel in times of war. And the League Assembly declared a state of war against the Swarmers several months back."

"I see. Well, Archea Station is bigger, and probably has more supplies to choose from. Let's set our course for there."

"She's on the bridge," Fergus said. "I can let her know, since things seem to be tense between you two. And, ah, something else."

"What's that?"

"Well, I've had some experience on long trips like this, and it's hard to stay sane, if I'm being completely honest. I think it would help for the crew to come together at least once a day to check on each other's status and such. Nothing too long, just five or ten minutes. Also, to have some optional things we can do together. Whether that's games, a holo night, whatever."

"Yeah, that makes sense. What were you thinking?"

"Well, I was thinking for our first night, we could all watch a holo together. Something recent, since all of us are so out of the loop. Serah still knows almost nothing about modern society, and Emma and Khairu have been at that Academy for several years. I've been on Psyche for several years myself, and Linus and Plato . . . well, they probably have the worst of it."

"That's a good idea, Fergus. Maybe we can rotate. Each crew member gets to decide what we do on a certain night."

"Sounds good. I already downloaded a lot of stuff to the ship's library. Maybe I can go first tonight."

"Yeah. Sounds good."

Fergus left, and Lucian found himself at a loss for what to do. He headed toward the cabin he and Serah were sharing.

When the door slid open, it revealed the tiny cabin. While private, there wasn't much space. Serah was lying on her back, mindlessly scanning her slate. She didn't even look at him as he approached.

"You mad at me?"

"I'm not mad." Her tone was even, as if she were trying to convey that fact.

When he plopped down beside her, her body stiffened. She didn't speak to him for a full thirty seconds. That wasn't a good sign.

Finally, she put down the slate. "Did you have a pleasant chat with your old girlfriend in the engine room?"

"Come on. We were just catching up. And for the record, she's happy for us. She's moved on, and so have I."

"Well, that's peachy. Thanks for letting me know. All my doubts and insecurities have magically evaporated."

Lucian resisted the urge to sigh. "How can I convince you?"

"Oh, I don't know. Maybe stop getting that weird longing look in your eyes whenever you look at her?"

Had he really been doing that? "I don't know what you're talking about. She's my friend who I haven't seen in two years. Am I just supposed to give her the cold shoulder because of your insecurities?"

"Yes."

"That's . . . real mature."

"I don't care what it is. It's how I feel."

"What about how *I* feel? Why should I be rude to someone who doesn't deserve it?"

She didn't have an answer for that. Lucian just wished she would admit he was right. Unfortunately, he knew that wouldn't happen.

Serah remained silent. "She's beautiful. You never told me she looked like *that*."

"She's not beautiful at all."

A smile tugged at her lips. "Just *look* at her. Little Miss Perfect. Tall, beautiful face, everything is where it's supposed to be . . ."

"What's *that* supposed to mean? I think you've been looking at her more than me."

"She's like, perfectly formed. And then there's *me*."

She was looking at her arm again.

"You think I'm going to dump you because of your arm?"

"Not just my arm. It's not really hurting too bad now. I still take pain meds for it since Halia. It's not spreading, at least. That's only because I'm not using magic as much. But I know as soon as we're back in the fire . . ."

She trailed off, as if she didn't have the wherewithal to continue.

"Point is," she said. "If it were me . . . I'd probably choose her, too."

"Why are you doing this to yourself?" He reached for her hand. "When we find all the Orbs, your arm will be fixed." He looked down at it. "You can still use it, right?"

She nodded. "Yeah. Usually, the fraying has to spread further before you lose control of your nervous system. It's just surface level for now."

"And it's going to stay that way. Now that we have more people, you won't have to stream as much. That gives us more time. And we can continue those things I've been showing you, strengthening your Focus to keep the impurities out."

"I'm not as strong as you," Serah said. "My way and your way are different. I've gone too far down the path to turn back."

As much as Lucian hated to admit it, maybe she was right. There wouldn't be time to fix how she streamed. She grew up on Psyche, and to survive there as a mage, one had to stream fast and hard. While Serah used a Focus to stream, as every mage did, for her it was more about raw bursts of power to accomplish her goals. Life expectancy on Psyche was so short that there was no sense of balance with streaming. Raw strength was the only thing that mattered.

"I'm here for you," Lucian said. "Okay?"

She gave a noncommittal grunt. Clearly, she didn't believe him.

"I think we're going to have a movie night tonight," Lucian said. "Will you be there?"

"Will everyone be going?"

By everyone, he knew she just meant Emma. "I don't know. I'll be. It's hard to imagine Khairu watching a movie."

"I'll go," she said. "I hate these long voyages. If I knew *this* was going to be life after leaving Psyche . . ." She trailed off. "No. I shouldn't say that. I wish it was possible to just sleep the entire time."

"Unfortunately, you can't go faster than light. And space is big." He thought for a moment. "Actually, we might get a bit of a break on the way. Fergus says we need to stop at Archea Station since we don't have enough food anymore."

She seemed to perk up at that, actually turning toward him. "Really? Maybe there'll be a fight again!"

"Why do you sound like you're looking forward to that?"

She shrugged. "I'm crazy. You haven't figured that out yet?"

His mind went back to the fight in the dockyards of Archea Station. He had killed, just as he has on the pirate moon of Kandi. The thought that *his* actions caused the deaths of several men was harrowing to think about, even if they were trying to kill him. If any sort of cameras had picked them up, they might be in for a bad time.

"Well, despite myself, I actually feel a bit better," Serah said. "As long as you aren't *too* nice to her, we won't have problems."

"Professional distance, then."

Serah smiled. "That's right." Her blue eyes became dangerous. "*Very* professional."

Lucian wondered for a moment what kind of woman he'd gotten involved with. She kept things interesting, especially as she finally relaxed her body against his.

As far as Emma, well, he had made his choice, and she had made hers. She would remain his friend, but she could never be more than that. Whatever they'd had was in the past. And Lucian meant to keep it that way.

15

DURING MOVIE NIGHT, Lucian's thoughts kept returning to the dusty old tome Transcend White had handed him. It was like a seed in the back of his mind. Having taken root, it was encroaching on all of his thoughts.

He stayed to the end, for Serah's sake, as well as the rest of the crew. Seeing her laugh lightened his mood, and he enjoyed answering her questions on random pieces of pop culture referenced in the movie. Usually, after his explanations, things still didn't make sense to her.

When everyone went to bed, he headed back to the cabin he and Serah were sharing. While she got ready for bed, he dug into his pack and pulled out the book, eyeing it for a moment.

Serah placed her hand on his, keeping the book shut. "Give it a rest. It's been a long day."

Lucian nodded, knowing she was right. "Soon, then."

They turned out the lights and went to bed.

———

As THE WEEKS PASSED, Lucian kept putting off looking at the prophecy. Instead, he fell into a routine designed to keep his mind fully occupied. He woke at six, made coffee, and prepared breakfast for the rest of the crew. They mostly ate together, though Khairu liked to remain solo on the bridge when possible. Sometimes Emma joined her in there to talk about Academy stuff Lucian wasn't privy to. That created some distance between them, but after his conversation with Serah, perhaps that distance was a good thing.

Fergus insisted on mandatory training, done in *Ethereal's* cargo hold, the only space large enough to accommodate it. He allowed no magic beyond what was necessary to keep their pools from overflowing. Many times, Lucian realized that one powerful burst of his Binding or Psionic Magic would be enough to breach the ship's hull. Having the ability to stream magic was like walking around with a high caliber carbine at all times.

They mostly limited themselves to spear work and the creation of various types of shields and wards. Binding, Dynamistic, and Psionic shields were all ideal for stopping bullets, something necessary to master against enemies equipped with guns. Wards of the same type, while longer-lasting, were weaker, so unless the ward was especially powerful, they weren't practical unless under sustained fire.

The key was maintaining the shield with an active stream while using a shockspear to cause massive damage. While Dynamistic Magic was most common to stream on a shockspear, other Aspects could be used as well. Binding, for example, allowed a mage to throw the spear at great distance with striking accuracy and speed. Thermalism could set clothing afire, or even create fireballs when combined with Gravitonics. Gravitonics streamed on a shockspear's tip could pierce armor that would otherwise be too thick to penetrate. Radiance at the tip of the spear worked similarly to a flash bang, blinding opponents.

Lucian learned all these things and more during training sessions. Besides incorporating various Aspects in his spear work, he learned to duel better. They drilled against each other for hours, and when Lucian forced himself to use Aspects other than Binding and Psionics, he lost more often than not. They held a tournament almost every day, a tournament Fergus almost always won, with Khairu winning perhaps a quarter of the time. No one came close to defeating either of them.

Of course, Lucian could have with his Orbs, but that was hardly fair, so he limited himself from using them, at least for active streams.

Emma was especially deadly with Radiant Magic. She showed no mercy when she blinded him with her streams, the ball of light at the end of her spear shining like a nova. She forced him to ward himself with Radiance to dim the effects of the light, which drained him from attacking her in other ways. Of course, he didn't just have to worry about her magic, but what she could do with her spear.

After their last bout, when Emma smoothly placed the tip of her practice spear at his neck, he raised his hands in surrender.

"You've progressed a lot," he said.

She smiled. "I wish I could say the same for you."

"Is that *sass* from *you*?"

She just smiled and went back to the side of the dueling ring.

Serah was watching him from the wings. He'd already risked too much by rising to the bait. He needed to treat even the smallest trace of flirtation as radioactive.

Serah stepped up, extending her spear. "I believe you're up against me now, Emma."

Emma's smile faltered for a moment before recovering. "Sure thing. Show me how they fight on Psyche."

Serah gave a smile that was almost a snarl. Lucian wanted nothing more than to excuse himself.

"Ha!" Linus barked. "Don't blow up the ship."

Khairu had barely lowered her hand, the signal to start the match, when Serah charged Emma. Emma yelped and immediately went down, a Gravitonic disc blooming beneath her feet. Serah immediately brought down her practice shockspear, but it was at that moment a zap of electricity extended from the tip of Emma's shockspear, singeing Serah's jumpsuit. Serah yowled, and the shock almost made her drop her spear. The distraction was enough for Emma to roll off the disc and regain her feet.

The two women circled each other, looking for an opening. The tension was palpable. Here in the dueling ring, all pretense was gone. It was about survival.

Emma charged, her spear flashing with each jab and swing. Serah dodged each attack, using a Radiant shield to block Emma's flashes. Serah swung her spear in a wide arc, its tip glowing with a silvery aura. The spear fell incredibly fast, so fast that if it made contact, Emma would be severely injured, if not worse. Emma thankfully stepped aside as Serah's spear thundered on the deck, making a dent.

Khairu raised her arm. "Enough! No harming the ship. You've been disqualified, Serah."

Emma took a few steps back, as if Serah were a snake about to strike. "She was going to kill me!"

"Please," Serah said. "Any mage worth their salt would've seen that coming from a light-year away."

Before Emma could say anything more, Lucian broke in. "All right, who's next? I believe it's Serah against Fergus."

Thankfully, the two women seemed to let it go, though from time to time, they cast each other angry glances.

Fergus defeated Serah handily, and Fergus, as usual, defeated Khairu. Fergus had already eliminated Lucian in the first round.

"Another day, another victory," he crowed.

Khairu seemed nonplussed. "Not for long. I think I'm seeing your strategy."

"Oh? Do tell."

"If I told you, you'd be able to correct the weakness, wouldn't you?"

Fergus smiled uncertainly.

"Good job, Fergus," Plato said. "I would've liked to have gone toe-to-toe with you in my prime."

Looking at Plato, Lucian couldn't help but notice the old man had lost a few kilos. He found it ironic, since the food situation here was more secure than back on the Isle of Madness. Or perhaps it was the lack of Sea Drink, a fact he and Linus bemoaned every day. Every *hour*, it sometimes felt. They had finished their stores of that in three days.

After training, it was usually lunch. Afternoons were for resting and catching up on galactic news, of which there was plenty.

The Swarmers were firmly moving out of the Kasturi System toward Djerrah, which the League wasn't even making a pretense of defending. Djerrah was a desert Border World with less than a million people in the entire system. It was horrible to realize the League had done nothing to prepare evacuation vessels.

Of course, the pundits were blasting the League Assembly on Earth for its heartless inefficiency, while protests and even riots were breaking out on nearly every world with a League presence.

"So many people," Emma said. "It could have just as easily been Sani."

"Which way will they go after Djerrah?" Serah asked Khairu.

Khairu shrugged. "Who can say? If they're gunning for Earth, the spinward way is faster. They'll have to go through Talesia and Karelia before hitting Alpha Centauri. But those planets are less developed, so there will be fewer resources for the Swarmers to exploit. If they go coreward, then they have to blast through Fessan, Malon, and Astravan before reaching A.C."

Astravan. Hadn't that been where Jagar was from, or was it Alsan? He couldn't remember. Lucian wondered if the old man was still alive. He hoped so. They would pass through the Psyche System on their way to Isis, but trying to visit that world on the off chance that he had survived was far too risky.

"They cannot let Chiron fall," Linus said. "That would spell doom for humanity."

"The defenses at A.C. are strong," Khairu conceded. "It's where the League turned back the Swarmers two years ago."

It was also the system where Lucian's mother had perished. He didn't want the reminder.

"All that is months away," he said.

The pundits began talking about a recent development in the League—the ousting of League diplomats from Zion in the spinward Mid-Worlds.

"That's the world the Unionists founded fifty years back," Khairu said.

"Unionists?" Serah asked.

"More commonly known as the Believers," Khairu said. "They've long wanted their own government, and mostly, they've run their affairs without infringement. That far out from Sol, they've always been their own planet."

"Looks like it's official," Emma said. "Though I doubt the League will recognize them as their own government."

"Does it matter?" Khairu asked. "The League is a dying

institution. Even without the Swarmers, how can one planet, Earth, exert control, however nominal, over dozens of worlds, most of which are months away on the fastest starship?" Her question went unanswered. "It's always been about Sol, and to an extent, the First Worlds. To the League, everything else is a wilderness, resources to feed the inner worlds." She nodded toward the viewscreen. "Take that. To the League, a million Border Worlders' lives aren't worth saving."

"That's harsh," Lucian said.

"Do you deny it?" Khairu asked, in challenge.

Lucian had to admit, it was a point many Earthers had. Earth came first. Hell, that had been the platform of Richard Palmer, the current League Hegemon. Some Earthers even looked down on the L-Cities and Earth habs that orbited the planet, not four light-seconds away. If they couldn't even accept them as equals, how much more so the people beyond the Solar System Gates?

Fergus cleared his throat. "More than that, the Trailing Border Worlds have long been under the thrall of Zheng Yang, and before her, various pirate lords. I doubt a League vessel has been seen out there since the Mage War."

To Lucian, it felt like the galaxy was unraveling. If this were the effects of losing one star system to the Swarmers, then what would it be like to lose several?

"Didn't the Swarmers make it all the way to A.C. a couple of years ago?"

"Well, that fleet came as a surprise," Khairu explained. "They went undetected until they passed through the Talesia Gate. Originally, they probably came through Moncierre. They flew without pause, and before anyone knew what was happening, they were three weeks out from A.C."

"That was more of a strike force," Fergus said. "*This* is something else entirely."

"What's that?" Serah asked.

He paused grimly. "A full-scale invasion, designed to end humanity forever."

It was hard for Lucian not to feel despondent. At a time where humanity needed to be coming together, it was splintering. If the Unionists formed their own government, nearby worlds could fall under their influence. That was fewer ships and men to fight the Swarmers, assuming the Unionists wanted to leave the League to die.

While Sol and the First Worlds were greater than three-quarters of the industrial capacity of the League, if not more, any lack of support could be enough to tip the scales toward defeat.

It was hard not to feel like this was already over.

16

SEVERAL WEEKS LATER, *Ethereal* was docking at one of the primary ports of Archea Station. After twenty-six days in space, everyone was antsy to get off board and see what the station offered.

Khairu said they could handily afford the prime hangar. Considering a berth cost fifteen credits per standard day, Lucian was glad the Academy had seen fit to load them with five thousand credits.

"Anything I need to add to the order form?" he asked. "I've got food and fuel to capacity. Any spare parts we're lacking, that sort of thing?"

"We're good on that," Khairu said. "Let me handle inventory. You can focus on . . . well, whatever it is you do."

Everyone watched Lucian for a reaction. If it had just been them two, he would have let it go, but he couldn't let her walk over him in front of the others.

"Are you questioning whether I can do my job here?"

She pursed her lips, but said nothing.

"Let's get out of here," Fergus said, changing the subject. "I need a drink."

"Can I come with, good sir?" Linus asked, sidling up to him. "I take it you've been here before. Wouldn't want an old man to lose his way, would you?"

"Maybe it's not the best idea for you to leave," Serah said, eyeing Fergus. "Remember last time?"

"I've been on this ship for over three weeks, and I'll be damned if I don't get to relieve some stress."

Serah looked to Lucian for support, but he just shrugged. Fergus was a grown man, and even if Lucian told him *not* to go, it wouldn't stop him.

"Just . . . try to keep a low profile, will you?" Lucian said. "I don't want anyone to recognize you."

Fergus cracked a smile. "You're acting like I'd be anywhere else."

"What's that supposed to mean?" Emma asked.

Lucian didn't want to explain that the station's night district was on the lower levels. Whatever adult activities Fergus wanted to partake in, it wasn't his or anyone else's business.

"I need to stay on board to make sure everything gets delivered," Lucian said. "The rest of you have the run of the station. Be back in twelve hours, and for the love of God, don't cause a scene. After that we're setting off for Isis."

"What if something happens out there?" Emma said. "You mentioned pirates attacked last time."

"Well, I'm not discounting the possibility. You're free to stay here if you're more comfortable with that, but we're a registered mage vessel. So unless someone recognizes Fergus, Serah, or me and immediately connects the dots, it won't raise any eyebrows."

"I hope so," Emma said.

"If something happens, just call. We've got a good berth, close to the central elevators. There will be sizeable crowds, and it shouldn't take you guys long to get around the station and find your way back. Questions?"

"Yeah," Plato said, patting his belly. "Any restaurant recommendations?" He held up his slate. "I tried consulting this thing, but I don't trust it."

Fergus clapped his shoulder. "I've got many, my friend. We can head to the Star Lounge. Good food, pleasant views, strong drinks, beautiful women. Maybe even a game on the holodeck. Then we hit the lower levels, get buzzed, do shots. We'll get the Archea Fire Sling, it's a classic. Then after that . . ." He smiled. "Well, we'll have to see what the night brings."

"I don't know what a Fire Sling is, but color me intrigued," Linus said.

"Can I come with?" Serah asked.

"Of course," Plato said. "Where I'm from, it's bad luck not to have a beautiful lady around."

Serah smiled graciously, then turned to Lucian. "Meet up later?"

"Of course. I'll let you know when I've finished up."

"I think I'll just find something to eat close by," Emma said, a bit uncomfortably.

"Come with us!" Linus said. "Let loose. You need to drive all that Academy rot right out of your skull!"

Emma stiffened. "Well, most of us here *are* Academy mages, though I understand if everyone besides Khairu and me is just a Talent in name. I think I'll stick to the proper codes of conduct."

Khairu nodded approvingly while Linus just waved his hand. "Your loss." He looked at Fergus. "Shall we, Mr. Madigan?"

"Twelve hours or less, and not a nanosecond more," Lucian said.

Once they left the ship, talking boisterously, the ship was

much quieter with just him, Emma, and Khairu. It was actually something of a relief.

Emma looked over at him. "That Fergus seems a wild one, doesn't he?"

"He's been cooped up on Psyche for a long time, and Linus and Plato even longer. If anyone deserves to paint the station red, it's them."

"I'm just not feeling . . . up to it, you know. Even before my time as a mage, I'd rather read a book than go out drinking."

"Yeah, I can see that." He looked over at Khairu. "Any word on the delivery?"

"Should be soon. We could organize the cargo hold while we're waiting. Make sure everything fits."

Lucian realized he'd made a mistake sending everyone off so early. While they were slaving away on the ship, they'd be having the time of their lives at this Star Lounge place. He remembered Fergus mentioning it on Halia. He had to admit, it might be fun to hit the casino for old time's sake.

"I hope we have the creds for their shenanigans."

"That's something you should have considered *before* you sent them off."

"Is this how this is going to work?"

"How what's going to work?"

"You criticizing every decision I make?"

"Not every decision, but it would be nice to be consulted sometimes. As far as your friends going out, as long as it doesn't affect their training or maintaining the ship, I don't care." She looked at Emma. "If you'd like, perhaps we could walk around the station a bit later. Once we're done here, of course. I . . . could use something of a break myself."

"I'd like that," Emma said. "A restaurant with a view of Archea would be nice."

"We'll find something nicer than this Star Lounge place. I looked it up. Looks like a smoky sports bar, not befitting mages of our stature. The mages also have an embassy here. It's small, but there's free food and drinks, and non-mages won't be able to bother us."

"An embassy?" Lucian asked.

"Most of the major stations in the Worlds have one. Obviously, we don't advertise that outside our own Academies."

"Would you like to join us, Lucian?" Emma asked.

With Khairu there, it would probably be the most awkward dinner imaginable. "That's all right. I've got some stuff to do around here."

Thankfully, she didn't ask for clarification.

They spent the next two hours organizing the cargo hold. They revamped the storage in the freezers to make space for new food crates. They reorganized spare parts inside their compartments, so they knew where to find them. Trash they hadn't already vented, they disposed of. The shipboard diagnostics guided them in needed maintenance tasks. Khairu ordered a tech to come out and inspect the ventilation system and air recycler just in case.

When the shipment arrived, mostly food, they stored it over the next couple of hours. Lucian's slate dinged with messages, mostly from Serah. It was hard to tell if the copious misspellings were from her lack of experience with a slate, or her current state of inebriation.

"Seems like they're having a good time," he said.

"They must be three sheets to the wind by now," Emma said.

"What's that?"

"Old Earther expression. Means drunk. Figured you would've heard it. Or maybe I just read too much."

"All done," Khairu said. "Sure you don't want to come, Lucian?"

From her tone, it was clear Khairu was only being polite.

"No, thanks. Someone needs to stay on the ship. And it would be nice to have some alone time."

"Suit yourself."

"I'll bring you something back," Emma said.

"You don't have to."

"I insist. No one should have to eat an instameal while we're in port. Take it easy, okay?"

Once they were gone, Lucian almost wished he hadn't insisted on staying behind, but someone needed to stay with the *Ethereal*, and it was better for him to just take the hit, at least until Khairu and Emma returned. It was a rich-looking ship, and that might attract attention, as *Wayfinder* had at Port Kandi. While Archea Station was not as run-down, being a solid Mid-World, it had its seedier elements, a lesson he had learned the hard way.

Lucian went to the bridge to make sure the security system was set. A needless task, since it would ping him the moment anyone who was not a crewmember was within line of sight. Nor could anyone open the airlock without the correct biometrics.

He went to his cabin and lay on his bed, opening his slate to see a video of Serah and the boys doing shots at the Star Lounge. Linus tittered in the background while stars spun beyond the massive viewing windows.

Maybe it was better he had stayed behind.

Despite trying, he couldn't get much sleep, especially with Serah continually asking him where he was. He ended up shutting the slate down and reaching for the long neglected book, which over the weeks had collected a thin layer of dust on its cover.

Lucian began reading. Of course, the words made little sense. He'd have to draw on the power of the Orb of Psionics.

He drew a deep breath. There was no more putting this off.

He formed his Focus, reached for the Orb, and streamed,

forming a Psionic link with the words as if they were another person, pulling them into his mind as he had done with Ansaldra's prophecy.

Instantly, visions assaulted him. Visions of madness. A vague shape floated in a maelstrom of what seemed to be swirling water, a shape that materialized into a long, flowing figure that was a part of the dreamscape. Long white hair flowed with the waves, and for now the figure didn't seem to know he was there.

Fear rose in his chest. Without asking, Lucian knew who it was: the Immortal of Starsea.

He tried to break the connections, but the words were a part of him now, and the Orb would not shut off, as if trying to connect to that figure. The grotesque face snapped toward Lucian, a face bearing an elongated half-smile that bled into the surrounding eddies.

"So, you've come," the Immortal said. "I was worrying about you."

Lucian, now locked in this place, had to do whatever he could to escape. Since he couldn't shut off his stream, he instead tried to redirect it. He held out his hand, ethereal in this place, his fingers bleeding into the surrounding whirlpool of colors. He streamed, trying to blast the Immortal with Psionic force.

To his surprise, the watery colors whirled out of the way, revealing a white void beyond. But the figure remained still and rooted, a tree with unshakeable roots.

"Weak," the Immortal crowed. "Do you think you can unlock the secrets of Starsea with such corrupt words? Vera played you for a fool."

Lucian realized what he meant. This wasn't the same prophecy Vera had taken with her all those years ago. It was a more imperfect copy, and a dangerous one at that.

"You are nothing here, Chosen. Do you really think these

mad words will help you? No. They will destroy you!"

"No . . ."

"Yes. It won't be long now."

Lucian's mind couldn't exist in this place. Without all the Orbs, he could not endure the Manifold. No mortal could.

In desperation, Lucian reached for the Orb of Binding, hoping it might prove some shield here. And to his surprise, he sensed a way back to his body, still locked in his cabin and kneeling on the deck. He tethered his mind there, streaming with everything he had.

Slowly, he pulled himself from the maelstrom, and the Immortal receded into the distance, his indecipherable whispers following him like a fell wind.

———

THE OPENING of the blast door woke Lucian from his haunting dream. He forced his eyes open, using his Focus to calm himself. It was several minutes before he could think straight.

He got up, washed his face at the cabin's small sink, then went out to the wardroom, where Emma was sitting.

She looked up at him, holding a greasy brown bag.

"Seems like you've lost," she said.

Lucian blinked. "What?"

"You probably don't remember, but back when we were Novices, you told me you'd buy me a burger once you became Talent." She nodded toward the bag. "I beat you to the punch."

He forced a smile. "I remember that, actually. Seems like a long time ago."

Her eyes became concerned. "Are you all right? You look a little sick."

He didn't want to get into it at the moment. "Bad dreams. No big deal."

"Well, dinner might help. Something that isn't instant crap."

His slate dinged again, a message from Serah telling them they were going down to the lower levels. He felt guilty that he hadn't joined them yet. He'd been out of it for a couple of hours at least.

"I should go," she said. "Khairu probably has some more things she wants me to do."

She left, and Lucian chowed down on the burger. It was just a small thing to remind him of home in this faraway place, even if Archea's version was spicy. By the time he was halfway done, his entire mouth was on fire, to where he thought Emma was pulling a fast one on him. He dutifully finished and took a long drink of the sweet, carbonated beverage she'd brought as well.

He left, heading out the blast door and toward the central elevator that would take him down to the station's lower levels.

17

THE DARK, smoke-tinged club was crowded, about half foreign spacers and half locals. The spacers mostly wore single-piece jumpsuits, gathering in small clusters by the bar and club's periphery, while the locals were dressed in normal civilian wear. The men wore flashy nano-tailored night suits and the women colorful and revealing dresses.

Lucian found the others in a booth near the dance floor. Linus's face was ruddy, while Plato was leaning back contentedly, his eyes hooded. Serah was absent, while Fergus had his arms around a beautiful young woman. From the way they were looking at each other, they seemed about ready to excuse themselves.

"Ha!" Linus boomed. "About time you showed up!"

"Seems like I missed most of the action," Lucian said. "Drinks?"

Fergus tapped his slate. "You've got your own money or something?"

Lucian had forgotten. "Right. Group tab, then."

When he went to the menu on the slate to order, he saw they had already racked up a bill of 5.14 credits.

"Geez. Looks like you guys bought out the place."

"We are grateful for the Academy's patronage," Linus said.

Fergus shot him a look of warning. Linus hadn't said "Volsung Academy," but the young woman thankfully missed the comment.

"Ready to get out of here?" she asked Fergus.

"Just a moment, my dear."

"Where's Serah?" Lucian asked.

"Out there," Plato said, pointing to the dance floor.

"Be right back," he said.

He headed to the dance floor, weaving through the thick crowds. He found Serah quickly, dancing with a group of girls who had let her into their orbit. A couple of young men danced nearby, as if deciding whether to make a move.

Lucian stepped up to claim her. The two men eyed him for a moment, and one of them seemed ready to start something, but one look from Lucian was enough for him to decide not to take his chances.

"You're late," Serah said, wrapping her arms around him.

"Sorry," he said. "Inventory."

From her smile, it seemed she'd already forgiven him. "Everyone here loves my moves. They work great in this gravity."

She demonstrated right in front of him, and it was almost enough to make him blush. He had far too few drinks in him to match that. "I think the others are about to get out of here."

"How about *we* go somewhere else?" she asked, drawing his face toward her.

"That's the idea," he said.

He led her away from the dance floor, and thankfully, she seemed to be ready to leave.

When they got back to the table, Linus and Plato had

already started on another drink, while Fergus and his plus-one had vanished. At least *he* knew how to enjoy himself.

"I think we're getting out of here," Lucian said to the table. "Did Fergus pay the bill?"

"I assume so," Plato said, rubbing his belly. "All that drinking has worked up quite a hunger."

"I could eat again myself," Linus said.

"Your drink is there," Plato said. "I've been guarding it the past five minutes from *him*."

Linus stuck out a tongue. "Try it, Lucian, my boy. You shall not be disappointed."

All watched him as he took up the drink, as if something funny were about to happen. His suspicions were stoked, but he didn't want to be the only one who *hadn't* had a drink. The liquid within was blood red and bubbling.

Lucian tossed it back, and as soon as he did so, a spout of flame shot up, engulfing his head. He cried out, spitting out some of the drink, until he realized the flames were painless, just some sort of light show. The others died laughing.

"You should've seen your face!" Linus squealed.

Lucian broke into a smile. "I guess this is the Fire Sling?"

He tossed back the rest, the drink giving him a mighty kick on its way down.

"All right," he said. "Let's get you guys some food."

To be honest, Lucian wasn't too hungry, but he ate again, if only because they had months of instameals to look forward to. The others seemed to be of a similar mind. They went to a ramen joint, and there were no complaints as everyone tucked into their bowls of noodles.

"Sublime," Plato said, licking his fingers. "I haven't partied like this since . . . well, since I was younger than you fellows."

Serah nodded. "There is so much to see! And I want to see it all!"

There was a note of frustration in her voice, which Lucian

understood. All the things he took for granted were like wonders to her.

A telescreen in the background suddenly blared, revealing a suited man with a wild mop of orange hair, blathering from behind a podium in a posh English accent.

"Fear not, noble citizens of the League. Even now, our fleets are converging on Alpha Centauri. We'll beat the Swarmers back. The First Worlds will not fall, and the worlds in the Swarmers' paths are little populated, so the damage will be limited."

"Did he seriously just say that?" Linus asked. "Who is this blowhard?"

"Richard Palmer," Lucian said. "The League Hegemon."

"It really has all gone to shit, hasn't it?"

"What's the League Hegemon?" Serah asked.

"He presides over the League Assembly, selected by the Worlds' Delegates."

Lucian noticed the restaurant's few patrons were glaring at the screen. Richard Palmer was little-liked, especially in the Mid-Worlds and beyond. It had a lot to do with Palmer's campaign slogan, "First Worlds First." Even without the Swarmers, planets breaking away from the League wasn't idle talk.

Reporters barraged Palmer with questions, but he merely waved his hand and walked away from the podium as if someone might shoot him.

Lucian checked his slate. They had four hours until it was time to go.

"We should probably head back," Linus said, stifling a yawn. "I'm beat."

Everyone seemed to agree.

They stumbled back to the ship, and most went directly to bed. Lucian stayed up, more to make sure Fergus made it back in one piece. Lucian went to the bridge, checking the ship's status. Its internal check revealed no issues, and Khairu had signed off on the inspection of the ventilation system and air recyclers. Fuel was at capacity, as was the cargo hold. It felt good knowing they had the resources to go for six months, if it truly came to that.

Lucian noticed Khairu had also ordered radiation meds for *Ethereal's* two auto-doc medical pods. He tried not to wince at the bill, which was just north of five hundred credits, the largest portion being fuel. That alone made their night out seem like peanuts in comparison.

An hour until launch, Fergus came stumbling back without comment, looking the worse for wear. He was alive though, and that was what mattered. He met Lucian's eyes and shook his head.

"You all right?" Lucian asked.

"Mistakes were made, Lucian. Let's speak no more of it. Just wanted to check in, let you know I was back."

He swayed toward his cabin.

Khairu entered the bridge a couple of minutes later and took up the controls.

"I can take it from here," she said. "Go get some sleep."

"Two systems left before Isis," Lucian said.

Khairu nodded. "Psyche, Pontus, and then Isis. I imagine your friends have made it by now."

"They're not my friends."

"Get some sleep, captain."

Lucian's eyes widened a bit at being given that title, a not-so-subtle acknowledgment that he actually was in charge. It was far more than he would have expected.

"Will do. And . . . thanks for everything you've done tonight."

"Just doing my job."

Lucian left her there. After a quick shower, he was in bed and fast asleep long before he heard the ship's fusion reactor come online.

18

THE SECOND DAY out from Archea, they gathered in the conference room, where Khairu and Emma were going to brief them on what to expect when on the surface of Isis two months later.

"Isis is a high-G world," Khairu said. "Its pull is fifteen percent greater than Earth's, so we're increasing the artificial gravity field by .1 per day until we reach that point. If after a month you're not comfortable, you'll have to have gravitational therapy in the med pod."

"Don't like the sound of that," Serah said. As a Psyche native, she would have the hardest time adjusting.

"More than that," Khairu went on, "Xara Mallis completely irradiated Isis's surface at the end of the Mage War. While most of the radiation should have cleared by now, there could still be pockets of it left. There will be life down there, but make no mistake. Isis is no longer the Jewel of the Border Worlds it once was. While we have medicine to cure radiation poisoning, it won't be enough to heal extreme cases. So we must proceed with extreme caution."

"Will the radiation get through the ship?" Emma asked.

"The ship's electromagnetic shielding can stand up to many times what Isis will throw at us. Even now, we're being bombarded with more radiation than we'll ever experience on the surface. It's once we're on the surface that we'll need to be careful."

"Will there be resistance?" Fergus asked.

"Not likely. Isis has not broadcasted in over five decades. If there *are* survivors, which is doubtful, they live deep beneath the surface. They've had fifty years to die off, either from old age or the fraying."

"That's comforting," Linus said. "Either way, Plato and I will be worse than useless. So, we'll hold down the fort."

"That's a good idea," Lucian said. "What about Vera and Xara? If they're going to Isis, then we might run into them."

"It's possible," Khairu admitted. "However, they have a head start on us, two months or even more."

"Enough time to set some traps, maybe," Serah said.

"I won't discount the possibility," Khairu said. "But my guess is, once they've grabbed whatever they've set out to find, they will take their next step. Whatever that is."

"If it's data they're after, can't they just erase it?" Lucian asked.

"Possibly," Khairu said. "But if they want to do it properly, the process would take weeks. Either they take that time, or keep their lead and continue on. They might do some damage to slow us down, but probably won't spend too much time with it."

"With either of her Orbs, she could bring down the Starsea Sanctum in its entirety," Lucian said.

"If that's the case, we'll have to pick up their trail from there somehow." Before anyone could sow any more doubts, she pressed on. "Now, on to the Starsea Sanctum itself. Emma, you want to take it from here?"

"Certainly." All turned to watch her. "I've spent much of the trip looking at any Academy record about the Starsea Sanctum. Even if Isis's surface is unrecognizable, we still have the proper coordinates. The Sanctum is located deep within a mountain, so there's reason to think it survived. League law forbids landing on the planet. It's not like Psyche, though. It's only guarded by one sensor station."

"That'll pick us up for sure," Fergus said.

"There is a way past it. The station dates from just after the Mage War, meaning it's quite dated. So, its detection range is small. More than that, back when the League built it, they didn't expect the advances in spacecraft speed and artificial gravity fields we have today."

"Meaning?" Serah asked.

"Meaning we have a narrow window of about fifty-two minutes where we can approach the planet without being detected. We have to wait for the station to become obscured by Isis's far side, at which point we'll have to burn toward the planet at maximum speed. By the time we slow down enough to enter the atmosphere, we should have some time before the station wraps around again. And Isis's clouds are so thick that no meaningful scan can penetrate them."

"How much time?" Lucian asked.

"As I said, we have a fifty-two minute window. Executed perfectly, the maneuver will leave us ten seconds to spare."

Silence met these words. Looking around, Lucian could see everyone was thinking what he was thinking.

"That's a razor-thin margin," Plato said. "A lot can go wrong in fifty-two minutes."

"There's no other way. There's a League base on a moon of Mensae, the next planet out from Isis's parent star. If we trigger an alert, we won't have time to investigate the Sanctum. However, it will be impossible to avoid being detected on the way out. But by then, our ship should be faster than anything the League can send at us."

"If we get away, they can just intercept us in another system," Fergus said. "Right?"

Emma's cheeks colored. "Well, it's possible that with the Swarmers, the League might not have the ships to chase us down across half the galaxy."

Fergus cleared his throat. "Well, we know where the Starsea Sanctum is. We know how to get down there, as impossible as it seems. We know our friends might have left behind some nasty surprises. Anything else?"

"That should be everything," Emma said. "It's anyone's guess what it will be like down there."

There were a lot of unknowns, but Lucian realized there was little choice. Though the day was still two months away, if all went well, they would soon set foot on Isis.

———

ETHEREAL WAS out of the Archea System in ten days and back in Psyche System. Though they were far from the prison moon and the Warden fleet guarding it, it did little for Lucian's confidence. Things remained quiet, much to his satisfaction, as *Ethereal* shifted its course toward the Pontus Gate, which would lead them toward the outer Mid-Worlds.

The Pontus Gate was on the far side of the system, meaning it took over a month to reach it. That month seemed to take forever, but Lucian sunk deeper into his training to make the time pass faster. Still, it was hard not to think about what he had left behind on Psyche, especially Jagar, who was likely dead for facing Queen Ansaldra.

At last, they passed out of the Psyche System, much to Lucian's relief.

"Welcome to the Pontus System," Khairu said.

"I hope it's safer than Psyche," Plato said.

Khairu gave a dry chuckle. "Unfortunately, it's known for its rampant piracy. Once you're this far out from the First Worlds, there's no such thing as safety. That said, I can almost guarantee that what we're flying is faster than any rusty pirate vessel we're likely to come across."

"They don't need to be faster," Lucian said. "Just have a lucky torpedo."

"Pirates want to take the ship intact," Khairu said. "From their perspective, it's the height of foolishness to destroy the mark."

"Does our course take us close to Pontus itself?" Fergus asked.

"No," Khairu said. "However, we will be close to Revati, the system's outer gas giant. Like Jupiter, it has quite the assortment of moons. And wherever there are dozens of unexplored moons, there are roaches hiding."

"Will they be able to pick us out on their scopes?" Lucian asked.

"Probably."

"Great," Emma said.

"Anyway, this is our course for the next twenty days. The Isis Gate is all the way across this system, so even with our speed, it'll be a jaunt to get there."

NOTHING HAPPENED . . . at least, not until they were two days out from the Isis Gate.

Lucian was eating in the wardroom with Linus and Plato when he heard the announcement from the speakers.

"Lucian, get up here," Khairu said. "We have a problem."

Linus arched his eyebrows. "You need us?"

"Maybe," Lucian said. "Hold tight."

He rushed out of the mess hall and toward the bridge.

"Bogey on our scopes," Khairu said. "Transponder is off."

"Pirate?" Lucian asked, feeling a weight form in his stomach.

Khairu nodded. "Yeah. They're about thirty minutes out and burning hard toward us."

"Can we outfly them?"

"No doubt. However, they are on an intercept course and will get close enough to get a lock on us."

"Don't we have point defense cannons?"

"We have two sternward, but this isn't a military ship. It's no guarantee, especially if they fire multiple."

"How likely is that? Didn't you say pirates want to take a ship intact?"

"Yes. I'm just outlining a worst-case scenario."

"Well, if they won't hail us, then—"

At that moment, the console dinged with an incoming voice request. By this point, Fergus, Serah, and Emma had stepped onto the bridge.

As soon as Lucian accepted the incoming message, a male voice came out, thickly accented with the drawl of the coreward Border Worlds. At these distances, the conversation lag was only a couple of seconds.

"*M.S. Ethereal*, match our speed and vector and prepare to be boarded. Failure to comply will result in your destruction."

"Who is this?" Lucian asked. "Why is your transponder off?"

Khairu spoke into her headset. "Unknown ship, we're a validated mage ship out of Volsung on a League-mandated mission to Mensae. The Mensae base expects our imminent arrival and will hunt you down if you interfere. If you value your lives, I advise you to close this channel and change course, otherwise we'll forward your ship's schematics to Mensae Command."

By now, everyone had arrived on the bridge. There was a

long silence as everyone held their breaths and awaited an answer.

"Mage vessel, eh? A fair amount of persons of interest on board, no doubt."

"Above your paygrade," Khairu said. "I advise you to turn aside and—"

"You wouldn't happen to have a . . .Fergus Madigan on board?"

Khairu's head spun and looked at Fergus. "No."

"A pity. He was last seen in the Archea system. If you know the location of this dangerous mage, Admiral Zheng Yang would be eternally grateful. Enough, perhaps, to give you carte blanche access in Pirate Space and five thousand credits to boot."

"This isn't Pirate Space," Khairu said. "The Pirates claim nothing this far coreward."

"Times are changing, and even Pontus pays homage to her Eminence, Admiral Yang. You're on our turf, and if you don't match our speed and vector, we will fire. Mage vessel or not."

A bluff? Lucian couldn't say. And after Khairu's assessment of the strength of their point defenses, it didn't seem worth the risk.

Fergus cleared his throat. "I'm on board." Everyone looked at him, shocked, as he just shrugged his shoulders. "It's the only way to guarantee they don't shoot us."

"You are wise to admit to it," the pirate captain said, seeming to be a bit surprised himself. There was a moment's hesitation, as if the dog were wondering what to do now that it had caught the car. "I assume you and your friends are armed and dangerous?"

"Very," Fergus said. "And I assume Admiral Yang wants me very much alive."

The captain was silent, something Lucian took to mean assent.

"Well, you have a few choices," Fergus said. "Shoot us down and piss off the Admiral. Chase us, and fail, since we have one of the fastest ships in the League. Or try to follow us to Mensae, which would be an exercise in futility."

The captain laughed. "You overestimate your abilities, Mr. Madigan."

"What's the point of shooting? You waste a few missiles and get no reward. Not even the ship."

"We have stun missiles, perfectly calibrated to incapacitate your fusion drive. Either you ease up or you'll get a taste of them."

How did a pirate get access to *stun missiles*? They were far more expensive than conventional, and could only be found on League military vessels. Either this pirate was lying, or they had taken them off a League corvette, something unimaginable to Lucian. If pirates could attack the League with impunity here in the outer Mid-Worlds, things were far worse than he'd thought.

"I think you're full of shit," Lucian said.

"We will see, *Ethereal*," the captain said smugly. "You have thirty seconds."

He closed the channel.

"*Nice* diplomacy," Khairu said.

"He doesn't have stun missiles," Lucian said. "The odds of that are so insurmountably low—"

"You sound *very* sure of that," Fergus said.

"What, you'd rather me hand you over?"

"No," Fergus said. "But their ship is no bigger than ours, and slower. Whatever crew they had, we could have let them board and take care of them then. You think they *really* want to go toe-to-toe with mages?"

"Probably not, thinking it through."

"So if they truly think they have a chance ..." Emma said.

The pirate captain came back on. "Time's up."

At that moment, red warning lights flashed on the bridge and a klaxon blared.

"Two missiles inbound," Khairu said, her voice tense. "At the current acceleration curve . . . they'll strike in four minutes."

"Rotting hell!" Serah said. "I'm not ready to die!"

Lucian watched the warning screen in disbelief. If those *were* stun missiles, it would force their engines off and place them at the vessel's mercy. If they were conventional missiles, then they had less than four minutes to live.

"Cutting acceleration and flipping sternward toward the missiles," Khairu said. "Computer is saying the PDCs have a thirty percent chance of taking them out."

"That low?" Emma asked.

"They're firing military grade missiles at us."

Lucian shook his head. Maybe they *had* pilfered some missiles from the League. He'd been a right fool, and because of his mistakes, they would likely pay with their lives.

"Wait," Lucian said. "I have an idea."

Khairu looked at him. "*What* idea? All your ideas have been terrible. There's nowhere to run or hide out here. Not in four minutes!"

"We could try calling him back," Fergus said. "Surrender. Maybe they can redirect them."

"No, we won't be doing that," Lucian said. "Everyone, in your EVA suits. I'm going to stop those missiles."

19

EVERYONE LOOKED at him in shock, but Khairu was the first to speak.

"How?"

"I'll shield them. I'll slow them down enough for the PDCs to target them."

Khairu shook her head. "No. By the time a shield takes effect, the missiles will be too close in for the PDCs to target."

"Not necessarily," Fergus said. "It would have to be a powerful shield, though."

"Three minutes," Emma said.

"Khairu, prepare the PDC's. Everyone else, suit up just in case. I'm going out there."

Before anyone could argue, he left the bridge and headed for the operations room, followed by everyone else. They had all prepared for this moment, and could suit up in less than a minute.

Khairu's voice blared from the speaker. "Two minutes to impact. I *strongly* advise a different COA."

Emma, already suited up, stepped up next to him. "If you're

just making a shield, going outside won't be necessary. You can just extend it from within the ship."

"I'm still going out there," he said.

"When the PDCs engage, it might be enough to jar you off the ship," Fergus said.

"I'll Bind myself to the hull."

"Lucian . . ."

"I'll be fine." His heart thundered in his chest. Did they believe that lie? Did *he*?

Before he could second guess himself, he entered the airlock and shut the door behind him. It was silent in here. He waited as the air evacuated through the vents, his breaths sounding rattled in his suit.

Khairu's voice entered his ear. "If you're set on being stupid and doing this, follow my instructions. I'm going to face you the right way and give you a countdown."

"Understood."

Soon, the sounds of the vents faded into silence. The outer blast door slid open, revealing the thick, star-studded inner band of the Milky Way. It took Lucian's breath. He was alone out here. Insignificant. He couldn't believe that not too far away was an enemy that wished him harm.

He reached for his Focus to steady his nerves. It was do or die.

He walked on the outer hull of the ship, engaging his magboots so as not to float away.

"Head to port," Khairu said. "Stop once you're in the middle of the hull."

Lucian followed her directions.

"Turn left about forty-five degrees."

Lucian did so.

"There," she said. "One minute to impact."

Looking sternward, the twin turrets of the PDCs were facing the same direction he was. All was utterly silent. Before he could doubt himself, he let his Focus steady him. He *became* it. He pushed fear aside until it was only himself and his intentions. He could feel both of his Orbs thrumming like second and third hearts within, and luxuriated in their potential power.

Would it be enough?

He began by tethering himself to the hull. He wanted to be sure he didn't go flying off in the wrong direction.

"Fifteen seconds," Khairu said.

"You can stop the count," Lucian said.

At that moment, the cannons roared to life. Twin superheated streams of flak shot outward in rivers of light, momentarily blinding him. Lucian reached for both the Orbs of Binding and Psionics, drawing so much ether into him that it felt as if he were drowning. The stars fell away, replaced by matrices of violet and blue light, all converging on him. Even in this great emptiness, there was ether in abundance. Ether waiting to be used.

He gathered it all, forming a mighty reverse Binding shield solidified by a shell of Psionic Magic. A bubble of indigo light pulsed around the entire ship, its intensity brightening. Lucian streamed and streamed, making the shield so strong that he went blind with the outward flow of magic pulsing from his hands and feeding the surrounding shield. He wanted no room for mistakes.

There was a blinding flash. After it faded, only he remained.

"Scratch two," Khairu said, her voice faint and unbelieving. "Did the PDCs get them at the last second?"

"No," Fergus responded. "If they had, we'd have some hull damage." There was a pause. "Lucian must have pushed them away."

"They're gone," Lucian managed.

He sunk to his knees and let go of the shield, his vision

going black for a moment. He felt divorced from reality, his mind seeming to float above him. He'd experienced this before, during moments of intense streaming. Sometimes, he saw the universe through his Focus, not his own eyes. The experience was always jarring. But given time, he would come back.

"You okay?" Emma asked.

Lucian couldn't respond. Not a minute later, he could make out a figure in an EVA suit coming toward him. Inside the faceplate, Serah's blue eyes watched him with concern. With that grounding, he felt himself returning to reality more fully. He could breathe without feeling like an elephant was sitting on his chest.

He tried to speak her name, but nothing escaped his lips.

She embraced him, and she held him like that, on top of *Ethereal* among the stars.

"I'm here," she said.

"I know," he said. "I . . . haven't streamed like that in a while."

Khairu's voice entered his ears. "They're hailing us again."

"Ignore it," Lucian said. "If they try again, we know we can stop them."

Taking his hand, Serah led him back inside *Ethereal*.

THE RADIO REMAINED silent as *Ethereal* passed through the Isis Gate, with nine days left on its voyage.

Because of the League station in orbit around Isis, they would have to decelerate far faster than the inertial dampeners could compensate. Khairu's projections showed them enduring five gravities for almost thirty minutes before the ship could slip past the planet's cloudy atmosphere. Normally, such a force would kill them in less than two minutes, so their only hope was for Serah to relieve the pressure with an anti-gravity stream.

Lucian didn't want her doing that for too long. Of everyone, she needed to be the *most* careful. But it seemed there was little choice.

Once *Ethereal's* trajectory took it beyond known inter-gate lanes, they switched the transponder off. If a League vessel detected them, they would be within their full rights to blast them into dust. But they could not risk being sighted heading toward the Tomb World. The League's base on Mensae was less than a standard day from Isis. A League vessel could easily intercept them if they kept the transponder on.

The days were interminably long, and it was hard to relax. On their own scopes, they detected no traffic—they were a fair distance away from the main space lanes. No one stayed in the Isis System for long.

They got into range of the world without incident. After over three months, they had arrived at this pivotal moment.

An hour from entering the atmosphere, they strapped themselves into their crash seats to best endure the harsh toll of deceleration. Serah believed her gravity stream could cut the force down from five gravities to three. An almost unbearable shock for the human body, but survivable for thirty minutes, assuming best conditions.

There were far too many assumptions for Lucian's taste.

Isis floated before them, only a fingernail's width in diameter. shining dull blue in the star-studded black. Lucian couldn't believe they would accomplish this slowdown in thirty minutes, when it should have taken half a day.

"Station wraps around in two minutes," Khairu said. "Double-check your restraints, and don't move a muscle." She turned her head toward Serah. "Are you ready, Talent?"

That title added additional severity to the situation. Technically, she *was* a Talent, even if it didn't seem like it.

"Ready as I can be," Serah said.

No one responded when one minute remained, as the ship flipped so its main thrusters pointed opposite of Isis.

Lucian closed his eyes, holding his Focus to separate himself from the situation. His stomach churned, knowing what they had to endure.

"Five seconds," Khairu said.

A moment more, and then Lucian was pushed into his seat, which absorbed only some of the force of deceleration. It only took a few seconds for the engines to bring them up to five gravities, and his vision almost immediately blackened as his lungs fought for breath. He wanted to scream, but could scarcely draw breath.

Serah?

His mind linked with hers, though it didn't seem as if she was there. Had she passed out? Why wasn't Khairu aborting the operation?

They would *die* at this gravity in two or three minutes.

That was when the deck shone with silvery light, taking the edge off the extreme force pushing them down. It was far heavier than what he was used to, but Lucian could at least breathe and turn his head.

In the seat on his right, Serah was just awakening, her eyes blinking in confusion.

If she wasn't streaming, then who was?

Linus grunted from the seat on his left, his jaw clenching. Gray magic streamed from his hands, spreading across the deck and making it shine with silver luminescence. Serah watched him a moment, her eyes widening, before her features firmed with resolve and she joined him. As soon as she set her own stream, Linus let go of his own and closed his eyes.

"Ten minutes to contact," Khairu said, her voice escaping at a rasp.

With great effort, Lucian turned to watch Serah streaming. Her expression was grim, a vein protruding from her forehead.

Isis was close now. Perilously close. If Khairu had the calculations wrong, even slightly, it would end in all of their deaths.

"Two minutes," Khairu said.

Serah gasped, and at that moment, Lucian felt the pressure increasing on his chest. They weren't decelerating more. Her stream had weakened too much to compensate. He tried to shout a warning, but it was all he could do to breathe.

A moment later, the pressure lessened as Linus picked up the stream where she'd left off. He had to hold on a minute more, no longer. His own features struggled with the load. Lucian tried not to think about how out of practice Linus had to be.

Just when it felt as if it would never end, the horrible downward force vanished. A collective sigh of relief escaped everyone's lips at the same time.

"Deceleration complete," Khairu said. "Flipping toward Isis's atmosphere."

The vista outside the viewscreen changed from the black of space filled with stars, to a tannish-blue and cloudy world that dominated the viewscreen. There was nothing but those clouds as far as the eye could see. The swirls of color reminded him of Venus, and he could only imagine what sorts of storms were raging on the surface.

He had little time to think about it as Isis's gravity pulled them into its embrace.

THE ATMOSPHERE ROARED AROUND THEM, shaking *Ethereal* as it dove headfirst into the thick, bilious clouds, like a peregrine toward its prey. After a couple of minutes of extreme g-forces, the ship drew up and Khairu took the control stick.

"We're in, with ten seconds to spare," she said. "The station never came on our scopes."

Lucian breathed a sigh of relief. "And the Sanctum?"

"Near," she said. "Heading down now."

Lucian could discern nothing through the haze of the viewscreen. They said that before the Mage War, Isis rivaled Earth in beauty. The planet was a key target of colonization during the first diaspora, despite its distance, because of its similarity to humanity's homeworld. Its citizens had planned great things for its future.

But after Xara Mallis and the Starsea Mages, all of those plans had been for nothing. Such was the destruction, that even after five decades, the League hadn't allowed for its recolonization, instead designating it as a Mage War memorial.

Fifty years after its nuclear winter, Isis had warmed somewhat, but the world would likely never return to its former glory without a few more centuries of uninterrupted time to recover. The clouds were white, strangely, while the sky was blue, if a more of a slate blue than Earth's. It was the only difference Lucian noticed as they descended toward the surface.

When *Ethereal* finally burst through, it revealed a dismal, gray wasteland bereft of life. In the far distance marched a line of mountains, Earthlike in appearance, with lofty peaks reaching into the white clouds above. It was toward these mountains that Khairu veered *Ethereal*, over a wide river running down from its foothills. Ruins of decaying towers clung to both sides of that river, ruins which had lain undisturbed for the past five decades.

All watched in silence. Though it was hard for Lucian to believe, fifty years was enough time for the atmosphere to be mostly breathable. That said, most of the danger from radiation didn't come from the nuclear fallout itself. It came from the UV radiation blasted out by Isis's sun. Xara Mallis's desperate gambit had not only destroyed the planet's surface and most of its life. It had also reduced the world's ozone layer to nearly nothing, something that would take many decades to recover without terraforming to speed it along.

All too soon, Khairu landed on the surface. The surrounding landscape reminded Lucian very much of the cold tundra of Volsung. He felt this world's gravity pulling down at him—hard. Here, he weighed fifteen percent more than he would have on Earth. They'd had the ship running at that gravity, but feeling the real thing made it seem heavier.

Before them stretched a broken road leading toward a high cliff set before the mountains. The road seemed to extend directly into the cliff without diverging.

"You sure this is the right spot?" Fergus asked.

"My coordinates are correct," Khairu said.

"Maybe there's a tunnel or something," Emma said.

Lucian watched the cliff closely. "We're in the right place. I just think Vera and Xara buried it."

"A trap?" Fergus asked.

"Possibly. Either way, we have to get moving. Everyone needs to get in their enviro suits."

Plato wrung his hands. "Ah . . . if you don't mind, I think I'll be staying behind. Don't know how much good a fat old man like me would be in this gravity."

"Nor will I be going," Linus said. "After that performance up above, I'm ready to puke my guts out."

"Of course," Lucian said. "And . . . thanks for your help."

"When we get back to civilization, you owe me a night's worth of drinks. If you need us, call us up on the radio."

Lucian nodded. "Will do."

They all went to the operations room, each to their separate locker. Within, they had their equipment—vacsuits for space, enviro suits for Isis, shockspears, coilguns, and lightweight packs that held water and rations. Split among their lockers were the parts to assemble a radiation and vacuum-resistant tent, though because of their proximity to *Ethereal*, they wouldn't need that. All had received enough simulation training on the coilguns to be proficient in their use, if not experts. For Lucian's part, he felt more comfortable using his magic and a shockspear.

Once suited up, the five of them stood before the blast door. Lucian pressed the exit button, and the door rolled back to reveal the gray, windswept plain. That wind pummeled him as he stepped upon the rocky, bare ground and faced the looming mountains toward the west. The road led to the cliff, several hundred meters high at its tallest point. Somewhere in that mass was the Starsea Sanctum, and with luck, answers.

They trudged up the road in silence. Turning back, Lucian lost sight of *Ethereal* in the gray landscape. The planet's tomb-like silence made the hairs on his arms stand on end.

"Is this thing on?" Serah asked, her voice entering his ear on a private channel.

"Yeah, loud and clear," Lucian said. "What's up?"

"Rotting creepy out here," she said.

"At least it's not the Darkrift."

"At least I *know* the Darkrift. All I can think about is the millions who died here. Kind of regretting all that reading I did on the way here."

"Well, they're gone now. No such thing as ghosts."

"Well, until a couple of centuries ago, no one believed in magic, either."

She had a point. He changed the band to the entire group. "Getting close. Stay alert."

Within a couple of minutes, they were standing before the giant rock wall, with no obvious entrance.

"Got to be a way in there somewhere," Serah said on the common band.

Lucian reached with his Focus, feeling at the rock for any obvious weakness. It all seemed to be of a single piece.

"Wait, I think I see something," Fergus said, his eyes shining with green Radiance. The light within them dissipated, and he approached the wall, feeling along its length.

"This rock was recently melted," he said. "Fused together."

"Covering their tracks?" Lucian asked.

He nodded. "Appears so."

"So what do we do?" Serah asked. "Blast it to smithereens?"

"Maybe," Lucian said. "Likely, Xara dragged down part of the cliff with the Orb of Gravitonics, and used Atomicism to meld it together."

"Anything you can take care of with your Orbs?" Fergus asked.

Everyone was looking at him, and Lucian felt the weight of that pressure. If he drew too deeply of the Orbs, that would cause his mind to skirt the surface of the Ethereal Background, the membrane separating this reality, the Shadow World, from the Light Realm, the source of the Manifold and magic. And within the Light Realm, his mind would only come in contact with the Ancient One, just as it had when he drew too much to read the Academy's copy of the prophecy.

"I don't see any other choice," he said.

He wasn't even sure where to begin. He only had access to Binding and Psionics, at least the power levels he needed, and he wasn't sure which would be most effective in this situation. He could Bind the mountain face directly to the mountain slopes far above and force them toward each other. But bridging that distance would be an incredible feat, even with the Orb of Binding. Then again, Lucian wasn't as experienced with Psionics, and wasn't sure how he might use it to his advantage.

"Maybe all of you should stand back," he said.

They backed away. Not far enough for Lucian's liking, but it would have to do. He reached first for the Orb of Binding and was just about to stream, when he felt a strong inclination to use Psionics instead.

An idea then entered his head. He knew not from where. He envisioned collapsing the rock wall, revealing the entrance behind it, and knew just how to achieve it.

The power required would be mind-boggling, but he *could* do it.

"Stand farther back," he said.

He didn't face the cliff again until he was sure everyone was halfway to the ship. He clenched his fists and closed his eyes, reaching for the Orb of Psionics. Its power waited for him to wield it.

He quickly saw it would not be enough to stream Psionics. He also needed Binding. Specifically, what he needed was a dualstream that harnessed the power of both.

He reached for the Orb of Biding as well, fusing that stream with the Psionic stream. Binding gave him control, while Psionics gave him power. Magic tore through him, exiting his hands in blue and violet streams. It entered the rock face, lacing a net of purple and blue lightning, pulsing with potential power as it spread up the cliff. Ether built within him, making him dizzy with vertigo. He pushed it along the streams, each push sending thunderous peals throughout the cliff. The rock *shifted* beneath the net as if it were his own hand. A hand that was tens of meters wide.

He wanted to exult at this amount of power. He drew more, and he did so, he could feel the rock before him crumbling. Dust and debris rained from the heights, coming perilously close to crushing him. Lucian didn't care. With each push of Psionic Magic, the mountain crumbled even further. And the Orbs didn't tire, streaming more ether into the net.

Emma's voice entered his mind, snapping him back to reality.

Lucian, get out of there!

He blinked and realized the predicament he was in. With the last of his stored magic, he dispelled a massive Psionic wave against the mountainside. With a thunderous crack, a rockslide began falling right toward him at an alarming speed aided by Isis's heavy gravity.

He turned, using the Orb of Binding to lock himself on the hull of the ship. A tether bridged the gap between his chest and *Ethereal*, yanking him from the ground and sending him flying from the landslide. Just a moment later, metric tons of rock buried the spot he'd once occupied. After a few seconds of flying, he cut off his stream, landing with a heavy thud next to the others.

When he turned back around, the rocks were *still* falling, and a great cloud of dust was rolling in their direction.

"I hope there's a Starsea Sanctum left after this," Fergus said.

"We should get back inside the ship," Khairu said, ignoring his point. "Let things clear up. Not like we can see anything with that dust."

The first wave of dust hit them just as they were climbing the boarding ramp. Lucian's suit read an increase in rads, but still within tolerable levels. The ship would protect enough until the wind dispersed the debris.

Plato was sitting in the wardroom, drinking a cup of coffee. "That was fast. What was all that racket out there?"

"Look out the bridge and see for yourself," Serah said.

He gave her a questioning look, but walked in that direction. Lucian and the others followed him. The viewscreen only revealed a scene clouded with dust.

"Can't see a thing."

"I opened the way to the Sanctum," Lucian said. "The dust will clear. Eventually."

Plato arched an eyebrow. "*You* did that? Those magic stones of yours are no joke."

They stood there another minute, watching the dust billow past.

"This might take a while," Khairu said. "I can stay in here until the dust is gone. Might be an excellent opportunity to rest before going back out."

Lucian realized resting might be a good idea, and something he sorely needed after his exertion from earlier.

"Let's regroup then. As soon as that dust is gone, we'll head out."

21

IT TOOK several hours before the air was clear enough to see ten meters at a stretch, but by then, night was falling, keeping them contained in the ship. They decided it would be better to wait for morning, to have a full day to explore the Sanctum.

They rose at the break of dawn, suited up, and approached the broken cliff. They climbed piles of broken rock and rubble toward an enormous gap in the devastation. Somewhere in this mess had to be *something*.

Once they reached the top of the debris pile, no easy feat in the heavy gravity, Fergus was the first to see something.

"Over there. Looks like a tunnel."

It took a moment, but Lucian saw it, too, a dark hole leading into the mountain.

"So, who's first?" Serah asked.

"I'll go," Lucian said.

Emma was quiet, watching the opening worriedly. "The question is how to get down there."

"One step at a time," Serah said, jumping and falling with sudden speed. Before she landed, an anti-gravity disc opened beneath her, breaking her fall. Lucian wished she *wouldn't* do that, but Serah was going to do whatever she wanted.

Everyone else went down far more carefully. Bits of rubble cascaded down with the odd footstep, but nothing that threatened their lives. Lucian worried the hole was just an opening with a dead end, but as they drew closer, it became clear it was artificial. The dimensions were square and wide enough for ten people to walk side-by-side, and ten meters high at least.

They entered the dark space, dust still clinging to the air. Fergus streamed a light sphere, its brilliance illuminating pillars of swirling motes. Above stretched skylights, but there was no sky beyond, only rubble from the collapse. Geometric designs ran vertically along the length of the corridor, which led into deeper darkness.

"I almost didn't believe this place would be real," Khairu said.

Silence met these words. Fergus led the way, his hand on the haft of his shockspear. Lucian didn't expect to find resistance, but it was better to be careful. Other than Vera and Xara, they were likely the only souls to have visited this place since the end of the Mage War. Lucian could hardly imagine that more than two of his lifetimes ago, this place had been the central hub of the short-lived Starsea Empire. Now, it was the abode of ghosts, its memories of grandeur present only in the minds of a few.

If they didn't find answers here, then Xara and Vera might actually recreate the empire. That left only one option: find answers.

As their footsteps echoed along the empty halls and ascending stairways, it became clear this place was far larger than the Volsung Academy many times over. Multiple paths branched off from the main corridor, leading to further hallways, arcades, grand spaces, and endless stairways. The tall, empty windows and high skylights suggested the Sanctum existed mostly within the mountain, following beneath its sloped surface. The hallways were dark, and dust covered everything. Lucian looked for signs of recent activity, some sign of disturbance, but there was nothing.

Maybe Vera and Xara hadn't been here at all. It was an uncomfortable thought. A thought Lucian didn't want to entertain.

They ascended a long flight of steps, rising seemingly without end. It was difficult with all their gear in Isis's heavy gravity. The echoes of their feet reverberated in the cavernous space. The stairs finally ended, opening ahead into a vast chamber.

"The Starsea Mages did not make this place, that much is clear," Fergus said.

"Who, then?" Serah asked, her face inquisitive before realization dawned. "Wait. The *Ancients* made this place?"

"Who else? It becomes clear why they set up their base here. They must've found something."

"I have a feeling we're about to find it, too," Emma said, her voice somewhat tremulous.

They paused at the top of the flight, catching their breaths. Lucian's heart thundered against his chest. Peering into the darkness, he could not help but hold the haft of his spear, as did everyone else. He'd almost forgotten the coilgun hanging from his right shoulder.

"Something up ahead," Fergus said, his eyes shining brilliantly green with Radiant Magic. "Let's get closer, so all of you can see it, too."

Lucian felt his skin prickle, though he couldn't have said why. All of this seemed . . . *familiar*, though there was no obvious reason it should be. He followed Fergus across the vast expanse, what seemed to be a vast circular area supported by columns. He realized then what this place *really* was, and why it felt so familiar, especially when he spied an empty dais in the center of the chamber.

"An oracle," Lucian said. "It's so much larger than any we've seen."

Because of the darkness, it was impossible to guess the entire breadth of the chamber. The stone pillars were thicker than most trees Lucian had seen. And there were at least seven of them that Lucian could count in the darkness.

"It's about to get a lot brighter," Fergus said. "Don't look directly at my sphere."

The sphere levitated about ten meters above their heads and shone with sudden brilliance, floating in the center of the chamber like a miniature sun. What it revealed made everyone gasp.

They stood in a massive, circular hall, surrounded by at least thirty of those massive pillars. All the surfaces appeared to be of sandstone, with intricate carvings still preserved despite the passing of time. In the center was a high dais with several steps leading up, at the top of which stood the empty pedestal Lucian had spied earlier, just large enough for an Orb to sit upon.

"I guess we know where she found the Orb of Atomicism," he said.

"Look!" Serah said from behind, her voice echoing.

Lucian turned in her direction to see a massive mural painted on the wall, a mural of such detail that it took his breath away. It wrapped around the entire domed space, and there were so many images that it was hard to focus on just one. His eyes first locked on a profiled image of a tall, willowy being that stood on two legs, with a long forehead, and a gilded cap set with a red ruby on its head. The being raised a long, thin arm as if in benediction. Great angel wings, larger than the figure itself, spread out, taking up almost the entire height of the wall. Lucian had guessed that the Ancients had been taller than humans by the height of the steps he'd climbed, both here and elsewhere. This artwork confirmed his suspicions. Did those wings suggest they could fly, or was it merely artistic expression?

To the right were three more similar figures, much smaller, each holding weapons like scepters with long, curved blades. Beneath their gnarled feet stood other figures, backs bent and kneeling as if in supplication, or perhaps surrender. To the right of that was the largest part of the mural, depicting a massive fleet battle between strange ships with ovoid curves. Long lances of light extended from the vessels on the left side toward the harsher angles of the ships on the right.

Something seemed familiar about those ships on the right. For good reason: Lucian had seen them in the news broadcasts not several days earlier.

"Swarmers," Fergus said. "And those on the left must be the armada of Old Starsea. Perhaps this is a representation of a battle."

"Look," Serah said, pointing to the other side. "The Septagon!"

Indeed, on the other side was a depiction of the Septagon, something he would have recognized anywhere. That it was something this alien race had *also* discovered, albeit over a century ago, almost gave him chills.

Only this one looked . . . *different*. There were still the Seven Aspects of Magic, their colors long faded, along with the lines connecting them one and two spaces apart. That was the same. What was different, though, was that every single one of those Aspects had a line going straight toward the middle, toward another Orb, the color of which was pure black.

This, too, seemed familiar. Lucian didn't know why at first, but memory slowly returned.

During his ether withdrawals on Volsung, when he had swum through his wild dreams, he had envisioned this version of the Septagon. Something had been in the middle of it, too, but it hadn't been this Orb.

From the others' silence, it seemed they noticed the difference, too. As if of a single mind, all of them approached the mural until it filled their vision.

"What does it mean?" Serah asked, her voice small in the grand space.

Lucian shook his head. "Hell if I know."

Though an idea was already tickling at the back of his mind. An idea counter to everything he had ever come to know about magic.

It was Emma who gave voice to his thought. "Maybe it's another Aspect of Magic."

All of them stood silent as they thought of the implications.

"That *can't* be true," Serah said. "If there were another Aspect, we'd know about it." She looked at the others. "Right?"

No one responded. Not at first. Finally, Khairu deigned to answer.

"There is so much we don't understand about the universe. Who is to say? There might be some Aspect that's hidden to us. The idea has been put forward before, by the Old Masters, but there was never any evidence of it. They theorized that the Lost Aspect bound the rest together, as depicted by this Septagon." She shrugged. "But, it could just be artistic license."

"What does it *mean*, though?" Serah asked.

"I . . . had a dream about something like this once," Lucian said. "While I was on Volsung. I didn't know what it was. All I knew was that it was . . . *wrong*."

"What do you mean by *wrong*?" Khairu asked.

He shook his head. "I don't know. Broken. Twisted. It's hard to describe. I couldn't look at it directly, like I am now."

"If there's another Aspect," Fergus said, "then what would its power be?"

Everyone tried to think of an answer. It seemed everyone was as clueless as he was.

"They *knew* about this," Lucian said. "The Starsea Mages were sitting on this information this entire time. And none of them breathed a word of it!"

"Maybe they didn't figure it out?" Emma asked.

"No," Fergus said. "We guessed the meaning after just a few seconds. Assuming we have the right of it."

"If this theory about the Lost Aspect is true," Lucian said, "then maybe the Ancients had the same theory. That doesn't mean they knew it existed definitively."

This entire time, Lucian had believed holding the Seven Orbs would be enough. But just knowing there was potentially an *eighth* Orb out there changed the equation. If he had to return the Seven Orbs to the Heart of Creation, would he not also have to bring a hypothetical eighth Orb?

He shook his head. "It's useless to speculate. We just need to remember our goal. Is there anything here that might lead us to the Prophecy of the Seven?"

"How about that?" Serah said, pointing.

Down the mural, in between the Septagon and the conquest reliefs of Starsea, stood a depiction of what could only be described as a map. But it was not just any map. It was a map of the stars and the connections between them.

"Might be something there," Fergus said. "Might as well see what it's all about."

He strode forward, and the others followed. Before long, they were standing before it. There were thousands of nodes that could represent nothing other than stars, and the lines between them had to be paths between the Gates. Instantly, Lucian recognized a certain section of the map that looked similar to League Space. Only that section was only a small portion of the overall rendering, perhaps as little as five percent.

Old Starsea had been far larger than he ever imagined. If the League had claimed almost a hundred systems, then Old Starsea had to encompass *at least* a thousand, if not more.

"It's a map of their empire," he said. He approached, pointing several meters above him at the star he knew to hold Earth. "See? That's Earth, and the one above that is Volsung. Which would make that one over here, Isis."

"That's nice and all, but what's the point?" Serah asked. "You mean *somewhere* in all those worlds is this Nai Shairen place? How are we supposed to know which one it is?" She placed her hands on her hips, as if angry at the monumental task before them. "What if it's all the way on the other side of this map? It would take *years* to get there. Decades even!"

"It can't be *that* far if Arian made it," Khairu said. "I guess it's *possible* it took him years, but something tells me it's closer than we think."

"What do we know about it?" Emma asked. "Arian said it's beyond the Dark Gate. Might that be on here, somehow?"

"Maybe," Fergus said, doubtfully. "From this map, it doesn't seem the Gates themselves have been depicted. Just the connections. You can't go anywhere unless you know where the proper Gate is."

Lucian wondered what this place actually *was* before the Starsea Mages had taken it over. Perhaps it was the palace of whoever had last controlled the Orb of Atomicism. Lucian could hardly believe that in this chamber, hundreds of thousands of years ago, the Ancients had lived. And, since the Swarmers had eventually wiped them out, they had likely died here, too, but not before the Oracle of Atomicism, that Vigilant of Starsea, had protected his Orb. At least, until Xara Mallis had uncovered it over sixty years ago.

The timeline was almost enough to boggle the mind, and it made Lucian feel very small.

At that moment, Lucian felt the Orbs stirring within him.

"The Chosen will know the way," he said.

All looked at him as the Orbs screamed to be used.

"Stand back a second," he said.

They did as instructed, and not a moment too soon. Twin lights shot from his hands, blue and violet, blasting the map.

"Lucian!" Khairu said. "What are you doing?"

She stopped short as the lights coalesced and spread among the various stars and interconnecting lines, like molten metal filling groves. Within seconds, the entire map shone with radiance.

But one of the stars looked different. Dark, and pulsing with potential energy.

"That one," Emma said. "It's Aurora! I know it is. Just three Gates coreward from Sani..."

Could that be it? Could Aurora be Nai Shairen, or at least where this Dark Gate was?

"Wait," Emma said. "I feel something. Someone who can use magic is close..."

At that moment, a bloodcurdling, inhuman shriek ripped through the air, making the hairs on Lucian's arms stand on end. He cut off both of his streams as more screeches sounded from somewhere in the Sanctum, echoing so much that it was impossible to tell where they were coming from.

"What's happening?" Khairu asked.

Lucian knew the answer just from observing Serah's ghostly white expression. Of everyone there, she'd had the most experience with this threat. They'd talked before about how a burner's cry could be heard for kilometers around in the Riftlands.

"Burners," she said. "A whole rotting lot of them."

22

A COLUMN of fire shot outward from a dark corridor and directly toward them. Serah raised a Thermal shield just in time, barely strong enough to eat the impact. Fergus fired off a few humming shots from his coilgun. A high, inhuman shriek sounded.

"Ward your primaries!" Lucian barked. "Get back to the ship."

They raced across the stone floor toward the corridor from which they had come. Fergus brought up the rear, firing a few more shots at skulking forms now materializing from seemingly every opening in the chamber. It was hard to say just how many burners there were, but at least a dozen slinking forms shambled toward them, with frayed, rotting skin and long cadaverous limbs. Their elongated hands were wrapped with various colored magical streams, waiting to be unleashed.

One burner shot a series of ice spikes, only deflected aside by Lucian's hastily raised shield. From another issued a fork of lightning, absorbed by Khairu's extended shockspear. Three burners lurched toward Emma with nasty snarls. Before Lucian could react, she raised her hand, where a sphere of green light collected before being dispelled into a thick green laser that sliced their heads off.

One burner, the largest of all with a mummified face and a nasty snarl, streamed a blue tether. Not at anyone in the group, but at the archway they intended to pass through.

The opening buckled under the strain. Lucian opened himself to the Orb of Binding, allowing its ether to infuse into his Focus. Immediately, he countered the burner's tether, causing it to dissipate. As soon as everyone was through, he allowed the archway to crumble behind them.

Hopefully, that would keep them from following.

They raced down the long stairway. After a couple of minutes, Lucian was thinking they'd lost them. But at that exact moment, two more burners appeared, blocking the intersection ahead, each wielding a shockspear in a decrepit, claw-like hand.

"Where did *they* come from?" Emma shouted.

Lucian reached for the Orb of Psionics, unadulterated ether pouring through him. He shaped it into a massive kinetic wave, which barreled down the stairs and blasted the two corpse-like beings against a wall. They twitched before fires consumed their wretched forms, the final petering out of their accumulated ether. As the group ran past, the fetid stench of burning, rotted flesh almost made Lucian heave. More howls from behind inspired him to keep running.

"They must be the remnants of the Starsea Mages who sheltered here," Fergus answered. "They've lost their humanity long ago."

"You'd think they'd have rotted away by now," Emma said.

"Burners can last a long time," Serah said. "Decades if there's nothing to disturb them."

Such a thing was unimaginable to Lucian. To think that could be *any* mage's fate gave him the creeps.

For the next ten minutes, they ran, never minding the strain of doing so in the intense gravity. When a light at the end of the tunnel materialized, Lucian had never seen a more beautiful sight.

From behind, the cries of more burners echoed. Holding his Focus, Lucian once again reached for the Orb of Binding, tethering the top of the corridor to the bottom. He streamed, forcing the two sides into one another.

"Out!" Fergus said. "He's bringing the whole place down!"

The others rushed outside just as the ceiling cracked. The crack spread, running the length of the corridor. Lucian cut off his stream, deciding it was time to run himself. Bits of stone broke from the ceiling, and one would have crushed Lucian had he not redirected it with a quick kinetic push.

Lucian leaped as the ceiling above buckled. He streamed a tether onto a piece of rubble where the others had gathered. He pulled himself forward as the rest of the corridor collapsed, a cloud of dust issuing from behind.

"Rotting hell," Serah said. "That was too close."

"We have to get out of this hollow," Lucian said. "I'll tether you up one at a time. Watch below for burners."

He tethered Khairu first. She'd have to get the ship warmed up and ready. Her only betrayal of surprise was a slight widening of her eyes when she shot toward the rim of the hollow above. Once she'd landed, Lucian streamed Serah.

A gurgling yowl sounded from somewhere in the basin, but Lucian didn't have time to look. Emma raised her hand, shooting off another quick laser. The burner gave a high screech before falling dead.

Lucian tethered Emma next, followed by Fergus. As scores of burners filled the depression, Lucian shot himself off last of all, surging toward the rim as fireballs, ice spikes, and bolts of lightning flew in his direction.

He touched down just in the nick of time, the edge of the

depression shielding him from further attacks. They raced across the blasted flatland toward *Ethereal*.

Linus's voice entered through his headset. "Uh, Lucian? We've got trouble coming."

"Yeah, I know!" Lucian managed between breaths. "We'll be there soon."

"What do you want me to do?"

"We're almost there. We'll blast off in a second."

"With the two League cruisers up above, I don't know what you're expecting to do."

"League cruisers? The hell are you talking about?"

"You said you knew!"

"No, I was talking about the burners in the Sanctum. What's this about cruisers?"

"They're hailing us. Apparently, the sensor station caught us and they know we're here. What's this about burners?"

"Rotting hell ..."

From the others' expressions, it was clear Linus had said it on the group channel. But there would be time to figure things out when they got on board.

———

"So, how screwed are we?" Lucian asked once everyone gathered on the bridge of *Ethereal*.

Khairu shook her head. "Well, no chance of escaping. We can out-fly just about anything, but you can't out-fly torpedoes."

"Lucian can stop torpedoes," Emma said.

"About that," Khairu said. "Each League Orion class cruiser comes equipped with *one hundred and twenty* torpedoes. Two cruisers will have two-forty. You think you can Bind your way out of that, even *with* an Orb?"

Did she have to put it *that* way? "So, we're screwed."

The console chimed once again with a hail request from an *LS Bolivar*.

"Not everything has to be a battle," Khairu said, hitting accept on the monitor before Lucian could say anything.

"Unknown vessel," came a commanding female voice. "This is Captain Alayna Solari of the *LS Bolivar*. You are in violation of Article III, Section Two of the Treaty of Chiron by passing within one million kilometers of Isis. You are also in violation of the League Safe Transit Act for traveling without a transponder. I order you to get off planet immediately and dock with us, or face annihilation."

Lucian cleared his throat, forcing himself to remain calm. "We're on a mission mandated by the Volsung Academy. And since the League is in a state of war, the mages have free rein to travel as needed within League borders."

There was a long pause after this. "Who are you? If you *are* a verified mage vessel, turn on your transponder code. You still have to inform us of any operations you intend to conduct. *Especially* those related to Isis."

"I'm Lucian Abrantes, Blue Talent of the Volsung Academy. We are here at the behest of the Transcends, on a secret mission that's *way* above your paygrade."

"Don't piss her off!" Emma whispered.

There was a long silence as the captain seemed to consider this.

"Regardless," Captain Solari said, "I order you off world and to meet us at the coordinates we're sending to your navigation computer. As soon as you turn on your transponder, of course. I will interpret any deviation from course as an attempt to resist arrest, and will shoot until dead. Rest assured, I will verify your story with the proper authorities."

"I don't have time to be waylaid," Lucian said. "We're in pursuit of two very dangerous criminals, and every hour we lose is an hour they have to get away."

"*What* criminals?"

"That's classified."

"Of course," she said, somewhat sarcastically. "Well, if you have any verified letters that prove that, we can talk about it. In a few hours at the coordinates I've sent you."

Rot it. There was no way he was getting out of this.

"Uh, Lucian?" Linus said, pointing. "You expecting visitors?"

Everyone's eyes darted up, where a long line of burners was shambling its way across the wasteland.

"Time to leave," Khairu said.

"Also," Captain Solari said. "Please turn on your transponder before you leave the planet. I wouldn't want to give you a second infraction of the LSTA."

With that, she cut out.

Lucian sat fuming. Even as the burners closed the distance, Khairu powered it on and followed the course given to them by the captain.

"The last thing we need," he said. "*Bureaucracy*."

"It'll get sorted out, I'm sure," Emma said. "As soon as Transcend White confirms your story."

"You're more optimistic than me, then."

At these distances, any "sorting out" would take days at least. Just when they had made this breakthrough, *now* they were getting held up?

Already, they were lifting off the ground. The burners were soon lost to sight as *Ethereal* rose into Isis's thick clouds.

23

LUCIAN HAD THOUGHT he couldn't wait to get off Isis, but knowing what they were about to get into made him want to duck back into its atmosphere.

His skin crawled thinking that *somewhere* out here in space, two potentially hostile cruisers lurked. If he tried to run right now, they would meet their end within minutes, if not sooner. Perhaps it was possible to stop a couple of hundred of torpedoes with the Orbs, but Lucian didn't want to chance it. And even *if* he could, the League would hunt their ship throughout the Worlds, anyway, which was the last thing they needed.

It was better to cooperate and clear things up so no one had to die.

"There they are," Khairu said.

Against the black backdrop of space, Lucian didn't see the cruisers at first. But as they drew closer, their long forms came into view. They sat side by side, twin beasts of darkness, and it didn't help that their bows were facing toward them, along with their full complement of gauss cannons.

Ethereal's engine shut off of its own accord, completing the program the *Bolivar* had uploaded. Almost at once, the cruisers moved in tandem, like a pair of sharks smelling blood in the water.

"Please tell me we're not about to die," Linus said.

No one answered as the nearer of the two ships, what Lucian assumed to be the *Bolivar*, slowed right above them. It came to a stop, and a moment later lowered itself over them. Soon, the panorama of space was replaced by a large hangar bay, the doors of which closed below them.

The console chimed again, and Lucian reluctantly answered.

"Stay on board," Captain Solari ordered, "and disarm yourselves. Open the blast door on our command."

The speaker clicked off, and Lucian slouched back in his seat.

"Do you think they'll confiscate our slates?" Fergus asked. "I got a recording of the map, in case we need to look at it later."

"I can back it up," Khairu said. "They won't find it."

Fergus handed his slate to her, and Khairu finished the task within moments.

Outside the forward viewscreen, a contingent of blue power-armored League marines clomped across the deck of the hangar bay. At their head was a red centurion, the leader of the troop. They carried heavy coilguns and personal energy shields.

"Sparing no expense, I see," Fergus said.

"Those are rangers," Khairu said. "A cut above the average marine. Ships this size usually have a squadron of them."

Several minutes passed with nothing happening. The soldiers remained stationed outside the ship, apparently waiting for further orders.

"What's going on?" Emma asked.

"Bureaucracy," Lucian said. "Trying to decide what to do with us."

"And how long will that take?"

Apparently, it took several hours. Enough for Lucian to fall into a light doze, along with some of the others.

A sudden pounding at the blast door woke him up. Lucian waited only a moment before allowing access, knowing the moment he did so, all hell could break loose.

"Comply," he said to the others. "We'll get through this."

The soldiers stormed on board, spreading to secure every section of the ship.

Lucian spoke into the ship-wide intercom. "All of us are on the bridge."

On the screen, they watched as the red-armored leader held up a hand, and the soldiers gathered in the wardroom. When those that had secured the anterior of the ship had finished, they pushed as a unit toward the front. The stomping of metal boots on the deck was almost deafening.

Lucian went to the door, sliding it open. Four rangers pointed their coilgun carbines at his face.

"Hands in the air!" the red leader barked. "All of you!"

Lucian did so, and reluctantly, the rest followed suit.

"They're armed, sir," one of the blue-armored soldiers said to the one in red.

"Shockspears only," Lucian said. "We're mages."

"The captain ordered you to disarm yourselves."

"Mages never go without their shockspears," Khairu said. "League Law recognizes that right."

"Set them on the deck," the leader commanded, clearly not caring. "Slowly!"

Growling, Lucian did so, and the others followed his example. He had the Orb of Binding in reach, just in case one of those rangers got trigger-happy.

"We won't attack," Lucian said. "All this is a misunderstanding."

"Are you the captain?" the leader asked.

"I'm the leader of this expedition, yes. Psion Khairu is the pilot."

"You're to come with me. Captain Solari wants to speak to you."

"And the others?"

The ranger ignored him, motioning him forward. "Step forward and turn around. Slowly place your hands behind your back. Comply, and no one gets hurt."

Lucian resisted the urge to sigh. "Fine."

He stepped forward, turned, and put his hands behind his back. Two blue-armored rangers patted him down and then clamped his wrists with magnetically sealed manacles. He didn't want to tell them, but he could easily get out of those with a reverse Dynamistic stream.

"He's clean," one of them said.

The leader nodded. "Good. Bring him in."

And just like that, they led Lucian off the ship and across the hangar bay. He held his Focus, keeping utterly calm, even if twenty of the League's most elite soldiers surrounded him. They didn't break step as they led him down narrow corridors, ostensibly toward the bow of the ship. After a couple of minutes of walking, they reached a pair of double doors that slid back, revealing a wide bridge where, behind a terminal, stood a blue-uniformed woman with blonde hair, blue eyes, and a sharp expression. Before her, the rangers stopped short, all of them saluting as a unit.

"Lucian Abrantes, Captain Solari," the leader said.

"As you were, Lieutenant Garcia. You and your men may vacate the deck and resume your former duties."

"Ma'am?"

"Immediately. And take those manacles off."

There was slight hesitation, but the burning blue fire in Solari's eyes left no room for doubt.

"You heard the captain, men."

After taking off the manacles, the rangers filed out of the room. The door shut behind and left the bridge in silence. A few other officers remained at their posts, not even looking up.

Solari placed her hands behind her back as she regarded Lucian. She had several medals pinned to her breast, including one he recognized to be the Sunburst of Valor, awarded only for soldiers whose actions had saved a hundred or more lives in a single engagement. She'd probably earned that one during one of the Swarmer Wars.

"I've sent a light-message to Volsung, top priority. It should arrive in eighteen hours, and with luck, we'll have a response in as much time."

"So, my crew and I are stuck here until then."

Her blue eyes narrowed. "Assuming everything checks out, yes."

"What if Transcend White isn't there? They were going to reinforce the fleet at Alpha Centauri. They might be gone by now."

"I've received no intelligence of the mages' deployment. I've addressed the message to her personally. Wherever in the Worlds she is, it'll find her." She leaned forward, her stoic face showing no emotion. "Now, in the interim, there are things I'd like to discuss."

"Such as?"

"What the hell are you doing in my system? You mentioned chasing two fugitives. Who might those fugitives be?"

"That's classified."

Solari watched him with a barely suppressed smirk. "I find it hard to believe I would not have been apprised of any special operations taking place here."

"It's mage business. That's all you need to know."

"Well, the mages don't run the League Fleet. Far from it. In fact, I outrank Transcend White in this system. The fact that you are interested in Isis is suspect. No one in their right mind goes there."

"Which should tell you we did it for a good reason. One we can't reveal."

"You *will* reveal that reason."

It was hard not to lose patience with her, repeating the same thing over and over. "I can't. What I can say is that our mission is vital to the war effort. Any delay—"

"I'm not letting you go until either you or Transcend White gives me a full explanation as to why—"

At that moment, her console chimed with an incoming hail. She watched Lucian a moment, as if this were some trick of his. She tapped a button on the terminal.

"Captain Solari speaking."

"I have a message from the mages."

"So soon? It can't have reached Volsung yet . . ."

"Not from Volsung," the voice said. "This is from the First Mage of Irion, a certain Quentin Vasser. All Fleet communication to the mages is forwarded to each Academy by default."

"Of course," Solari said, not missing a beat, though Lucian knew from her face that the fact must have slipped her mind. "Play message."

"Captain Solari," came a rich, engaging male voice. "I'm Quentin Vassar, First Mage of the Irion Academy. I've been told a vessel known as the *Ethereal* has passed into Isis space. More than that, it's landed on the planet."

Captain Solari looked annoyed. Lucian figured anything that gave her reaction was probably good for him.

Vassar continued. "It might confuse you why I'm responding to you instead of Transcend White of the Volsung Academy. As you know, the Irion Academy is closest to your position, which is why we received the message first. As First Mage of the Irion Academy, please do nothing rash. The *Ethereal* is on a mission sanctioned by the Full Spectrum of the

Volsung Academy. Whatever help they need, it is paramount you provide it. Thousands, if not millions, of lives are at stake. I also ask that you relay a message to the crew of *Ethereal* as soon as they've finished with their surface operations. The message is: come to Irion. The ones you seek just passed through here, and more, they are heading into the frontier."

Lucian couldn't help but widen his eyes. Vera and Xara passed through *Irion*? What were they doing there?

"Whatever they're searching for," Vassar continued, "I think they've found it. I won't risk revealing sensitive information, but we can speak more in person when you arrive. Please, make all haste. It's what Transcend White would want you to do."

With that, the communication cut off.

Captain Solari turned to Lucian for an explanation, but he was just as dumfounded as she, if not more so.

Solari's cold blue eyes weighed on him for a moment, and then she nodded. "Well, you're one lucky son-of-a-bitch is all I have to say."

"Can we go?"

Her eyes narrowed for a moment before she gave a brute nod. "You may. Your ship will be ready to launch within the hour. But make no mistake: we will watch your every move. If you aren't going directly to Irion, then everything I said before applies. Understood?"

Lucian met her gaze. "Got it."

She called Lieutenant Garcia back in, who led him back to *Ethereal*.

24

BY THE TIME Lucian finished explaining, Linus whistled.

"So they're just going to let us leave, then?"

"Looks that way. On the condition that we go to Irion."

At once, everyone looked at Fergus. From the way he was staring balefully out the front viewscreen, he was less than thrilled at the prospect.

"They are the ones responsible for sending me to Psyche," he said. "Quentin Vassar in particular. I would not return there, if possible."

"Seems we have no choice," Lucian said.

"What can we expect from him?" Emma asked.

Fergus shook his head, not wanting to get into that. "The Irion Academy isn't like the Volsung Academy. It would be more accurate to call it the Irion Mage Corporation. They lease out their mages to the highest bidder. They use the lucrative proceeds of that to invest in various opportunities in the Worlds."

"Even if that bidder is an infamous pirate, like Zheng Yang?" Serah said.

Fergus nodded. "If we go there, I don't know what will happen. Irion prides itself on never failing a contract. Until me, no mage had ever voluntarily left an employer. I'm still the only one, as far as I know. For that, I went to Psyche."

"Don't you want to tell them off?" Serah asked. "Think of how good it would feel!"

His shoulders hunched, a strange gesture for a man of his size and strength. "I don't know *what* I would say. I was loyal to a fault. At least, until I couldn't take it anymore. I paid the price."

"What could they want with us?" Lucian asked. "Vassar said he wants to give us info on the *ones we* seek. I can't believe Vera and Xara just passed through there like it was nothing."

Fergus let out a labored sigh. "We can try sending a light-message, but I doubt they'll give any details. They want us there, and they seem to have information regarding Vera and Xara. The mages of the Irion Academy are shrewd negotiators."

"He said they'd passed through," Emma said. "If they came here first, *then* headed there, they went through the Pontus and Quassel Systems. The only question is, where did they go from there?"

Lucian's thoughts returned to the map, to the star that pulsed with dark energy. Could *that* be where they were heading?

"You said that planet was Aurora," he said. "How sure are you, Emma?"

"One hundred percent. If they're heading to the Aurora System, then it would make sense for them to pass through Irion. Of course, Sani is the more common route, but there's probably a way there from Varda, too. I just don't know of it."

"Varda is the one beyond Irion, right?"

Emma nodded.

Lucian frowned in thought. "I just want to know how this Vassar knew about our mission. Is it common practice for the leaders of each Academy to keep each other up-to-date on everything, *including* the missions their mages are on?"

"Yes, and more so in war," Khairu said.

Lucian supposed that made sense. "Well, this is all we've got for now. We know Vera and Xara went that direction, so we can suppose that there's something there worth finding." He looked at everyone, all watching him for the next move. He could never get used to that. "That's what we'll do. Head to Irion, see what we can learn. That's all I've got."

"We should tread with caution," Khairu said. "Our loyalty is to the Volsung Academy and the Spectrum of Transcends."

Lucian almost wanted to contradict her, saying their loyalty was to the mission. But he realized that was a convincing argument, at least for Khairu and Emma.

Outside the viewscreen, some harbor operators signaled their departure. Khairu immediately powered on the engine before Captain Solari had a sudden change of heart.

"Did they finish refueling?" Plato asked.

"Yes," Khairu said. "And they refilled our food and water stocks as well."

"That was charitable of them."

"Well, it wasn't free. We paid above market price. Solari's revenge, perhaps, at not being able to blast us out of her system."

"Was that a joke out of you, Khairu?" Lucian asked. "I'm impressed."

"I don't know what you're talking about."

In the next moment, the ship dropped through the lower hangar doors. Within the minute, they were jetting away from *Bolivar* and toward the Pontus Gate.

———

LATER, Lucian met with Fergus in the conference room to quiz him on what to expect with the First Mage of Irion. Fergus didn't seem to want to have the conversation, but Lucian needed to know.

"Quentin Vassar has been First Mage for about ten years now," Fergus said. "They are a major political force on that world. And beyond. Their mages have concessions from the League that the mages of Volsung or Mako could only dream of."

"How so?"

"The Irion Mages make themselves useful, and don't have the moral hang-ups of the other two Academies. Of course, none of this on the surface. They are business managers, and their business is to operate from the shadows as spies, saboteurs, and bodyguards. Of course, they also have their hands in many investments, a lot off the books."

"I guess that . . . surprises me," Lucian said. "I'd always assumed the Volsung Academy's structure was the default. Khairu told me a long time ago that they are the ascendant academy."

"They are in times of war," Fergus said. "But the academies operate independently of one another. Most of the time, they only have to answer to the LHA, which runs them with a distant hand. If Volsung is about training the mages to be defending the Worlds in times of trouble, the Irion Academy is more self-interested. They see mages as a business opportunity. They use the proceeds of licensing them to various entities to get a foothold in politics and business."

"Sounds morally dubious."

"Perhaps, but there is nothing illegal about it."

"Makes me wonder what the Mako Academy is like."

"As opposite of Irion as you can imagine. Isolationist and monastic. It's basically a more extreme version of the Volsung Academy."

"Okay. So, what do you think Vassar wants with us? It can't just be about wanting to help us. If he's such a good business-man, he'll want something in return."

"Well, I'm glad you're smart enough to see that. He sees an opportunity for himself, that's for sure."

"Vera and Xara visiting them must have been quite the shock."

"Yes, it certainly changes the equation. At some point, the Worlds will learn the truth, and it's hard to predict what exactly will happen when that happens. It'll take time for rumors to become fact, at least in the minds of the general population."

Serah popped her head into the conference room. "Uh, guys? We have a situation."

Before Lucian could ask, she was heading toward the wardroom.

Sharing a look, Lucian and Fergus followed.

The entire crew had gathered to watch a news broadcast from the Pontus System. The shot showed angular Swarmer vessels passing through a Gate. Emma's face was ashen at the sight, and for good reason.

The ticker at the bottom of the screen revealed the system to be Sani, the system where she'd been born.

Lucian could only watch in disbelief. *Sani*? That was on the opposite side of the League compared to Kasturi. That meant the Swarmers were invading from *another* direction. How could such a thing be possible unless the Swarmers had taken years to surround the League, unknown and unnoticed?

Emma shook her head and left the wardroom. Lucian watched her go helplessly, the words of the news anchor a muddled blur.

Sani. That was just four Gates away. By the time they passed into Pontus, it would be *three* Gates away. Not enough time for the Swarmers to reach them, even in the best conditions, but still too damn close. And with Xara and Vera likely going to Varda and beyond, was there any connection?

"If Nai Shairen is close to Aurora, like we think," Plato said, breaking the heavy silence, "we may all be royally screwed."

Lucian couldn't find any counter to that. He cleared his throat before answering. "The plan remains unchanged. We still have time to get to Irion, learn where they're heading. After that . . ."

"Into the hornet's nest?" Serah asked.

Lucian nodded. "Looks like it."

———

Once everyone had gotten their fill of bad news, Lucian went to the back to check on Emma. He hesitated a moment before knocking, not sure if it was his place to check on her. Before he could doubt himself, he knocked twice.

"Come in."

Lucian pressed the entry button to find Emma sitting on her bunk, her eyes puffy with recently dried tears. He watched her for a moment, feeling her sorrow, before he sat at the foot of her bed.

He didn't know what to say to make things better until he realized there probably wasn't anything he *could* say.

She didn't speak for a long time, seeming to be in a state of shock. "Sani. How is it possible? I *know* people there. Sani doesn't have the ships to get people out. It's a farming world. There's only a few people, just under a million. But that's a million lives, and some of them are my friends, even if we haven't talked in years . . ." She shook her head. "They'll be dead soon. It'll be like Kasturi all over again. And with the League fleet at Alpha Centauri, there's no way they'll get there in time. It won't just be Kasturi, Djerrah, and Sani. So many worlds are going to burn . . ."

Lucian couldn't argue with her assessment. "I'm sorry. I wish there was something I could say, but that doesn't change the facts."

"It feels so hopeless sometimes..."

Lucian couldn't force himself to lie. It wouldn't do much good, anyway. "I'm sorry. I can't imagine what you're going through."

"I... think I need time to process this. Sorry..."

"Sure. Let me know if you need anything."

At that moment, the door to the cabin slid open, admitting Khairu. She stared hard at Lucian for a moment, as if he were infringing on her space. Perhaps he was. That glare took him back to his Novice days.

"I was just leaving."

Emma didn't respond as Khairu went to comfort her.

He left the cabin, feeling absolutely useless, before feeling guilty for having that sentiment. He wasn't all-powerful, and it wasn't about him. Khairu was from Sani, too, if he remembered right. Maybe he *was* overstepping.

"You all right?"

He looked up to see Serah approaching from down the corridor. She stopped, placing a hand on his arm.

"Bad news earlier, huh?"

He nodded, drawing her close. "I can't believe this is happening."

"You're doing too much. How about taking a break? It's nearly two in the morning."

With that realization, a wave of exhaustion hit him. "Not a bad idea. It's hard to imagine sleeping, just knowing what's headed our way. What's headed *humanity's* way."

"Well, when you're rested, we can try to make sense out of things."

Lucian nodded. He didn't have a better idea, so that was what they'd do.

25

THE NEXT DAY, as *Ethereal* sped toward the Pontus Gate, they deciphered Fergus's footage from the Starsea Sanctum over breakfast and well into lunch. By then, they were fairly sure which stars were which. Their positions on the map had shifted slightly from the time of the Ancients over a million years ago.

Lucian focused on the black star, the one that was different. Did it mean anything, or were they grasping at straws?

At that moment, Emma stood in the doorway of the conference room, circles underlining her eyes. She focused on the holographic map they had projected on the table before them.

"We need to know where the right Gates are," she said. "Otherwise, we can't get there. You can buy the Sani-Aurora route off the black market, but with things the way they're going . . ." She trailed off. "Point being, we need a real map and hard numbers to plug into our navigation program. I'm sure it's possible to reach Sani through Varda. Like Vera, we'll have to pass through Irion to get there."

"From this map, it looks like we can expect three Gates," Khairu said.

Serah looked crestfallen. "And how long will *that* take?"

"I don't know," Khairu said. "Three months, if we're lucky. Six months counting a return journey."

"We don't *have* six months!" she said. "Half a year has passed since I left Psyche. And I've spent almost every waking hour on this rotting ship."

"If that's a problem for you," Khairu said, "I'm sure they'll accept you for training at Irion."

The two women locked eyes for a moment. Lucian had to step in before this could deteriorate further.

"This isn't helping." He looked at Khairu. "You're estimating six months to get to Aurora and back. How long until Irion?"

"That'll be shorter. Less than two months."

"I think we can hold on that long."

"This is what we signed up for," Emma said. "It hasn't been easy. For any of us."

"Especially for an old fart like me," Linus said. "Space doesn't agree with old bones and joints." He looked at Lucian. "You know, I often curse the day you took us off the Isle of Madness. Don't look at me like that! I know I should be grateful. But me and poor Plato don't have a home in all the Worlds, and somehow, this tiny, enclosed place has *become* home. If we're going to be in this spaceship for another six months . . ." He shook his head. "Am I crazy? These numbers just aren't adding up! Might be a year before we've finished this whole rotting business. Does humanity even *have* that long?"

"Thank you," Serah said. "My point exactly. After six months, half the League could be burning."

"It's impossible to predict just what's going to happen," Fergus said. "One year ago, I was living in a cave on Psyche. So was Serah. I refuse to believe this is hopeless."

"Some rough math," Khairu said, bringing out her slate. "I've just input a course to the Varda System, with a three-day stop at Irion. Add three months to Aurora, assuming that's where the Dark Gate is. From there, I've charted a course to Hephaestus for the Orb of Thermalism. Add an extra month, just to be conservative . . ."

She stared at the screen, her eyes widening slightly. From that alone, Lucian knew the prognosis couldn't be good.

"This entire enterprise will take . . . just over nine months."

All were silent at that news. Two Swarmer fleets had already entered League Space in the last half year. If more came, it would all but spell doom for humanity.

"Rot me," Serah said.

Fergus shook his head. "We can only hope the Alpha Centauri fleet wipes the floor with the Kasturi fleet. And then somehow turn to meet the second one. Travel time alone will take many months . . ."

"The most likely outcome," Khairu said, her face grave, "is that the League will leave this part of space for the Swarmers. In a few months' time, it'll be a wasteland. Humanity will withdraw toward the First Worlds and a few key planets in the Mid-Worlds. Of course, it's impossible to say just how bad it'll be. But it'll be bad."

"We're not giving up though, are we?" Emma asked. "I don't care *what* we have to do. We need to find the Orbs and end this, even if it kills us!"

"We'll make this go faster," Lucian said. "We *have* to."

Khairu looked as if she wanted to contradict him, but thankfully, she kept her mouth shut.

Lucian looked around the table. Everyone seemed to be lost in their own thoughts. He couldn't keep them from fighting, he couldn't keep them from losing hope, and he couldn't give them a plan that was going to work.

Some leader *he* was.

"Maybe we should all break here," he said. He couldn't mask the disappointment in his voice. That disappointment wasn't with the others. It was with himself.

He left, the others remaining silent.

He wasn't sure where to go, what to do. This ship was too damn small, and he wanted to be alone. It was strange that the last thing you could find in space was . . . *space*.

He ended up settling for the galley. No one was there, which was good enough for him. He leaned his head against the microwave and closed his eyes. He felt as if he would go crazy at any moment. How was he supposed to do this? Millions would die before they even *reached* Aurora. And that assumed that was actually where they needed to go.

It was impossible.

A few minutes later, footsteps thudded from behind. He turned to see Plato, his prodigious gut almost wide enough to brush the counter in the small confines of the galley.

"Don't mind me," he said, reaching for an instameal. His expression became concerned. "You all right, lad? That was rough in there."

"To be honest, no. How could I be all right when everything's going to shit?"

"Fair point," he said. He nodded toward the microwave. "Mind if you move? Never stand between a fat man and his next meal."

"Yeah, sorry."

It was silent as Plato watched his food warm up.

"If I might say so myself," Plato rumbled, "you're not doing a terrible job. Can't be easy, being the bloody Chosen and all."

"I'm not the Chosen. I thought that was established. It's rotting Xara Mallis, and from the looks of it, she's getting to the prophecy before us."

As the microwave beeped, Plato shrugged. "Might be. Might not be. From everything you've said so far, isn't the Chosen the one who has all the Orbs at the end? Last I checked, no one does yet."

"Remember what I told you about what Arian said? The

Chosen is supposed to know the way to the Dark Gate. It certainly seems as if that's describing Xara, too. We're riding on her coattails right now."

"Could be. We don't know enough. I think this First Mage fellow will know a few things. That's my bet."

"Yeah," Lucian said. "But what'll he want in exchange?"

"Won't know that until we get there."

Lucian wasn't sure if he should be annoyed with this attempt at a pep talk. It made him feel guilty, since Plato was just trying to help.

"What's your reason for going on, Plato?"

"You're looking at it," he said, slurping some spaghetti.

Lucian didn't get it. "*Food*?"

Plato swallowed. "Food, wine, holo-films, conversation, seeing new things. Or at least, the future promise of them. And right now, I'm on an adventure to save the entire bloody galaxy. What could be a better reason for going on?"

"I don't know. It all just feels . . . hopeless sometimes."

"Nothing's ever over until you decide it is. That's how I look at it."

"Even you have to see how the odds are stacked against us. It's hard to say, but Aurora is *at least* another three months away on the short end, and probably much more. We just can't be fast enough, and we have one of the fastest ships in the Worlds."

"When have the odds ever *not* been stacked against us?" He leaned back against the counter. "I lived over twenty years on that damn, rotting island." He paused reflectively. "Wonderful word. *Rotting*. It should really enter the proper lexicon." He cleared his throat. "Any time in those twenty years, I could've walked off a cliff, because there was no way to escape aside from the Mad Moon."

"Why didn't you?"

He shrugged. "You can get used to anything."

"So, you're saying I can get used to being under the gun every minute of every day?"

"Well, anytime you enter a crisis state, and that state never ends, it becomes the new normal. You adjust. My point is, if I'd walked off that cliff, I wouldn't be here now, in a future I could have never foreseen. I was a goldfish in a bowl, unable to see the hand that was about to throw me back in the pond."

Lucian realized he had something of a point there. "So, just wait for the hand to throw me out?"

Plato nodded. "It's not guaranteed. Hell, it probably won't even happen. But it *definitely* won't happen if you give up." He patted Lucian on the shoulder, put his tray in the recycler, and brushed off his gut, where a few crumbs had collected. "Anyway, it's normal to want a moment to vent, or feel despondent sometimes. But as long as there is something you can do to better the situation, it's never over. Not until you say it is."

"It's not over," Lucian said. "I still want to get back at Vera for what she did."

"There you go," he said. "She's convinced she's right, too. Don't take this the wrong way, but her and Xara have something of a point, too."

"What are you talking about?"

"They see what they're doing as the only way to stop the Swarmers, to save humanity. The only question is, is the society they want to create worth saving?"

Lucian tried to imagine that future, where Xara Mallis had ascended to become a new Immortal Empress, leading humanity into an infinite future. Concentrating that much power in a single person was a terrifying thought, especially one that had the blood of billions on her hands.

"I don't think so," Lucian said. "They know more than us. It's enough to keep me up at night. Even if I *had* the Orbs, I wouldn't know the first thing to do with them."

And more than that, whether he had the mental fortitude to

achieve the impossible. To enter the Manifold through the First Gate. Assuming he could even find it.

"You're thinking too much, lad," Plato said. "Just keep your eyes on the next goal. Don't even think about what has to happen in the end. A man can drive himself mad thinking too much." He clapped him on the shoulder. "We're in for a long journey. Spend some time with your girl. Try to remember the things that make life worth it"

Lucian wasn't sure how much this was helping, but he certainly didn't feel any worse. "I'm glad you're here, Plato."

"I've sort of been coming to terms with something myself."

"What's that?"

His hand glowed red for a moment, producing a ball of ice.

Lucian's eyes widened. "You broke your block?"

"Right before we went down on Isis, Linus and I had a talk. I said this wasn't a holiday. That we needed to make ourselves a bit more useful. Both of us could have got off on Archea Station, but we stayed. Now, we need to pull our weight."

"How did he react?"

He laughed. "Quite indignant. He would've been quite content to just sit in his cabin, watch holos, and eat endlessly. So when he streamed that anti-grav ward during our descent to Isis, I'm not sure whether that was him changing his mind, or his realization that all of us were in this together."

"Whatever the case, I'm grateful. That couldn't have been a simple decision for either of you."

Plato shrugged. "It is what it is. You're down a Thermalist, and having a second Gravitist in Linus won't be a bad thing." He pushed himself off the counter. "Just thought you should know. I'm here to help, and I'm as good as any Thermalist I know. At least, I was back in my day. Well, Lucian. Keep your head up. That's what's most important."

When Plato left, Lucian hoped he could come to believe that. Someday.

26

OF COURSE, it was hard to maintain belief that things could get better when everything just kept getting worse.

Sani fell with almost no resistance. Tens of thousands escaped, but League sources estimated hundreds of thousands were dead. Emma became even more withdrawn, while Khairu snapped more than usual.

Estimated death counts piled up, refugees gave panicked interviews on the newsfeeds, and more Swarmer vessels poured through the Coreward Border Gate. It was clear there were just as many vessels in this fleet as the Kasturi one. Perhaps even more.

In the end, they turned off the newscasts. They passed through the Pontus Gate, and from there, it was only a four-day connection to the Quassel System, and then another eight days to Irion itself. System chatter was panicked, with the local government commanding every ship in the system to be requisitioned for official use. Lucian wondered how they planned to use these ships. Would they distribute the limited capacity in a fair way, or would the politicians give priority to their families and the rich before anyone else? Lucian had seen enough of human nature to know the answer.

Lucian did his best to put all that out of his mind, keeping everyone busy with training. Linus and Plato also joined them. Plato was adept at reverse Thermal streams, preferring to work with ice rather than fire. In his bouts, he was famous for making the deck slick with practically invisible black ice that caused even Fergus to stumble.

Meanwhile, Linus was skilled at amplifying Gravitonic streams—those that increased the force of gravity. One of Linus's tricks was making his opponent's spear impossible to lift. He also liked to stream a Gravitonic brand at the point of his spear just as it was about to strike. It added incredible force to his attacks. Though in his late sixties, he could hit almost as hard as Fergus.

As the days passed, Lucian was recognizing everyone's strengths. Fergus was unmatched in melee combat, and he became *more* dangerous when he blinded with light. Or worse, he would *bend* light for fractions of a second, causing his opponent's eyes to misinterpret his actions. He preferred to work with wards and brands rather than active streams, leaving most of his concentration for dismantling his opponent's defenses with his spear. None on board could match him, though Khairu came closest.

As far as Khairu, she was equally adept at forward and reverse Dynamistic streams. Not only did electricity add a bite to her attacks, but she also *reversed* the streams to use magnetism to her advantage. It had little practical use against a mage using a carbon-based graphene shockspear, but outside the ship, there were countless applications. Drawing metallic weapons away, neutralizing electromagnetic coilguns, launching projectiles, to name a few.

Since the invasion of Sani, Emma trained harder than she ever had. She used her shockspear mostly in a defensive capacity, while relying on offensive magic to attack. While she was proficient in Dynamism, her true talent was Radiance. Unlike Fergus, she favored active streams, mostly lasers. She couldn't stream those on a spaceship, for obvious reasons, but she'd used them to deadly effect against the burners on Isis.

As far as Serah, she could be anywhere she wanted to be with her anti-grav discs, making her incredibly difficult to hit. When she leaped, she could fly high and come down hard and fast.

Which left Lucian himself. He was unmatched in both Binding and Psionics, both forward and reverse streams. He could end any physical fight immediately with a reverse Binding shield that was practically impenetrable. His tethers allowed him to move far quicker than his feet could take him, and turn his spear into a targeted missile that would never miss.

As far as Psionics, he'd had less practice than Binding. Tele-kinetic waves and pushes were simple enough, and required nothing more than a concentrated, forward stream. Though he didn't practice it on his friends for moral reasons, he was equally capable of reverse Psionic streams that would allow him to tamper with others' minds, either by implanting thoughts or doubts or reading their next move before it happened.

They drilled as much as their ether would allow. It was tempting to push beyond his limits, to overdraw. Magic felt *good*. *Power* felt good. It sometimes felt like the only thing Lucian was living for, since there was nothing else happening in the long days of travel.

Falling into this rhythm, they came to the Irion System far faster than he would have imagined.

———

LUCIAN STOOD ON THE BRIDGE, watching the gray-clouded world approach. He turned to Fergus. "Where is the Irion Academy, anyway?"

"Should be a program on the navigation computer to take us down. Though knowing the Academy, they might charge us to dock."

"Found it," Khairu said. "Engaging now."

The ship entered autopilot, picking a smooth trajectory into the atmosphere. The burn of reentry only lasted a few moments before the ship slowed enough to glide among the thick, lightning-laced clouds.

"Is the whole world like this?" Serah asked.

"The clouds cover most of the planet, yes," Fergus said. "Rarely do you get to see the sky."

"Sounds like Psyche."

"There are similarities. Most people live in the mountains, because it's far too hot at lower elevations. Upwards of seventy centigrade on the equator."

It didn't take long for the cloud layer to break and reveal a landscape of high, pointed peaks. Atop the highest in the far distance stood a single tower thrusting into the sky. Fergus's expression seemed to become somber upon seeing it. Such was the distance that it didn't seem large at first. But as they drew nearer, the silver tower was clearly at least half a kilometer tall, rounded and with a spire stretching into the gray clouds above.

It couldn't have been more different from the Volsung Academy—more like a corporate office than a place of learning.

At that moment, a voice request chimed from the dash. Lucian accepted.

A male voice spoke. "*Ethereal*, you are cleared for docking. Welcome to the Irion Academy."

The voice cut out, and the ship crawled slowly forward, decelerating as it angled below the tower.

"Where's it taking us?" Serah asked.

"The hangar is underneath," Fergus said.

Ethereal slipped into a wide opening in the mountain, coming to rest in a spacious hangar. Theirs was not the only ship. There were at least a dozen others, all modern and sleek. Several long-limbed droids labored, doing inspections and maintenance work.

The ship settled into its berth and powered off. Now that he was here, Lucian found he didn't want to get out. Maybe it was from his time at the Volsung Academy, but the commercial atmosphere of this place felt . . . *wrong*.

"So, what now?" he asked.

"We wait for the welcoming committee."

At that moment, a pair of double doors leading from the hangar slid open, revealing a pair of attractive young women in heels and business attire. They walked across the hangar with an air of confidence, each beaming an artificial smile.

"What the rotting hell is this?" Serah asked.

The two women disappeared under the ship, and a moment later, there was a knock at the blast door.

"Let's go," Lucian said.

The others followed him to the door, which he pressed open.

The smiles of the two women, one blonde and the other brunette, beamed even wider. The first one spoke.

"Welcome to the Irion Academy, Mr. Abrantes. It's so wonderful to meet you." The way she said that made it sound like as if she truly *was* excited for his arrival. "I'm Delphine Moneaux, and this is my associate, Arith Sones." Each held out a hand in a move that seemed eerily coordinated. Lucian just blinked.

Delphine cleared her throat awkwardly, quickly recovering. "The First Mage of Irion is eager to meet with you and . . ." She produced a slate and squinted. "A certain Fergus Madigan?"

Fergus gave a derisive laugh. "As if they don't know that name from hangar to Skyloft here."

The women's smiles faltered for a moment. "Yes, the First Mage is a very busy man. As his executive assistant, he relies on me to maintain his schedule, and he has indicated he wishes to speak with you both immediately. If you would, Mr. Abrantes and Mr. Madigan, please follow me." She took in the others. "Of course, you are also welcome here at the Irion Academy. We have a comfortable waiting area, filled with many forms of entertainment, along with food, drinks, and refreshments. Arith will show you there, if you please."

Serah looked at Lucian, seeming to wonder if it was safe.

"It'll be fine," Fergus said. "Stretch your legs. This might be a while."

"I'm coming, too," Khairu said. "I'm Psion Khairu Diseth, the ranking member of the Volsung Academy here. I will not be passed over."

Delphine's eyes seemed unsure. "Well, I was only told to allow Mr. Abrantes and Mr. Madigan . . ."

"I insist," Khairu said. "Or he won't see us at all."

Lucian wasn't sure why she was pushing so hard, but he was grateful for someone else to have his back.

"I see," Delphine said. "Very well. I will let the First Mage know you're on the way." She swiped out a message on her slate. Though she smiled, her expression was tense, as if she feared retribution for doing something that wasn't ordered. "Now, if the three of you will follow me." She turned to the others. "Arith will take good care of you. Of course, we will refuel and restock your vessel, no charge."

That made Fergus's posture stiffen a bit, though Lucian couldn't see why. Khairu didn't seem to like it either. He supposed he was missing the point.

Delphine led the three of them across the hangar. Fergus

must have seen Lucian's confusion, because he leaned over and whispered in his ear.

"Here, they give nothing for free. Nothing. It's enough to make my hackles rise."

"Makes sense," Lucian said. "I'll keep my eyes open."

Delphine turned her head and plastered on that fake smile of hers. Lucian wondered if *she* was a mage. She didn't exactly fit the profile for one, with the business attire and all. But then again, everything was different here. Maybe the mage's uniform at Irion was suits and business dresses, not the customary robes of the Volsung Academy.

They left the hangar and entered a long, white corridor filled with abstract artwork hanging on the walls. Lucian felt as if he were in a museum.

"The Hall of Canvases," Delphine said, somewhat proudly. "The Irion Academy has been fortunate enough to gain many masterworks, many that were believed to be lost during the Climate Wars of Earth. Monet, Gavrikov, Albrecht, to name a few."

She led them into a circular glass elevator and within, a scanner reading her biometrics. She input the top floor of the building, labeled Skyloft, and the doors closed without sound.

The elevator rose as quickly as it did smoothly. Through the glass exterior, they lifted above a vast lobby, at least twenty floors tall, filled with a maze of curved stairways, balconies, alcoves, pillars, and multi-tiered dancing fountains. The extravagance made Lucian's eyes pop. To Fergus, it was nothing impressive, while Khairu didn't seem surprised at all.

Watching the people below milling about, he realized that most everyone here *couldn't* be mages. This was merely the headquarters of a corporation that was *run* by mages. In fact, the Academy must have only comprised a tiny part of this place's overall operations.

After a couple of minutes, the elevator doors opened,

revealing a sumptuously appointed waiting lobby filled with red couches, a dancing fountain, and a pretty secretary sitting behind a massive mahogany desk. The secretary's attire was strange, something that was a cross between a traditional mage robe and business attire. The upper part of the cloak almost functioned as a designer jacket, opened at the front, while she wore dark pants and leather boots. She gave the same saccharine, professional smile as Delphine.

"The First Mage will see you now," the secretary said, pressing a button behind her desk to buzz them in.

Delphine led them around the fountain and toward a pair of pointlessly tall and ornate doors that swung open automatically, revealing a room far too large to be called an office. It was an open concept, with tall windows, an upper balcony, and two sleek staircases on either side leading up to it. Another elevator rested precisely between the staircases. It was to this that Delphine led them.

They rose to the second balcony, entering an area that seemed more like an office. Behind a desk that was at least half the size of Lucian's old condo sat a bespectacled, dark-skinned man, wearing a rich designer suit-robe hybrid. Gray touched his temples, adding a layer of dignity, but the severe lines of his face suggested he smiled little.

He didn't look away from his thin computer monitor, as if he were so completely absorbed that he didn't notice the new people standing in front of him. He worked half a minute longer, and Delphine waited patiently, as if knowing better than to interrupt. Lucian rolled his eyes, and when that didn't work, he coughed.

Quentin Vassar looked up, giving Lucian a hard gaze that he felt to the marrow of his bones. A curious coolness tingled him from head to toe. By instinct, he streamed a Psionic ward, and the prickling sensation ceased.

"Nice to meet you, too, First Mage," Lucian said.

Delphine looked at him as if horror-struck. She was about to leap to her boss's defense when Vassar held up a hand.

"Please, Delphine. It's quite all right. You can resume your duties."

Her composure, which had wavered for a moment, instantly reformed. "Of course, First Mage. Call if you need anything."

As she passed Lucian, her eyes were nearly murderous. No one spoke until she had entered the elevator and the clacking of her heels had faded from below.

Vassar leaned back in his executive chair. "You'll have to forgive that I couldn't meet you personally at the hangar. I had some bad news with our companies in the Coreward Border Worlds. In short, recent events have been a terrible disaster, and I need to clone myself a hundred times just to have a hope of addressing it all." His eyes next went to Fergus, and a small, knowing smile formed on his lips. "It's good to see you again, old friend. I should have known not even Psyche could keep you in its employ."

Fergus's face darkened. "What do you want, Quentin?"

"Straight to the point, as always. Well, we are old friends, so why not? I'm sure you've briefed your friends on what to expect from me." His hard gaze took in both Khairu and Lucian. "Trust me. Everything he's said about me is true. And more."

"Like you," Khairu said, "we're pressed for time. You're the one who invited us here, so let's hear it. What do you know about Vera and Xara?"

Vassar turned to Lucian. "You're awfully quiet. Not even a *thank you* for extricating you from your predicament?"

"Fergus says you do nothing for free, so why should I thank you?"

Vassar gave a shrewd smile. "Ah. Well, he may be right." He steepled his fingers. "While I'm a businessman, I consider myself a mage first, believe it or not. I will die before I let the suits take over the Irion Tower."

"Looks like they already have," Fergus said. "More suits than robes down there since the last time I was here."

"Yes, things have changed. However, the mages are firmly in control. As we always will be. And like all mages, I believe in the Manifold and its plans for us all. Irion, Volsung, and Mako. All of us play our role in the Worlds, and we all have our gifts. Some would consider us . . . *money-grubbers*, for lack of a better term. As if sitting in a meditation cell all day somehow makes you holy and unassailable." He scoffed. "I digress. You're not here to discuss the details of my philosophy. As Psion Khairu has said, we're here to discuss Vera Desai and Xara Mallis."

"Did you really just let them walk in and out of here like it was nothing?" Lucian asked.

Vassar gave an amused smile. "What would you have done in my place, Mr. Abrantes?"

"I don't know. Anything but aid and abet the enemy."

"Now, that's the strange thing. After hearing them out, I'm not even sure they *are* the enemy, despite what Transcend White says. They make an interesting case, and Xara's determination to gather all the Orbs is admirable."

Lucian supposed he shouldn't have been surprised that Vera and Xara had told him about the Orbs. He wondered what they'd mentioned about *him*.

"They proved it to me, of course. My point being, even if I were inclined to stop them on their mad quest, I would have been unable to."

"Why did you ask us here?" Fergus asked impatiently. "You said you could help us."

Khairu clenched her jaw. "More than that. If you're so supportive of their goals, then *why* help us?"

"Unless this is a trap," Lucian said.

Vassar chuckled. "You give me far too much credit. I'm a scoundrel, undoubtedly, but not *that* bad."

Lucian was fairly sure Vasser was telling the truth, which only left him more confused.

"Quentin," Fergus said, with forced patience, "why did you invite us here?"

"To tell you the reason Vera and Xara paid me a visit. I had something they wanted. The Irion Academy has the most complete knowledge of Gate locations and orbital paths outside League Space. As you know, it's illegal for League vessels to store that information on their navigation computers. It's the League's way of preventing an uncontrolled diaspora of humanity from escaping its clutches."

"People still find a way out," Lucian said, thinking of how Emma's family had gone to Aurora, a world well outside the League.

"Of course. Where there's a will, there's a way. Many Gates have been discovered outside League space, but once you go a certain distance, a lot of it is guesswork. Such information is scattered, and most of it is unreliable. But for the last fifty years, the Irion Academy has been compiling this information, confirming it with hard evidence and at great expense. We've had to deal with many unsavory people—corrupt politicians, pirates, smugglers. You get the idea."

Lucian saw where this was going. "You gave them the locations of every Gate outside the League?"

Vassar nodded. It was hard for Lucian not to think of the implications. That information was vital for going into the frontier. There might even be information about the Dark Gate itself.

"Do you know about anything called the Dark Gate?"

Vassar frowned. "Can't say I do. Xara and Vera omitted that. What is it?"

"More than you deserve to know," Fergus said.

"Be that way, if you wish. Of course, I haven't gone over

every bit of data. Perhaps there's something there that reveals a Dark Gate. I wouldn't know."

"We'll take it," Lucian said.

Vassar smiled graciously. "I'm pleased with your interest. I'm sure we can cut a deal."

"And the price?" Fergus asked.

Vassar shrugged. "Well, I'll tell you what I charged Vera and Xara."

"They didn't force it from you?" Lucian asked.

"Now, why would they have done that?"

"Because they could."

It was hard to tell, but Vassar seemed to sober a bit at that.

"How much do you want for it?" Fergus asked.

Vassar watched him, deadpan. "I gave them a very fair price, mage to mage. Five hundred thousand credits. They gladly paid."

Even Khairu gawked at that sum. And for Lucian, it was ten times the amount they'd offered him to give up his Orb. And they had paid that for a *map*?

"They rotting low-balled me," he said, somewhat indignant.

"What's that?" Vassar asked.

"Err . . . never mind. Obviously, we can't pay that."

Khairu was still white as a sheet. "I . . . could speak to Transcend White. See if she'll sync the funds."

"The Volsung Academy *has* that much?" Lucian asked.

Khairu frowned. "Liquid, no. But it might be done. It would hurt. A lot."

Vassar watched them coolly. "I've already spoken to Transcend White, apprising her of the situation. Because of the war effort, the Volsung Academy cannot pay such a price. I even bent a little, offering it at four-fifty. Alas, she showed no interest, even knowing your situation."

"It'll be impossible to reach Aurora without knowledge of those Gates," Lucian said. "Especially going through Varda."

If Aurora was even where Xara and Vera were going. It was all they had to go on.

"Obviously, we can't pay that price," Lucian said. "Don't you realize we need that information? If we don't have it, civilization itself could collapse."

"Yes, I realize that," Vassar said, somewhat solemnly, though it looked as if he were fighting a smile. "However, I cannot let that information go for less than a fair price. Mages died gaining it, and great resources went into verifying its authenticity. To merely *give* it to you would dishonor their sacrifice. I would have you know that we've licensed this very information to the League itself at a rate of two and a half million credits *per month*. As you can see, I'm giving you quite the bargain."

"That's the rotting League of Worlds," Lucian said. "They have cash flow in the *billions*. How do you expect us to pay for that?"

Fergus's expression darkened. "What is it you really want, Quentin?"

Quentin watched him matter-of-factly. "It's time we cleared the air, my dear Fergus. As a token of old friendship, I'm willing to impart the data entirely for free. Only if you can impart a token of similar value."

"I don't see what that could be—"

"Word has gotten out, Fergus. An agent of Zheng Yang saw you on Archea Station. Admiral Yang contacted us a couple of months ago, asking about having you continue your contract with her. She has graciously agreed to amend the previous contract. You know, the one you broke. All the details are exactly the same. As you surely remember, you had two years, four months, and some days left by the standard count."

Vassar spun his monitor around, revealing the very contract he was talking about. Fergus watched it, stunned.

"No," Fergus said. "Absolutely not! Are you rotting mad?"

"I'm far from *rotting* mad," Vassar said. "You, Fergus Madigan, hold the distinction of being the only mage at the Irion Academy who has failed to complete his contract. *That* cannot be allowed to stand. You know I never, ever back out on a deal."

"You can't do that," Lucian said. "Fergus is working with me now."

"Do you have a contract with him?"

"What? No! I'm not a rotting psychopath."

"More fool you, then."

"She'll kill me for what I did," Fergus said. "Or worse."

"I'm sure she'll find a better use for your talents, Fergus. I'm sure she misses her former paramour."

Lucian watched Fergus, stunned. "What is he talking about?"

Fergus's expression was furious. "You had no right."

"We have *every* right to know the details of every mage's assignment. While your . . . *liaisons* . . . with Admiral Yang went against protocol, it didn't interfere with your duties, and the client reported . . . *full* satisfaction with the arrangement."

"Come on, now," Lucian said. "*Really?*"

"Regardless, this is your only option. Either pony up the credits. Or renew your contract to serve Zheng Yang and follow that contract until completion." Vassar leaned forward mercilessly. "Do it, or get the hell out of my tower."

27

EVERYONE WAS silent as they absorbed the news. Lucian was so shocked that he didn't know what to say. Fergus and Zheng Yang had been *together*? That was definitely not how Fergus told the story.

But looking back, it made sense. Lucian thought back to the first time on Archea Station. Fergus's vehement dislike of the pirate queen seemed to go beyond the horrible things she had done. It was personal. Could whatever had happened between them be his main reason for breaking the contract?

"I would never have expected even you to be this cruel, Vassar," Fergus said. "I would rather return to Psyche."

Vassar shrugged. "You had a contract. You broke it. And now, you must rectify it. I told you my price. This is not just about money. It's about the Irion Academy's honor."

"Honor!" Fergus scoffed. "*What* honor? Whatever honor this place had departed ten years ago with your ascension to First Mage. You've *always* been jealous of me. You've always believed I wanted to be First Mage. *Never!* And it pissed you off that I could have had it. The board was ready to vote for me.

But when I spoke in favor of you, you hated me even more. And ever since that day, you used your power to screw me over. First, you contracted me to that reprehensible woman, for God knows how much?"

He gave a ruthless smile. "Oh? She never told you?"

"I don't care to know. I hope it was worth it."

"It very much was. Believe me, I've never had such entertainment from spending one credit."

Lucian gawked. Vassar had contracted Fergus to her for *one credit*? Fergus's reaction was of shock and rage.

And then he exploded.

"One credit! You hate me that much, Vassar? Is this Academy a joke to you? You didn't sell *me*. You sold whatever honor this place had left."

Vassar slammed his fist on the table. "I sold *nothing*! You were an impediment to the Academy's future. It was *my right* to contract you to Admiral Yang, as it was my right to send you to the pits of Psyche!"

Fergus shouted, thrusting out his hand and pushing Vassar with a reverse tether that threw him against the glass. While the pane cracked, it held firm. Vassar gave a somewhat maddened chuckle as he stood.

"See? You prove my point. I've won, Fergus. Don't you see that?"

Fergus's chest was heaving. "You won when you consigned me to Psyche. How much more until you're satisfied? How much more must you break me?"

From Vassar's hollow expression, Lucian already knew that answer. It would *never* be enough. Not until Fergus was dead. Lucian wondered at their enmity. Only envy could drive a man to be so ruthlessly cruel.

"Let's just settle down," Lucian said. It seemed such a pithy thing to say, given the circumstances. "You're both grown men. Act like it."

By now, Vassar was standing. "That wisdom comes with age is a lie, Lucian. People don't grow up. They just become older."

Fergus looked out the glass, now dark with night. His eyes were distant, defeated.

Lucian realized there might be a way to get that information out of Vassar. He could *force* it out of him.

"Do you know what the Orb of Psionics can do? Let's just say we can do this the easy way, or the hard way."

At this, Khairu put her hand on the haft of her shockspear.

But the threat was not effective. Vassar just smiled in a way that said he'd already won. "Of course, Vera and Xara warned me of your capabilities. As soon as you attack me Psionically, it will trigger a ward that will alert Delphine of your ill intent. Over a hundred mages will come to my defense." His smile widened. "Nice try, though."

Could that be true? They needed the Gate map, but kicking this hornet's nest wasn't a risk he could take. It seemed Vassar had prepared for this contingency, but more than that, they had his ship while his friends were down below.

"That will do no good," Fergus said to Lucian. He turned back to Vassar. "Quentin, let's talk this out man-to-man. We were friends once. I don't know what happened, what darkened your heart against me. We'll . . . figure something out. This is bigger than the two of us. The Worlds are in our hands."

Vassar watched Fergus a moment, and from that look, Lucian knew these two had been like brothers once. Only brothers could hate each other this much.

"You heard him," Vassar said. "Leave us."

Lucian watched Vassar for a moment, knowing deep down there was nothing more he could do. Defeated, he and Khairu exited to the waiting room outside.

———

Fifteen minutes later, Fergus threw open the doors, his face a storm cloud of anger. He walked directly to the elevator.

"Fergus!" Lucian said. "Wait up."

He didn't seem to hear him. He was in the elevator, with barely enough time for Khairu and Lucian to join him before the doors closed. Khairu watched him with concern, but Fergus was seeing nothing but red. To say anything would undoubtedly cause an explosion of epic proportions.

As the elevator began its long descent down, Khairu looked up at Fergus.

"The map?"

He grimaced, but in the end, reached into his Talent's robes. He thrust a data drive in Khairu's direction, which she took quickly, before he could do any potential damage to it.

At that point, Fergus withdrew a pill from his robe pocket. It seemed he would crush it in his open palm. But in the end, he popped it and swallowed it down.

"What was that?" Lucian asked.

He thought Fergus wouldn't answer at first. But in the end, Fergus managed a terse answer. "My doom."

Khairu watched him worriedly. "Fergus, if you just did something that will affect your performance—"

"Nothing like that," Fergus said. "It's a timed nano sleeper and tracker. I have exactly one year to contact Zheng Yang and resume my contract, or it knocks me into a coma. Either I die from it, or the Irion Academy's agents will deliver me the hard way."

Lucian watched him in shock. He'd only heard of those pills. They were highly illegal, but it seemed Vassar was the type of person to not care.

"Surely it can be extracted?" Khairu said.

"It can't," Fergus said, despondently. "It will replicate and exist at the cellular level. And worse, if it detects anything it deems to be an invasive operation to remove it, it will trigger immediately. Unless I replace every cell in my body, I'm not escaping this."

"That isn't legal, Fergus. If we could just ..."

He trailed off, knowing it was pointless.

"Who will we go to, the League?" Fergus scoffed. "I'm done, Lucian. We've got our map, and I was the price. It's just how it worked out."

When the elevator came to a stop, the doors slid open. They walked down the white corridor toward the hangar. An open archway on the left led into the waiting room. Inside were Serah, Linus, Plato, and Emma. The room was filled with couches, monitors, and what looked like VR panels.

Serah and Emma were each immersed in their own VR realities, while Linus and Plato were drinking some sort of alcoholic beverage, eating popcorn, and watching a comedy holo, with Linus laughing uproariously. Well, it was great *they* were having fun.

"We're leaving," Fergus boomed, before walking toward the ship.

Immediately, Emma and Serah took off their headsets, while Plato switched the holo off. Emma seemed embarrassed to have been caught having fun, while Serah was blinking in confusion, unable to snap back to the real world.

"Hey!" Linus said. "I was *watching* that!" Noticing everyone looking toward Lucian and Khairu, he grew more serious. "Oh. All finished, then? Can't we stay longer? This was getting good!"

He was like a child begging to stay longer in an arcade or an amusement park. It might have been funny in another situation, but not now.

"It's time to leave," Lucian said. "We won't be welcome here for much longer."

"What *happened* up there?" Serah asked.

"We'll explain on board."

———

As they left Irion's atmosphere, Lucian's stomach was doing flips that had nothing to do with the turbulence. In orbit above the planet, he gave Khairu a nod.

"All right. Let's load up that map data."

It felt wrong to do that, given the circumstances. But if they didn't load it, it would make Fergus's sacrifice pointless.

She inserted the data drive, and immediately it loaded the ship's star navigation program. It logged hundreds of Gate entries, all of them outside the League's borders. There were so many that the display had to expand to accommodate them all.

"Looks like a lot of info," Lucian said.

It was a vast understatement. Khairu had to play with the parameters to get the star map to shrink again.

"Anything that looks like the Dark Gate?" Lucian asked.

"What's a Dark Gate supposed to look like?"

Hell if he knew. "I was hoping you would know."

Khairu gave a rare, if bitter, laugh. "Well, we can get to Aurora from Varda now, so that's something at least." She plotted the course. "Not so bad. Only thirty-eight days. Three Gates."

"They must be getting close."

Serah stepped onto the bridge. "Are we allowed to ask questions yet? Fergus is in his cabin and looked like he wanted to punch a hole in the bulwark."

"We're about to get underway," Khairu said. "Just a few more minutes until we're on the right trajectory."

"Let's meet up in the conference room," Lucian said. "And put on some coffee."

Once everyone was situated and the ship speeding from Irion, only Fergus was conspicuously absent. Lucian and Khairu took a few minutes to explain everything. Everyone listened in shock as they learned about Fergus's old friendship with Quentin Vasser, the First Mage's treachery, and Fergus's relationship with the pirate queen, Zheng Yang, all before being consigned to Psyche. It was Fergus's story to tell, but the crew needed to know, and there was no knowing when Fergus might emerge from his quarters.

It was a moment before anyone could think to speak.

Plato cleared his throat. "He's lived enough lives for ten men. Maybe more."

"What are we going to do about this sleeper pill?" Emma asked. "We can't allow him to be delivered to her!"

Lucian shook his head. "Fergus made it sound impossible to counteract. More than that, the pill has spread to the cellular level. Whatever that means."

"It means it's not coming out," Khairu said.

"And we have one year?" Emma asked. "It would take the better part of a year just to *reach* Pirate Space. It's far, both fringeward and spinward."

Pirate Space. Though the League claimed the ten stars centered on Brennus as its own, they actually fell under the purview of Zheng Yang and her Golden Armada. Such had been the case for the past seven years.

"It means we have to work quickly," Lucian said. "Find the Prophecy of the Seven and go after Zheng Yang. Try to convince her to end his contract."

"She won't do that," Linus said. "There's a bounty on his head. She wants revenge."

"She might still be in love with him," Serah said, a bit too wistfully.

"She's a murderous tyrant," Khairu said sharply. "You shouldn't romanticize her."

At that moment, Fergus appeared in the doorway. The anger on his face was gone, though it still smoldered in his dark brown eyes.

"I suppose everyone's caught up?"

"Yeah," Lucian said. "We told them."

He nodded. "Then you know what I have to do."

"There *has* to be a way to stop it," Emma said. "It's not fair!"

Fergus chuckled darkly. "*Nothing* in my life has been fair, Emma. Why should things change now?"

She looked at him with pity, but he didn't seem to notice.

"Quentin and I were friends once. I might have even called him my best friend. I always thought I was helping him, doing what made him happy. But the whole time he was unhappy. He claimed I had it easy. That I had the looks, the skills, the charisma. That I would be First Mage one day. I always denied that. I never wanted the big job." He smiled grimly. "I've often wondered. Would it have been better to take it? To allow myself to be better than him for once? Would he have resented me less for it, if only I'd behaved in the way *he* would have?" He sat in his chair, filled his mug with coffee, and took a deep sip. "I was blind to his motivations, because you don't expect your friend to stab you in the back. To learn that all the pain he inflicted was for the sum of one credit . . ."

He went quiet, seeming to think dark thoughts.

"I'm not the same person now as I was back then. I'm not innocent in this, either. I knew Zheng's past, what she was capable of. But still I fell in with her. Became worse because of it. But in the end, it got to be too much, even for me. She never told me the truth. I guess she knew it would kill me. Zheng may be cruel, but she never was to me. She has that going for her, I guess. Still, I abetted so much that was wrong in the Worlds. All for one credit. Before that, I could just tell myself this rich contract was going to benefit the Academy in so many ways. And yes. I received a handsome payout, too, far more than the contract itself. I never would have guessed the truth." He stared at the table. "I had to get out of there. I ran from the Academy's agents, and was caught. For that, Vassar and the board sentenced me to Psyche."

"Was there a trial?" Lucian asked.

Fergus shook his head. "Did *you* have a trial?"

Lucian saw where he was going with that. If a mage was not a part of an Academy, they were a criminal.

Fergus sighed. "The masters of each academy have complete discretion on who to send to Psyche. It's one of their privileges."

"Why not just send you to Psyche right off the bat?" Emma asked. "Why go through the pretense of contracting you to Zheng Yang?"

"Because Quentin Vassar wanted me to suffer as much as possible. Even before Zheng, he gave me dead-end jobs that consigned me to mediocrity. Anytime things went well, he would interfere. Anytime hope kindled, he doused it." Fergus shook his head. "And he did it all with a smile, all the while holding a knife behind his back. I never suspected him."

"What a vile man," Emma said.

"He'll get his just desserts, Fergie," Serah said, in rare agreement with Emma. "You'll see."

"I don't *want* revenge," he said. "I just want to live my life without his meddling. After he hailed us in the Isis System, I knew it was going to be bad. To the marrow of my bones." He sighed. "Perhaps I'm the stronger, the more likeable, and yes . . . more handsome, if I do say so myself. But Vassar is the craftier. Even when we were students, he had a devious mind, playing pranks on the other students. And sometimes, even instructors." He smiled a bit in memory. "He hadn't gone bad, then. I never thought he'd use that sharp mind of his to prank *me*, in a much more painful way."

"That's not your fault," Emma said.

"It's not," Fergus said. "But I have to live with the consequences of my ignorance." He looked at Khairu. "Is the information loaded, at least?"

"Yes. It appears authentic. We'll be at Aurora in thirty-eight days, if all goes well."

Fergus nodded. "Well, at least there's that."

"They must be weeks ahead of us by now," Emma said. "Hopefully, they've found nothing."

"Do they know we're following them?" Linus asked.

"I'm positive," Lucian said. "Vera branded me, remember? It's how she knew exactly where to find me on Psyche. It would take a fair bit of magic on her part, but she'll be able to feel where I am."

"So, you're from Aurora, right?" Plato asked Emma. "What can we expect?"

"Well, at the time I lived there, there were only a few settlements, all within walking distance of each other. Mine was the main one, called Vale. I don't know what's changed since then. A lot of Ancient ruins, though."

"Is it possible that Aurora could be Nai Shairen?" Khairu asked. "Does Aurora have a moon?"

"Yes," Emma said. "But what about the Dark Gate, and the Chosen knowing the way?"

"I don't know anything," Lucian said.

Lucian left the rest unsaid. What if Xara *was* the Chosen? What if *she* knew the way, and he was just trailing her dust? Maybe it *was* his lot to give his Orbs to her.

But then reason won over, especially as everyone watched him. They had come too far to give up this easily.

"To Aurora, then," Lucian said. "I don't know what we'll find, but maybe we can put down by the ruins Emma knows about. Do you think you could get the coordinates for them?"

"I've uploaded them to the ship already," she said. "The entire planet is mapped."

"Good," Khairu said. "It's something."

"Thirty-eight days," Serah said. "Glad I downloaded a lot of those VR's and took about five hundred sim pills. If we're done here, I have a character I want to continue."

She was already getting up. Serah was the last person Lucian would have expected to get into simulation games. And had she been playing with Emma earlier? The idea of it made him antsy.

Serah looked Lucian's way. "Meeting adjourned?"

"Unless anyone else has something, yes," Lucian said. "Meeting adjourned."

As people got up, Emma headed his way. "Sorry. I showed her this old RPG I used to play. I . . . might've created a monster."

"That's all right. At least something good came out of our stay at Irion."

"You can pop in with us, if you want."

Us? He wasn't sure whether to be grateful they were getting along, or nervous that their conversations might go beyond surface level.

"Um, that's all right. I have things I need to do."

"Things like what?"

"Well, checking on Fergus, for one."

"Do you need help with that?"

"I'll be fine. So . . . I guess you and Serah are good now?"

Emma shrugged. "I'm not sure. It seemed we were getting somewhere back in the waiting room, so we'll see. If you change your mind, you know where to find me. Might be fun, for old time's sake."

"I don't know. Maybe."

"See you around."

She left him there, and Lucian frowned. He was glad things were less awkward with her, and glad that she'd made a friend. But did it *have* to be Serah?

He put it out of his mind and went to find Fergus.

28

FERGUS, predictably, was nowhere to be found. The cabin he shared with Linus and Plato was empty, along with the engine room, wardroom, and bridge.

Lucian eventually took the ladder down to the cargo bay, finding him practicing his spear work among the crates the Irion Academy had loaded. He regarded Lucian for a moment before going back to his forms.

Lucian wondered if he should bother him. It might be better to give him space.

It was at that moment that Lucian felt his shockspear yanked right out of his belt. It flew toward Fergus, who had tethered it. Fergus regarded the weapon for a moment.

"Such carelessness can have you easily killed."

Lucian wondered if he was being serious. "I don't expect my friends to kill me."

"One almost did, just a few months ago. You should be wary of even friends, Lucian. Too much is at stake."

Lucian was ready to argue that Vera *hadn't* been his friend, but in the end, he refrained. He knew where this was coming from. Fergus was projecting what Vassar had done to him.

"I trust everyone on this ship. I get your point, though."

"Care to go a round?" Fergus asked.

Normally, Lucian would have said "no," especially given Fergus's foul mood, but it might help Fergus blow off some stream.

Lucian entered the principus position, spear pointed out and legs bent, just as Khairu had taught him at the Volsung Academy. Fergus faced across from him, assuming the same form.

"No limits," Fergus said.

Lucian arched an eyebrow. A "no limits" duel meant Lucian could use whatever Aspects he wanted, in any amount he wanted, so long as it didn't risk the integrity of the ship.

"You sure?"

"Just fight me!"

Lucian nodded. He began by warding Radiance and Dynamism with a Binding shell, committing most of his ether to the stream. His skin tingled once he set the ward, while a curious pressure released in his mind.

Fergus threw out his palm, which became awash in violet light. He didn't aim at Lucian, though, but at a crate between them. It shot across the deck with surprising speed, but Lucian streamed a quick reverse Binding shield, making the crate ricochet and fly back toward Fergus. Fergus leaped high with the aid of an anti-grav disc, and the crate slammed into the hull with an uncomfortably loud reverberation.

But Fergus was already falling down, his spear point surrounded with a Binding brand designed to pierce Lucian's shield.

Lucian tethered himself to the bulkhead to dodge the blow. Fergus came down hard on the deck.

They faced off again, getting the measure of each other.

Fergus's eyes were thunderous. Lucian got the feeling that he was treating him as he would Vassar.

Fergus pulled two metallic crates with two reverse Dynamistic streams, causing them to clamp toward Lucian like a pincer. Lucian raised a Binding shield, but not quickly enough to thwart the impact. His legs became pinned, and as Fergus leaped forward, his Binding-branded spear pointing out, Lucian streamed a kinetic wave that blasted in all directions. Not only did the crates slide away, but the blast hit Fergus, sending him flying with a startled yell.

Before Fergus could pancake against the bulwark, Lucian brought him under control with a tether. Fergus's face was fuming, his breaths haggard.

"Why are you doing this, Fergus? Do you have a death wish?"

Once Lucian lowered him to the deck, Fergus remained kneeling. "Even when . . . I try my hardest . . ." He paused a moment for breath. "I can't come close. My ether is rotting gone. And still . . . you stand. Barely touched."

In a limited duel, Fergus *would* have defeated him. But Fergus couldn't seriously expect to beat Lucian in a no limits duel.

"I'll probably get some bruises from those crates."

Fergus chuckled darkly. "You insult me."

"I have two Orbs. There's nothing you can do against that. There's nothing *anyone* can do against that." Vera and Xara were likely exceptions, but Lucian didn't want to mention that. "If I didn't use them, you'd get me every time."

"I want to win with no limits. Just once."

Lucian didn't understand why. "Are you trying to prove something?"

Fergus stood, dusting off the lower part of his gray Talent robes. "I don't know. I'm trying to prove that I have some power left, maybe. That I'm not useless."

"You're definitely not useless," Lucian said. "If you want me to, I'll turn this ship around and blast Vassar right off that rotting tower of his."

"That would be a sight," Fergus said. "But we both know that can't happen. He's won. He always does."

"It's not over. We have a year, right? A lot can happen in a year. We'll get the contract nullified. Perhaps Zheng Yang will be met with an unfortunate accident."

Fergus guffawed. "You've an imagination, I'll give you that. That's no easy feat, even for the Chosen. She has tens of thousands of soldiers and an armada of a thousand ships, and ten worlds that pay her some form of tribute. If not more by now." Fergus nodded, as if to confirm that. "We'll have to deal with her, eventually. If things are moving in the Worlds, you can bet your life she'll want a hand in it."

"A thousand ships," Lucian said. "You think she'd help the League in the defense? Mutual preservation and all."

"I highly doubt it," Fergus said. "So far out from the First Worlds, the Pirates rely little on Earth and the First Worlds. It takes upwards of six months for freighters to reach Pirate Space, and up to a year for them to reach their capital world of Brennus. But she has a part to play, of that I assure you. What that part is remains to be seen."

"You think she wants you dead?"

Fergus's eyes were distant. "That's . . . hard to say. Something tells me she'll behave much like Vassar, but in her own way. Will she keep me around as some sort of pet, taunting me for leaving her? Will she forgive me and put me to good use? Or shoot me out an airlock?" He shook his head. "The third option might be the most merciful. And the least likely."

Lucian supposed they'd only find out when the time came. For now, they were about as far from her as they could get, at least on this side of the Worlds.

"Just take it easy, okay?"

Fergus nodded, streaming some quick magic to put the crates back in their proper positions.

"Don't worry about me. I have plenty of time to mope on the way to Aurora. By the time we're in the Varda System, I'll be back to my old self. You'll see."

Lucian wasn't sure that was true, but could tell Fergus wanted to believe it was. "I'm sure."

"Thanks for the fight, captain," he said.

Lucian's eyes widened a bit. To be called that by him was strange. After all, Fergus had been the captain on Psyche, and back then, Fergus saying that to him would have been unimaginable.

Lucian returned to the bridge to check on the ship's progress. He found it empty, so he sat in the captain's chair and checked the system position. They were already two million klicks out of Irion, and the ship's acceleration was picking up all the time. They would get up to four percent light before being forced to slow down for Aurora.

Lucian checked his slate to see an incoming message from Serah.

Where are you?

He swiped out a response. *Bridge.*

A minute later, she appeared in the doorway. She sat next to him in the seat, forcing him to scooch to the side. She wrapped her arms around him and laid her head on his chest.

"You smell . . . *sweaty*."

"Fergus and I had a bout."

"So *that* was all the noise. Almost brought me and Emma out of the sim to see if things were okay."

"Oh?"

She laughed, her blue eyes becoming mischievous. "*Oh?* That's all you have to say?"

"I'm glad you've made a new friend."

"She's actually kind of . . . okay. You know, when I actually let myself talk to her. We have something in common at least."

"Games?"

"Yeah," she said. "You should've seen this raid we did. I think Emma saved the replay if you want to watch." She paused. "Well, nothing like what we did on Psyche, but this was better because you can't . . . you know, *die*."

"I see. Well, not dying is always a plus."

On one hand, he was happy about their budding friendship. But it also made him nervous. What if they started talking about *him*? Comparing notes, even? It was hard not to worry about it.

"Did you talk about me?"

"No," Serah said. "Why would we do that? Since when are *you* the center of the universe, Mr. Chosen?"

"All right. Be that way"

She gave a girlish giggle. "You're getting a big head. Maybe I'm not teasing you enough."

"No, that's *definitely* not it."

"*Someone* needs to cut you down to size. Who won the fight down there, anyway?"

"Me, of course."

"Oh, no. Your head is in grave danger of exploding from pure arrogance."

"I can think of worse ways to go."

"You *ever* tire of winning, Lucian?"

"Well, I can't win with you."

She smiled. "Don't be so glum. It's a mismatch of epic proportions, to be sure."

She kissed him, and Lucian lost himself in the moment. Well, it was better for her and Emma to like each other than *not* to like each other, he supposed. He just had to learn to let it be. Knowing Serah, the minute he said he approved, she would probably go back to hating her guts again.

"What's wrong?" she asked.

"I'm worried about Fergus."

"I . . . feel bad for him. The poor guy can't catch a break."

"What would *you* do? I went down to talk to him, and he just wanted to fight me. He went all out, Serah. Like . . . he wanted to kill me. Without the Orbs, who knows what would have happened."

"He only went that hard *because* of the Orbs. He wouldn't actually kill you. He's just trying to push you, test your limits. Strengthen you."

"You think?"

Serah nodded sagely. "You need to be strong enough to beat Xara Mallis. Eventually."

Yes, there was that. The thought made him go cold.

"I don't know how old she is," Lucian said, "but probably in her late seventies by now, if not older. The Orb of Atomicism has made her look like she's still in her forties. She's had all this time to learn about magic, how to use her Orb. And it's *Atomicism*, the most terrifying Aspect of all. To top it off, she has the Orb of Gravitonics, too. Those two Aspects can be dual-streamed in terrifying ways. Fusion reactions, instant elemental shifts, enormous blasts of radiation. I just don't see how beating her is *possible*. She could probably do things with magic we can't even imagine. Vera only covered so much with me on *Wayfinder*, and I doubt she came even close to teaching me half of what she knew."

"That's why *you* have to become stronger. You can combine Psionics and Binding in terrifying ways, too. Didn't Vera teach you anything about that?"

"She did, but if Vera taught me, Xara will know, too. Binding and Psionic dualstreams *are* powerful, but nothing like Atomicism mixed with literally anything. I have to gather more Orbs. We can't let her have another one. And because I was dumb and told Vera everything, they know the Orb of Thermalism is on Hephaestus."

"Well, I *warned* you not to tell her."

Lucian sighed. "You were right."

Serah smiled. Lucian supposed that to her, those three words were the most beautiful words imaginable.

They sat quietly for a while, just watching the stars out the forward viewscreen. It might have been a pleasant moment, but all he could think about was whether he was up to the task.

29

TWO FIGURES SAT around a fire under a starry sky. A molten moon glowed above high, ruinous towers from a bygone age. Lucian didn't have to ask who or what he was seeing. This was Aurora, and the two figures could be none other than Vera and Xara.

This had to be a dream. He tried to force himself awake, but one figure looked at him, revealing a long, wrinkled face and eyes so dark that they were almost black.

Vera rose and walked toward him, and the closer she came, the more she locked him into the dream. He struggled like a bug caught in a spider's web.

"Getting close, now," she said. "But you are too late."

"Let me out."

"Not until I'm through with you. And it would seem the Manifold is not, either." She regarded him for a moment. "You escaped the burners of the Starsea Sanctum, and you somehow convinced that insufferable First Mage to give you his map. And now, you think you'll beat us to the Dark Gate." She gave a thin smile. "Does it scare you to not know what you're doing?"

"Neither do you."

"That's where you're wrong. In time, we'll discover the location of the Dark Gate, and we'll pass through it to Nai Shairen. It won't be long before the prophecy is ours, and with it, any hope you have." She leaned forward until he could see every line of her face. "The next time we meet, Xara will not ask nicely for the Orbs. If you wish to prove yourself the rightful Chosen, you must defeat her."

"Your days are numbered."

Her smile widened as she let out a cackle. "I like you, Lucian. Even now, I don't think of you as an enemy. There is still time to realize your error and return the Orbs to their rightful owner."

"Your and Xara's plan is . . . *vile*. You would let the Ancient One return and rule humanity as slaves?"

Her smile fell away, and Vera watched him almost with pity. "It's the only option we have. And the mages would profit from it. I don't pretend to know his plans for humanity, but I doubt it is outright slavery. It will certainly differ from the League's vision of disunity and atrophy."

"You *really* believe he won't turn on you?"

"And the option you espouse?" Vera asked, ignoring his question. "Returning the Orbs to the Heart of Creation." She scoffed. "I fight for the only future we have. If you were wise, you'd join me. With four Orbs, Xara would be nigh unstoppable. The *Alkasen* have enclosed the Worlds. They are tightening like a noose, constricting the League's breath. Millions have died already, and hundreds of millions more will in the coming months. There is a year left, perhaps two, before hope is lost entirely. Only the Chosen can deliver humanity from darkness. Only Xara has the power and the will."

"She's not the Chosen until she holds all Seven."

Lucian then remembered the Lost Aspect, or at least, what *could* be the Lost Aspect. Vera and Xara surely knew about it, since they'd once lived in the Starsea Sanctum. But there was no need to bring it up.

She seemed to guess his thoughts. "You've learned about the Lost Aspect, then? I need not even use my brand to read your face. You make it so easy." She watched him for a moment. "At your lack of surprise, I suppose you figured that part out. Either that, or my meddlesome sister told you."

"Ironic that you would consider her meddlesome. So, the Lost Aspect is real?"

She hesitated, as if wondering whether she should explain it to him. "I see no harm in telling you what we know. Which is nothing. It seems the Ancients believed in it, and searched madly for it, to no avail. Whether it exists, or doesn't, I cannot say. But only Seven are needed to end the fraying. Seven to stop the *Alkasen*. Such are the words of Arian himself."

"If you want Xara to fuse with the Ancient One, then you've frayed."

Vera chuckled. "You have spirit. I'll grant you that. But I know which horse I'm backing. Don't think I'll underestimate you. We'll be waiting, Lucian, on Nai Shairen. And without the Prophecy of the Seven, your pursuit of the Orbs is as good as over."

With that, the dream ended.

LUCIAN SAT up in bed with a shout, his arm extended and wrapped with violet magic. His retracted shockspear shot forward and landed hard against the bulwark before he could curb the stream. Various articles exploded outward, caught in the discharge of energy.

Serah woke with a start, her eyes wide. "What the hell's going on?"

Lucian assumed his Focus to force calm. Now in control, he slowed his breathing and closed his eyes.

Serah's hand touched his shoulder. "Lucian. Are you all right? What happened?"

"Vera."

"A dream?"

He nodded shakily. "She's . . . on Aurora. Whatever they're looking for, they're going to find it. If they haven't already."

"What did you see?"

"Ruins," he said. "It seems they know where to look."

Lucian told her the rest of it, and she listened quietly.

"No new information, really," Serah said. "Sounds like she's just taunting you."

He looked around at the mess the cabin was in. "I was streaming Psionic Magic in my sleep. When I woke up, I must've changed the direction of the stream to cause *this*." He nodded toward the disaster that was their cabin.

"Well, that's easily cleaned up. What's important is that you're okay."

Lucian wasn't sure he was. Mentally, at least. "I hate how she can just . . . *intrude*. I need to get this rotting brand off me."

"We'll find a way."

"How? Not even the Transcends could manage it. Not without breaking my mind, anyway."

"There *is* a way," Serah said, somewhat forcefully. "Just as you think there's a way to save *me* from the fraying."

Serah got up and started putting things back in order. Lucian joined her. Within a few minutes, everything was in its proper place, and the dream was already receding.

The next few days passed as the Sani refugee crisis swept the newsfeeds. Only a lucky few escaped, usually those with the creds to buy their passage off from smugglers, pirates, and profiteers. Lucian could hardly bear to watch the broadcasts, where the estimated death counts climbed by the tens of thousands every day.

On the sixth day after they'd set out, they passed into the Varda System, the border of the League of Worlds itself. Varda itself was a small world of less than fifty thousand souls, annexed by the League twenty years ago. After the buzz of the Irion newscasts, Varda was strangely quiet, as if bracing for a coming storm. But there were no Swarmers passing through its Border Gate, toward which *Ethereal* flew.

They would pass through in another six days. Lucian was all too aware that the Swarmers might pour through at any moment. Surely, beyond that Gate in the Coreward Frontier, thousands upon thousands of Swarmer vessels lurked.

But Vera and Xara had made it. Perhaps it was not too late. It wasn't like they had a choice, anyway. They had come this far.

———

SEVERAL DAYS FROM THE GATE, with no broadcasts from Varda and only old news beamed from Irion, Lucian was sitting on the bridge. Khairu was almost always there, whether or not it was her shift. Lucian didn't really mind. Things had been amicable with her ever since Isis. Getting ambushed by dozens of burners had the tendency of making people set their differences aside.

Driven by impulse he didn't understand, he told her about his dream.

She listened quietly, and said nothing for a long while, just staring out the front viewscreen at the stars.

"A confrontation with her is inevitable," Khairu said. "It's time you learned the magic you would have learned as a Psion of the Volsung Academy."

"There's special magic you know?"

She nodded. "I've . . . only had the training for a couple of years by now. And technically, I shouldn't teach you such things. You may have already learned most of it from Vera, for all I know. Still, maybe there are a few things I can show you."

"I'm willing to learn," Lucian said.

"Xara is an Atomicist, as you well know," she said, "while Vera is a Psionic. Together, they will be practically unstoppable. But against one, you may have a chance. Given you understand how to use magic effectively."

"I'm listening."

She hesitated for a moment. "Let's begin tomorrow at nine in the cargo hold."

"Sure. Sounds good."

"I can take over your shift," Khairu said.

"Tomorrow, then."

———

LUCIAN WAS EARLY for the training session. When Khairu arrived, she faced off from him where he and Fergus had sparred.

"We have about twenty days until we reach Aurora," she said. "No matter how hard you train, you won't be ready in time. But you might learn *something*. If you *listen* and follow my streams. Can you do that?"

In the past, Lucian would have given a prideful response. But now, he simply nodded, and awaited further instructions.

"Your obvious strengths are Binding and Psionics, but so far, you've limited yourself to those two Aspects streamed singly. Unfortunately, they are not my specialty, and to discover the true extent of your power, you must seek training from a true master. For what it's worth, though, the true strength of magic becomes apparent in the dualstream. Not every mage can effectively dualstream, and certainly not in every Aspect, and none can for great lengths of time. But you are in a unique position because of the Orbs you hold. You can create Binding and Psionic dualstreams with impunity. *That* should be used to its fullest strength. It's time you learn to combine them in the four most basic configurations."

Lucian was with her so far. Vera had taught him about psychic streams specifically, what he'd used on Halia to read his opponent's poker hand. But that was about the extent of it.

"Have you learned about forward and reverse streams, how the properties of an Aspect change depending on direction?"

Lucian nodded. Each Aspect manifested differently depending on how it was streamed. Forward streams had different effects from reverse streams.

"This also applies to dualstreams," she said. "Every dualstream has four configurations, based on the four variations of forward and reverse streams. For example, forward Psionic streams are telekinetic, while reverse streams are telepathic. For binding, forward streams are pushing, while reverse streams are pulling."

"Okay. With you so far."

"So, each configuration of forward and reverse can exist in a dualstream, for a total of four. And effects are different depending on the configuration."

Lucian understood so far. "Okay. So what are the four configurations of a Psionic and Binding dualstream?"

"First, you have Forward Binding and Forward Psionics. This creates a *controlled telekinetic stream*. Normally, when you do a kinetic wave, or a pushing tether, the movement is more or less uncontrolled, but simple to stream in the heat of the moment. However, combining both Aspects allows greater flexibility. Observe."

Khairu raised her hands, finding a small crate to tether, one hand wrapped in blue magic. As soon as she did so, her other hand became wrapped in violet magic, joining the tether. She moved the crate around the area with great precision for a few seconds before allowing it to drop to the deck.

She wiped her brow once she was done. "This . . . is not my area of strength. You get the picture. That's a controlled telekinetic stream."

Lucian immediately saw the implications. It could be useful for moving heavy objects with greater precision than allowed by a simple tether or kinetic wave. And of course, he could precisely aim heavy objects at enemies. The Binding tether grasped and aimed, while the Psionic push provided power.

"Now," Khairu said, "for Forward Binding and Reverse Psionics. Because of the reversal of the Psionic stream, the effects are *completely* different. You are *pushing* with the Binding stream, but telepathically controlling with the Psionic stream. Thus, you have the building blocks for a mind domination stream."

"Okay. So, how's mind domination work?"

"It's just what it sounds like. This dualstream is Ansaldra's bread and butter, though she makes brands out of them."

"I don't want to control someone's mind."

"You must keep the option open, Lucian. It could one day save your life, or the life of one of your friends."

She had a point there. "So, what about Reverse Binding and Reverse Psionics?"

"That would be a psychic stream, the one used on Halia and the one Vera taught you. It's self-explanatory, too. It allows for the reading of others' thoughts. It's what Vassar *tried* to do to you before you warded against it. The Binding stream pulls, while the Psionic stream establishes a telepathic connection."

"I see. Makes sense."

"That leaves the last Binding-Psionic dualstream. Reverse Binding, Forward Psionics. This creates a shattering stream. This is how you broke that iceberg back at the Volsung Academy, and also how you caused that mountainside to crumble on Isis. It is by far the most deadly attack possible with a Binding-Psionic dualstream."

Lucian thought back to the night he broke his block. It seemed so long ago. After learning about his mother's death, he'd unleashed all his magic on that distant iceberg. Transcend Green said the feat had been accomplished with Binding. However, Lucian had been sure it was Psionics.

As it turned out, it had been both.

"The way a shattering stream works is you pull with a tether, and meanwhile, apply kinetic force at the end of the tether. While a forward reverse stream provides direction and control, the forward Psionic stream creates chaos. It causes the tethered object to fragment."

"Even . . . a person?"

Khairu nodded. "Yes. *Even* a person. Anything you can reach with a reverse tether. It takes a lot of magic to create a dualstream that powerful, but after what I saw you do to the mountain, I know you're more than capable. During the Mage War, the Binders and Psionics powerful enough to shatter their opponents were greatly feared. And rightly so."

"Sounds like a terrible way to die."

"Make no mistake. It is. Of course, the simplest Binding or Psionic ward can dampen the effects of a Binding-Psionic dualstream, rendering it useless. But the defense must be as strong as the attack, counting both Aspects."

"What do you mean by that?"

"For example, say I attack you with a shattering stream. You can ward or shield it with either Binding or Psionics. But remember, dualstreams require four times the ether of a single stream. Therefore, you must ward or shield four times more strongly to compensate, otherwise, you risk being overpowered."

"And I would only need to ward one of those two Aspects?"

Khairu nodded. "All this to say, while you have unlimited

power in Binding and Psionics, Xara has the same advantage with Atomicism and Gravitonics. Unfortunately, those two Aspects can also be dualstreamed."

Lucian felt his stomach fall. He remembered what he'd told Serah about it, things he had learned in passing from Vera. But now, he was going to learn more fully just what he'd be up against.

"Perhaps first it would be best to become acquainted with what each Aspect does individually. You are probably more familiar with Gravitonics, so we'll start with that. Forward Gravitonics is gravity amplification, reverse is gravity reduction. Simple enough. With Atomicism, forward simulates fission, while reverse is elemental transmutation."

"Okay. I'm with you so far."

"When you combine the two, it makes for a potent concoction. A forward Atomic stream merely creates the fuel for fission, so to speak. It still needs a spark to create the atomic blast. So, a forward Thermal stream is also part of it. However, Forward Gravitonics and Forward Atomicism transforms the reaction from fission into fusion, creating something far more powerful."

"So, you're saying Xara can drop *hydrogen bombs* on me with reckless abandon?"

"Not if you're warded or shielded properly. The more time she has to draw ether from her Orbs, the more time she has to overpower your defenses. The key is to interrupt her concentration, to not give her time to set up. If she opted to do such a thing, she would likely do so at a distance. Such a stream takes a lot of time and care to set up. That is to your advantage."

Even with that qualifier, it was almost enough to make Lucian lose hope. Hydrogen bombs with *magic*? But she went relentlessly on.

"Reverse Gravitonics and Forward Atomicism creates something just as terrifying, but in a different way. It allows radiation to diffuse and spread far more than it normally would. Commonly, it's called dirty bombing."

"Dirty bombing?"

"Depending on power, it can diffuse for up to a hundred kilometers all around. This was part of how Xara and the Starsea Mages irradiated Isis during their last stand."

Lucian didn't want to know the rest, but he figured he had to know what he was up against.

"Forward Gravitonics and Reverse Atomicism is an elemental amplification stream. It allows for a more drastic transmutation of elements, unlike an isolated Reverse Atomic stream. With elemental amplification and enough magic, you can create lasting transmutation from a lighter element to a much heavier element. Reverse Gravitonics and Atomicism produces a similar effect, though in the opposite direction, in a stream called elemental reduction."

"I see," Lucian said. "When we fought Nostra, she somehow took the oxygen out of the air. She changed it into nitrogen or something."

"That might have been a dualstream, though such a thing would have been possible with an Atomic brand, too."

That went to show that transmutation could be deadly, too. In short, Xara had no shortage of tools to dispose of him with.

"To defend yourself against these dualstreams," she said, "you'll need to ward either Gravitonics or Atomicism. I suggest Gravitonics since it's your secondary. However, today I would like to focus on Atomicism. Xara can still come after you with that Aspect alone, and by itself, it needs to be shielded appropriately."

"Is streaming Atomicism different from the other Aspects?"

"It's probably most similar to Radiance. Its chief strengths, aside from the raw power of nuclear reactions, come from how it combines with other Aspects, as well as various brands. You must learn to stream *at least* Atomic wards and shields, or Xara will likely destroy you."

"Not pulling punches, are you?"

"I'm not, because Xara won't."

"Atomicism is my weakest Aspect," Lucian said. "It's a quaternary."

"You still have to try. Likely, you'll have to commit everything to your ward and lean on the Orbs of Binding and Psionics for the rest. But for a mage of your experience, and the development of your Focus, streaming Atomicism should be fairly straightforward."

"Guess I'll get started, then."

Lucian closed his eyes, reaching for the Atomic Aspect. It felt . . . unfamiliar. Heavy. Cumbersome.

But Lucian had to learn if he was to survive.

He released a breath, holding his Focus and forcing calm. He streamed, feeling the magic tingle beneath his skin. A sudden wave of nausea overtook him. He remembered how the Elders of Kiro had discussed stream purity. Atomicism had to be his least pure, meaning he was getting less magic and more poison than he was used to.

If he streamed this too much, it would make him fray.

But he forced himself to draw more, forming a Gravitonic shell around the ward to set it. Khairu watched him closely, and a moment later, he felt something pricking at his ward, and the resistance of his magic pushing back.

"Not bad," she said.

But was it good enough? Lucian had the feeling that even *she* couldn't say.

"Now," she said. "Use the Orbs."

He reached for both Orbs in tandem and went through the Binding-Psionic that didn't involve reading thoughts or mind domination. He moved crates around with relative ease and precision, and reversing the Binding stream caused the metallic crates to become misshapen. Lucian cut off the shattering dual-stream before too much damage could be done.

"You learn . . . quickly," Khairu said. "I thought we'd be working on this for a few weeks at least."

"Good to know I'm not hopeless."

Lucian had always intrinsically known what to do, at least as related to Binding and Psionics. He tried not to think about *where* that knowledge came from. Perhaps the Orbs not only supplied power, but knowledge.

"I'm not sure if there's anything more I can teach you, at least regarding those Aspects. If you want to learn more about dualstreams, I can teach you about Dynamism and how it works with its complementary Aspects. Chain lightning, a more powerful version of a basic lightning stream, can be streamed with Forward Binding and Forward Dynamism. I'm sure the others have their own tricks they've learned over the years."

It was a good idea. Things were coming to a head, and all too quickly. He had so much to learn, and not enough time to do it in.

30

AS THE DAYS PASSED, Lucian learned. Not only from Khairu, but the other crewmembers.

From Emma, he learned lasers were actually a dualstream of Radiance and Dynamism, and not pure Radiance as he had first supposed. Serah taught him a few tricks, how combining Gravitonics with Thermalism could produce streams of fire or freezing cold, depending on the direction of the Thermal stream. Khairu showed him how he could reflect magic off his Binding shield by dualstreaming it with Reverse Dynamism.

He learned all this, and more. Even if most of it wasn't practical to try in the confines of the ship, just knowing it was possible gave him a lot to think about.

He practiced what he could as they passed through the Border Gate into the Thalia System, which was directly beyond Varda. Two more Gates remained until Aurora.

The system was uncannily quiet. They turned their transponder off and detected no ships or signals as they passed from Thalia into Xyri, and twelve days later, into the Aurora

252

System. With five days left, they were slowing and entering an orbital trajectory.

And with the clock counting down, they sat down in the conference room to decide what to do.

Emma was the only one with any idea worth its salt. "If anyone knows anything about the ruins on Aurora, it's my old friend, Mathias. Last I saw him, he lived in a mage commune about a day's walk outside our village."

"You think Vera and Xara would have gone there?" Fergus asked.

"No idea. There are a lot of ruins on the planet, so they could be anywhere."

"That's what we'll do," Lucian said. "You have the coordinates?"

Emma nodded. "I downloaded them on Irion."

"Sounds like it's settled," Linus said.

All that was left was to land on a new world.

———

AURORA WAS a world of white mountains and clouds, the only blue and green on the surface being a narrow, two thousand kilometer band on the equator. They detected no orbital traffic, nor did they detect anything on the surface below.

"That's strange," Emma said. "There should be *something* going on down there. Radio broadcasts, at the least."

Her voice seemed strained, as if she were already expecting the worst. So far into the frontier, it was quite possible that what few people lived here had met their fate months ago. It was a silent world whose thick clouds seemed to hold dark secrets.

Lucian reached with his Focus, trying to feel if anything was down there. It was too far to detect anything. Likely, Vera already knew they were here, and that made him wary. He put the thought from his mind. Hopefully, they had moved on by now.

"Prepare for atmospheric entry," Khairu said.

Not a moment later, *Ethereal* shook as it burned through the atmosphere. They endured the intense gravity before the ship leveled out, heading toward a snow-filled, forested valley between two mountain ranges. Emma looked out the viewscreen with intense concentration, as if searching for any sign of destruction.

But there was no destruction at all. Only a world of untamed wilderness. Before long, a clearing and a town of wooden buildings materialized on the snowy surface below.

"Vale," Emma said. "It's still there!"

Despite the lack of destruction, there seemed to be something wrong with the town. But it wasn't until they'd landed that it became apparent.

Debris lay scattered outside the front viewscreen, half-buried in snow. Doors hung open. Windows were broken, while chimneys were empty of smoke. There was not a single soul.

"Abandoned," Khairu said. "And it looks like it has been for some time."

"Maybe they escaped," Emma said, her voice filled with hope.

"Looks damn cold out there," Linus said.

"Nothing you're not used to," Plato put in.

"I've gotten used to comforts again," Linus said. "If I don't have my coffee and holo by six at night, I'm calling for a general strike."

Plato sniffed. "Your lack of contribution likely wouldn't be noticed."

Lucian wasn't in the mood for bickering. "Everyone, suit up. Remember, Xara and Vera might be out there."

"What do we do if we come across them?" Plato asked.

"If they want my Orbs, they'll have to take them over my dead body."

Linus sighed. "I was *afraid* of that . . ."

"No drive signatures detected in the last few days," Khairu said. "Of course, they could be powered down somewhere nearby."

With luck, they were long gone. Lucian was nowhere near ready to deal with them.

He looked at Emma. "Ready?"

"I think so." She seemed a bit rattled. It had to be strange to be back in a place she spent much of her formative years. "I'm worried the mage's commune will be empty."

"They wouldn't return to the League, like the general population," Khairu said. "We may still be in luck."

"Our luck will be their lack of it," Fergus said.

"We're burning daylight," Lucian said. He looked at Emma. "How long's a day here?"

"Twenty-two hours," she said. "No axial tilt, so it's uniform from pole to pole. Judging from the sun, we probably have a few hours until sunset, when it gets really cold."

"It's cold *now*," Linus said.

"How far is the commune?" Lucian asked.

"Thirty minutes up the trail."

"No chance of landing the ship up there?" Linus asked.

"Afraid not," Emma said. "It's too hilly."

"Lucian's right, we should get moving," Khairu said.

Somehow, Khairu's words were the impetus to finally go, not his. Within minutes, they were standing outside in the ankle-deep snow. The air was still and frigid, and the clouds hung heavy, as if they might release snow at any moment.

Emma led the way, at first facing the village. She was staring at a particular building, what looked to be a two-story log cabin. Inclement weather had stripped most of the shingles on top clean off, while almost all the windows were broken.

"If we have time, I'd like to go inside. On the way back, maybe."

"Your house?" Lucian asked.

She nodded. "Once upon a time. Four years ago now. Still feels like yesterday."

As if of their own will, Lucian's eyes roved upward, down the snowy lane toward a large central tree. Something about that tree seemed . . . *familiar*. It was where he and Emma had met during the dream on Psyche. Why there, exactly, and not at the Academy? Lucian never thought to question it.

But the reason suddenly struck him. And it nearly took his breath away.

"That's it," he said, feeling the hairs on his arms rise. "*That's* the tree from the vision!"

Serah's eyes widened. "When Ansaldra's prophecy dissolved?"

Lucian nodded. "I'm sure of it. It's the same!"

"That would mean . . ."

All just stared at the tree as the same realization hit them all at once.

If the vision he'd seen was true, they had just stumbled, by pure happenstance, onto another Orb of Starsea.

————

THEY DIDN'T WALK. They *ran*.

All but Lucian, who felt a sudden sense of vertigo. He knew he should run with them, but he could hardly believe it. What were the odds that *this* tree, the one with ties to Emma's past, would be the one to show the way to the Orb? Was it within the tree itself, underneath it?

There was only one way to find out.

Within a couple of minutes, they were standing before it, breathless.

Emma looked up into the tree's wide boughs. "I've always felt some sort of . . . *resonance* emanating from this tree. Ever since I first started having emergence dreams. Maybe it was just me sensing what was inside."

"Can you feel anything now?" Lucian asked.

". . . Yes. It's here. Underneath."

"Then how do we get to it?" Linus asked. "Start blasting?"

Emma's eyes widened. "No! It . . . might be *convinced* to show us a way in."

"And how would we do that?" Plato asked.

Emma closed her eyes, reaching for her Focus. A moment later, she was streaming Radiant Magic on the tree's trunk. Lucian wasn't sure what she was doing, but there seemed to be some sort of connection. The green magic spread along the trunk and limbs, but nowhere near enough to diffuse evenly.

That was when he joined in, opening up his own stream and adding to hers in confluence. More magic left her hands.

One by one, the others added their own strength. Fergus joined last of all, and with that, a blinding stream of green light left her hands. There was a sudden crackling boom. The stream was cut off, and the green aura surrounding the tree faded.

Then, another crack sounded as a green light rose upward from the ground.

Immediately, Lucian knew what he was expected to do. He moved forward.

"Lucian?"

He turned back to see Emma's worried expression.

"Please be careful."

He nodded. "That amount of magic might have tipped off Vera and Xara. Be ready."

The others nodded, and he went forward. Without hesitating, he reached for his Focus and stepped into the light.

31

HE WAS NO LONGER on Aurora, or at least, so it seemed. He kneeled on a plain of translucent green light, and when he rose, stars and darkness extended in all directions. His breath caught at the sight. Had that light *teleported* him, or was all this happening in his mind?

The only thing he knew was to walk forward. Forward, toward a pedestal he knew all too well, the same kind he'd seen on Volsung, Psyche, and Halia.

And sitting upon it was the Orb of Radiance, seeming to beckon. The Emerald of Starsea.

He approached until he was just a few meters away, its radiant light bathing his face in blinding green. For all that light, however, he didn't close his eyes.

He watched for any sign of the Oracle bound to the Orb, but so far, he was alone. So he strode forward and reached.

And instantly clasped it in his hand.

A shock of power ran through his arm, its green light absorbing toward his Focus. Was it really going to be this easy? No resistance, no challenge, no test of his worthiness?

It is yours, a tired female voice said. *Long have I, the Oracle Noxolo, waited. No longer.*

As Lucian absorbed the streams of green light, he felt the power of the Orb's potential.

But perhaps the challenge was not in obtaining of the Orb, but in keeping it. He rushed back from where he came, but the light that had taken him in here had vanished. And looking in all directions, there seemed to be no escape.

Perhaps *this* was the test. Not in gaining the Orb, but in getting it out.

Lucian willed the mounting panic to settle and tried to think things through. Radiance was the magic of light, in all its various forms.

Using the Orb, perhaps he could find something that was invisible to the naked eye.

He reached for the Orb and drank deeply of its power, creating a ward around himself to sharpen his vision, to see in spectrums far above and below what was natural to the human eye. A new walkway revealed itself, stretching into infinity.

At its end rose a Gate that had been invisible before. He was seeing millions of kilometers into the distance, the power of the Orb of Radiance somehow amplified in this space.

Lucian walked forward, but he never closed the distance. It was too far. This wasn't the way out of here.

This was the *Dark Gate,* visible only with the Orb. But how could it be in this reality, wherever *this* was?

A voice entered his mind. *Lucian?*

Emma?

You can hear me?

Yes. I've found the Dark Gate. Or what I think is the Dark Gate.

Never mind that. Where are you?

I don't know. I've got the Orb, though. Somehow.

Come back. Do you know how?

No. That light is gone now. Maybe it's like a Gate, but more . . . localized. I don't know.

Maybe the Orb will show you how to do it. Try going to where you went in and streaming.

Lucian wasn't sure why he hadn't thought of that. He returned to the spot, just a few meters away. There was a strange sigil there. Looking up, he saw only darkness.

He reached for the Radiant Aspect and streamed magic directly on the sigil. It glowed with emerald luminescence. He streamed until it was as bright as a star.

Then, just as with before, it seemed to absorb him entirely, carrying him with it above the shining floor.

LUCIAN BLINKED awake in the snow, a crowd of blurred faces staring above him.

"He's back from the dead!" Linus shouted.

"I wasn't dead," Lucian said with a groan. He sat up, his vision slowly returning. "I . . . have the Orb. Assuming all that wasn't a massive trip."

"No, you were gone," Plato said. "Disappeared into the light!"

"We should get back to the ship," Khairu said. "At any moment, they'll—"

Something *pushed* against Lucian's mind. By pure instinct, he reached for the Orb of Psionics and streamed a shield as strong as any he'd ever made.

Seeing his reaction, the others' eyes went wide.

"They're here," he managed. "Back to the ship. Now!"

They ran. Lucian didn't have time to look for Vera or Xara, but Vera was accessing the brand she'd created, and was probably powerful enough to do some damage at a distance. Looking up at the sky, a ship was now breaking through the clouds.

The *Wayfinder*.

"Rotting hell!" Serah yelled.

They clambered up the boarding ramp and onto the ship. Khairu, who had run ahead, was already firing it up. They were moving before anyone had time to strap themselves in.

Lucian crawled into a jump seat built into the bulwark, slamming it down and forcing himself in. He tried not to heave from the extreme g-forces pushing against him.

They endured a jarring passage out of Aurora's atmosphere, things not exactly calming until they were well into space. Lucian stood as soon as there were a few seconds of peace and ran to the bridge to see what was going on.

"They're hot on our tail," Khairu said, switching to the LADAR interface. "We got out just in time."

Serah rushed onto the bridge, along with the rest. "Are they going to shoot us down?"

Lucian shook his head. "No. *We're* the ones leading them now." Again, Lucian felt Vera pushing against his mind, demanding access. He kept himself completely insulated in a Psionic ward. There was no chance she was busting in.

"Where are we going?" Emma asked.

Lucian could remember the Dark Gate in the starscape where he'd found the Orb of Radiance, but he could not recall exactly where it was.

The Chosen will know the way. The words of Arian echoed in his mind. Was he the Chosen, if he had seen the Dark Gate? Could he find it again?

The Orb of Radiance was the key. *It* would show the way.

But first, he wanted to make sure it wasn't a fluke. That he actually had it in his possession. He closed his eyes, accessing his Focus. He willed the Orb of Radiance to release itself and appear in his hand.

If nothing happened, then he would know it was all a dream.

Almost instantly, green lines streamed from his chest toward his hand, swirling and materializing into the Emerald of Starsea. Lucian was just as shocked to see it as the others.

"It's real," he said. "I . . . wasn't sure if it was."

"Use it," Emma said.

Lucian nodded. "I'll try."

He absorbed the Orb once again, and its brilliant light dissipated. As soon as he was sure it was a part of him, he closed his eyes, reaching for the Radiant Aspect.

Show me the Dark Gate, he said, willing the Orb to understand. *If I'm the Chosen, show it to me.*

He reached with the Orb, willing himself to see something that was impossible without it. The bridge of the *Ethereal* faded, and all he saw were thousands upon thousands of stars, more becoming visible as he drew more ether. It was like peering into the most advanced telescope known to humanity; he could see across billions of light-years toward the dawn of the universe if he wanted.

In all that information, though, he only needed one thing.

The Chosen would know the way.

Lucian let go of the Orb.

"This isn't my strength," he said. "Fergus? Emma?"

Each of them looked at him as if he were crazy.

"I'm serious," he said. "Maybe I'm the Chosen, maybe I'm not. But maybe the Chosen knowing the way is also the Chosen knowing his limits."

Fergus watched Emma. "Want to flip a coin?"

She shook her head. "I'll take it." She watched him closely. "Don't worry. I'll give it right back."

Once again, Lucian willed the Orb into his hand. He watched it a moment, marveling at its splendor, before forcing himself to hand it over. It wasn't easy doing that, but his trust of

Emma won out. It pulsed a bit when it touched Emma's hand. Perhaps it recognized her abilities.

"What do I do with it?" Emma asked.

"Assume your Focus, and draw it into you with a reverse Radiant stream," Lucian said. "When it's in there . . . you'll know."

She swallowed, her face pale. "Well, here goes nothing."

She closed her eyes and instantly, the Orb of Radiance seemed to melt into her hands, bleeding along her arms toward her heart. When she opened her eyes, they were wide and shone green. She gasped.

"*This* is what you feel all the time?"

"You'll get used to it," Lucian said. "The Dark Gate is out there somewhere."

"Right." Emma kept her eyes open, advancing to the front of the bridge. She peered into the distance, as if she could see into those stars.

"I can see . . . *everything* I want to see. I can even see the Gate we used to get here!"

"Look for others," Khairu said. "See if you can track all of the ones we know about. If you find another, that might be the one. We know it's in this system now."

All watched as she worked for the next few minutes, her entire body shining with green radiance. Though her eyes were closed, she could see without them. Lucian couldn't imagine what kind of power she wielded.

"I . . . see something," she said. "It's a Gate, somewhere out there."

Her eyes were facing the bulwark. Such was the power of the Orb that even *it* wasn't a hindrance to sight.

"Scanning," Khairu said. She frowned. "Nothing coming up. You sure?"

"Yes, I'm sure."

"Any idea where it leads?" Fergus asked.

"That's it," she said. "Sweep that patch of stars out there. I .. . can see it moving. It's on a different orbital path, not even on the same plane as the planets of this system. That must be why it was never found."

"How can we interpret whatever she's seeing?" Linus asked.

"Don't worry," Emma said, her eyes opening and the green aura around her fading. "Check the navigator."

Khairu checked the program, finding that there was a new entry. "Wait. How'd you *do* that? You broke the encryption on *my* machine?"

"*That* was the easy part," she said. "With *this* . . . I can do *anything*."

"Plotting a new course now," Khairu said, her voice impressed. "Good work, Talent Emma."

Now, everyone watched what she would do, whether she'd give the Orb back.

"Just keep it for now," Lucian said. "You might need it later."

For a moment, it looked as if she were about to argue, but then she nodded. "All right. If you're sure."

Ethereal veered course as it picked up speed for the new Gate, going as fast as its fusion drive could push it. Unfortunately, *Wayfinder* seemed to keep pace easily.

"Four days until we reach the Gate," Khairu said. "And after that . . . who knows? Ladies and gentlemen, it seems we've found Nai Shairen."

———

As those four days passed, *Wayfinder* only fell marginally behind. *Ethereal* was faster, but the difference was practically negligible. Two minutes out from the mysterious Dark Gate, they only had an hour on the ship.

"Closing in," Khairu said.

Plato gave a dark chuckle. "Soon, we'll find out whether we live or die."

"Silence," Linus said. "The Dark Gate might sense our ill thoughts."

"We don't even *know* if it's the rotting Dark Gate," Serah said.

"It is," Emma said.

"One minute," Khairu said.

They waited, nothing in the viewscreen changing in appearance. Lucian held his breath when, suddenly, it was as if he *blinked*, though his eyes never closed. In the next moment, the stars had changed.

"New system," Khairu said. "Scanners are cataloguing orbital bodies. Should take a few hours."

"Just blast us toward the star," Lucian said. "How long until we're in the inner system?"

"Five days," Khairu said. "Less if we're willing to put up with some uncomfortable g-forces."

"How much less?"

She shrugged. "Doesn't change by much. Six hours, at a guess."

Lucian thought for a moment. "They can't find anything without us. And we still have an hour on them, so let's just make sure we get there fresh and ready."

"Alternately, we could decelerate slowly most of the way," Khairu said, "and do what we did for Isis. Burn hard in reverse and take off the edge with an anti-grav aura."

"No," Lucian said, thinking of Serah. "That almost cost us last time."

"It would give back . . ." Khairu did the calculations. "About two hours."

"Let's do it," Serah said. "Every minute matters. And you can bet they'll be trying the same thing, only they have the Orb of Gravitonics. They can push their ship to the breaking point, and the Orb will keep them from being squashed like a pancake."

She had a good point. "Okay. You and Linus can work together, then. Be sure to stream the disc before we start deceleration this time."

Serah nodded. "I know what I'm doing."

Lucian let the point drop. It wouldn't be long now, assuming the scanners logged the orbital bodies in time, including planets that were likely candidates to be Nai Shairen and its one moon, Nai Elyn.

And failing that, they had the Orb of Radiance. It would show the way to Nai Shairen. It was hard to believe they were here, after such a long and dangerous journey.

Arian's prophecy would be found.

32

AN HOUR LATER, *Wayfinder* appeared from the Gate behind them, matching their speed and vector into the Nai Shairen System.

The system scan added several planets to *Ethereal's* database, including four rocky inner worlds, much like the Solar System, along with several gas giants and icy planets outside what seemed to be an asteroid belt. They focused the ship's sensors on the inner system. Only the fourth planet out had a moon, and a sizeable one at that.

"That has to be it," Khairu said.

Lucian watched the display, remembering the words spoken to him several months ago: *Find me beyond the Dark Gate. And, if the passing of long years has ended me, I have my prophecy, kept safe in this tower, the only edifice on the moon beyond the Dark Gate that looks upon Nai Shairen, the Cradle of the Ancients. Find me before it is too late. The Chosen of the Manifold will know the way.*

All watched in silence.

"Vera called that moon Nai Elyn," Lucian said. "Nai Elyn

was the Immortal's home, where he lived in paradise as he looked down on the Ancients' homeworld. I doubt it's the same paradise it once was, but if Arian went there, his prophecy would be there, too."

Along with whatever else he had been looking for. That seemed the greatest mystery of all.

Whatever happened, they could not allow Xara and Vera to reach it first. Lucian would die before he let that happen.

"I have a course plotted toward the moon," Khairu said. "Four days from our current position."

"If there's any way to shave off some time, do it," Lucian said.

"We'll go in with a hard approach, like Isis," Khairu said. "We're so close now. We can't lose after coming all this way."

Lucian had to agree. "Whatever happens, it's been a hell of a trip."

Serah seemed about to say something when the display dinged a warning. Lucian's heart dropped.

"Are they shooting at us?" Linus squawked.

Khairu watched as shapes materialized, not from *Wayfinder*, but from the Gate they'd just left behind. "Bogeys. They . . . don't seem to be of League make."

Lucian didn't have to ask what they were. There was only one way in or out of this system, and somehow, some way, Swarmer vessels had followed them in.

"Well," Plato said, "looks like it's about to be even *more* of a trip."

THE NEXT THREE days were the most tense Lucian ever remembered. They raced as fast as possible toward the Ancient world of Nai Shairen, with *Wayfinder* just an hour behind, and behind them by another two hours, a growing fleet of Swarmer vessels. *Hundreds* of vessels, including one gargantuan one that could be nothing other than a carrier for the forerunning strike craft.

They were well within range of torpedoes, so Lucian didn't know what the Swarmers' game was. As long as it was possible to gain the prophecy, he would do so. They had nothing left *but* that vain and slender hope.

Though it felt pointless, they had to keep going.

"Orbital entry programmed," Khairu said. "Seems Nai Elyn has an atmosphere. Rather thick, too."

"That's . . . unexpected," Emma said.

"The moon is enough to keep something of an atmosphere, it seems. If the Ancients terraformed it a million years ago, that's rather recent on the scale of stars and planets. It may take millions of years before that atmosphere erodes, assuming a low gravity."

"Is the air breathable?" Plato asked.

"It'll be impossible to tell until we're on the surface. But I'm getting high readings of oxygen and nitrogen. Carbon dioxide levels are still a question mark." She tapped the screen. "Thirty seconds out. Double-check your straps, have anti-grav auras streamed."

Within seconds, both Linus and Serah were sharing a stream, which she led. Lucian felt himself instantly lifted in his seat, almost as if in zero gravity. The ten seconds counting down seemed to take an eternity.

The ship flipped and burned, shaking mightily as Lucian felt himself pushed back into his gelled gravity seat. He closed his eyes to better endure that hell.

A couple of minutes into the maneuver, Khairu spoke. "They're not slowing. They'll shoot right past us if they keep going like that."

Lucian watched helplessly as *Wayfinder* shot past them on the LADAR screen. There were still twenty minutes to go.

"Running some quick calcs," Khairu said. "They'll get there fifteen minutes before us."

"Rotting hell," Serah said.

"Fifteen minutes is nothing," Linus said. "We shall prevail!"

Well, at least *he* could be positive.

Wayfinder disappeared off LADAR, a sign it was entering Nai Elyn's atmosphere. Lucian closed his eyes, centering himself on his Focus to calm his nerves. The dash beeped angrily at the approach of the Swarmers, still two hours out. Assuming they didn't change speed, they had that much time to get on world, fight Xara and Vera, and find the Prophecy of the Seven.

Impossible didn't even begin to describe it.

A large blue world with a single, massive continent dominated the viewscreen. And in front of that world hung a gray-clouded moon directly in their path. So fast was their approach that Lucian could see the size of both growing ever larger by the second.

"One more minute," Khairu said. "Prepare for atmosphere reentry."

It didn't take long for the ship to shake with the speed of their descent. They roared through gray clouds, where Lucian could see flashes of lightning. He remained calm, focused on his goal.

"The tower is facing the planet," he said. "We need to get the ship to the other side."

"Hold on," Khairu said.

The vessel gave a sudden jolt, Serah crying out as her stream was interrupted. The sudden shift in g-forces made Lucian black out for a moment. When he came to, they were well below the clouds, a heavy rain pouring onto a dark surface below. It was hard to tell, but there appeared to be jungle thousands of meters below them, along with the surface of a dark, still sea.

They ripped with incredible force through Nai Elyn's dark sky. They actually weren't too far from their target. The world of Nai Shairen hung above, an imposing presence in the distance, seeming almost close enough to reach. Its blue oceans and white clouds recalled Earth. And under the light of that world, Lucian could see ruins rising from the surface below. Destitute cities, broken bridges, empty canals.

Far ahead in the distance, a strange sight took his breath away. A tall tower rose toward the stars, illumined behind by the surface of Nai Shairen. Sheer and pointed, Lucian knew this tower was where they needed to go. Perhaps it wasn't the only edifice on the world, as Arian had said. But it was the only edifice of any scale.

"Down there," he said.

Khairu angled the ship down, past a deep canal and ancient, crumbled city. There, he saw his worst fears manifested. *Wayfinder* sat before the tower.

"Be ready for anything," Lucian said.

"You want the Orb back?" Emma asked.

This entire time, he'd let her hold it, in case she needed to guide them again.

"Keep it," he said. "I need someone who knows how to use Radiance."

"You sure?"

Lucian nodded. "Positive."

They said nothing more about it as *Ethereal* landed, a little too close to *Wayfinder* for Lucian's taste, but it was the only area clear of debris.

"Atmosphere's completely breathable," Khairu said.

"Let's roll," Lucian said. "Ward your primaries." He looked at Emma. "Stay close to me. I don't know if they can tell you have the Orb or not, but I'd rather not take chances."

She nodded.

They exited the blast door and down the boarding ramp to

stand face to face with the mighty tower. It was even taller from the ground, and Lucian knew that this was where Arian had gone all those years ago. He felt a power resonating from it, though it was hard to say what exactly it was.

The air felt thin to breathe, as if some of the atmosphere had indeed escaped over the long, silent years. The Tower, shining by the light of Nai Shairen and a multitude of stars in the black sky, seemed to be made from some silvery alloy. It stood high, proud, and unbowed by the passing of eras. A subtle glow emanated from its surfaces, a shell of magic that was no doubt seven-sealed to have lasted this long. This Tower, like the Gates, would remain standing as long as magic existed. Time would not touch it, even if extinction had laid low the one who built it.

Lucian took all this in, and more, as he led the others across the metallic walkway leading toward the Tower's wide, arched entrance. On either side grew a lawn of green grass, perfectly manicured, as if hundreds of servants tended to it every day. Despite this, the air seemed dead, without fragrance or wind. Nothing had stirred on this world for eons. Arian must have been this world's last visitor, and before that, only the ghosts of the past.

Lucian streamed a Dynamistic brand at the tip of his shock-spear. Streams of electricity flowed from hand to brand, and back again, magic that could weaken and puncture any mage's shield, given it was strong enough. Fergus, Khairu, and Emma followed his example, streaming their own brands, while Linus, Serah, and Plato opted for Thermal brands that caused the tips of their spears to glow white-hot. Between the seven of them, they had every Aspect of Magic warded. So long as they stood together and didn't waver, neither Vera Desai nor Xara Mallis could break them. At least, not without concerted effort.

It was three Orbs against two, as it was seven mages against two. But the two Starsea Mages had a head start. For all Lucian knew, they would secure the prophecy first and find some unknown way to escape. If so, they had less than two hours if they wanted to have any hope of escaping the approaching *Alkasen* fleet.

They entered the Tower's cavernous entrance, finding themselves standing in a dark, hollow chamber not dissimilar to the Spire in the Burning Sands of Psyche. Only this chamber was larger. *Far* larger. Lucian gaped at the scale of the interior, at the countless winding stairs circling the periphery. There were not only these steps to contend with, but hundreds of open archways set at regular intervals along the encircling stairway. The prophecy could be through *any* of those entrances.

Before he could feel too hopeless, Lucian noticed something familiar emblazoned on the floor ahead. It was an engraving of the Septagon, at least fifty meters across, with two of its points shining like beacons in the gloom. The position of Atomicism was lit bright orange, along with that of Gravitonics, shining like quicksilver. The others remained dark, waiting.

Lucian did not have to ask what was expected of him. Emma watched him nervously, seeming also to understand her role. Ahead of the others, they walked toward the center of the Septagon, toward the central nexus node that connected all Seven to the periphery.

As they walked across the silent surface, their steps echoing in the massive, solemn place, Lucian watched the many archways above where Xara and Vera could be lurking. The quiet was truly unsettling; *someone* was watching him, that much he could feel. He strengthened his Psionic ward even more. Whatever was watching seemed to mark his every move, to lay him bare, to make him feel weak, despite the enormous power he held.

At last, he and Emma stood at the center of the Septagon. Each of his Orbs pulsed within, demanding that their power to be released. He had never felt such a longing to use the Orbs, and judging from the tension on Emma's face, the fear behind her eyes, she was feeling a similar pull.

"Together," Lucian said.

"What will happen?"

He gave a nervous laugh. "You think *I* know?"

"That was what I was afraid of."

They were stalling and he knew it. Where were Vera and Xara? Had they even left their ship? Of course they had; why else would those nodes on the Septagon be lit? They corresponded to Xara's Orbs.

They could deny the power of the Orbs no longer. Lucian streamed, and twin beams of violet and blue emitted from his either hand. Emma streamed as well, a green beam from her left hand. All three streams joined as one, fusing together on the node beneath them, feeding it. Then, the colors diverged and raced along their respective lines toward their nodes on the exterior of the Septagon, filling them with brilliant color, illumining the dark interior of the Tower.

Five of the Seven were now lit. Only two, Thermalism and Dynamism, remained dark and empty. The node on which they stood, which had been mostly colorless before, now shone dark gray. Lucian had the feeling that if they'd had the two other Orbs, it would shine completely black, as black as space itself without stars, as black as beyond the event horizon of a black hole from which no light could escape.

A resounding click sounded from directly ahead. A stone wall folded back opposite of the entrance, revealing a new, dark chamber.

Along with a new Orb that seemed to drink in the light of the others. A *black* Orb.

Lucian knew what it was without having to ask.

The Lost Aspect. It was here.

He immediately started forward, rushing to secure the prize.

Serah screamed from behind. "Lucian!"

He turned and followed her eyes upward, to see two figures falling with incredible speed, following a blue tether that extended to the floor between him and the black Orb. An anti-grav disc bloomed at the point of contact.

Landing lightly upon it, as if they hadn't been falling at breakneck speed just before, were Vera Desai and Xara Mallis, smiling victoriously.

33

TEN METERS in front of him, Vera and Xara watched him, still as statues. Behind them, the black Orb still pulsed with potential power, seeming to call to anyone willing to wield it. It sat on its pedestal, seeming to drink the surrounding auras of the shining, colored nodes.

"Stand aside," Lucian said, knowing even as he said that they would not listen.

"This is the end for you, Lucian Abrantes," Xara said. "I will give you one last chance to hand over your Orbs before I take them by force."

"Only the Chosen could have found the way here," he said. "You're just riding on my coattails."

Xara gave a sharp smile. "Oh, that's what you think? Well, I'll take your stubbornness as refusal. Prepare to be destroyed by the true Chosen!"

But neither Lucian, Xara, nor Vera were the first to strike. It was Emma. With a shout that could only be described as a war cry, she thrust out her hands and a powerful beam of green light shot in Xara and Vera's direction. Lucian had *never* seen a laser that bright or powerful, so much so that it almost blinded him. She screamed as the light tore out of her.

Quick as lightning, Xara and Vera raised a green Radiant shield, which shrieked under the sheer impact, the light intensifying at the point of contact. Their eyes widened in surprise, clearly not expecting this level of power from her. Emma's laser was pushing the two of them back, little by little, toward the newly opened chamber.

"Go!" Emma called. "Grab it!"

Lucian didn't waste any time. He streamed a tether at the base of the pedestal. He shot along the tether's length, opening himself to the Orb of Psionics to unleash a kinetic wave at Vera and Xara as he passed.

But before he could complete the stream, Xara broke from streaming the Radiant shield, leaving only Vera to contend with the massive laser, which was weakening somewhat. Xara raised her hands, streaming a cone of orange light laced with silvery magic in Lucian's direction. Lucian recognized it to be a Gravitonic and Thermal dualstream, but couldn't guess its purpose. The answer came when Emma's laser ignited the cone, causing it to erupt into a prodigious spout of flame aimed right at Lucian.

Lucian raised a Thermal shield just in time, but such was the attack's strength that it did little to take the edge off. He cried out as he lost control of the tether, crashing against the black marble floor.

Others rushed to join the fray. Fergus had his spear extended, lightning flashing from the point. Serah, hands wrapped in Gravitonic Magic, floated above the sigil and was readying to join the melee. Linus, face twisted in rage, was throwing his spear laced with Gravitonic Magic, to strike hard at whoever was unlucky enough to be in its path. And Plato, running with speed that defied his heft, had his hands wrapped with red Thermal magic, with a stream of what appeared to be pure cold blasting toward the two Starsea Mages. From Khairu's hands flashed lightning, which forced Vera to raise another shield, this one Dynamistic. Emma's stream seemed to slow, the laser from her hands petering out, though she was trying her best to continue the attack.

Even with the Orb of Gravitonics and Atomicism, Xara had plenty to contend with.

"Run, boy!" Linus called. "Get that Orb!"

Vera, with a snarl, grasped Linus's spear, still airborne, with a telekinetic tether, a dualstream of Binding and Psionics. She redirected it right back at him with deadly speed and precision. Lucian streamed from the Orb of Binding, neutralizing Vera's stream, allowing the spear to return to Linus's hand.

Vera's attention shifted to Lucian. She raised her hands and directed a stream of deadly fire in his direction, her eyes narrowed in fury. Lucian streamed a more powerful Thermal shield, burning through the rest of his ether to do so. Even so, the blast knocked him back, causing him to roll across the floor.

He had a moment's reprieve as the others pressed the attack, forcing Vera to fight for her life. Fergus and Serah forced her back with their shockspears while she had nothing but her Psionic shields and kinetic waves for defense. Emma, Linus, Khairu, and Plato teamed up on Xara, who was shooting more flames in their direction, only neutralized by Plato's strong Thermal shields. The two of them fought like cornered badgers.

Lucian ran, despite the pain of the burns along his skin. Just when he gained some speed, he felt himself crushed from above. He slammed into the ground, his vision darkening. Through the haze, he could see a gravity amplification disc glowing under him—a stream held by Xara, even as she was fending off four of her own attackers.

When Lucian streamed a Gravitonic shield, it was like trying to use an umbrella against a hurricane. The gravity lessened somewhat, only enough for him to gain sight of the chamber beyond.

But that was all Lucian needed. He streamed from the Orb of Binding again. Now free of the gravity disc, he could finally breathe as he raced toward the pedestal and the black Orb. Xara shrieked, shooting a column of fire toward the pedestal. Lucian cut off his tether, allowing the flame to dissipate before tethering it again.

"Stop at once, you fool!" Vera said. "You'll kill us all!"

He disregarded her, landing lightly in front of the pedestal. He wasted no time in reaching for the Orb. There was no barrier to his touch, and time seemed to stop as he made it his.

Immediately, it absorbed into his arms, trailing toward his chest, infusing into his Focus. He whipped around, raising his hands and reaching for the new Orb. Black light wrapped around his hands . . .

. . . and he appeared right in front of Vera. He stabbed with his shockspear, driving it right through her abdomen.

Her eyes widened in surprise. Everything seemed to go still. Everyone watched in shock as Vera's dark eyes glazed over, as blood dribbled from her thin lips.

She tried to form a word, but ended up falling to her knees in front of him.

Lucian took a few stuttering steps back, unbelieving of what he'd just done. He'd *killed* her.

"Master!" Xara cried. She ran to Vera's side and touched her shoulder. Her eyes met Lucian's, smoldering in the darkness. "What power is this?"

Lucian couldn't answer her. As if he could tell her. "Hand over the Orbs, Xara. It's over. Don't make me do to you what I did to Vera."

"Fool," she said. "You're not the Chosen. *I* am!"

"Last chance," Lucian said.

"If you won't hand me the Orbs," Xara said, with a manic

smile. "If you won't let prophecy be fulfilled . . . then I will fulfill it right here, right now."

The Black Orb was still pulsing with power. Lucian smiled, unable to help himself. This euphoria and sense of dominance was unstoppable.

"You can try," he said. "But you will fail."

With a scream, Xara stood and cupped her hands, creating a ball of orange energy wrapped in gray light. Lucian knew exactly what she was doing: using the Orbs of Atomicism and Gravitonics, she was creating a fusion reaction, one that would obliterate every single one of them and smite the landscape for kilometers around. But it would take time for it to build.

"Run!" he said. "Get off this world. I'll find you later."

"How?" Serah screamed.

"No arguing! Go." He didn't understand what he was doing, or why he was doing it, but it felt right in the moment. This wasn't their fight anymore. It was *his*.

Thankfully, the others listened and started running as Xara continued to gather her energy.

"You can't stop me," she said with a wicked smile. "Go ahead. Try. I outmatch you in everything." Her eyes seemed to follow Emma as she fled the Tower. "I'll find the girl later. But for now—your three Orbs will suffice!"

Lucian wasn't concerned in the least. The Black Orb demanded to be used, and so he streamed. Instead of streaming forward, as he'd done last time, he streamed backward, creating a brand of the Lost Aspect around the fusion reaction Xara was preparing to unleash, which had grown to be a meter apart by now. He didn't know what he was doing, or how he was doing it. Like with the other Orbs, the knowledge seemed to be intrinsic. He knew he couldn't think about it too hard, or he'd mess things up.

A black matrix of lines surrounded the ball of light like a

net, leeching onto it. The lines swirled, faster and faster, as the ball of light started shrinking. Xara's eyes widened in dismay.

"How are you doing that?"

"Hand over the Orbs. Now."

Xara shrieked, leaping high with a gravity assisted jump, extending her shockspear. While in the air, she pointed her spear down, as a sphere of orange-yellow light coalesced at its tip. She aimed it directly at Lucian as a chain of fiery lightning dispersed from the spear. This was not typical lightning, but something else. Something he intrinsically understood to be far deadlier.

He forward streamed with the Black Orb, appearing in the chamber where he had found the Orb. Xara looked for him for a few seconds, before blasting him with the strange lightning again. Lucian *jumped* again, appearing near the entrance. Masonry and stonework fell where he had been standing not a second before.

Xara watched him a moment, her chest heaving from exertion. Lucian wondered what exactly he could do with this new Orb that could kill Xara. It still pulsed with power, but eventually, the tap was going to run out.

He streamed and appeared behind her, but she was ready. She blasted him backward with a kinetic wave, a wave that caused him to fly back despite the strength of his Psionic ward. Sensing a momentary advantage, Xara streamed her orange lightning again. Just in the nick of time, Lucian teleported to the staircase on the opposite side of the Tower.

"You will fall to my death lightning," she said. "It vaporizes *anything* it touches. During the Mage War, it laid waste to entire squadrons of marines. It kills so fast, you don't even scream." She laughed. "I *would* hear you scream before the end, Lucian, for what you did to Vera."

As if her name were some form of benediction, Vera sputtered. She was *alive*? The old woman was clawing her way off the floor, trying to force herself to stand.

Lucian saw his chance, streaming his own lightning from the tip of his spear, guided with stunning accuracy with a Binding tether. The lightning spread, simultaneously striking at both Vera and Xara. Still, Xara whipped it away with a flick of her spear, which was branded with Dynamistic and Binding magic. Lucian expected that magic to only neutralize his attack, but somehow, it *reflected* it. Before he could think to *jump* away, the lightning connected with his own spear, throwing him against the wall behind him.

He had time enough to warp away just before a new stream of Xara's death lightning struck him.

But this time, he stood *outside* the Tower, at least a hundred meters away. *Ethereal* was gone.

He sought a Psionic link with Khairu. *Khairu? You still here?*

His link was interrupted when two figures appeared at the entrance of the Tower, one standing tall and sure, the other hobbling. He was far enough to where they didn't see him. Not yet.

He spied a stand of ruins and warped himself behind them. He hid there, waiting a few moments to make sure that they couldn't see him. Of course, he realized the uselessness of this. They *knew* he was there, only they weren't going after him. Xara was carrying her master on board *Wayfinder*, and after another minute, they were blasting off, apparently to live and fight another day.

When Lucian looked up into the sky, he could see exactly why they made that choice. The faint outline of a Swarmer carrier was materializing against the backdrop of Nai Shairen.

34

LUCIAN IMMEDIATELY SAW THEIR PLAN. Let the Swarmers deal with him, and then pick over his remains to find the Orbs. Of course, that plan was flawed because the Swarmers would want his Orbs, too. Xara had simply chosen loyalty to her master over finishing the job. A questionable choice, but one Lucian didn't begrudge her.

It was just as well that they had left him behind because the power of the mysterious Orb was ebbing. And he had no desire to face an enemy that no human had ever seen face to face.

Instead, he ran back toward the Tower, figuring that it was his only refuge. The carrier above was lowering over the surface; in minutes, whatever beings were on board would be coming to fight him directly.

Once inside, Lucian tethered himself up the central shaft toward the top. He figured if there was anything of interest, it would be up there. He bridged the gap in seconds, landing before a pair of ebony doors. He pushed them open, revealing a vast, empty chamber. Empty, save for the remains of an old fire and a tent in the far corner next to a large, empty window, over-looking the courtyard far below and the planet of Nai Shairen.

Lucian ran forward, finding what he feared inside the tent; a skeleton clothed in violet mage robes, the same as worn by Transcend Violet. A shockspear had been extended through the skull below the chin, making the manner of death obvious.

It was Arian. It could be no one else.

Lucian knew these remains had been here almost a century now, and he couldn't help but feel that *something* lingered here. He kneeled down, noticing what appeared to be a data drive held in the skeleton's left hand. If this was not what he was looking for, then nothing was.

He reached for his slate, which thankfully still had a full charge. It was pure luck that Xara's attacks hadn't fried it.

He plugged the data drive into his slate and the files installed immediately.

Outside the window, the carrier thundered down from the dark sky. Lucian knew he should run, but he had come this far. If he was going to die, at least he might die knowing exactly where to find the final two Orbs, even if the knowledge would prove ultimately useless.

His slate projected a holographic visage of Arian, a with-ered old man with a long, white beard who was the picture of complete exhaustion. His hooded eyes watched the camera as he began his monologue.

"Chosen, you have come. At long last, after a long journey, of which I will see neither beginning nor end. I speak to you across years, perhaps even centuries or millennia. However, I have faith in my revelations, in what the Ascendant Beings of the Light Realm have deigned to share. That you would come in thunder and power, that I might lead you to this place where I first found the Lost Aspect."

Lucian leaned in, watching attentively. All the death raining down outside might as well have not mattered.

"You must blame me for beginning the Starsea Cycle," he said. "It was I, as a young man, who birthed magic once again among the stars. I was exploring the Gates with Erik Nielsen himself in the days of the first diasporas. Whether by fate or chance, we happened upon the ruins of this nameless world. And in these ruins, I found the Orb you no doubt now hold in your hand. For if you are indeed the Chosen, you would have had the requisite Five Orbs required to unlock the chamber, as I've related in prophecy."

Lucian tried to ignore that he did not *have* five Orbs. He, Emma, and Xara combined held five, something Arian had likely overlooked. He wasn't sure what to make of it.

"For as long as magic has returned to the galaxy, you have likely not guessed at the existence of the Eighth Aspect. Likely, you are wondering at its powers, and how it fits into the scheme of things. For in my original Prophecy of the Seven, the Seven whom you know as the Oracles of Starsea, insisted that the only way to stop the fraying was to gather the Seven Orbs of Starsea. And that is true, but the solution is imperfect. The Aspect of Space-Time was a myth to the Ancients, though the Immortal sought it with all his might. While the Madness will end with the gathering of the Seven, you cannot mend it fully without the Eighth Aspect. The Aspect of Space-Time serves as the connection between all Aspects, allowing for magic to flow properly, preventing the Madness from visiting the mages. So long as you hold that Orb, Chosen, you will not fray, no matter what Aspect you use. However, the Aspect of Space-Time will not carry over to the galaxy at large until you've gathered every Orb in your Focus."

Lucian was wondering if he understood right. While Seven Orbs in a single mage stopped the fraying, it did not stop it at its source. The Eighth Aspect somehow fused them all together.

The only thing Lucian didn't understand was what Arian

expected him to do with all Eight Orbs. Would everything fix itself if he gathered all eight, or did he still have to find the Heart of Creation?

Lucian glanced outside, noting bipedal beings filling the courtyard below from the landed carrier. Highly coordinated strike craft by the dozens teemed in the sky above. If there had been the possibility of escape before, there was none now.

The beings, the *Alkasen*, were starting toward the Tower as if of a single mind.

"I have loaded the prophecy wherever you're playing this message. You must read it under Psionic hypnosis which, if you have the Orb of Space-Time, you can delve without fear of the fraying, assuming you don't have the Orb of Psionics. The prophecy works with magic, serving as a hearkening to the Light Realm itself. It will reveal the way to the Orbs that remain hidden to you.

"And as far as me . . . the prophecy led me here to fill my last role. To pass my words down to you, along with the Orb that started the Starsea Cycle. If you hold that Orb in your hand, by the words of my prophecy, you are the Chosen. Space-Time is the most powerful of Aspects, but as long as magic is broken, it will not function properly. It requires the other Orbs to work. Without at least one other Orb, it proves useless. With all the Seven other Orbs, it proves almost limitless. That was why I could never use it; it was the only Orb I ever possessed. The more Orbs you hold, the more capable the Orb of Space-Time becomes. The Orb controls its namesake, allowing you to bend time and space itself. It takes a great deal of magic to do so, and feeds from the power of other held Orbs. Only the strongest of mages can hope to wield it, and the Orb will only accept the strongest of the strong as its steward. Until you gather the rest of the Orbs, as is your destiny, it will be of limited use. The power to reverse time or bend space, even for a moment, is great."

Lucian understood then that was what he had done to stop Xara's fusion reaction. And his "warping" was actually him existing in two places at once. Only when he reappeared in the second location, he ceased to exist in the first.

With a start, he realized that *this* was how the Gates worked. They had to have been forged with this Orb, all those eons ago by the ones who came before the Ancients, the Gate-Builders. Perhaps even by the First Immortal himself. And the magic of those Gates endured because they were simply seven-sealed Space-Time brands that would last until the death of the universe.

So, even if the Second Immortal of Starsea had not had access to this Orb, the Immortal before him did. Whoever *he* was.

The only question was, how did the Orbs become separated in the first place? What caused magic to be broken?

On this point, Arian seemed to have no answer.

"That, Chosen, is the extent of my knowledge. Paltry, I know, but it will be up to you to discover the rest. Good luck. Even with such power, you will certainly need it. I wish you well. You are the Worlds' only hope. Though the days are dark, never lose hope."

The hologram disappeared, leaving Lucian stunned and alone with his thoughts. But there was little time to be surprised at Arian's revelations. He had to find a way out of here.

He reached for the Orb of Space-Time, but as Arian had hinted, its power was extinguished, at least for now. He could not use it without restriction until he had gained the rest of the Orbs. Which left only the Orbs of Binding and Psionics at his disposal.

He reached for the Orb of Psionics, seeking a connection with Khairu. He found it in just a few seconds.

Khairu? Did you escape?

Yes, Khairu said. *But the Swarmers are too thick by the Tower. Vera and Xara are heading back for the Dark Gate.*

I'm going to try to get out of here. I have the prophecy, but the Orb of Space-Time doesn't work.

The Orb of Space-Time? Is that what that thing is?

There's no time to explain, Lucian said, looking down at where the *Alkasen* were entering the Immortal's Tower. *Try to find me in the wilderness of this world.*

Lucian, they are blockading everything. I'm not sure it's possible.

Lucian struggled for what to do, but there was no time to think. The doors to his chamber blasted open, revealing two tall, thin beings that had to stand at well over two meters each. Their bodies seemed stretched, their limbs long with dark violet, reptilian skin. A protruded brow ridge supported three rows of short spikes along their skulls, and they wore gray robes and each carried long, curved scepters.

It was hard not to stare in surprise. It was the first time a human had ever seen an alien, and they were not what he expected. These were the same ones on the murals of the Starsea Sanctums, minus the angel wings. These were Ancients, not *Alkasen.* Or were they?

Their scepters lit with electricity as they advanced with deadly grace.

Lucian streamed a kinetic wave, the distortion of air advancing quickly across the stone floor. The wave was powerful enough to knock them back as they gave low, garbled cries. Lucian turned, leaping from the open window and tethering himself to a distant set of ruins about half a kilometer away. His tether took it up immediately, pulling him along at breakneck speed. The Orb supplied the power with ease.

Several tiny strike craft teeming above the carrier shifted their trajectories, shooting off a few projectiles at the ruins he'd attached himself to. The tower crumbled, and so did his tether. As he fell, he reached for a more distant tower, drawing more ether from the Orb. He pulled himself far beyond the lower courtyard and the carrier that rested there.

Serah's voice entered his mind. *Lucian?*

Serah. You okay?

We're on the other side of Nai Shairen now. Khairu won't turn the ship back . . .

It's all right. She shouldn't until it's safe.

Are you crazy? You're going to die, Lucian!

I just need time for my new Orb to recharge. If she can get the ship close enough, I'll be able to warp on board.

Warp? Now I know you're crazy.

You need to trust me, Serah. I'm not dying. Not yet.

In truth, Lucian didn't think the odds were great. He just didn't want her to lose hope.

Lucian re-tethered himself on another broken tower. It seemed he was gaining some distance, at least. The strike craft were changing course, shooting after him as he fled.

One ship fired upon the tower he was streaming for. Like the other one, it disintegrated into dust. Lucian would have righted himself with another tether, but another ship whooshed by, causing him to lose his balance. He spun around and couldn't get an accurate read on his environment. The ground rushed up to meet him.

The last thing he could do was create a kinetic wave that pushed against the ground. It buoyed him for a moment, allowing him to right himself and land on his feet.

That was when four separate crafts landed on the surrounding ground, completely boxing him in. Dozens of Ancients poured out, each with magical shields deployed and scepters laced with lightning at the ready. Lucian tried his best to defend himself, but there were simply too many. He felt his Psionic ward under assault such as he had never felt before. Even streaming the full might of the orb of Psionics, he was no match for their combined power. His knees buckled as he fell to the ground. He closed his eyes, fighting to remain conscious.

But it simply wasn't enough. His vision darkened, and his last sight was a blue alien face in front of him, leering down at him with the dark orbs for eyes.

35

WHEN HE AWOKE, he knew he was on a spaceship, probably the carrier. The thought should have terrified him more than it actually did.

It was hard to tell just how much time had passed. Probably hours, judging by the throbbing in his head. When he tried to reach for his Focus, he couldn't feel it. Blocked, then.

Well, at least he had the privilege of being the first person to see what a Swarmer vessel was like. If these *were* Swarmers. Maybe the Ancients weren't extinct after all. Vera had mentioned the Swarmers were emissaries sent by the Light Realm. Lucian wasn't sure *what* to believe now. Were these creatures from the Light Realm, or were they from his own existence? And why were they keeping him alive?

Without his magic, there was little he could do besides wait.

He took inventory of his surroundings, finding himself in a small hold with white walls. There was no door. Lucian wondered how they had gotten him in here. Clearly, they were magical beings, mages like him. For the first time in his life, they had overpowered him, even when he was using an Orb. That alone told him he should tread carefully. Then again, if they wanted to kill him, they probably would have by now.

They were keeping him alive for a reason. But for *what* reason?

An opening in the wall appeared, peeling itself apart. It seemed organic rather than artificial. Whatever it was, it was no technology Lucian was aware of. There was nothing to do but start forward, to meet his fate, good or bad.

He walked down a long white corridor, a corridor that seemed to stretch forever. He was most definitely on the carrier. He tried to hold his Focus to calm his nerves, but it was impossible to do when he was blocked. He thought of Serah, wondered if he would ever see her again. That was all he wanted right now, to hold her, for everything to be okay.

Whatever he had to face, he had to do it on his own merits, without magic.

The corridor eventually opened onto a larger bridge. There were no instruments, panels, or even seats. But there was a tall being, an Ancient, standing with his back facing Lucian before a wide set of viewscreens revealing the expanse of space before him, along with the world of Nai Shairen. He turned as Lucian approached, regarding him for a moment with silent eyes and an unreadable expression. It was tall, unknowable, judging. It seemed to know things beyond Lucian's conception. It wore a snow-white robe with a long cape trimmed with gold, and in its hand it held a scepter, containing at its hilt a shape Lucian would have recognized anywhere: the Septagon, this one with the middle node denoting the Lost Aspect. Its features were proud and haughty, and it was obvious this one was a cut above the others that had overwhelmed him.

"Chosen," the being said, its voice deeply resonant.

Lucian regarded it for a moment. "Who are you?"

The being watched him for a moment in silence, ignoring Lucian's question. "You are the one prophesied by Arian. Do you know who *I* am?"

"How can you speak my language?"

"I'm not speaking to you in your language. I am speaking in my language, and my Psionic Magic is translating it in your mind."

Even as the alien spoke, Lucian noticed that the movements of its mouth didn't seem quite right. It *was* speaking another language.

"You're an Ancient."

"Yes. But not quite."

"What do you mean?"

"I am one of the Preserved."

As if Lucian was supposed to know what *that* meant. "What does that mean?"

The alien watched him without blinking. It was hard to meet its gaze, but Lucian forced himself to.

"We are those saved by the Ascended Beings to accomplish their ends in the Shadow Realm. We are not organic beings, but an amalgamation of them. We are the Preserved."

"That . . . makes sense."

"We are of the Light Realm, but to be present in the Shadow, we must have bodies. How I look is of no consequence. What matters are my words and thoughts."

Lucian saw he was getting nowhere with him. If "him" was even the proper word. "What do you want with me, then?"

"You are the Chosen of the Manifold. And I am the Emissary of the Ascendant Beings, sent to the Shadow Realm to ensure the Chosen of the Manifold finishes his task. In my previous life, my name was Silumko. You can call me that, if you wish, or you can call me Emissary. Whatever is more comfortable for you."

"Okay, then. Silumko, why are the Swarmers attacking us?"

"We are not attacking you. We are attacking humanity."

"Okay. Why are you attacking humanity?"

"Because the Orbs do not belong in this realm, and humanity holds the Orbs. The Orbs belong to the Light. Long ago, the Shadow Lord of the First Empire of Starsea stole them from us, and the Ascendant Beings swore eternal vengeance on whoever held the Orbs in this realm. Return them to their rightful owners and rid this plane of existence of magic, and we will depart this plane of existence."

"That's what I'm *trying* to do," Lucian said. "But killing innocent people who have nothing to do with the Orbs is not just cruel. It's actually making my job a lot harder."

"I can't change the rules," Silumko said. "The Ascendant Beings are the perfect manifestation of reality. Who is the shadow to argue against the caster? How can the imperfect find a flaw? Without the Light Realm, Chosen, your reality is nothing. It would cease to be. The Orbs are part of a higher reality, and until you return them, *your* reality is cursed. As the Chosen, the Ascendant Beings tolerate your use of the Orbs, but only if you return them to the Heart of Creation."

Lucian had to swallow his pride. He did not like being told his reality was nothing, because to him, it was everything. He needed to learn answers. "Where is the Heart of Creation, anyway?"

"That will be revealed when you gather all the Orbs, Chosen."

"I'll just . . . know?"

"The Seven-Sealed path will show the way," the Emissary said. "That's the path only the Chosen can see once he gathers the Orbs. And the Orb of Space-Time, the ultimate key, must be fully powered. You will have everything you need to return the Orbs to their rightful place soon."

"How does the Immortal Emperor fit into this? You might

know him as the Ancient One."

Silumko watched him closely. "Though he calls himself Ancient One, by the measure of the Ascendant Beings, he is a babe still drawing his first breath. He is a pretender we will destroy as soon as you complete your mission. He held all Seven, and only the Aspect of Space-Time eluded him. With the power of the Seven, he elevated himself to the Light Realm, forced his consciousness into a place it did not deserve to go. But he is weak here. Imprisoned for his transgression. However, we cannot fully expunge him without the Orbs."

"But he becomes stronger with each Orb I gather. He said so himself."

Silumko only stared at him, not denying it.

"Did these Ascendant Beings create the Orbs?" Lucian asked. "Where did they come from?"

"The Orbs have been since the dawn of creation. And the Light Realm is a byproduct of the Orbs. They cannot be destroyed, only returned."

Lucian wanted to ask what would happen if he kept them. Arian had mentioned he could fix magic as soon as he'd gathered the Seven in his Focus, along with the Orb of Space-Time. But that would cause the Lost Aspect to diffuse into the universe once again. When that happened, *any* mage could use it. It seemed too powerful. Too dangerous. What would the effects be? Arian also suggested that magic would remain here in the Shadow Realm, even if Lucian returned the Orbs.

But so long as he kept the Orbs here, where they didn't belong, the *Alkasen* would not stop their attacks. These Ascendant Beings considered the Orbs theirs, and returning them to the Heart of Creation was the only way to save humanity.

That was, unless he wanted to keep the Orbs and fight them head-on. Lucian didn't see the appeal of that, though Xara obviously seemed to.

"I'll bring them back," Lucian said. "Just . . . stop attacking us."

"That cannot be," Silumko said.

"Isn't my promise enough? Millions have died already. Millions more will die. For what purpose?"

"I sympathize," Silumko said. "But I am only a messenger. There are some of my masters who wish even for your death, Chosen, for profaning the Orbs with your touch. Magic is a gift for the Ascendant Beings, not Beings of Shadow."

"Why do they even care? How does our using magic harm them?"

"These things . . . are beyond you. You must be content to do what I ask. Gather the Orbs. Find Xara Mallis, the Champion of the Ancient One. Defeat her. You are the Chosen of the Manifold. You are your kind's only hope."

Lucian didn't have all his questions answered. Not even close. And yet, this Silumko was folding his arms within his robe and lowering his face.

"This audience is over," he said. "Enough time has passed now for you to return to your ship."

"What do you mean? Where is my ship?"

"You have the Orb of Space-Time," the Emissary said. "You may return to any place you've previously visited, assuming it isn't too far, and you have the requisite power.

Any place? "You're saying I can leave this place *right now* and get back on my ship?"

"With enough magic, yes. The Orb's capabilities will grow greater as you gather more of the Seven. As it stands, with enough magic, you will no longer be confined to the Gates."

"What do you mean?"

"You'll be able to warp your entire ship near any place you have a memory of. Or even from world to world, if you wish. The Orb has its limits, of course. Limits you must discover on your own."

Lucian was speechless. *Warp* the entire ship? It made what he'd done during his battle with Xara Mallis seem like child's play.

"Assume your Focus," the Emissary said. "And remember every detail. Remembering is important."

Lucian nodded. "Right."

He closed his eyes, imagining the cabin that he and Serah shared. He'd seen the place so much that it was no trouble recalling the bed, wardrobe, and bits of dirty clothes strewn across the deck, since Serah was a slob. He smiled at a memory of them lying in bed together, feeling almost as if he were actually there. The Orb of Space-Time thrummed with potential.

Magic rushed through him, and the bridge and Silumko disappeared.

THE HUM of *Ethereal's* fusion engine surrounded him. He was alone in his cabin in bed, and it was like waking up from a dream. Indeed, that seemed a greater possibility than what had just happened to him.

He headed out into the corridor to find the rest of the crew sitting at the table built into the bulwark. All were looking at the deck or wall listlessly, or facing away from him.

"Miss me?"

As one, they turned around, and the collective shock on their faces was enough to make Lucian laugh.

Linus was the first to recover, his gray-bearded face brightening. "Lucian? How'd *you* get in here?"

"What in the Worlds . . ." Plato said. "How did you ever . . . ?"

Fergus watched him, his eyes wide, while Serah ran forward and threw herself on him. Her eyes were puffy and red.

"I didn't think you were coming back."

"I told you to trust me, didn't I?"

She held him tighter.

"Where are Emma and Khairu?"

"Khairu's up front," Fergus said, finally standing. "I'm . . . grateful you're alive, but was this *really* the best time for a prank? How did you sneak on board, anyway?"

"I'll explain everything soon," Lucian said. "Emma?"

"Resting," Plato said. "Poor girl. I think streaming that Orb did a number on her."

"Go grab Khairu," Lucian said. "We have a lot to talk about."

He went to Emma's cabin and opened the door. She was lying on her side, her back facing him.

"Emma? You all right?"

She turned and looked at him as if he were a ghost. "Lucian?" She sat up and came to him, hugging him tight with tears in her eyes. "I thought you were dead!"

"It'll take more than a Swarmer fleet to kill me," he said.

"How did you ever . . . ?"

"I'm about to explain," he said. "I'm all right. Are you feeling okay?"

"Just . . . dazed. Wondering how everything could've gone so wrong . . . I can't believe you're here!"

Serah stood in the doorway. "Hello? All of us are waiting out there!"

They gathered in the wardroom over tea and coffee, and Lucian explained what happened. How things had ended with Xara and Vera, how the *Alkasen* carrier had landed in the courtyard, and his finding of the Prophecy of the Seven on the topmost level of the Immortal's Tower. He explained Arian's revelation, as well as how Arian had been the one to spark the Starsea Cycle anew by finding the Orb of Space-Time, the Orb lost even to the Immortal and the Ancients of Starsea.

Emma spoke. "He had it the *whole time* and didn't tell a soul?"

"He must have," Plato said. "If so, then why didn't he use it?"

"I was getting to that part," Lucian said.

He talked about how he tried to escape the *Alkasen*, but was captured and ended up on their vessel. He related his audience with Silumko and what he had revealed about the Orb of Space-Time, along with the *Alkasen's* motives for attacking humanity. All of them just listened in stunned silence.

"So," Lucian said, "I just used the Orb to get back here. It doesn't work like the other ones. It needs the other Orbs to power it. And the more Orbs I have, the stronger it gets."

Khairu frowned. "The effects are *already* pretty strong, if it could warp you here. We are several million klicks out from Nai Shairen by now."

"Bound for the Dark Gate, I guess," Lucian said.

Khairu nodded. "Yes. However, if you can just use the Orb . . ."

Linus shook his head forcefully. "Heavens, no! I'm not getting warped *anywhere*."

"You already have, several times," Emma pointed out. "How do you think the Gates work? I think we just solved another mystery." The others didn't seem so quick to catch on, so she explained. "People have always wondered how the Gates worked. They were obviously magic, but not any magic we recognized. No Aspect we knew of bent space-time. Now, we know there *is* an Aspect for it. Whoever made the Gates had the Orb of Space-Time in their possession."

"So, it's true?" Serah asked. "You can warp this whole ship and everyone on it *anywhere* in the Worlds? No more waiting weeks between Gates?"

"No, I can't go just anywhere. Just places I've been before that I have a powerful memory of. Silumko seemed to say distance was a factor, too. The more distance, the more magic required. The Orb has its limits, and he said I'd have to figure out what those are."

"Meaning?" Fergus asked.

Lucian shrugged. "Don't know. All I can say is, the more Orbs I have, the greater the capabilities of the Orb of Space-Time."

"You already warped yourself during the battle with Xara and Vera," Khairu said. "Multiple times. And you even reversed *time*, if only for a moment and in a confined area. How much more powerful can that Orb get?"

Certainly, the Orb of Space-Time seemed to be the most powerful of the Orbs he'd found, as Arian had suggested. "I can say that it runs out of juice fast. During the battle, it worked great for a while. Until it didn't. Likewise, if I did something big, like warping an entire ship, it would probably take a long time to recover its power."

"Don't the other Orbs work the same way?" Serah asked.

"They do, but not to the same extent. I can always use those Orbs, though of course, if I pull a lot of ether from one of them to do something huge, it'll need time to recover, too. The effect seems to be more pronounced with the Orb of Space-Time, though."

There was one other thing Lucian forgot to mention. Perhaps the most important thing. But he didn't want to say it in front of the others. Not yet, anyway.

"Let's keep on a course for the Dark Gate for now. Where are Vera and Xara?"

"Ahead of us, and gaining distance," Khairu said. "They'll reach the Gate a day before us."

So, *Wayfinder* was the faster ship. Assuming the Orb of Space-Time worked, that wouldn't matter for much longer.

"That's all for now. I need some rest."

"Boy, we need to *celebrate*!" Linus said. "I think the Irion Academy gave us some champagne. I hid it in the back of the fridge, just in case the occasion called for it . . ."

"I could whip up some food," Plato said. "The waiting room

at the Academy had some cheesecake I nabbed. Should still be frozen."

"Later," Lucian said.

He took Serah by the hand, and at her questioning look, he nodded toward their cabin.

"What's this?" she asked.

"There's something I need to tell you."

They entered their cabin, and Serah watched him curiously. "What's going on?"

"There was something I didn't say about the Orb of Space-Time," Lucian said.

"Okay. Why are you hedging?"

Lucian sighed. "I don't know. Just wanted to run it by you first. Would you be willing to take control of it?"

Her eyes popped. "What?"

"Silumko said that whoever has the Orb of Space-Time won't fray. That includes *every* Aspect."

She watched him skeptically. "You serious?"

"That's what he said. He said something about how the Orb is required for magic to work properly. It won't apply itself everywhere until—"

She put a hand on his arm. "Lucian. You're the Chosen, not me. What if me taking it messes something up?"

"But don't you want to try? We've been working so hard to find a cure for you, and this could be the answer."

She looked at his chest reluctantly, as if the Orb was some-where around his heart. "Are you sure?"

"Yes. Emma took one, so you can take one, too."

Her eyes narrowed. "I might be friendlier with her now, but don't bring her into this."

"I meant nothing by it."

"I know. That's what's so annoying." She sighed. "Well, let's see it, then."

Despite Serah's words, he could see hope building in her eyes.

Lucian closed his eyes and reached for his Focus. He reached for the Orb of Space-Time, willing for it to materialize in his hands.

And was met with resistance.

"Come on," he said.

He streamed, trying to force it out of his Focus. The thing was stuck, though. Frustration rose. Why was it doing this?

"Useless, rotting piece of shit," he said. "Maybe it just needs time to recover."

"Lucian."

"Seriously, I can get it out."

Lucian focused again, drawing magic from every Orb he had: Binding, Psionics, and Space-Time. He channeled all that energy toward the Orb of Space-Time, willing it to dislodge from the central space on his Focus.

It only drank in that light, darkening with power, becoming *more* rooted to his Focus.

Lucian yelled in frustration, punching the bulwark.

Serah placed a hand on his shoulder. He closed his eyes and felt the onset of a sob.

"You need it," he said. "Not me."

"It's okay," she said, holding him. "We'll figure it out the old-fashioned way. You're the Chosen, Lucian. And that Orb seems to have chosen you."

"Rot the Orb," he said. "I want you."

She looked at him with a strange combination of sadness and amusement. "You *have* me. And we'll figure this out, okay? Don't go punching holes in this ship. We still need it."

Lucian looked away. "I'm a failure."

Serah just smiled. "*Still* trying to do everything by yourself, aren't you?"

Lucian realized she was right. "I . . . guess I am."

She cupped his face in her hands. "You're *not* a failure. You literally did what we came out to do. Now, let's take that prophecy and see where the rest of these Orbs are."

"I still have to read it," Lucian said. "It won't make any sense unless I use the Orb of Psionics."

"Just rest for now," Serah said. "Okay? We won the battle. Let's go eat cake and drink."

36

WHEN LUCIAN AWOKE the next day, he could tell that he'd been asleep for a long time. And he was quite hungry, not having eaten a proper meal since well before the operation on Nai Elyn.

He went to the galley and warmed up an instameal. Because of his hunger, it tasted far better than it should have. After getting a cup of black coffee, he went to sit at the conference room table, being the only one awake.

He dug into his pocket and took out his slate. The data drive was still plugged in. Not that it needed to be, since the data was loaded, but it seemed better that way. This antiquated data drive had been owned by Arian himself. It should be in a museum or something.

Once he finished eating, he took the slate to the bridge, his only company the thousands of stars outside the viewscreen. Settling in with his coffee, kicking his feet up on the dash, he read.

As he suspected, not a word was intelligible. But all that would change. He reached for the Orb of Psionics, forming a telepathic link with the words, as if they were someone to connect to and not words on a screen. As magic poured through him, he read in a hypnotic state where his mind swam through worlds, realities, and memories, forming an experience like a dream, except more visceral.

He saw the Orbs as they came into being at the beginning of time, how the Orb of Space-Time was first. From Space-Time itself came the other Orbs, all at once, until they had joined in a crown of light. This, he knew, was in the Light Realm, the source of all existence. The Manifold was here, the center of reality, the mover of all things, but that which remained unmoved.

Though the Orbs dictated the reality of the Shadow Realm, here they existed in a sort of stasis. Until there was an incursion. The Shadow Lord entered the Light Realm, an indistinct figure that was strangely familiar. He took the Orbs, just picked them up, and left through the rending in reality created by the Forerunners, those who came before even the Ancients. This rending in reality, this opening into the Light Realm, Lucian knew to be the First Gate.

The Orbs stayed with the Shadow Lord for a long while. Eons. Enough time for the Ten Thousand Gates to be created. Ten *Thousand*. How could there be so many? Enough to bridge most of the habitable worlds in the Milky Way.

But the Gates also sealed their doom. The First Starsea Empire fell, and so did the First Immortal, the Shadow Lord, at the hands of the *Alkasen* sent by the Ascendant Beings of the Light Realm. But with his mighty power, the First Immortal sent the Orbs forward in time. Ten million *years* forward in time, where the *Alkasen* surely would not remain. And with his magic, he bound himself to the Orbs, so that a part of him could always live on, to return when a new being regathered them.

To the Ascendant Beings, however, time is no barrier, even

ten million years. The Gates remained functioning, as they would until the end of time, though who could say what would happen when the stars they orbited finally died? When the Second Immortal, a poor slave thralled to a cruel and wealthy master, happened upon the Orbs during the colonization of a new world, he took them and revenged himself. Magic was reborn, but so was the spirit of the First Immortal . . . the Ancient One. Over the long years, after fusing with the Second Immortal, the Ancient One created a society where the Ancient Mages ruled over all.

But the Orb of Space-Time was still lost. During the time transition, and unintended by the First Immortal, it never traveled forward with the rest. The *Alkasen* found it, those who were Preserved, who knew it to be the key to everything. They took it with them deep into Dark Space, intending it for one of their choosing. One who was powerful enough to cross the First Gate to reach the Heart of Creation, the source of the Manifold.

They allowed a young man named Arian exploring the Gates to find that Orb. Of course, it did not work, but it was enough to awaken magic once again. To fulfill the *Alkasen's* goals of gathering the rest.

It was Arian's task to keep that Orb safe, as revealed by the Ascendant Beings as magic sparked within him. Long did he put off that destiny, but eventually, the need to fulfill his task drove him mad. He left with the Orb, and a prophecy, that would guide the Ascendant Being's Chosen on his path to return that which was lost millions of years ago.

Arian returned to the Second Immortal's Tower on Nai Elyn, the place where he had originally found the orb of Space-Time. And he died, knowing that long after his death, the Chosen would know the way.

ARIAN'S LINES, slavishly read over by countless mages, including the likes of Vera and Ansaldra, could only reveal part of the truth. Only the Chosen would know the way. The *full* way.

When Lucian awoke from his trance, he was bathed in cold sweat and beset with dread.

He knew beyond any shadow of a doubt now.

"It's not Xara," he said. "It's *me*."

At least, it was as long as he stuck true to his task. As long as he remained determined to complete that which the Oracle of Binding long ago prescribed for him. The minute he turned aside from that, the Orb of Space-Time would no doubt find another more worthy.

Xara held the Orbs of Gravitonics and Atomicism. They would deal with that later. Emma had Radiance; that was right, at least for the moment. The Orb of Thermalism was still untouched, ready and waiting for the Chosen to find it.

The Orb of Dynamism was the remaining mystery. Lucian could sense it, faint as a whisper, calling him spinward across the Worlds. Lucian did not know *exactly* where it was, but things would become clearer when he got closer.

For now, though, Lucian knew his path. And that path was leading him to Hephaestus, and the Orb of Thermalism.

THE DREAD PIRATE ZHENG YANG, the Terror of the Stars, gave a pleased smile aboard the bridge of her flagship, *Stars' Blood*.

"You've done well, Altan."

The bald man, who had a score of boils on his pockmarked, oily face, flashed a toothy, yellow smile. He answered in the rasp of a heavy smoker. "Aye, the First Mage of Irion dances upon your strings, Admiral. As it should be."

"It would seem I didn't misplace my faith in you."

It was music to his ears. His performance had raised him in her mental calculus, distancing himself that much farther from the threat of an unfortunate death. Such considerations were important with the Terror of the Stars, whose moods were as unpredictable as the tidal fluctuations of the Ice Rings of Brennus. Many a captain thought they knew their way in those deadly tracts, only to be terribly wrong in the end.

Altan Gan Baatar would make no such mistakes. That was how he had survived this long as the Golden Armada's First Quartermaster.

Admiral Yang's face suddenly sobered, as if remembering something. "You mentioned you had lost signal several days ago. Do you *really* think he'd run? Doesn't sound like the Fergus I know."

"Possibly, possibly . . . greater men have surely fled the Terror of the Stars. Aye, that be true."

Judging by the Admiral's slight frown, calling her that was a mistake. Not a deadly one, but a mistake all the same. Once upon a time, Admiral Yang had been proud to bear that title. But perhaps things had changed.

Altan would not make the same error again. It wasn't easy, being second to the Admiral of the Golden Armada. Few could hold the position longer than six months. Before he had become First Quartermaster, Altan had seen many good men take a one-way trip out the airlock. When she was merciful, she sent them without a helmet. The unmerciful had plenty of air and water to think about their wrongdoings, and of course, no radio to lament their fate to any passing vessel. That Altan had held the position of Fleet Quartermaster this long was less a testament to his effectiveness and more a testament to his lightness of foot upon eggshells.

He sometimes wondered why he'd allowed himself to be promoted upon the untimely death of his predecessor. Then he remembered. With the right amount of plunder, and the right amount of daring to navigate the Admiral's erratic moods, one might be fool enough to try.

And there was some perverse pleasure in skirting the line of death. His pirate's blood went back generations, and he was more pirate than any of his ancestors. Aye, that was true enough.

But the Admiral's next words drained his confidence.

"There is *none* greater than Fergus Madigan, Altan. Even *you* should know that."

Altan's face paled at the severity of her voice, but her eyes were distant with thought, her right hand bracing her chin as she ruminated. Altan knew better than to interrupt his master's train of thought. That mistake had cost many foolish crewmen their jobs, and just as often, their presence inside the shelter of a ship in deep space. One could take nothing for granted with the Admiral.

The Admiral looked out the viewports as the wintry world of Brennus slipped into view. Brennus was a world of extremes—ten standard years of winter followed ten plentiful years of summer. Brennus now stood locked in the middle of its winter. Except for a narrow band of green and blue on the equator, the world was an inhospitable surface of mountains and ice. It was bleakly beautiful, a bleakness only accentuated by the thick band of icy rings surrounding it, along with its four small moons, which altogether were a world unto themselves. Brennus was a wild planet, a far cry from the arid warmth of Altan's homeworld of Archea. He suspected no one could tame Brennus's wilds, not even Zheng Yang. Wisely, he kept that thought to himself.

At last, she stirred upon her ivory seat, carved from the tusks of the arcto-bears native to the Southern Reaches of the Pirates' homeworld. Hundreds of the noble beasts had died to assemble that throne, and it shone resplendent under the starlight beaming from the massive forward viewports. The plush, white fur from one of those same animals enveloped her thin neck. Her coldly beautiful face was framed by shoulder length coal-black hair. Her dark brown eyes, deadened and unfeeling, held no soul behind them.

Sometimes, he wondered how many she'd killed for her eyes to look like that. Altan had killed his share of men. Women, too. Aye, there was no escaping that in the pirate's life. But her eyes were almost enough to make his hairs stand on end, and the woman scarcely reached his shoulder. He could never look into them for long. What man could? This Fergus must be a hard man to face them. He was also a mage. Perhaps that changed the equation.

"We cannot stay here, Altan. The Worlds are stirring like a breached anthill. But chaos is opportunity for those with the valor to seize it."

Altan felt a stirring in his blood, an echo of what he always felt right before a battle. "What do you mean, Admiral Yang?"

Her dark eyes glittered. There *was* a soul, then. But all that soul wanted was to consume, to burn unabated until there was nothing left.

"I want you to muster every ship fit for war in the Eleven Worlds. Too long have we hid in the dark. Too long have we feared the League, a dying institution rotting from within. Too long have we been the villains of history. How would you like to be the hero for once?"

Altan could not hide his disappointment. He expertly erased his frown, but not quickly enough. Admiral Yang smiled as if she'd caught him in a faithless act.

Altan cleared his throat, embarrassed. "I'm . . . not sure I catch your meaning, Admiral."

"Let me be more clear. I'm not content with Brennus. I'm not content with Lubben, Tannia, Alren, Sulisto, and the rest of the worlds that pay me tribute. The colonization of the Fringe proceeds too slowly. I will not live to see the results. The real power, the real wealth, is spinward. Coreward."

Altan's blood stirred again. *This* was why he'd pledged herself to her. "Aye. That be true, Admiral. Very true indeed."

"The League's days are numbered. I don't dream of picking over its remains, like some half-starved jackal. Not when the High Prophet Sharo Khalin and the Oneists dream bigger things. I must forge a new destiny for the Golden Pirates. Our enclaves are in place, ready to pounce on my word. The time is now."

Altan Gan Baatar drew himself up proudly, puffing out his

chest. "What is your plan, Admiral? I will execute it without fail. Aye, that I will."

"That remains to be seen. As soon as you've mustered the Golden Armada, how soon can we reach the Fire World of Hephaestus?"

Altan did not understand. *Hephaestus*? What in the Worlds could be there? *That* wasn't a First World. *That* wasn't Sol. What was the Admiral thinking?

"Well," he ventured, "it would be about six months, including the time to muster our forces. Hephaestus is eight Gates away."

"I hear the doubt in your voice, Altan. It might behoove you to mask that doubt in the future."

"No doubts here, Admiral. Only questions."

"I know what you're thinking. Why not Sol? Why not the First Worlds? In time. You must remember, Hephaestus contains most of the League's industrial capacity outside the First Worlds. If we seize it and keep it safe, then every world trailward from it will pay us tribute. More ships, more resources, more manpower. Committed as the League is to the Swarmers, as fearful as they are of an attack on Alpha Centauri, do you really think they can *defend* Hephaestus? Will they not thank us for our foresight and service to humanity for guarding such a key star system from the dreaded alien menace?"

How had he not seen it before? Altan smiled. "Aye, a brilliant ploy, Admiral. Why, with Hephaestus and the Elevator under your command, none could withstand you!"

"It will be no simple thing. For most, Brennus and its surrounding stars would be enough. A Star Queendom. But I desire a *Star Empire*, like the mages dared of old. If we do not grow, we will perish. If not soon, then one day. Now is our opportunity. The only one we will ever have. It is time to throw the dice."

And what would the First Quartermaster of the Golden

Armada be in this new empire? Highly placed indeed, given he played his role to perfection.

"Aye. On your command, I will muster the fleet. It's been too long since we've seen the Thousand Ships gathered in their full power and glory. Not since the Exodus from Archea!"

Admiral Yang flashed a sharp smile. "You will feel the rays of Archea's sun on your face before long, rest assured, my faithful captain. But Archea will be the least of it. The Worlds will sing the praises of Zheng Yang. From the deserts of Sulisto to the tundra of Terminus, they will love and fear me. An Empire composed of all humanity. And those who help me there will be well-rewarded."

In the near-term, Altan knew there would be more fear than love. The Golden Armada did not have the supplies to reach Hephaestus. As First Quartermaster, he knew that well. Some, if not all, worlds on the way would have to burn, but there was no avoiding that. With the Swarmers, burning would be their fate, anyway. Better to put those resources to proper use, and of course, to skim some well-earned fat off the top.

Altan Gan Baatar so very loved burning.

As for Fergus Madigan, the Empress's former paramour . . . well, there was nothing they could do about him for now. Fergus could run, but soon, he'd have no choice but to complete his contract. Having a mage in the Admiral's employ, especially one as capable as Fergus, would present new options. After all, the Radiant had been instrumental in Admiral Yang's rise to power on Archea. How much *more* could he extend her reach in this brave new era?

Once they found him, they had him for two years, four months, and seven days. Fergus had last been seen in Varda, so Hephaestus would get them closer to him. Who knew? Perhaps going to Hephaestus would put them in contact faster. While Fergus was not the end, he was a powerful means. A means they could scarcely ignore.

And of course, Admiral Yang would want her revenge. She would want that very much.

"Ready the fleet, Altan. We sail for Hephaestus as soon as the Golden Armada has gathered."

"Aye. It shall be as you say."

"Oh. And one more thing."

"Yes, Admiral?"

"No longer can the Worlds know me as the Terror of the Stars. It sends the wrong message." She gave a chilling smile befitting that moniker. "How about *Grand Empress* of the Stars?"

Altan laughed. "That is most fitting . . . Grand Empress of the Stars. I can send the message out on wide-band."

"See that you do. Great things are coming, Altan. Prepare yourself to face them."

Yes. Change was coming to the Worlds. Not just with the Swarmers, the fracturing of the League, or the rumblings of the Oneists on Zion.

The Golden Pirates would shake the Worlds to their foundations.

THE END OF BOOK FIVE

THE STARSEA CYCLE CONTINUES IN BOOK SIX

THE FIRES OF HEPHAESTUS

ABOUT THE AUTHOR

Kyle West is the author of a growing number of sci-fi and fantasy series: *The Starsea Cycle*, *The Wasteland Chronicles*, and *The Xenoworld Saga*.

His goal is to write as many entertaining books as possible, with interesting worlds and characters that hopefully give his readers a break from the mundane.

He lives with his lovely wife, son, and two insanely spoiled cats.

 twitter.com/kylewestwriter

ALSO BY KYLE WEST

THE STARSEA CYCLE

The Mages of Starsea

The Orb of Binding

The Rifts of Psyche

The Chosen of the Manifold

The Prophecy of the Seven

The Fires of Hephaestus

THE WASTELAND CHRONICLES

Apocalypse

Origins

Evolution

Revelation

Darkness

Extinction

Xenofall

Lost Angel (Prequel)

THE XENOWORLD SAGA

Prophecy

Bastion

Beacon

Sanctum

Kingdom

Dissolution

Aberration